The Gilded Fan

The Gilded Fan

Christina Courtenay

Sequel to *The Scarlet Kimono*

Published 2013 by Choc Lit Limited
Penrose House, Crawley Drive, Camberley, Surrey GU15 2AB, UK
www.choclitpublishing.com

A CIP catalogue record for this book is available
from the British Library

ISBN-978-1-781890-08-0

MIX
Paper from
responsible sources
FSC® C014728

Printed and bound by CPI Group (UK) Ltd, Croydon, CR0 4YY

To Paul Tapper,
the best brother in the world,
with love

Acknowledgements

The idea for this story came to me while listening to the song 'The Temple of the King' by Ritchie Blackmore's Rainbow (on the album of the same name), so I have to thank Mr Blackmore and Ronnie James Dio for writing such an excellent and evocative song! And thanks to my brother Paul for sending me the album.

Huge thanks to the Choc Lit team and Choc Lit authors – you are fantastic and so supportive, it's a joy to work with you all!

Thank you to my writing buddies who keep me sane (or as sane as an author can be!) – Henriette Gyland, Gill Stewart, Tina Brown, Sue Moorcroft and Myra Kersner, among others, and all my friends in the Romantic Novelists' Association and the Historical Novel Society.

Special thanks to my sister-in-law Jacqueline Oishi Tapper for helping with Japanese phrases and for providing inspiration for my heroine; to Margaret James who really believed in this story right from its first incarnation; and to Rachel Summerson for invaluable critique and for pointing out that initially I had the wrong hero – you were right. Hope you like this one!

To Dr Janet Few and Christopher Braund at
the *Torrington 1646* permanent exhibition in
Great Torrington, Devon, many thanks for the
demonstrations and for patiently answering my questions.
Thanks also to Ken Clayton and his friends in the English
Civil War Society for additional help. And I'm indebted
to Professor Mark Stoyle as well – his book *Loyalty and
Locality: Popular Allegiance in Devon during the English
Civil War* explained it all brilliantly.

As always, I'm very grateful to Richard, Josceline and
Jessamy for putting up with me, and to 'the boys' for
keeping me company as I write.

Prologue

On the coldest day of the Year of the Dragon the great temple bell tolled, keeping time with the heavy steps of the mourners as they trudged through the snow. The deep, resonating sound echoed around the nearby hills and across the valley. Its harsh notes were as unyielding as death itself.

The snow which had arrived so unexpectedly the night before was soft and malleable, clinging to every surface as if to shield it from harm. The silhouettes of the rooftops were blurred and merged with the white-frosted trees behind them. On the ground an endless vista of smooth, shimmering surface assaulted the eye. It was almost blinding in its intensity, but so beautiful it was impossible to look away. The whole created a pleasing effect which, at any other time, would have delighted Midori Kumashiro. Today she felt nothing but a hollow emptiness at the sight, because her mother, Hannah, was no longer there to see it with her.

With heads bowed in respect, the silent group followed the urn towards the temple, high up on the hill opposite the castle, where Buddhist monks and priests awaited them. Their low-pitched voices, chanting prayers for the deceased, could be heard despite the din of the bell. Midori suppressed a shudder. To her, it was an eerie sound, as if the whispering of their ancestors' souls mingled with human voices to lament her mother's passing. The sad truth, however, was that her mother didn't have any ancestors here and there was no one who really cared apart from Midori herself.

Hannah had been a *gai-jin,* a foreigner from a land so far away Midori had trouble even imagining it. She'd come to Japan by stowing away on a trading ship and once there she had met and fallen in love with Taro Kumashiro, Midori's father, a powerful *daimyo* warlord. Her parents had loved each other deeply and, despite their cultural differences, lived happily together until the previous year, when Taro had been killed in a hunting accident. From that moment on, Midori knew her mother no longer wanted to live.

Well, you have your wish, she thought now, *but did you think of me?*

She knew she was being unfair. Her mother had loved her very much, but that love was as nothing compared to her feelings for Midori's father. The two belonged together, in death as in life, and it was something their daughter knew she'd have to accept.

The cortège reached the gates to the temple, and as she passed through, she looked up briefly at the chanting monks. Forty days had passed since her mother had died and they had first come to begin the rituals of death, but the pain was still intense. Midori felt it twisting her insides and struggled to breathe. She knew it would become easier to bear with time, if only she could endure the here and now.

The procession moved on and Midori was nudged slightly from behind as a reminder to keep going. She followed the others to the burial ground in a numb haze, instantly forgetting everything else as she caught sight of the small hole in the ground. It was the place where her mother would now rest for eternity. Midori's entire body felt as frozen as the earth all around them and she didn't register any of the priest's words.

A crow sat silent and watchful in a nearby pine tree and Midori concentrated her gaze on his magnificent black plumage, fluffed up to withstand the cold. It helped her to keep the pain at bay and as she noticed the bird's stoic acceptance of everything around him, she straightened her backbone, determined to copy his example. Somehow, she got through the ordeal in this way, and when her half-brother, Ichiro, touched her arm, she jumped and stared at him with unfocused eyes.

'It's time to go,' he whispered.

'Go? Oh, yes of course.'

She caught a brief glimpse of grief in his eyes, but it was quickly masked. It made her realise she wasn't as alone as she'd thought, however, and this gave her added courage. She turned to follow him, after one last glance at the small pit in the ground, so dismally black against the white of the snow. The dark soil echoed her mood and the white no doubt reflected her pallor, but she refused to give way to her emotions. She was the daughter of a *daimyo*; she would endure this with dignity.

She squared her shoulders and made her way down the hill with her head held high and the grief locked away inside until later.

Chapter One

Nico Noordholt, first mate of the *Zwarte Zwaan*, sat cross-legged on a large silk cushion, fighting a desperate battle to keep his back straight. The Japanese officials seated opposite him, in their costly robes of smooth silk, seemed to have no difficulty in maintaining their upright positions. Nico envied them as his back muscles were beginning to twitch from his efforts. On his left, Corneliszoon, chief factor of the VOC – the Dutch East India Company – in Japan, didn't even make the attempt, but squirmed and slouched repeatedly. The man on his right, however, Captain Casper de Leuw, sat as if he'd had a fire iron rammed up his backside, but Nico could see the effort it cost him.

Damn it all, he should be lying down!

Nico had said as much to his superior before the meeting. 'You're not well. Let me handle this for you, please.'

'No, not this time. I trust you, you know that, but it's my responsibility and mine alone,' de Leuw had grunted, mopping his sweating brow with a somewhat grimy handkerchief. 'I must negotiate a good cargo now the officials have finally consented to come. Besides, there's nothing wrong with me other than a little bit of fever.'

That was an understatement, as they both knew, but Nico wisely held his tongue. He'd known de Leuw for more than a decade now and the word 'stubborn' didn't even begin to describe the man. Arguing with him would only have the opposite of the desired effect.

Underneath the cushions they were sitting on was a floor woven of tightly matted rice stalks. It felt soft and springy and gave off a fragrance that reminded Nico of a dewy meadow at dawn. He wished he could fall backwards on to these wonderful *tatami* mats and stretch out his long legs before his knee joints became permanently stuck in the unnatural position they were in at the moment. However, to do so would mean to lose face to these strangers. And since they were willing to trade, despite their reservations about foreigners, that was unthinkable. He couldn't let de Leuw down.

'*Ah, so desu ka, demo …*'

Nico liked the sound of their language, but the business discussion seemed to be taking forever. Although the translator did his best, Nico still had trouble understanding all the nuances of the conversation and didn't feel part of it for most of the time. Corneliszoon yawned openly, earning himself a glare from the translator, which he ignored. Nico prayed a cargo would be negotiated as quickly as possible, before the officials lost all patience with the rude man.

'We need to return to Amsterdam soon, and it's absolutely essential that we bring valuable goods,' de Leuw had told the translator. 'We'd be very grateful for your help.'

Having command of a VOC ship was a huge honour and failure was not an option for a man like de Leuw. He'd always been successful before and if the Chief Factor ruined everything now with his cavalier attitude, Nico knew he'd never be forgiven. He tried to send Corneliszoon a warning glance on de Leuw's behalf, but the man's attention was elsewhere.

While the others droned on, Nico stared out of the window, across the narrow strip of water which was all that separated him from the city of Nagasaki. The Dutch trading post was situated on a man-made island called Dejima, just outside the town, but the foreigners weren't allowed to go any further. Entering this exotic country was forbidden and Dejima was the only place where they were permitted to trade with the Japanese. Indeed, it was lucky their ship was Dutch, since that was the sole nation allowed any trading rights at all now. The Spaniards had been banned years ago, the English had given up of their own accord and Nico had heard that the Portuguese had been thrown out of Japan only two years ago.

'The only way on to the mainland is across a small bridge, which is guarded at all times,' he'd been told on arrival. 'Don't ever cross it.'

Nico didn't even try – he knew it would have been a pointless exercise – but he'd spent many hours gazing longingly towards the other side. Japan fascinated him. It was like no other place he'd ever seen during his extensive travels. He admired the orderliness with which everything was conducted – be it negotiations, cooking or gardening. The Japanese seemed to have rules governing all aspects of life, and if some of them seemed cruel to outsiders, at least they were effective. From what Nico had seen, their society ran very smoothly indeed.

Nagasaki harbour was ringed by hills and a scenic coastline. It was beautiful and it irked him that he couldn't see it up close. *I've come all this way, only to be left on the outside looking in.* It seemed like a wasted opportunity. Soon, however, they would leave it all behind and return to Holland, hopefully with a highly valuable cargo, which was all that mattered. The profits in the Far East trade could be enormous and well worth the risks of the lengthy journeys.

'De-ruh-*san*, Nohduh-hortuh-*san*, Kohnehlison-*san*,' the translator said, standing up to bring the meeting to an end at last. Nico smiled inwardly at the man's inability to pronounce their names, but made no comment.

He helped de Leuw to his feet, and steadied the captain when he swayed slightly. The man's skin was so hot to the touch, Nico felt as if his hand had been scorched.

Damnation! Little bit of fever indeed … Nico tried not to show his concern. Only a few more minutes and the captain could go and lie down.

De Leuw drew in a deep breath which seemed laboured. '*Hai,* Ito-*san*,' he replied with a bow. Nico followed suit and nudged Corneliszoon into doing the same. Both Nico and his superior had attempted to learn a few Japanese words and phrases, and it hadn't proved too difficult.

'Dutch traders will be respectfully and considerately treated by Japanese officials if they make an effort to understand their hosts and their customs,' an older VOC official had told them before they left Amsterdam. 'I should know, I've made the journey myself, twice.' It had proved good advice.

'Negotiation finished, cargo ready in one week. This good?' the translator asked.

Nico stifled a sigh while de Leuw nodded. They'd already been kicking their heels here for long enough and the crew were becoming a nuisance, with their constant demands for whores and entertainment. There was nothing to be gained by impatience though, especially not when it came to trade.

'Very good. Thank you. *Domo arigato gozaimasu.*' The party all bowed once more, Nico and de Leuw slightly lower than the Japanese officials to show them respect. The foreign men's expressions gave nothing away, but Nico had the distinct feeling they appreciated the gesture.

'Thank goodness that's over with,' he said as soon as the officials had gone. He turned to smile at de Leuw, but the smile died as he saw the older man turn a waxy shade of pale. With a faint cry of distress, de Leuw's legs crumpled and he started to sink towards the floor. Nico lunged, his reflexes honed by years aboard a pitching ship, and managed to catch the man before he hit his head on the corner of a low table.

'Captain!' He lowered him on to the fragrant *tatami* mat and slotted a cushion under his head, then shouted at Corneliszoon, 'We need a physician, now. *Go!*'

The chief factor blinked as if he hadn't quite taken in what had happened yet, but Nico's words finally registered and he nodded. 'I'll send for the ship's surgeon immediately.'

As he hurried out of the room, Nico knelt on the floor by the side of his captain, friend and mentor. 'Don't leave me yet, Casper,' he whispered. 'We're in this together.'

But judging by the unnatural colour of de Leuw's face, he wasn't long for this world.

'You must go ... and see *Mijnheer* Schuyler.'

The rasping voice startled Nico awake and he sat up straight. He'd been leaning against the wall next to de Leuw's *futon* on the floor and had nodded off. The room was in near darkness and he had no idea how long he'd been dozing, but it must have been a couple of hours at least.

'What? Casper – how are you feeling?'

'Been better.'

Nico lit a lantern and could see that for himself. Three days had passed since de Leuw's collapse and his face appeared to have shrunk in on itself. The colour was now more ash than wax. *Not a good sign.*

'Well, don't talk. You must rest and conserve your strength if you're to get better. Would you like some water? Something to eat?'

'No, listen please.' There was a pause while de Leuw drew in a few more laboured breaths, then he continued, 'I'm not going to make it. You must see Schuyler ... he knows ... left you something.'

Nico gripped de Leuw's hand, which felt like mostly skin and bone. It wasn't hot any longer, but an icy cold that sent a chill through Nico. The frail hand trembled and he squeezed it as if to imbue it with his own strength, but he knew it was no good. 'You mustn't talk like that. Of course you'll get better,' he said bracingly.

The older man slowly shook his head on the pillow. 'Nico, let's not pretend. You're strong. I've prepared you. You must take over now. Your turn.'

Nico blinked away the sudden stinging in his eyes. He hadn't cried since he was a little boy and he wasn't about to now, but ... *Damn, this is so unfair!*

He'd first come across Casper de Leuw when he signed on as a crew member on a ship under de Leuw's command. Nico was only seventeen at the time and new to life at sea. For some reason the older man singled him out and took him under his wing, teaching him all there was to know about sailing a ship and trading. A strong bond grew between them and Casper was everything Nico had never had before – kind father-figure, mentor and friend. Ever since that first journey, they'd sailed together, and Nico knew life without Casper would be very empty.

'You don't need to give me anything,' he muttered. 'I've made enough from our trading ventures and my share of the profit from this trip will ensure I can live well for years to come. Besides, you've already given me more than you know and your personal possessions should go to your nieces and nephews.' He knew there were several of each and was sure they'd expect to inherit everything Casper owned. 'I'll be all right.'

'I've left them something, too.' The breath hissed out of Casper with a harsh rustling that sounded painful. 'There's enough for you all. Too late to argue ... my will is signed and legal.'

'Well, thank you,' Nico whispered. 'Thank you for everything.'

Casper's feeble hand managed to squeeze Nico's and the

older man smiled. 'No, thank *you*. You've been the son I never had. Live your life to the full and be happy! You're the captain of the *Zwarte Zwaan* now ... you'll do me proud, I know.'

Nico could only nod, and watched as Casper's chest rose and fell one more time before he breathed his last breath. No one else had ever believed in him or been proud of him, and he was determined to prove Casper right.

'I'll do my best. Rest in peace, my friend.'

'I really don't think this is wise, Midori. You should wait until I can find some official to bribe so I can go with you.'

Midori glanced at her half-brother and tried not to show her impatience. They'd discussed this already, at length, and she thought he had reached a decision. 'You agreed it might be too late then. The foreign ships are leaving soon, your informant said so. Please, Ichiro, let me try this on my own.'

So much had changed in a year and Midori didn't really want to think about it. She needed to act, and fast, before it was too late. There was no time for arguing, no time for regrets.

They were standing in the grounds of a small temple near the island of Dejima in Nagasaki's harbour. The little island, curiously shaped like the *Shogun's* fan, housed foreign traders and it was these they'd come to see. They were Midori's only hope now. She needed to buy passage on one of their ships, back to her mother's country. It wasn't something she'd ever wanted, but she had no choice.

She had to leave Japan.

How has it come to this? She suppressed the thought and tried to focus on the task at hand instead.

It was after dusk and the temple gate shielded them from view, but someone might come along at any moment. Midori drew deeper into the shadows and listened for the sound of footsteps. All was quiet.

'The foreigners may not speak Japanese,' she whispered, 'and although you were taught English, you're not as used to speaking my mother's language as I am.'

'And what if these Dutchmen don't understand you, either? We know nothing of their language.' Midori could see Ichiro frowning, despite the gloom.

'I have no idea. We'll have to hope they understand at least a little. How else do they trade with the English?'

'Going alone isn't seemly. You'll be among men who are not your family nor your equals. Under normal circumstances I should go with you.'

'Yes, but these are not normal circumstances, are they?' Midori pointed out gently, but firmly. 'I'll be alone during the journey, too. I can manage. I have to.'

Ichiro argued against her going by herself for quite a while longer, but in the end he admitted it seemed the only way. She had to start to look after herself at some stage, and now was as good a time as any.

'But my men and I will hide near the gate and if there is any sign of trouble you call for help, is that understood? If the island is as small as they say, we should hear you easily.'

'Yes, brother.' She was grateful for his concern, but at the back of her mind lurked the thought that very soon now he wouldn't be around to help and protect her.

'I really ought to send someone with you to England,' Ichiro muttered, as if he'd read her thoughts. 'Take Satoshi, he'll not refuse if I ask it of him.'

Midori caught the horrified look on the servant's face before he hurriedly assumed his usual blank expression. She shook her head. 'No, Ichiro. He has a family and if he comes with me he might never see them again. I couldn't do that to anyone. It wouldn't be right.'

'Very well, have it your way. Go now and hurry back!'

Chapter Two

As she approached the foreign enclave, Midori tried to quell her misgivings. There was a fluttering in the pit of her stomach, and she swallowed hard before setting foot on the narrow bridge. Then she took a deep breath and clenched her fists inside her sleeves, holding tight to the handle of the sword she'd hidden there. It was always best to be prepared and she was. Holding on to that thought, she marched across the bridge, breathing evenly to calm her spirit so she could concentrate on the task in hand.

'*Konbanwa*, I have come to see the foreigner in charge here,' she said politely to the guard on duty, bowing with respect and hiding her gaze under the brim of her straw hat. Above all, she knew she mustn't show him her eyes, which were a murky green rather than the usual brown. She doubted he could see them in the dark, but it was best not to take any chances.

'Corneliszoon-*san* or the captain?' he asked.

Midori hesitated. 'Er, the second one,' she muttered. If he was a captain, that must mean he was in charge of a ship, and therefore exactly the man she needed to speak to.

The guard's insolent glance travelled over her from top to toe and back again, but she just waited patiently until he had finished. Normally she would never have tolerated such blatant disrespect, but now she couldn't afford to be so sensitive, even though it set her teeth on edge.

'I don't think you'll have much luck with him dressed like that. Very particular about his women, is the captain. In fact, I don't recall him asking for any at all.'

'His women?' Midori wondered what he meant by that, but soon had her answer.

'I assume you've been sent to entertain him, since whores are the only women allowed on the island, but I doubt you'll entice anyone dressed in *hakama*.' The man chuckled, as if the thought of a courtesan dressed thus was ridiculous. Midori could see his point.

So that was it. She swore under her breath, but recovered quickly from this unwelcome news. Ichiro's informant had told them only Japanese women were allowed on the island, apart from the officials in charge of foreigners and any servants. He hadn't told them what kind of women, though, the fool. Still, it didn't matter if the guard thought her a courtesan, she thought, so long as she could speak to the captain. Once she had stated her business, she was sure he'd understand. It was a nuisance about the clothing, but she'd dressed in men's clothes on purpose. If there was any trouble, she needed the freedom of movement in order to defend herself properly.

'He apparently asked for something a bit different this evening,' she lied. 'Besides, I hardly think he cares what I'm wearing, but rather what is underneath.' She adopted a flirtatious tone of voice, giggling slightly, and saw a slow smile spread over the guard's face as he digested her words.

'I suppose you're right. Oh, very well, you may pass. Go straight on, then turn left and it's the second house on your right.' He waved her through and Midori hurried past him.

A Japanese servant was just coming out of the main building when she entered a small courtyard and he bowed when she told him who she'd come to see.

'Please wait here and I will find out whether the captain-*san* is ready for you.'

'Thank you.'

Midori looked around the yard and wrinkled her nose in disgust. Large lanterns had been placed at intervals and cast their pale light over the scene, showing her it was none too clean. There were piles of animal excrement dotted everywhere and hens picking their way between them, clucking gently. A couple of pigs fought over the contents of a trough and an unsavoury smell hung about the place. It was a far cry from the well-kept grounds of Castle Shiroi, her home. Making her way carefully through the mud and dung, Midori walked over to a small bench which leaned against a wall. She sat down, after first checking to make sure it was clean and wouldn't collapse under her weight.

She heaved a sigh of relief. It was wonderful to have made it this far. *I should be safe enough here with all the other foreigners.* After all, they were allowed on this island by order of the *Shogun*, and she was one of them now. She refused to think of what lay before her and she wouldn't contemplate failure. These Dutchmen had to take her to Europe. *I have to persuade them somehow.* Neither did she allow herself to think of the people she would leave behind. Her fate lay elsewhere.

Midori watched the pigs for a while in horrified fascination. They were ugly, loathsome creatures who seemed to be eating nothing but rubbish. Midori couldn't understand how the foreigners could actually want to eat something so repulsive. Samurai hardly ever ate meat. And although Hannah had occasionally made her try it on the few days when she hankered after her own native food, Midori had never liked it and had struggled to hide her distaste. Looking at the pigs now, it made her shudder to remember the leathery texture of it in her mouth.

From the little she knew about them, the foreigners were dirty and disgusting in their personal habits too, not much better than the animals they ate, in fact. And yet, she herself was half-foreign, so what right did she have to criticise them? Wasn't she betraying her mother by having these thoughts? Midori felt guilty and resolved not to make any hasty judgements. Perhaps she was doing her mother's relatives a great injustice? She would just have to wait and see.

'Upon my word, it must be my lucky day!'

The exclamation made Midori's head jerk up. It was the first time she'd heard English spoken by anyone other than her mother, father or Ichiro, and she stared intently at the three men approaching across the mire. At first, she couldn't see them properly, but soon they were close enough for her to make out their features in the light of the lanterns.

Large and hairy, with straggly beards and strange clothes that looked as if they hadn't been washed for years, they were like no one she'd ever met before. One had a huge, porous nose, the other two had long, sharp ones. They looked similar enough to be brothers. Unfortunately all three wore identical, leering expressions which weren't difficult to interpret. She stood up and readied herself for confrontation, reaching inside her left sleeve to grip the handle of her sword.

'Good evening,' she said, keeping a wary eye on the three men while bowing slightly the way she'd seen her father do when acknowledging someone of inferior rank.

'"Good evening"?' one of the men mimicked and they all burst into laughter. 'D'you hear that, Barker? 'Struth, a whore what's been trained by someone with manners. And in English, too!'

Midori frowned, wondering what she had said that was so amusing. She thought she'd greeted them correctly, but then she had never lived among her mother's people and therefore had no way of knowing what they considered proper. No doubt she would learn in time.

'You are English?' she asked, thinking that perhaps she could keep them distracted by small talk until the captain arrived. Unless one of them was the captain? She hoped not. 'I thought only Dutchmen lived here.'

'We work for 'em, though the Lord only knows why,' one of the sharp-nosed men replied.

'They pay better'n most of ours. Which leaves us with extra money to spend.' The man with the porous nose, who was apparently called Barker, wriggled his eyebrows suggestively at Midori. He looked so idiotic she had to stop herself from laughing out loud.

'Kimura-*san*'s outdone himself this time,' he said to his companions. 'A pretty little piece he's brought us and no mistake.' He crooked his finger at Midori. 'Come here, my sweet, and show me what you can do.'

'I'm here to see the captain, no one else.'

'Captain Noordholt? No, no, we're not lettin' him keep a tasty little morsel like you all to hisself.'

'Definitely not,' the others echoed. 'Whores are shared equally around here. Not that he normally takes part, but then I can see why he's been saving hisself for the likes o' you.'

They advanced on Midori, who warned them, 'Do not come any nearer.'

'Why not? Are you going to stop us?' The men started laughing again, one of them going so far as to clutch his stomach in mirth.

'Enough o' this nonsense.' Barker walked forward and stretched out a hand to grab Midori's arm, only to stop short as a very sharp curved sword appeared in front of his face.

'I *said* … do … not … come … any closer.'

The man glared at her for a moment, before turning bright red with anger. 'What's this? Fight me with a sword, would you? We'll just see about that, wench.' He stepped back a few paces and whipped out his own sword. It was badly made and of inferior quality, and Midori wondered vaguely how he'd survived as long as he had.

The other two men watched the ensuing fight in open-mouthed astonishment, oblivious to the fact that they should be helping their friend. Midori soon forgot about them as she concentrated on the man in front of her. He came at her like an enraged bullock and almost went charging straight into the wall when she simply stepped to one side. It was easier than she had imagined to whack him on the side of the head with the hilt of her sword, but apparently he had a thick skull, since this only served to annoy him further. Turning faster than she'd thought him capable of, he swung his sword over his head while shouting some unintelligible curse, then brought it down hard. She parried, but it took all her willpower not to show that his blow had jarred her arm. The clanging of steel on steel rang in her ears and she shook her head slightly in order to concentrate.

As Barker feinted clumsily to the right, she quickly slashed to the left, cutting a hole in the fabric of his sleeve. He bellowed and brought his sword down again, but this time she'd learned her lesson and jumped away from him, instead of trying to meet his thrust. He followed her, slashing wildly, and she moved out of the way again and again. This strange dance continued for a while until his breath started to come out in great gasps and sweat poured down his face, as if he wasn't used to such exertion. Midori recoiled from the stench of him, which was vile in the extreme. She decided to end the fight as quickly as possible so she could remove herself from his vicinity.

If she hadn't been trained never to show her emotions during a fight, she would have laughed out loud at the look of incredulity which crossed Barker's features when, after a swift attack when he least expected it, she sank her weapon into his sword arm. He uttered a harsh cry of pain and stumbled backwards, where his companions caught him.

'She cut me! My arm!' The shout echoed round the courtyard, galvanising the others into action.

'Bloody impudence!'

'She's got to be taught a lesson.'

Midori gritted her teeth and prepared to take on the other two men, her heart pounding with indignation and fury. They were the ones who needed to be taught a lesson, both in how to treat a lady and in sword fighting.

I'll show them.

Nico sat on a verandah, staring across the bay, his thoughts still with Casper. The older man's body had been taken away to be prepared for burial, but although Nico had watched him being carried out, it still seemed a bit unreal.

He had informed the crew members and Corneliszoon, as well as a Japanese official, and everyone had immediately started calling Nico 'Captain'. It felt wrong to him, since it had been Casper's title for so long, but he knew he had to get used to it, and fast. As first mate, he'd already been in charge of the crew on a day-to-day basis, but now he had to show them he was truly in command.

He heard shouting from somewhere on the island, but ignored it. The crewmen were forever brawling, but he was too tired to care right now. Sighing, he prepared to go indoors to start checking the list of goods to be loaded on to the ship in the morning. *Better to keep busy than wallow in unproductive thoughts.*

In the doorway he almost collided with a servant. 'There is lady to see you,' the man said, bowing politely.

'A lady?' Nico was well aware what the man meant by that euphemism. 'I'm sorry, but I didn't ask for one. Please, either send her away or tell her to speak to the other men.' He nodded to dismiss the servant. He had to immerse himself in his new role and didn't have time for whores. They would only distract him.

To his surprise the servant stood his ground. '*Sumimasen*, but lady ask for captain. Said she want speak to you.'

Nico stifled another sigh. It amazed him how enterprising some of the courtesans could be, not to mention tenacious. If he didn't go and send her away in person, she might make a nuisance of herself. 'Very well, I'll see to it. Thank you.'

Nico made his way towards the little yard outside the house. As he approached the door, he frowned at the sound of steel clanging on steel. He also heard voices raised in anger and they were speaking English.

'Damn it all,' he muttered. 'What are they up to now?' The English crew members were a constant source of trouble and he was tired of dealing with them. They were a particularly rough bunch, but he hadn't had much choice when he signed them up during a brief stop in Batavia on the island of Java. Sailors frequently jumped ship in various ports and then found themselves needing passage home. Unfortunately, the Englishmen had been the only ones available when Nico was short-handed.

Stopping in the half-open doorway, Nico blinked at the sight that met his eyes. It certainly wasn't one he'd ever thought to see. John Barker, one of the Englishmen, was leaning against a wall, clutching his arm, which seemed to be bleeding profusely. From time to time he swore out loud, in between making a keening noise to show he was in pain. Meanwhile, a Japanese woman fought with two of Barker's compatriots, and she wasn't intimidated in the least by the look of things. Nico stood rooted to the spot, watching her with growing amazement.

'A pox on ye, wench!'

Abe Jessop, Barker's friend, charged at her first, with a murderous look in his eyes. It was clear his anger ruined his concentration, however, and when the woman's foot shot out to deliver a well-placed kick to the stomach, Abe wasn't prepared and fell heavily. The second man, Abe's cousin Peter, launched himself at her from the other side, brandishing a long knife. Nico watched as the woman turned just in time to knock the weapon out of Peter's hand with a few thrusts of her own. She had a short, curved sword, which flashed in the light from the nearby lantern. Nico could see it was honed to perfection and she wielded it with expertise. Peter didn't stand a chance – the woman made besting him look as easy as stealing from a child.

Abe had recovered by now and made as if to charge her once more, but Nico decided it was time to intervene. No matter how skilled she was, the men were still fighting with a woman. He couldn't allow that.

'Enough! What's going on here?' His curt command stopped both Abe and Peter in their tracks.

They turned as one to face him, wearing identical expressions of frustration and rage. Nico would have laughed if it hadn't been for the fact that the woman swivelled round to look at him as well. Suddenly he forgot everything else as he gazed into quite the most perfect face he'd ever seen. In fact, it was so exquisite that for a moment he wondered if she was actually real.

Large, slightly almond-shaped eyes, fringed with dark lashes, under perfectly arched brows. A small, tip-tilted nose, high cheek-bones and a mouth just the right shape and size, all set in a heart-shaped face with flawless, porcelain skin. The woman may be dressed in what appeared to be men's clothing, but she was female in every other way. Soft curves were hinted at by the silk of her robe and her backside was delineated by the strange, skirt-like breeches. Thick, shining tresses of hair cascaded down to her knees, tied back loosely with a ribbon.

Nico had to remind himself to close his mouth. 'Well?' he prompted. 'Have you all lost your tongues?'

Chapter Three

Midori turned to see who had come to her rescue. The voice belonged to a man who was much taller than the others, broad-shouldered and not quite as ill-kempt. He seemed to have made an effort to tame his beard by clipping it very close to his skin and had tied his hair into a short tail to keep it tidy. It was of a colour she'd never seen before, like shiny but tarnished gold, and it swept back from what her mother had called a widow's peak. Midori found it impossible to stop staring at him.

His beard and eyebrows were darker and showed off the sharp planes of his face. Deep-set eyes, a determined jaw and straight nose with a slight bump in the middle gave him character. Although he was wearing the same type of baggy knee-length breeches as his compatriots, he had a clean Japanese belted jacket on top. He stood with his legs apart and arms crossed, a fearful scowl directed at the other men as he asked them to account for the scene before him.

'Oh, Captain Noordholt, sir, this here wench dared to cut Barker in the arm.'

'Yes, we were just havin' a bit o' sport with her, like with the others, but she got all uppity and took offence at somethin'.'

'And she drew a sword on us. Just look what she's done, sir.'

Barker made an elaborate show of uncovering his wound, adding a great deal of noise to the process. It was deep and blood flowed freely, but it was hardly a mortal wound. Midori sent him a scornful look. She hadn't behaved like that since childhood, and he was a grown man. *Pitiful!*

'Leave us,' the captain ordered. 'Go and have Barker's wound seen to.'

'But Captain Noordholt, sir ...'

'Do as I say,' he snapped. 'I will speak with you later.'

The three grumbled, but took themselves off at last, leaving Midori to face the man she'd asked to see. His scowl disappeared and he studied her with a calm blue gaze, so like her mother's it made her breath catch in her throat. He bowed to her, then spoke in halting Japanese, his voice gentle and kind now.

'I apologise. I am the captain-*san*. You wish speak to me? Please state business.'

Midori bowed, lower than she had to the others to acknowledge his attempt at politeness, before answering him in English. 'It is no matter. I believe they mistook me for something that I'm not.'

'You speak English?' His eyebrows shot up and Midori was tempted to laugh again. These foreigners were so transparent.

'Yes, I'm half-English.'

'I see. And what brings you here, if I may ask?'

'I'm on my way to visit my relatives and have come to buy passage to England on board your ship. That is, if I'm speaking to the owner of the *Zwarte Zwaan*?' Satoshi had reported the name of the only foreign ship in port at the moment and Midori hoped she had pronounced it correctly.

'Not her owner, but her captain, yes.' He hesitated. 'Er, you are travelling alone?'

When Midori nodded, he frowned.

'Perhaps you're not aware of the fact that females seldom travel unaccompanied, especially not on a ship, unless they are the kind of woman my men took you for?'

'*Honto, neh*?' Midori thought quickly. She wouldn't have travelled by herself in Japan either, but this time she didn't have a choice. Although she supposed she could hire some hapless servant to accompany her on the journey, it was hardly fair since she didn't intend to return. She said as much to Captain Noordholt.

'You don't plan to return?'

'No.'

'Not ever?' He opened his eyes wide and in the light from the lantern they glittered with sapphire sparks. Midori was momentarily distracted by the sight, then realised he'd asked her a question. She shook her head.

He stroked the stubble on his chin while apparently thinking this over. 'If you don't mind my asking – are you expected by your kin?'

'No, but I don't think it will be a problem. I carry a letter for them.'

'Hmm. Well, Mistress, er …?'

'Midori. My name is Midori.' She thought it best not to mention the name of her father's clan, just in case. Her first name would do for now.

He looked her in the eyes and smiled briefly. 'Very fitting, to be sure. Your green eyes must be much admired where you come from, being rather unique here, I take it?'

Midori gathered he knew her name meant 'green' in Japanese, and he'd seen the colour of her eyes in the light from the lantern, but she didn't understand his strange question. She frowned. 'No, no one liked them apart from my parents. And Ichiro, of course.' She stopped, realising she may have said too much. 'But what has that to do with anything?'

'Oh, nothing really, I beg your pardon. I shouldn't have mentioned it.'

Midori was becoming impatient and didn't want to discuss the colour of her eyes. 'Well, are you going to let me travel on your ship or not?' she asked.

'No, I'm afraid I can't help you. Allowing you to sail alone on a ship with upwards of a hundred and twenty men would be madness.' He shrugged apologetically.

'Why? I won't mingle with any of them. I'll pay you for a private cabin.'

He frowned at her again. 'Mistress Midori, you don't appear to lack sense. Surely you can understand that you would represent a great temptation?'

'I can defend myself. Haven't I already proved it?'

'Against three men perhaps, and three of the clumsiest at that. What of the other hundred-odd? Cabin doors are rather flimsy.'

'Surely they wouldn't all … at once …?' Midori tried not to feel intimidated by the image he'd conjured in her mind.

'Wouldn't they?'

The quizzical expression on Captain Noordholt's face as he stared down his haughty nose at her riled Midori. She decided he was just being obstinate, trying to put her off going. She clenched her fists inside the sleeves of her robe as she tried to compose herself. A Japanese lady never lost her temper and she had no intention of letting this irritating stranger provoke her.

'Maybe you underestimate your own charms, Mistress Midori,' he added in a kindly voice, which annoyed her even more.

'Aren't you man enough to ensure complete obedience in your crew?' she challenged.

He looked surprised. 'Of course, but tempting them with a tasty female isn't a normal occurrence on board any ship. I would be a fool to do so and I really don't need any more complications on this journey. I've only recently taken over as captain, so it's important that nothing goes wrong.'

'*Tasty*?' Midori almost raised her voice, but managed to resist the temptation at the last moment. 'If you must know, I have never yet met a man who was tempted by what you call my charms.' She didn't count the episode with the three

Englishmen as they had thought her a whore and therefore fair game. 'If your men are so desperate, you should bring along some other females.'

'By all that's holy, woman, have you lost your mind? I'll have enough trouble keeping the crew adequately fed during such a long journey. And I don't need any hangers-on for them to fight over at every opportunity. God's teeth, but there would be a mutiny before we'd sailed a hundred leagues.' He shook his head at the thought.

Midori stepped closer to him. 'Well, I don't care how you arrange matters on board your ship. All I know is that I must sail with you and I have plenty of silver to pay for my passage. If I stay here, I die. It's as simple as that.'

'What do you mean, you'll die?'

Nico frowned at the woman, trying to make sense of her words.

She glared at him. 'Haven't you heard? The *Shogun* has decided to persecute all foreigners and Christians. We're to be evicted from the country, even half *gai-jin* like me. I have no choice but to leave, don't you see?'

Nico had heard vague rumours to that effect, but hadn't taken much notice. Corneliszoon assured everyone on the island they were safe since they had permission to trade and weren't staying long, so it didn't concern him.

'I'm sure there must be other options open to you. I've been told there is a thriving Japanese Christian community in the Philippine Islands. Couldn't you go there?' he suggested. 'It's much closer, for one thing, and you could sail on a Japanese vessel.'

It was a reasonable proposition, but apparently it wasn't to the lady's liking. 'I don't want to go there. I'm going to England,' she insisted.

Nico sighed inwardly. He hated arguing with females;

their logic was not like his. In this case he had to stay firm, though. 'Not with me. I'm sorry, but there it is.'

Although he didn't raise his voice, there was a steely quality to it that should have told her he wasn't prepared to back down. He'd practised it on the crew of the *Zwarte Zwaan* often enough and it usually procured instant obedience.

Her eyes narrowed and she took a deep breath, then asked in a softer tone of voice, 'Have you by any chance heard of the *ninja*?'

'I believe so. Trained assassins or some such thing? What of them?' Nico felt his frown deepening. *What is she up to now?*

'My brother happens to know where to find them and, as you may know, they'll do most anything for a price. Unlike some people.'

He crossed his arms over his chest again, fixing her with a stern gaze. 'Where is this conversation leading, Mistress Midori?' he asked, although he was perfectly able to guess. 'I have other calls on my time.'

'Oh, yes, of course. You were expecting a whore. I'm so sorry to take up your valuable time, but then …'

'I am *not* entertaining any whores,' he gritted out between clenched teeth, trying not to let her goad him. 'And it's not a word any respectable female should be familiar with in any case. Your parents should have taught you that.'

'Really? How strange. What should I call them then?'

'Nothing! If you're a lady, you don't mention them at all. Now could we get to the point please?' He was fast losing his patience.

'The point, Captain Noordholt, is that unless you change your mind and allow me on board your ship, you yourself might not be sailing on her. The *ninja* are known to be swift and deadly and they're trained never to fail in their missions.'

He stepped closer and glared at her. 'Are you threatening

me?' Since he was at least a head taller than her and possibly twice as broad, this should have made her back off, but she didn't seem intimidated in the least.

She looked up at him, as calm as you please, and assumed an innocent expression. 'I wouldn't call it that exactly. I'm just informing you of the consequences should you persist in your refusal.'

He fumed silently for a moment, unable to believe this slip of a woman would dare to give him an ultimatum. Then he realised the absurdity of the situation and gave a short laugh. 'And what's to stop me from murdering you right here, right now? Or taking you captive?'

'My brother is expecting me back shortly. If I don't return, he'll come looking for me.'

'Then I would be ready and waiting, with my men.'

Midori shook her head at him. 'He wouldn't come charging in, he would use stealth,' she scoffed. 'He's not a fool. Besides, I don't believe it will be necessary.'

Before Nico had time to do more than open his eyes wide in surprise, he found himself lying on his back in the dirt with all the air knocked from his lungs. Midori sat on top of him pointing a very sharp knife at his throat as he gasped to regain his breath. He stared at her in shock.

'What the hell ...? How did you ...?'

A wave of fury surged through him, but he managed to hold his temper in check. This had gone beyond absurd. It was downright ridiculous.

It had been almost too easy and Midori knew she'd taken him by surprise only because he hadn't expected to be attacked by a female. He was a big man, after all, and she was tiny in comparison, so he hadn't been on his guard. She'd simply hooked her right leg behind his left one and pushed hard, then quickly jumped down on top of him as he fell, pulling out her knife. Luck had been on her side this time, but she was sure he'd never allow it to happen again. She would have to take advantage of her victory immediately.

The interview hadn't been going according to plan, so Midori had known she had to do something drastic. She couldn't fail. To go back to Ichiro without securing passage on board the captain's ship would be to lose face. She had to prove to her brother she could fend for herself. With renewed determination, she gripped the handle of her knife and drew in another calming breath. It wouldn't do to sink to this barbarian's level; she must stay calm and reasonable. Slowly, she felt her inner harmony returning.

Several expressions flitted across the captain's face – astonishment, anger and possibly a small measure of admiration. Midori waited in silence, her knife poised by his neck. She could see him debating with himself, but his next words indicated that although he wasn't prepared to give in gracefully, he was wavering slightly.

'We're not going to England, so you'd have to find your way from Amsterdam to wherever you're headed,' he growled. 'By yourself.'

'Well, there must be ships that sail to London. It's not that far, is it?' Midori had no idea if this was true, but decided to take a chance. She wasn't actually going to London, but knew it was England's main city, so she was sure she could reach her destination from there somehow.

'London?' His eyebrows descended even further. 'Your relatives live there?'

'Um, nearby I believe, yes.' To distract the man from the fact that she was lying, Midori gave him a dazzling smile. 'So, you see, I'll be all right if only you can take me as far as Amsterdam.'

The captain blinked and stared at her. She saw him swallow hard, then he closed his eyes and uttered what sounded like a groan. 'Very well,' he gritted out. 'You may sail with us. I can't guarantee your safety, but I'll do my best. It might not be enough, though. Do you understand?'

'Perfectly. I'll leave you to your, er … pleasures now. When do we sail?'

'For the last time, I'm not indulging in any …' He muttered a curse, then made a visible effort to calm himself. 'We're sailing with the tide the day after tomorrow. I'll require your payment by tomorrow evening. A thousand pieces of silver.'

Midori didn't bat an eyelid at this preposterous amount, although she couldn't help wondering if Ichiro had brought such an enormous sum. 'Five hundred,' she said. 'I'll bring you half of it tomorrow, and the rest I will give you when we reach Amsterdam safely.'

'I didn't say the price was negotiable.' His blue gaze had turned to steel.

'No?' Midori smiled sweetly and lifted her eyebrows, while pricking him with her dagger. A tiny droplet of blood appeared on his sunburned skin.

Captain Noordholt gave her a furious look, before turning the tables on her with a minimum amount of effort. He grabbed the hilt of her knife with lightning speed, twisting it out of her grip and throwing it to the ground. Then he shoved her off and jumped to his feet in one fluid motion. With another glare he turned on his heel and stalked off.

'Six hundred and not a piece less,' he called over his shoulder before disappearing inside the house.

Midori sat in the mud and stared after him. 'What an extraordinary man,' she muttered. He could obviously have heaved her off at any time, but he'd let her think she had the upper hand. And then he gave in to her demands? It didn't make sense to her, but she was grateful all the same.

She wondered if she would ever understand these foreigners.

Nico stopped just inside the door and leaned his back on it for a moment. His heart was racing as if he'd been running, and he clenched his fists. 'Damnation, but you're a fool, man, a complete lackwit!' he berated himself. Of all the stupid things to do, he'd let a pretty face sway him and cloud his judgement. *Well, not just pretty, dazzlingly beautiful! But I'm still an idiot …*

And yet, how could he leave a woman like that here to die? She was half-English, after all, as much a foreigner to the Japanese as he was. A lady, alone and defenceless, who'd asked for his help. It put him in an impossible position.

He'd been determined to refuse her request. As he'd told her, it was sheer madness to allow her on board the *Zwarte Zwaan* and he doubted she understood what she was asking of him. But one smile, one incredible smile, and all his good intentions had flown out of the window.

Nico slammed his fist into the nearest wall, then regretted it when he made a huge dent in the flimsy wood. 'Damn it all to hell!'

But he'd given his word now and he couldn't take it back.

Chapter Four

'Off so soon?' The guard by the gate looked taken aback when Midori appeared behind him and demanded to be let out.

'Yes, the captain is a busy man, but he asked me to return tomorrow, so you had better warn your colleagues to expect me. Oh, and some of my servants might be bringing a few of my possessions, so kindly let them on to the island as well. I shall be sailing with the captain.' She swept past the slack-jawed man and disappeared into the night.

As soon as she was out of sight of the guard, Ichiro and his men came out of their hiding places to join her on the walk back to the inn.

'You are well?' Ichiro fell into step beside her and looked her up and down to check for any signs of violence.

'Yes, thank you. I have successfully negotiated a passage on board the *Zwarte Zwaan* to er ... the captain's country.' She didn't want to tell him the ship was bound for Amsterdam. It would only complicate matters and she was sure she could find a way to reach England from there.

'Your negotiations took place on the ground?'

'What?' Midori looked around to find Ichiro staring at her dirty clothing in the light from one of the lanterns his servants carried. 'Oh, no, but you wouldn't believe how disgusting their island is. They have livestock walking around the place. I sat on a bench to wait and it must have been filthy.'

'I see.' He gave her a penetrating look, but let the subject drop.

Midori hesitated slightly before voicing her main worry. 'Ichiro, how much silver did you bring?'

'Quite a lot. Why?'

'Well, the captain is asking for an incredible amount as payment and although I haggled, I wasn't sure whether I should have tried to make him lower the price further.'

'How much does he want?'

'Six hundred pieces.' She saw her brother's eyebrows go up and hurried to add, 'Although I said I would only pay half now and the rest on safe arrival in England.'

'Hmm. It's a lot, to be sure, but if that's what it takes to see you safe … No, we can't argue with the man. You need him to be on your side.'

Midori thought she'd better not tell Ichiro it was much too late for that. The captain would no doubt honour his word and try his best to protect her, but he was most definitely not 'on her side'.

'When do you leave?'

'The ship sails with the tide the day after tomorrow. We have one more day together.'

The thought that this was probably the last day she would ever spend with her brother suddenly hit her. An acute feeling of loss slammed into her gut and made her gasp for breath, but when Ichiro gave her a worried glance, she turned it into a cough and pretended she had choked on some dust. *One more day, and then what?*

She would have to make the best of it. It would never do to leave him with the memory of a sister who looked desolate. She wanted him to remember her in a happy mood. If it was their fate, they would meet again. Midori comforted herself with that thought.

He was the best of brothers and he'd tried to give her the bad news gently, but it had still come as a shock …

Just over a week earlier, she'd been in her suite of rooms at Castle Shiroi arranging flowers when her maid came to give her a message.

'Lady Midori, the lord Ichiro wishes to speak to you. He is by the pond.'

Midori looked up from the *ikebana* she was creating to find the maid bowed low and on her knees next to her. 'Thank you, Kumi, then I will go at once. You may accompany me.'

She wondered if the summons had anything to do with the arrival that morning of a messenger from Edo. Midori had seen him come galloping into the main courtyard. There had been an urgency to the man's mission which boded ill and she hated not knowing what was going on. If anything bad was to happen, she wanted to be told so she could prepare herself and meet the danger head on. It was what her father had taught her to do.

It was a clear autumn day, perfect for contemplating the beauty of nature, and there was no better place in all the world to do this than by the castle pond. Midori made her way along the garden paths, the maid following at a respectful distance behind her, and looked around at the glorious riot of colour. The acer trees were clad in their most brilliant hues, from palest orange to deep burgundy red, and Midori couldn't resist a brief smile at this display. It was as if nature was trying to make up for the barren, dull months that were to follow, leaving something spectacular to remember when all the colours had faded.

The pond was really a small lake, used for the breeding of carp as much as for decoration. She found Ichiro sitting on a jetty which was reflected in the calm water. Cross-legged, he was as still as the stones all around the shore, his eyes far away and his mind obviously in harmony with his surroundings. Midori hesitated, not wanting to disturb his tranquillity. When she took a step on to the jetty, however, this made it shake and alerted him to her presence. He turned and smiled, stretching out a hand in invitation.

'Ah, there you are. Come, sit by me.'

She saw that he was on a silk cushion and there was another waiting for her. She sank down on to her knees and folded her hands in her lap, waiting for him to speak. Although she was longing to question him about the messenger, she knew it wasn't her place. Such impertinence wouldn't be tolerated, even by a beloved sister. Ichiro would reveal all, if and when he felt so inclined and not a moment before.

He took his time, as if he had to weigh his words carefully before speaking. Finally he said, 'Midori, you know I have your welfare at heart and I want you to be happy?' She nodded. Despite an age difference of ten years and the fact that they had had different mothers, they'd always liked each other and dealt well together. 'Then if I tell you the time has come for you to leave, you'll understand it's not because I, personally, want you to go.' It was a statement, not a question, but Midori heard the slight hesitation in his voice, as if he wasn't sure how she would react.

'Leave? You mean you've found a husband for me at last?'

Ichiro sighed. 'No, I wish I had, but I'm afraid that's not what I meant.'

For several years now, her brother had tried his best to find her a husband noble enough to befit her station as the daughter of a *daimyo* and poor enough to overlook her mother's provenance. It had proved an impossible task.

Midori didn't think of herself as ugly, but she knew she was different from all the other girls in the castle. Although her hair was as straight and shiny as theirs, it was a dark auburn in colour and much softer besides. She supposed she could have dyed it black, but since she couldn't change her green eyes to brown there was no point. She'd noticed that whenever her prospective suitors looked into their depths they either gasped or blinked in horror, and soon after made their excuses. The plain truth was she frightened or repulsed them.

'You have to return to your mother's country,' Ichiro said, cutting into her thoughts, and Midori looked up at him quickly. It sounded like an order, the words uncompromising, which was most unlike the gentle brother she knew and loved.

'To England? Why can't I stay here with you? I can make myself useful in one way or another. I don't need a husband, really.'

'That's not the problem.' He was silent for a while, then continued. 'I had news from Edo this morning. My closest friend and ally sent me a warning I can't ignore. Have you heard about the persecution of Christians by the *Shogun*?'

'Well, yes, I know they're not much liked, but—'

'That is a huge understatement. They're simply not tolerated any longer. In fact, they are being hunted down like prey and soon they'll all be exterminated.'

'But what does it have to do with me? I'm not a Christian, you know that. Mother did try to teach me, but to be honest, I didn't really pay much attention to what she was telling me about her god and his son.'

'I know. Nevertheless you're half-foreign and as such, more likely to be a Christian in the eyes of the authorities. These people risk a lot for their beliefs, their very lives in fact, and none worship openly, as far as I know. Therefore suspicion can fall on anyone and you'd be a prime candidate. Had Hannah still been alive ...' He shook his head. 'We must be grateful she's not. Men, women and even children by their thousands have been executed already. I've heard many gruesome tales of torture and people being burned alive – alive, do you hear? – simply because they follow this foreign god and his teachings.'

He paused and took a deep breath before continuing. 'The present *Shogun* is even more determined than his predecessor to be rid of all foreigners, and now he has apparently ordered the expulsion of all children of mixed parentage as well. Those who don't leave will be put to death. I'm afraid that includes you.'

'But surely he doesn't know I'm here? Your castle is so far north, he never comes this way. When you next go to Edo, I can stay here.'

'Don't underestimate the *Shogun*. He has spies everywhere and, believe me, he knows of your existence. Someone made sure he knew.'

'What? You mean, someone deliberately informed him?'

'Precisely. I don't know who yet, but I will find out. Meanwhile, your life is in danger. You must leave while there is still time, Midori.'

She struggled to take in the news. Someone had informed the authorities of her existence. 'I don't understand, Ichiro. Why? Who wants me gone from here? I may not be universally liked, but as far as I know there's no one here who hates me.'

This wasn't strictly true. Lately there had been many instances where she'd come across groups of people whispering in corners, and whenever she appeared, they stopped abruptly. She was left in no doubt as to whom they were talking about, and she had caught several malicious glances coming her way as well. It had puzzled her at the time, but now she understood.

'It's a mystery, and I'll get to the bottom of it, never fear, but it doesn't make any difference who the culprit is. The fact is you have to leave, and soon, and although I am reluctant to let you go, we have no choice. Hannah was the only mother I ever knew and I held her in high esteem. I swore to her I would keep you safe and I intend to keep my promise. Did you know she saved my life once, here in this very pond when I fell off the jetty and nearly drowned? Now I have to do the same for you.'

He turned back to stare across the mirror surface of the water and when he spoke again, it was with the voice of one who is accustomed to being obeyed. 'I will escort you to the coast and together we'll sail south to Nagasaki, where I believe the foreign ships come to trade. I'll give you enough silver to buy yourself passage to your mother's country, and wait until I know you're safe on board a foreign ship. I will also provide you with a dowry. It's the best I can do in the circumstances. Do you know where to find Hannah's family?'

'Of course, she talked of her home often. It was in a place called Plymouth, but I had never thought to go there myself.' There was a hollow feeling inside Midori. She suddenly felt as if she were talking to a stranger, one who wanted to be rid of her. How could she leave all that was familiar and dear, to travel to a country which, by all accounts, was barbaric in the extreme? Where the people were dirty and discourteous, had no manners and ate strange food. She bowed her head to hide her tumultuous thoughts.

'And you know how to take care of yourself?'

Her head snapped back up and she frowned at him. 'Of course I do. You trained me yourself in swordplay and defence techniques, as well as archery. So did Father.'

He smiled and raised a hand to stop her. 'Yes, yes, forgive me, I didn't mean to cast doubt on your abilities. As you say, I've done my best to prepare you for life, although I hadn't thought you'd have to go quite so far away.'

Neither had she.

They sat in silence for a while, then Ichiro patted her hand awkwardly. 'It is for the best, and it's your fate. We must accept that.' He drew a sealed letter out of the capacious sleeve of his robe. 'Your mother and I discussed the possibility of you leaving one day, and she prepared this letter for you to give your relatives if the need should ever arise.' He handed her the rolled-up document.

'Why didn't she give it to me?' Midori frowned.

'Perhaps she didn't want to upset you? She knew your thoughts on the matter.'

Midori nodded slowly and recalled her mother's last words, whispered and urgent, her thin, clammy hand clutching Midori's. 'You must leave this place, return to England and seek out my family. There's nothing for you here.'

'If that is your wish, Mama,' Midori had replied, but she'd said it only to placate her mother and keep her from fretting. She'd never had any intention of travelling to a country on the other side of the world. Japan was her home.

'So it's all settled? There really is no other way?'

Ichiro nodded slowly. 'We leave tomorrow at first light.'

'So soon? But ...'

'Go and make your preparations now, and remember to take only as much as you can carry yourself. Who knows whether you'll find assistance en route. I'll send someone with your dowry so you can hide the coins in your clothing.'

'May I not even say goodbye to your wife, and my nieces and nephews?' Somehow the thought of leaving without bidding her sister-in-law and the rest of Ichiro's family farewell made it seem even harder.

Ichiro shook his head. 'I'm sorry; it's for the best. Just visit them as usual and pretend you'll see them tomorrow afternoon.'

Midori stood up, knowing the discussion was at an end. There was no choice and she had to abide by her brother's decision. He was the *daimyo* now, but even he couldn't save her from the *Shogun*'s men if they came for her, and she wouldn't want him to try. It would bring dishonour to the family and put both Ichiro and the entire clan in danger. She couldn't ask him to risk it. She bowed and turned to go, then hesitated.

'Ichiro? If I can't bear it in England, may I come back?'

He nodded without looking at her and Midori understood he was hoping it wouldn't come to that.

Slowly, she made her way back to her quarters. She tried to let the brilliance of nature soothe her troubled mind, but found it impossible to concentrate on the autumnal display. The shock of having to leave the only home she'd ever known, and so suddenly, was too great. *What if I never see this place again?* Midori drew in several calming breaths to stop her heart from beating faster, but she couldn't rein in the feelings of anger, sadness and resentment that surged through her.

She was still in a state of turmoil when she reached her suite in the east wing of the castle. Situated at ground level, with a tiny private garden, she had the luxury of two large rooms and one smaller one all to herself. *Tatami* mats of the highest quality and thickness covered the floors, and there were costly painted scrolls covering many of the walls. On a built-in shelf precious items of porcelain and lacquerware, which her parents had given her over the years, were displayed. In an alcove stood a low table with the half-finished flower arrangement she'd been working on earlier.

She had been spoiled, and she knew it, but that would now come to an end.

She wondered what kind of accommodation awaited her in England? Her mother had talked about sharing a small chamber and even a bed with her sister. Would that be Midori's fate, too, or worse? And what if her relatives weren't there any longer or wanted nothing to do with her? She sighed and tried to put such thoughts out of her mind. They were pointless.

In a corner of one room she had set up a small shrine in honour of her parents and she went to kneel in front of it. Two miniature urns held part of their ashes and there were wooden tablets with their names carved in Japanese *kanji*. A small bowl filled with sand held burning incense sticks which filled the room with sweet scent and early that morning she'd left an offering of food and drink.

She clapped her hands twice, bowed deeply, then began to pray for her parents' help.

'Please, give me the strength to meet my fate with courage, as you would have done. Help me to overcome any obstacles and to accept with fortitude that which can't be changed. Please, I beg of you, stay with me always and protect me,' she whispered. 'I need you both to guide me now as I journey into the unknown.'

She bowed once more and waited for a response. She believed with every fibre of her being that her parents were still with her, although as *kami*, spirits, and she had no doubt they were benign ones since they'd both been good in life. This was part of the Shinto religion she'd been taught by her father, and she much preferred it to her mother's Christian belief in an afterlife where the choice was only between heaven and hell.

'If the *Shogun* could see me now,' she whispered, 'then perhaps he wouldn't doubt me.'

A small wind stirred the hair on the nape of her neck and she knew her parents had heard her. Immediately she felt reassured. She must remember she wasn't alone and never would be. The prayers finished, she took the urns and tablets and began to pack. Wherever she went, her parents would go too.

There was one other thing she couldn't leave behind. From a small chest of drawers, she retrieved a tiny silk pouch. It contained a golden cross hanging on a chain and Midori held it up to the light. She shivered at the sight of the tiny symbol, glinting in the sunlight. She hadn't realised that to own it was to put oneself in the greatest of danger, but after what Ichiro had just told her, she understood now. It had belonged to her mother though, so how could she possibly leave it behind?

The safest course of action would be to throw the necklace into the pond and never set eyes on it again, but images of her mother wearing it kept intruding into Midori's mind. Hannah would have wanted her to keep it and surely, if it was well hidden, no one would ever know? Midori looked at the offending object again, then made up her mind. Soon, she'd be on her way to a country where such things were not forbidden – were encouraged even – and it might come in useful. She tied it into a piece of cloth, then fetched a garment and slit open a seam. Sewed safely inside, no one would ever find it, she was sure ...

Chapter Five

Nico lay on the soft *futon* with his hands behind his head, contemplating the dancing dust motes. It was only just after dawn, but he couldn't sleep. His mind was still whirling from his encounter with the sword-wielding Midori and his gut churned at the enormity of the tasks that lay before him.

How could I have agreed to take her with me? I must be mad!

All his arguments against letting her buy passage on his ship were definitely valid. Bringing one woman to live among over a hundred men was asking for serious trouble, no doubt about it. And not just any woman, but a young and breathtakingly beautiful one at that.

'Aaargh!' He punched his pillow to give vent to some of the frustration.

She had surprised him by attacking him like that, but he'd never been in any real danger. He could have said no and walked away, then put her out of his mind forever. There was nothing that said he had to be the one to rescue her, after all. *Except my conscience, devil take it!* He happened to be the man she chose to ask and once he'd seen her, talked to her and been dazzled by that amazing smile, he was lost.

Dear Lord, but she was so determined! Something about her resonated within him – perhaps an echo of the young boy he'd once been during that first voyage with Casper. Because, despite her bravado, he knew she was as vulnerable as he'd been then. No matter how many fighting tricks she knew, how skilled with her weapons, she'd been no match against a big man like himself. How then would she fare on a ship full of rough sailors without someone to protect her?

He dry-washed his face. *Well, I've taken on the task and I'll do my best.* The Lord only knew how.

Her beauty had disturbed him, more than he cared to admit. He'd seen pretty women before, had even been lucky enough to bed a few, but never had he met anyone like Midori. Perhaps it was her mixed heritage, he thought. The combination of European and Asian features made her looks exotic, yet not as different as the pure Japanese girls. She was somehow much more appealing and he couldn't deny that her fighting skills had fired his blood, too. *Such courage!*

'Struth, but I don't need this complication and I can't be lusting after her all through the voyage. I'll go insane … No, enough! No more thoughts of her.

He tried to concentrate on something else. *Anything other than Midori!* He let his gaze roam the plain interior of the house he was in. The spartan furnishings really appealed to Nico's aesthetic sense and he wanted to remember them when he left. Raised wooden floors supported the *tatami* mats, and the walls were made up of unpainted wooden pillars interspersed with removable panels, sliding doors and screens which partitioned all the rooms. The screens were fashioned of plain, oiled rice paper. Shiny and soft, with silvery strands of fibre forming a pretty pattern, they were very unlike the coarse material he was used to writing on. The only other furniture in the room, apart from the odd silk cushion, were some low tables.

If only his life were as simple, but fate seemed determined to play nasty tricks on him. Well, there was nothing for it but to grit his teeth and cope.

He'd had a lot of practice at that.

'We must buy you provisions for the journey,' Ichiro said to Midori the morning after her visit to Dejima. 'No doubt you'll find the ship's fare inedible so it's best if you cook your own food. I'll have my men deliver a small brazier to the ship and enough fuel to last you six months if you're careful.'

'What if it doesn't fit? I'm not sure how big my cabin will be.'

'We will make sure it's big enough for your needs.' There was a determined set to Ichiro's mouth which stopped Midori from arguing the point. 'Is there anything else?'

Together they made a list, and a servant was sent to buy the required items.

'Now I must go out for a while, but I think it's best if you stay here, just in case anyone should catch sight of you and report it to the authorities.'

Midori agreed, but as he'd said nothing about her having to remain in her room, she soon made her way into the tiny garden at the back of the inn. It was a haven of serenity, with a tiny water feature ringed by moss-covered stones and clumps of bamboo. The garden hummed with the drone of busy insects and a tiny frog croaked forlornly from under the shelter of a huge leaf. Midori sank down on to a rock nearby, breathing in the air that was moist with a tang of greenery. She stared at the tranquil scene, trying to come to terms with the unknown future she now faced.

It's odd how life can go on for years in the same old routines, then suddenly something happens to turn it upside down.

She had been so sure the biggest challenge she'd ever encounter would be marriage. But the older she got, finding a suitor became less likely with each day, and she had accepted her fate and settled into a peaceful existence where nothing much happened. Of course, she'd had to cope with the loss of her parents, but that was something everyone went through at some stage. Hard though it had been, it was nothing compared to what she now had to endure.

She took a deep breath. *Perhaps it won't be so bad?* After all, her mother had done much the same thing, all those years ago, hadn't she? Hannah had left her friends and family in England, never to return, and she'd been blissfully happy. Not once had she ever said she regretted her decision to stay. There was no reason why Midori shouldn't find joy in a strange country, as well. *Whatever happens, it must be better than staying in a place where I'm not wanted?*

Midori clenched her fists and silently cursed the *Shogun*.

'I wish he hadn't taken against foreigners,' she whispered. 'If only he would let me defend myself so I could convince him I'm not a Christian.'

And if only the *gai-jin* had kept their religion to themselves …

She sat by the little pond in the garden behind the inn for what seemed like ages. Completely lost in thought, she didn't realise she wasn't alone any longer until she was suddenly grabbed from behind.

'Got her!'

The harsh voice sounded triumphant and Midori twisted frantically to see who her captor was, her heart pounding with shock. To her consternation, there were several men crowding into the small, enclosed space, all dressed in identical clothing, which looked alarmingly official. A lightning streak of fear shot through her and she tried to struggle, but it was futile as she was completely outnumbered and there was no chance of escape.

'You're to come with us, *gai-jin*. The authorities have issued a warrant for your arrest.'

'I'm not a *gai-jin*, I'm the daughter of a *daimyo*,' she said, trying to sound confident and haughty. 'Release me, or it will be the worse for you.'

Her words were greeted with laughter and derision, and no one paid her the slightest heed. Instead, her hands were quickly tied behind her with a tight knot and she was hauled away through the inn. Just before they passed the front door of the *ryokan* and out into the city, she caught a glimpse of Satoshi, Ichiro's servant, hiding in a dark corner of the hallway. He seemed to be cowering in terror, but there was a strange look in his eyes which had Midori puzzled. There was no time to dwell on it, however, and knowing he'd seen her lessened some of her fear. Ichiro would be told what had happened, then he'd help her somehow. The thought gave her courage and she shrugged off the tight grip of her guard to walk unaided with her head held high.

'Lead on,' she commanded.

Some of the courage left her when she arrived at her destination, however. Her bonds were removed and she was shoved into a small room, filled to overflowing with pitiful individuals. They stank something dreadful, and she gagged as she landed on the floor with a thump. Gnarled hands reached out – some to help her up, some just fingering the fine silk of her clothing – but she shrank from them all and shot to her feet in record time. The hands continued to paw at her and she batted away a few, shrugging off others, looking around for some corner to shrink into.

'Have you any food? Give us something?' a voice pleaded, but Midori just shook her head, feeling too nauseous to speak.

'Oh, she's a haughty one, but they'll soon beat it out of her, won't they?' someone else cackled. 'What're you here for? Stealing? They'll cut your head off, so they will.'

'Leave me alone,' Midori muttered, shivering with delayed reaction. Seeing a free space by the wall at last, she stumbled towards it and sank down with her back against the rough surface. She pulled her knees up in front of her and hid her face behind the curtain of her hair, which had come undone

The less she saw of this place the better.

Nico was in the middle of his evening meal, enjoying the tranquillity of the night and the exotic dishes laid out for him so artistically. Casper had insisted on hiring a Japanese cook for the duration of his stay as he liked to try new things. Nico was all for it as well and so far he'd loved everything the man had served him. He would be very sorry to have to go back to the indifferent ship's fare in the morning.

He didn't hear anyone approaching, but an unexpected draught of air made him aware he wasn't alone in the room. Taken by surprise, he choked on a piece of shrimp *tempura* while staring at the menacing figure who had appeared, seemingly out of nowhere. The man stood before him, calm and unmoving. Dressed all in black and with a face like a threatening thunderstorm, he was a formidable sight. Nico immediately noticed the two shining swords at his side, their hilts glittering with his every move, and he felt sure there would be other weapons hidden among the man's clothing.

Throughout the bout of coughing which accompanied his attempts to dislodge the piece of shrimp, thoughts of the *ninja* Midori had threatened him with earlier streaked through his brain. He dismissed them almost immediately, though. From what he'd gathered, *ninja* never showed their faces and this man was staring at him openly, almost appraisingly. Besides, he'd already agreed to take her on board, so there was no need for threats.

Breathing normally again at last, Nico slowly stood up and bowed. '*Hai, nani desu ka?*' He wasn't sure he'd said that right, but thought the man would understand his meaning anyway.

To his surprise, the intruder replied in accented English. 'I am Kumashiro, brother of Midori-*sama*.' The polite phrase, '*Yoroshiku onegai shimasu*,' that roughly equalled the English 'how do you do' was tacked on almost as a grudging afterthought, but Nico barely noticed.

Brother? Nico studied the man's features again, but

couldn't see any trace of European blood. *So, a half-brother then*, he surmised. And obviously high-born, judging by his clothing and weapons. *How strange.* That must mean Midori was the child of a noblewoman. Why had such a lady married an Englishman? It seemed unlikely in the extreme, but there was no time to think about that now.

'How did you get in here? I thought no one was allowed on to this island without approval,' Nico said, vaguely irritated that the guard system didn't seem to be working both ways.

Kumashiro smiled briefly. 'Guard is … incapacitated.'

'I see. Well, to what do I owe this honour?' Nico crossed his arms over his chest to show he wasn't intimidated.

'You made bargain with my sister yesterday and I trust you keep it?'

Nico nodded. 'Of course. I'm a man of my word.'

Midori's brother looked as if he doubted whether foreigners could be honourable, but he didn't say this out loud. 'Hmph,' was all he said. 'Your ship sail tomorrow? This is certain?'

'Yes, unless your fellow countrymen find some way of delaying me. The cargo has been loaded and the ship is ready to leave at first light. I believe Mistress Midori's possessions are already on board.'

'My men have seen to it. There is slight problem, though.'

'Oh? Has she changed her mind?' In Nico's experience, that was something ladies were very prone to doing, and it drove him to distraction. He hoped he wasn't to be kept waiting, especially since he hadn't wanted this particular passenger in the first place.

'No, she has been arrested.'

'What? Why?' Nico felt himself go tense at this unexpected turn of events.

'She is *gai-jin*, like you. If I can't free her from prison, she be killed soon, tomorrow maybe.'

A cold grip took hold of Nico's gut. How could Midori be arrested and executed simply for being foreign? *So she was right then, she really did need to leave, and quickly.* He could see now why she'd been so insistent on buying passage immediately. He frowned and looked at the man before him. 'Can you free her?'

'Perhaps. But if I do, she must disappear straight away, or bad consequences for me and my clan. I must not be seen with her now.'

'Surely you'll be watched?'

'Yes, but there are ways of becoming, er …'

'Invisible?'

'*Hai.*'

Nico thought it best not to ask any further questions. The less he knew, the better, so he simply nodded.

'If I bring her during night, you be ready to receive her?' Kumashiro asked.

Nico didn't hesitate. This complicated matters even more, but he couldn't refuse. If he'd had doubts about helping Midori before, they were all gone now. She was in serious danger. 'Yes. I will go on board as soon as I have finished eating. I was all set to leave in any case.'

'Good. Thank you.' Kumashiro looked as if he wanted to say something else, but wasn't sure how to phrase it and Nico thought he could guess what it might be.

'Don't worry, I will look after your sister to the best of my ability. It may not be enough, but I'll do all I can. She is … a very brave woman.' Despite his anger earlier, he respected Midori for the way she had tried to force him to do her bidding. He'd never met a woman like her before, so sure of her own abilities and so unafraid.

Kumashiro narrowed his eyes as if he was sizing him

up again, judging what manner of man he might be, then unexpectedly he smiled once more. 'Thank you. I hope you really are man of your word.'

He turned to leave, but before he had reached the door, Nico realised he couldn't leave it at that and blurted out, 'Wait! Can I help in any way?'

Kumashiro swivelled round, his eyebrows raised in surprise. '*Nani?*'

'I would like to offer my assistance. You know, to free your sister …' Nico trailed off, realising he was probably insulting the man. After all, what could he do? A foreigner who wasn't even allowed to set foot on the mainland? His offer was genuine, though; he really wanted to help.

Kumashiro stayed silent for a while, deep in thought, then he nodded. 'Maybe, but you are putting self in danger, you know this?'

It was Nico's turn to nod. 'Yes, I know. Now please tell me what you would like me to do.'

Chapter Six

Despite the fear, Midori dozed for a while, but raised her head when the door was opened and something was thrown in by the guards. She wondered if it was another poor condemned soul, but then realised that what had arrived was their supper in a sack. Her fellow prisoners dived for the floor, fighting tooth and nail for the meagre rations of what looked like stale rice cakes. Midori shuddered and wondered how any of them could even think of eating. Bile rose in her throat and she swallowed hard.

For a short while, she'd thought perhaps she was just having a nightmare, but this was all too real. The hard, cold dirt floor she was sitting on smelled as if a hundred latrines had been emptied into it. The damp wall behind her back and the unbelievable stench of accumulated filth on the people all around her – no brain could have dreamed up any of it. Cockroaches scurried across her legs and a moment ago she had seen a rat peeping out through a hole in the corner. Her skin crawled and she scratched repeatedly at real or imaginary itches that were driving her insane.

I mustn't panic. Keep calm, breathe.

But never in all her life had she felt this afraid, this helpless and so utterly, devastatingly alone. There were people all around her, but they weren't the kind of people she was used to associating with. Most were not of her rank, just common persons, even *hinin* – beggars and other social offenders – and *eta*, the extremely unclean, lowest of the low. She pitied them, naturally, but wanted to shout out loud that she didn't belong here. Her status as the daughter of a *daimyo* should have afforded her better treatment and saved her from this, but the truth was they were all equals here. All at the mercy of their gaolers. *Here, I am nobody.*

'Father, Mother, please help me,' she prayed. She doubted if anything but the intervention of spirits could save her now.

An all-pervasive fear spread through her veins, paralysing her from head to toe until she felt as though she'd never be able to move again. She wanted to scream, but her jaw was stuck, so she couldn't open her mouth wide enough. And she couldn't breathe properly because her ribcage wouldn't budge.

Where is Ichiro? Would no one help her? But then how could he when to do so would be to risk his own life and the honour of the clan?

He'd already done so much …

The morning after Ichiro told her she had to leave, a small party assembled in the castle courtyard just after dawn. Midori looked around in surprise. She had expected a retinue of well over a hundred men, since Ichiro never travelled anywhere with less, but today there were only ten mounted guards and no baggage of any kind. She frowned as she walked across the cobbled stones.

She had dressed in clothing similar to the men's. This made it easier to ride and protected her legs from scratches and cuts. By the time her brother emerged from the main building, she was already astride her horse, having mounted without assistance. She liked to be self-sufficient in everything.

'Where is my hawk?' Ichiro's voice rang out, imperious as always and so like their late father's it made Midori's heart constrict.

'Here, my lord.' A man ran forward and handed his master the hooded bird of prey with a deep bow.

'Are we ready?' There were murmurs of assent. 'Then,

let us depart. I wish to find some sport before the sun is too high.'

As they clattered out through the gates and across the moat, Midori rode up beside him and leaned over to whisper, 'Where are my things? Aren't we leaving today after all?'

'Yes, but I think we're being watched, so we have to pretend we are only going hawking today. I sent someone ahead into the forest last night with our belongings and provisions for the journey. More men will follow us in a couple of days and when they catch up with us, I'll send someone back with the bird.'

Midori nodded. She trusted Ichiro implicitly and if he thought this subterfuge was necessary, she wouldn't argue with him. No one watching their departure would assume Ichiro was going very far, she thought. Her brother had planned well.

'The castle was rife with rumour all day yesterday and I also thought if I was seen to go hunting, seemingly without a care in the world, it might calm everyone down,' Ichiro said.

'Good point. If there was truly any danger, you would hardly risk venturing into the woods with so few men.'

'Precisely.' Ichiro smiled at her, then spurred his horse into a canter.

They rode up the hill towards the temple and she restrained the urge to turn and look back at the castle more than once. Although she knew this was probably the last time she would ever see the place which had been her home for nineteen years, she didn't want to raise anyone's suspicions. Besides, if she closed her eyes she could easily conjure up an image of the castle and its surroundings and she doubted she would ever forget it.

'Here, take the bird for a while.' Ichiro handed over the beautiful creature, obviously in an effort to divert her from her sad thoughts.

Midori sent him a smile of gratitude. 'Thank you. Am I that transparent?'

'Only occasionally. There are times when you are a little like your mother. She never could hide her emotions.'

'I know.' It was one of the things about Hannah that her father had loved and Midori remembered him teasing her mother about it. With an effort she put thoughts of her parents out of her mind and adjusted her glove to protect her wrist from the sharp talons of the bird, which shifted restlessly from one foot to the other. She concentrated on admiring the creature as its feathers gleamed a deep amber in the rays of the morning sun and the slight breeze rippled through the shiny surface.

The temple bell clanged as they rode past, stirring up memories of that cold day last winter. Midori shivered. It didn't matter whether she ever saw her mother's grave again, since her spirit travelled with her. Nevertheless, she glanced towards the burial ground out of the corner of her eye and sent up a prayer to the gods to keep the rest of her mother's and father's ashes safe.

A short distance along the track a man waited with spare horses loaded with provisions for the journey and Midori's belongings. She had only packed a single bamboo basket, lined and covered with oiled cloth and tied at the top so the contents couldn't spill out. As the servant brought the pack horse alongside Midori's own she noticed the fastenings had come undone on her basket and ordered the man to halt for a moment so she could retie them. As she bent to perform this task, however, she drew in a sharp breath.

'Ichiro, someone's tampered with my things.' She looked at her brother, who came over to peer into the opening.

He frowned. 'How do you know? It looks undisturbed to me.'

'I packed my amber-coloured *kimono* last, as it's my least precious one, but now the blue one is on top. See?'

'Hmm. Well, you'll have to check later to see if anything is missing. We don't have time to stop now.' Ichiro looked around them with narrowed eyes, as if he was afraid they were being spied on at this very moment. 'We must make haste, away from here.'

Midori nodded. He was right and, if anything had been taken, there was nothing she could do about it now.

Later, when they stopped for a quick meal, Midori emptied out the contents of her basket to see if anything was missing, but everything was still there.

'I think someone just searched through my belongings, then put them back, although in the wrong order,' she told Ichiro. 'As far as I can tell, all the silver you gave me is still sewn inside my garments and the few trinkets I brought are intact.' She didn't tell Ichiro about the golden cross, but she had squeezed the seam in which she'd hidden it to make sure the package was still where she had put it and to her relief had felt the small bump inside.

'Good. Perhaps they were just checking to see what you brought.' Ichiro didn't seem unduly concerned and Midori tried to relax. She was probably making too much of this, but it was hard to quell the anxiety altogether.

'You really think someone's watching us?' she asked him.

'Yes. Whoever told the *Shogun* of your existence must bear us a grudge. There wouldn't be any point in informing the authorities unless you knew something was going to be done about it. They will have made sure the *Shogun*'s men know your whereabouts.'

'It still doesn't make sense. What have I ever done?'

'It's not you personally they're after. If you were taken and burned, it would be seen as confirmation that I had harboured a Christian in my household and therefore brought dishonour on the entire clan. There are certain of our neighbours who wouldn't be unhappy if such a fate should befall us.'

'Yes, of course.'

Ichiro put a hand on her shoulder and squeezed. 'Stop worrying. I know my lands better than anyone. Father taught me well. I will take you to Nagasaki safely.'

'Thank you. For everything. I'm sorry to be putting you to so much trouble.'

'Think nothing of it. You're the only sibling I have left, so of course I'll do everything I can to help you.' Midori could see the deep affection in his eyes and knew that although he'd never say it out loud, he loved her, as she did him.

Midori thought of the others, two older sisters she had never known who had died young, and a little brother who hadn't made it past his first birthday. 'I suppose it's just as well there is only me,' she said. It had made the bond between them stronger. 'Can I write to you, do you think?' She didn't want the link severed completely, even if they never saw each other again.

'You can always try. Perhaps the trading ships could bring your missives. I will have to find a trustworthy individual in Nagasaki who can forward any letters to me. I'll see what I can arrange …'

Midori had thought imprisonment would become easier to bear at night, when she couldn't see the filth around her or the other miserable inmates, but she soon found out she was wrong.

With darkness came all sorts of sounds, magnified by her suddenly more acute hearing, and they all increased her terror tenfold. The rustling of the cockroaches and rats on the floor made it seem as if it was teeming with wildlife, even though she knew there probably weren't as many as she was imagining. The sinister wheezing of someone's breath appeared to be right next to her ear, rather than at arm's length. Worst of all, the screams of some poor soul being tortured echoed around the prison with alarming clarity now they were no longer drowned out by everyone else's chatter or moaning.

As the hours passed she started to calm down and tried to make her brain function enough to make some sort of plan. She had to help herself, and there must be a way out of here, if only she could think of something. Unfortunately, being terrified had a way of freezing her thought processes, which didn't help. Pulling herself together, she took some deep, calming breaths and tried to meditate.

She heard the door being opened, but kept her eyes closed and continued with her soothing mantra. Going deeper and deeper inside her own mind, she attempted to reach a state of utter calm. She was almost there, when a hand grabbed her arm and she was roughly yanked to her feet.

'Your turn. The judge wants to see you,' a harsh voice informed her.

'What? Who? No! Where are you taking me?' Midori felt dazed and confused, her brain not yet fully returned to earth, but she knew one thing for sure – she didn't want to be taken anywhere else. This room may be a nightmare, but there was a certain safety here, nevertheless.

The guard didn't pay any attention to her protests, but hauled her out through the door and across a courtyard. Through a gate they went, Midori digging in her heels as best she could. It was to no avail as he was a strong man. They continued along a corridor where the sounds of the torture victim's screams became louder. Midori's stomach cramped with fear. She wasn't afraid of the kind of pain encountered in normal, everyday life, such as could be caused by accidents or fighting, but the excruciating pain inflicted here, on purpose, was something else altogether. Thinking about it would only make matters worse, however, so instead she tried to memorise details of her surroundings. If she was to escape, knowing her way around would be vital.

The man came to a halt at last and knocked on a door, which was thrown open from inside on squeaking hinges. With his hand still clamped around Midori's arm, he pulled her through, leading her down the middle of a long, dimly lit room. It looked a bit like Ichiro's Great Hall, although on a smaller scale. The painted scrolls decorating the walls were slightly frayed at the edges and the *tatami* mats none too clean. Nevertheless, it was an imposing chamber, no doubt designed to intimidate the accused prisoners brought here. There was a distinct smell of fear in the air, making Midori take shallow breaths in order to avoid breathing it in.

'I can walk by myself,' she hissed, but the guard refused to let go of her arm.

Her eyes darted around to see what or whom she was up against. On the dais at the other end sat a small, wizened man in black robes and with a black hat set on top of his white hair. A pointy goatee beard and drooping moustache, together with the oblong shape of his face and barely visible eyes, made him look like a disaffected rat. When he started to speak, Midori wasn't surprised to see that he had rather large, protruding front teeth. She concentrated on the image of a rodent in order to distract her mind from all the other thoughts crowding into it, so as not to show any signs of fear. *I'm not afraid of rats.*

'Kumashiro Midori,' the man stated. 'You have been arrested by order of the *Shogun* as a *gai-jin* and traitor. Do you have anything to say?'

'I am not a *gai-jin*, my lord, I am a true *Nihon-jin* and I would fight to the death for my country and the *Shogun*. I have been falsely accused, I know not by whom,' she stated boldly, raising her chin a notch for added measure.

'We have it on good authority your mother was a foreigner and a Christian. You have been tainted by her,' the man said, his tone emotionless.

'No!' The word came out a bit too forcefully, so Midori took a deep breath before continuing. She had to stay calm, had to convince them somehow. 'That is, yes, my mother was a foreigner, but I didn't adopt her faith. I follow my father's teachings, nothing else.'

'I think not. You have been observed.' The man rustled some pieces of paper and peered at one. 'It says here you have been heard praying to the Christian god and that you own a symbol which signifies your acceptance of this faith.' He beckoned to someone next to him who held up a small gold cross on a chain. Midori blinked.

No, it can't be!

'This belongs to you, *neh*?' Rat-face took it from his henchman and threw it at her contemptuously. With quick reflexes she caught the offending object, staring at it in disbelief and almost with loathing. *Such a small, pretty thing, but so dangerous. I should never have kept it.*

'I ... it was my mother's. She left it to me as a keepsake, but it means nothing to me other than that. I swear.' Midori clenched her fists in frustration, slipping the offending item into a secret pocket inside her sleeve. How had they got hold of it? She'd been so sure it was well hidden, but she realised now that whoever had searched her basket must have unpicked the seam, then put the parcel back inside without the cross. She cursed inwardly; she should have made sure. But who had done such a thing and why? There must have been someone in Ichiro's household spying on her, perhaps even one of her own servants.

'I see you are proving difficult.' The man nodded to

himself, as if this was something he had already expected. 'Well, we shall soon see if you change your tune. Tie her up and take her away.' With a flick of the wrist, he dismissed her from his sight and the guard shoved her in the direction of two coarse-looking individuals.

'No! I can prove it. I'll sign a declaration, anything ...' Midori tried to protest further, but was cut off by a cuff across the cheek.

'Let's go.' The taller of the two men dragged her away and she knew then that Ichiro had been right all along – no one would listen to her. No one would believe her.

She had lost.

Chapter Seven

Outside the main gate of the prison, Nico was wondering if he'd taken leave of his senses. *What on earth possessed me to offer to help?* Any sensible man would have boarded his ship, not become embroiled in some doomed rescue attempt because of a misguided sense of duty towards a woman he'd only met once. *Even if she is an outsider here like me.* He didn't have any guarantees that Kumashiro wouldn't just use him and leave him to his fate. After all, he barely knew the man.

Nico sighed. *Obviously I'm not sane in the least, but now the die is cast and I have to go through with it.*

Following Kumashiro's instructions, he had poured an entire keg of *sake* down the front of his jacket and drunk a few mouthfuls as well. The alcoholic fumes and cloying smell of the rice wine was making him feel nauseous, but he swallowed hard and tried to ignore it. Summoning up his best acting skills, he began to make his way along the street outside the prison. He weaved drunkenly from side to side and made sure he stumbled on anything big enough to trip over. He filled his lungs with air and began to sing a loud and raucous ditty, the only one he could remember the words to at the moment. Inwardly, he prayed.

The effect of his little charade was almost instantaneous, as Kumashiro had predicted. The gate was flung open and guards swarmed out of the prison compound as if they were under attack, surrounding him faster than he had thought possible. Swords were pointed at him, and he held up his hands in mock surrender and laughed out loud. Then he ended his song with a large belch and a hiccough.

'What's this? *Nani?* Are we having a parade?' He swayed

exaggeratedly on his feet, danced a little jig, then took a step backwards, almost tripping over his own feet.

A stream of Japanese words were fired at him by the man who appeared to be in charge. Although Nico understood the gist of it, he pretended ignorance and raised his *sake* bottle in a clumsy salute. '*Kampai!*' He nodded at the man. 'Bottoms up.'

More angry words followed, but Nico became engrossed in the fact that his bottle was now empty. He shook it repeatedly, as if to see whether there was anything left inside. 'I want more!' he bellowed. '*Mo ichi,*' he repeated in Japanese, pointing at the bottle.

The head of the guard was now holding a whispered conversation with a fellow officer and Nico heard him muttering, '*Baka gai-jin*' – stupid foreigner – several times, which he took to be a good sign. If they thought him a fool, they might consider him harmless. There was a lot of pointing towards the prison, as well as in the opposite direction towards the harbour, as if the two men couldn't agree on a course of action. Nico ignored them and started on another ditty in a voice which was anything but melodious.

The muted conversation was interrupted by some newcomers on the scene, a group of men seemingly on their way home from a night on the town.

'What's going on here? Can we help?' one of them shouted.

'Yes, we'll do our civic duty,' called out another, or at least that's what Nico had been told he'd say. Kumashiro had prepared him so that he'd know if things were going wrong. He pretended he wasn't paying attention, but he listened closely and picked up the words which told him the conversation was going mostly as Kumashiro had planned.

'It is none of your concern,' the head guard replied haughtily, but his fellow officer whispered something in his ear which made him look at Nico again and mutter, 'Hmm.'

'Is the stupid foreigner bothering you?' the civilian persisted. 'Shall we throw him in the harbour for you?' His companions erupted into loud guffaws, shouting agreement.

'Yes, yes, let's dunk him, serve him right. They are too full of themselves, these *gai-jin*.'

'No, thank you. He is to be arrested. I have the matter in hand.'

Loud protests followed by the civilians. 'No, surely not!'

'He's probably just lost, didn't mean any harm.'

'Yes, look at the state of him!'

'We've all been there, a bit too much *sake* and before you know it …'

The second officer again whispered something to his superior and Nico wanted to shake the man. His nerves were stretched to breaking point; this was all taking too long and he wished himself a hundred miles away.

'Very well, I will let him go,' the man said at last. 'Perhaps you could take him back to where he came from? I can spare you a small escort in case he becomes troublesome, but most of my men are needed here at this time.'

'Back to where?' The civilian peered at the guard, as if he didn't quite understand.

'To the island of Dejima, of course,' the man snarled. 'Take him to the gate there and tell the fool of a guard on duty that next time he lets one of these idiots on to the mainland, he's a dead man.'

'Oh, I see. Very well, we can do that, can't we?' The civilian looked at his friends, who all nodded. Two of them came forward and took Nico by the arms, dragging him along.

'Come, it's time for bed. Bed, understand?'

'I want *sake*.' Nico frowned petulantly and dragged his feet. 'More *sake!*'

'Yes, yes, we'll find you some, now come along.'

The man waved away the guards, saying, 'We'll be all right, we don't need help. It's only one man, and a foreigner at that, we can manage.'

'Very well. Thank you.' Everyone bowed politely, including Nico whose head was unceremoniously pushed downwards by one of his new friends. The prison guards then began to disappear into their compound once again, like ants into a nest. The drunken party wended its way along the street and turned a corner. Out of sight of the prison they all began to run as if the hounds of hell were after them, and they didn't stop until they reached the very darkest part of the harbour.

At first, sunk in misery, Midori barely resisted the pull on her arms and didn't look to see where she was being taken. She assumed she was to be tortured, and it didn't matter where that was to take place. All she could pray for now was that they would kill her by mistake. Better that than …

Her mind suddenly rebelled and a steely resolve spread through her, taking her by surprise. *No, I don't want to die!* And she most certainly didn't want to be tortured. *It's up to me to do something about it.* Acting on impulse, she hurled herself at the guard on her right, taking him by surprise. She flung her arms round his neck from behind so the rope her wrists were tied with cut off his air supply. She crossed her hands behind his head, making the improvised garrotte squeeze him with all her might, her strength born of desperation and fear. Exhilaration flowed through her. She was in charge of her own destiny again and it felt good.

'*Chikusho!*' She shouted out her father's favourite curse.

She thanked the gods she was still wearing *hakama* and not hampered by a *kimono*. With her legs wrapped round his waist the man was hard put to stay upright, never mind shake her off. He struggled to pull her hands and the deadly rope away from his windpipe. In his frantic attempts to dislodge her, he swivelled from side to side. This protected Midori to a certain extent from attack by the other guard, who was trying to lunge at her. She kicked out several times, aiming for the second man's most vulnerable parts, and had the satisfaction of hearing him grunt.

The guard whose back she was clinging to suddenly charged backwards and slammed her into the wall, knocking the air out of her lungs and dealing her head a heavy blow against a door post. She blinked to clear her vision and gasped for breath, but didn't loosen her hold on the man's throat. She could feel him panicking now, then weakening, and prayed he would die quickly.

As he fell to the ground at last, however, the other guard pounced on her and she wasn't quite fast enough to escape his vice-like grip. His face was a contorted mask of fury only inches away from hers and he snarled, 'Get up,' and yanked her to her feet. She tried to resist, kicking out at him again, but this time he was ready for her. 'Oh, no you don't, you little *ama!*'

He grabbed her by the hair, while he kicked at the lifeless form of his comrade to check whether he was dead. 'You'll pay for this, just you wait.' With a vicious yank, he lifted her up and threw her over one shoulder, knocking the air out of her again. Despair flooded Midori's brain and all the fight went out of her as suddenly as it had come. *I have failed.*

A small rustling noise to one side penetrated the fog of despondency. In the next instant the man carrying her lost his grip on her and she fell to the ground, jarring her shoulder painfully. Looking up, she saw him staring at her strangely, before making a gurgling noise. He slumped to the ground, but a black-clad figure caught him from behind to stop any sound. Midori's breath stuck in her throat and she watched the attacker remove a knife from the guard's thick neck. Her rescuer had eyes that Midori would have recognised anywhere.

'Ichiro!' She mouthed his name, but no sound escaped her.

'Come,' he breathed next to her ear. 'There is not a moment to lose.'

Her heart, which had been doing somersaults, returned to its normal position, and she moved with lightning speed. She followed the hand that tugged her along and whipped her through a nearby door before anyone else came.

Several sombre shadows followed them. Others detached themselves from obscure corners of the courtyard to run in silent procession towards freedom. There was no time to look around as, with calm efficiency and speed, the shadowy men all climbed a blackened rope ladder slung over one wall. There didn't seem to be any guards on duty here, but Midori didn't have time to wonder about it. When her turn came, she climbed as fast as she could, helped by someone pulling her from above and hands pushing from below. At any moment she expected to hear a cry go up as her absence was noted, but nothing happened. There was the sound of people talking and laughing in the distance, but no alarm raised.

On the other side of the wall a palanquin waited, as dark as all her rescuers and barely visible. She almost dove into it head first and it started to move immediately. Someone running on either side pulled down the flaps to leave her in darkness. Jolted along like that, Midori should have felt sick, but she didn't. Instead, jubilation swelled through her and she breathed in the slightly stale air inside the conveyance, which, compared to the odours of the prison, was like perfume to her senses.

Ichiro had rescued her and she would be forever grateful to him.

By the time she was allowed out of the palanquin her brother was waiting near the shore, dressed in clothing identical to that worn by his men. They all blended into their surroundings and only his voice gave away his exact position. 'Are you hurt?' he asked, an anxious note in his voice which she had seldom heard.

'No, I just feel indescribably dirty.' She felt for his hands in the darkness and gripped them tight once she found them. 'I can't thank you enough. It was … You have no idea what … They were just about to …'

'I know. Don't think of it now, it's over. You did very well to kill one man, it helped us to rescue you more quickly. There is very little time, we must make haste out to the ship. The captain awaits us. And remember, don't show yourself until well after the ship has left in case there are other vessels around.'

'I promise. But Ichiro, you must take care, too. There is a traitor in our midst.' She told him quickly about the cross and Ichiro swore when she brought it out of her sleeve to show him.

'I knew it. Don't worry, I'll get to the bottom of this, never fear.'

Just at that moment, the moon came out and Midori caught sight of a pale face which stuck out briefly from behind a nearby tree, then disappeared almost as quickly. It happened so fast, at first she wasn't sure she had really seen anything. Then a memory flashed through her brain and she suddenly knew without a doubt who the traitor was. Fury threatened to choke her, but she quelled it and instead pretended to stumble. When Ichiro caught her, she whispered to him urgently.

Ichiro set off towards the tree straight away and whoever had been hiding behind it burst out of the cover and ran for his life, thereby proving his guilt. The other men had by now realised something was going on, and followed their master, converging on the fleeing individual from different angles. The traitor didn't stand a chance and, in the end, he was lucky to end his life swiftly with a knife between his shoulder blades. It was far too lenient a fate for such as him.

Midori waited by the shore and when Ichiro returned, panting slightly, she asked, 'Was I right?'

He nodded. 'Yes, Satoshi is dead. If I hadn't seen it with my own eyes, I would never have believed him capable of such treachery. That will teach me not to trust so easily in future. Thank you, you have no doubt saved me a lot of aggravation.'

'I'm glad.'

It was time to go. She was led down to the shore, where a tiny rowing boat waited. Ichiro took her hand to steady her, then jumped in swiftly behind her.

'Are you sure you should come?' Midori whispered.

'Yes, I want to see you settled.'

'But it's too dangerous. Someone might see you.'

'If they do, they'll be dead soon after.' He nodded towards the shore, where dark shadows moved into position behind trees and boulders. If anyone else had followed them, they would be dealt with ruthlessly.

To Midori's surprise they all bowed low to her as a gesture of farewell. She understood that they were honouring her, the *daimyo*'s *gai-jin* sister, and this was totally unexpected. She was deeply touched and, with equal respect, bowed back. She owed them her life.

The enormous ship lay anchored in the middle of the bay and, as they rowed out across the dark water, it rose before them until Midori felt completely dwarfed. It was moving slowly up and down with the almost non-existent waves. For a moment Midori felt like turning round and running as fast as she could, away from this hulking monster, but she took a deep breath and composed herself. No matter how terrifying her journey would be, surely it couldn't be worse than what she had just escaped from?

The smell of salt water mixed with the acrid stench of tar and there was a tang of wet wood hanging in the air, as well. A few lanterns were dotted around the deck, but the ship was in darkness for the most part. It was also strangely silent as they climbed a long rope ladder to reach the top. Midori jumped down on to the deck, then waited for Ichiro to join her.

'Where is everyone?' She looked around with interest. This ship wasn't like anything she'd ever seen before – it was big and unwieldy, with a seemingly well-scrubbed deck and huge, folded sails. Ropes as thick as her arms lay coiled in neat heaps at intervals and above her the many masts reached towards the sky. She wondered how such a heavy thing stayed afloat.

'Perhaps taking the chance for a last night of carousing before their departure?' Ichiro was looking round as well, but with a more critical eye, as if he was making sure all was in order. He nodded, apparently satisfied with what he saw.

A man came towards them from the back of the ship and Midori saw that it was Captain Noordholt. His tall, muscular frame was unmistakeable, even in the semi-darkness, and for some reason her heart skipped a beat at the sight of him. The light from a single lantern emphasised his features and made him look other-worldly. He stopped a few paces away from them and bowed, slightly awkwardly as if he hadn't quite figured out the correct angle expected of him yet. They followed suit and Midori was baffled to see Ichiro bow almost as low to the foreigner as he would to someone of superior rank.

'Welcome, Kumashiro-*sama*, Lady Midori,' Nico said in halting Japanese.

'Thank you.' Midori saw the two men eyeing each other

up, then some sort of silent message passed between them and they nodded. Both men smiled, which confused her even further, and she wondered what was going on. Before she had time to ask, however, Ichiro began to give her last-minute instructions in a quiet voice, and the moment was lost.

When he had finished, he turned to the captain. 'Is everything ready for departure?'

'Yes. Lady Midori's quarters are over here. If you would come with me, please?' He indicated the way and they followed him to a small cabin in the stern, which was reached via a hatch and down a set of steps. The captain had to duck his head to avoid hitting it on the lintel, unlike Ichiro, who, being shorter, was able to enter without any trouble. 'This is the best I can do, I'm afraid.' He sent Midori an apologetic glance. 'My cabin is right above yours. If you have need of me, just call out or thump the ceiling with something.' He bowed again.

'Thank you, Captain. I'm sure I'll be more than comfortable here.' Looking around, she knew that was an outright lie. But under the circumstances she had no choice and she didn't doubt the man's words – it probably was one of the best cabins on board.

Ichiro handed over a large pouch of silver and thanked the captain formally for conveying his sister to England. Captain Noordholt threw Midori an enigmatic look, before replying, 'It's my pleasure. I will leave you now.'

Midori surveyed her belongings before turning to embrace her brother. The European gesture felt unfamiliar, but still right somehow and he didn't pull away. 'Thank you again. You are the best of brothers,' she whispered, trying not to think about the fact that this may be the last time she ever saw him. He returned the hug awkwardly and they clung together for a few moments. She felt him shaking with emotion and knew it was the same with her. *I will miss him so much!*

'I'll not forget you,' he whispered back. 'I will pray to the gods and spirits to keep you from harm and I hope you can send me word of your safe arrival eventually.'

Midori's vision blurred and she blinked furiously. 'I won't forget you, either. Stay safe and well too, and write back if you can. Takano-*san* has promised to act as a go-between, right?' she said, trying to keep her voice from quivering.

'Yes. Anything you send him will be forwarded to me.'

'Good. Go now, I'll be all right.' Suddenly she wanted this leave-taking out of the way. It was too painful to suppress her emotions and if Ichiro didn't leave soon she knew she'd break down and beg him to let her stay. She couldn't dishonour their family in such a way.

He seemed to understand and didn't linger. 'May the gods be with you, little sister.'

Chapter Eight

Midori sat on her narrow bunk and listened to the waves slapping against the hull of the ship. As they were still anchored in the harbour the rocking motion was hardly noticeable, just a soothing background rhythm. The ship's timbers creaked continuously and she could hear footsteps as someone made the rounds to check everything was in order. When they came close to her cabin, she tensed, but they moved away again. Then there was only silence.

She felt utterly alone for the second time that night and in a moment of self-pity wondered if perhaps it would have been better if she had died after all. It was only a fleeting thought, however, because she definitely wanted to live. Even if it meant leaving everyone she knew behind and forging a new life for herself.

A sense of having been unfairly treated rose within her, but she quickly cut the thought off before it even took root.

'Never feel sorry for yourself and never complain about your lot in life,' her father had taught her. 'It is pointless.' Naturally that edict had been easier to follow as the pampered daughter of a *daimyo,* but she knew whatever fate threw at her, she could endure. She was a fighter.

She had proved to be a good sailor on the journey south and therefore had no qualms about going to sea. Her stomach was even now beginning to accustom itself to the undulating motion of the ship. And even though the noxious odours coming from the bilge water in the lowest deck tainted the air slightly, she didn't feel nauseous. There was a slight fluttering in her stomach, however, as she remembered the captain's words at their first meeting.

'Allowing you to sail alone on a ship with upwards of a hundred and twenty men would be madness.'

Midori took a deep breath to steady her nerves. 'It's too late to worry about that now,' she told herself. She had to hope he could keep her safe from his crew. In order to make his task easier, she decided to remain in her cabin as much as possible, only venturing up on deck if the captain had time to escort her.

There came a sudden knock on her door and she stood up, instinctively reaching for one of her swords, which she had put out in readiness for any possible attack. 'Yes? Who is it?'

'Captain Noordholt.'

She opened the door and there he was, as if conjured up by her thoughts. He looked enormous in the low-ceilinged corridor, and Midori couldn't suppress a sudden shiver of fear which slithered down her back. He stared at her for a moment and she couldn't read the expression in his eyes. This made her more anxious. Was he dangerous? Could she trust him? She remembered the strange exchange of smiles between Ichiro and the captain and wished now that she'd had time to ask her brother about it. It would seem Ichiro had given the captain his seal of approval, but why?

'I just wondered if you have everything you need?' Captain Noordholt asked. His voice was deep and slightly husky, soothing her frayed nerves a little, but at the same time the sound unsettled her further, albeit in a different way. She took another steadying breath and tried to appear calm.

'Yes, thank you. My brother's men have brought all my provisions, as you know.' She hesitated, not wanting to ask him for anything. 'Although, might I have a bucket of seawater every day, please? I could fetch it myself, only ...'

'Naturally you will be provided with drinking water daily.'

'No, no, I meant water to wash myself.' For some reason talking to the captain about such an intimate thing made her feel uncomfortable, although she had no idea why. She'd never been embarrassed about her body before, but somehow even thinking about being undressed while he stared at her with those blue eyes of his made her skin heat up. Midori swallowed a curse. *What is wrong with me?*

'Oh, I see. Yes, of course, I'll have some brought.' He added, 'If he can be spared, one of the cabin boys will be assigned to serve you during the journey, but I'm afraid you'll have to do without the sort of pampering you are no doubt used to.'

'Thank you, but I'm sure I can manage on my own.' Midori didn't want to be beholden to Captain Noordholt any more than she already was.

An awkward silence fell between them.

Finally he said, 'So you decided not to hire the *ninja*, then?' It was more a statement than a question. His mouth quirked up in one corner and his eyes twinkled.

'They were needed to rescue me instead.' Midori tried to make light of the threat she'd made, unsure why he found it amusing. Doubts assailed her once more. What if he went back on his word, now Ichiro was gone, and told her to disembark? 'And as you agreed to take me with you, there was no need to call on their services,' she added brusquely, emphasising the word 'agreed'.

'Indeed.' His smile widened for a moment, but then his expression grew serious again. 'I know some of what happened today. Are you ... I mean, were you hurt in any way?'

Midori wondered whether he really cared. After all, it would have been better for him if she'd been prevented from boarding his ship. 'No, not really. Ichiro came in time.' She turned to stare out of a small porthole, not wanting to dwell on what could have been her fate. 'I should never have been arrested in the first place. We were so careful. As I told you, the *Shogun* won't tolerate foreigners, and even children of foreigners have been ordered to leave the country on pain of death, but someone tried to make sure that I was unable to do so.'

It was his turn to frown. 'Why?'

She shrugged. 'I don't know. Perhaps he had a grudge against Ichiro, although more likely he was paid by someone else to spy on us. At least he's dead now, so there's no immediate threat to my brother.'

'Well, whatever the case, you will stay in your cabin until we sail,' he ordered.

Midori bristled at his peremptory tone even though she saw the sense in this command and had been intending to do so in any case. 'Very well. How many members of your crew know that I'm here?'

'Only a handful.'

'We must hope they've kept their mouths shut then.'

'I've made sure of it.'

'Have you?' she challenged and saw his mouth tighten. She wondered how trustworthy his men really were and whether they always obeyed their captain.

'Yes.' His reply was curt and Midori thought it best not to anger him further. Captain Noordholt was silent for a moment before asking, 'Why does the *Shogun* hate foreigners so much?'

'He believes us to be a threat to his regime. Because of the Christian faith.' The captain looked confused, so she elaborated. 'The Christian god claims that he is to be obeyed before everyone else. Naturally the *Shogun* can't allow such a thing; he's the absolute ruler of Japan. So we must go.'

'And if you convert back to … whatever religion you have?'

'I have no need to convert, I was never a Christian myself.

It's just that they wouldn't believe me. I tried to tell them.' She shuddered as she remembered the cold stare of the rodent-like man. He had wanted her dead, had relished the prospect, she was sure, and wasn't prepared to listen to anything she had to say.

'I see. I take it none of this applies to visiting merchants like myself? I'm only asking in case I have to come back at some point, you understand.'

'No, I don't think so. Foreigners are safe so long as you stay on Dejima.'

He looked away for a moment, as if pondering her words, before returning his gaze to her. 'You were wrong, you know,' he said gently, a strange look in his eyes.

'About what?'

He opened his mouth to reply, then appeared to think better of it and shook his head. 'Nothing,' he snapped.

And with that, he was gone.

'Damn her!'

She was definitely a complication he could well have done without. And he'd almost told her she was beautiful enough to tempt any man. *Even me. No, especially me!*

Nico sat in his cabin, staring out of the windows into the darkness of the night while the ship gently rode the waves of the harbour. Lights flickered along the shore as people made their way home carrying lanterns, but apart from that nothing stirred. *Except her.*

He could hear her moving around in the little cabin below his and he could picture her getting ready to bed down for the night. She would shed the mannish clothing which gave away the contours of her body as no female apparel ever would. Then she'd lie down in the bunk and close those magnificent eyes and spread the fan of her dark eyelashes against her soft cheeks ... Nico swore again at the image he was creating in his mind and tried to will away his body's reaction to them.

'By all that's holy,' he muttered. If he couldn't even keep from lusting after her himself, how was he to stop the rest of the crew from having similar thoughts? And acting on them?

'I can't afford to waste time like this,' he grumbled to himself. So why then was he sitting here thinking about her?

She was just another woman. The world was full of them. He'd make sure she reached England safely, then he could put her out of his mind, secure in the knowledge that he'd done his duty as a gentleman.

'But why the hell was she sent to plague *me* of all people?' he grumbled.

There had been at least three other Dutch ships that had sailed to Japan this year alone; why couldn't she have asked for passage on one of them? He sighed and drew his fingers through his hair, massaging his scalp to soothe the ache that had begun to build there.

And yet, he knew she was probably safer with him than she would have been with any of the other captains of his acquaintance. Most of them would have considered her fair game once the ship was under way. They would no doubt have protected her from the common sailors, but that wouldn't have precluded them trying to seduce her themselves, despite the fact she was a lady of high status. Nico had given Ichiro his word he would protect her as best he could, and he'd meant it.

'As if I don't have enough trouble with my crew already.' But he was fairly sure he could keep them in check, if only he could rule by example. And that, he now realised, was going to be the hardest thing of all.

By the time Midori woke up the next morning, the ship was already far out to sea. Her cabin had two tiny portholes, but when she looked out all she could see were the frothing waves caused by their progress and a dark shape in the distance. She swallowed hard and decided it was probably for the best that she hadn't seen the coastline disappear.

A knock on the door drew her thoughts back to the present. Her heart thumped uncomfortably as she asked, 'Yes, who is it?' Visions of coarse crew members come to harass her rose in her mind, but she pushed these thoughts away.

'Jochem, mistress,' came the reply in a voice that sounded young and far from threatening. 'Captain said as how I was to fetch you sea water every day.'

The door had a stout bar, and she lifted it out of the way before admitting a gangly youth. 'Thank you, Jochem. That's very kind. If you could put it over there, please?' She pointed to a corner and he carried the pail carefully over to where she had indicated. 'You speak English, then? I thought most of the crew were Dutch.'

'I'm a Dutch citizen, mistress, but my parents were English, same as the captain's. My father was in the wool trade and there's a fair bit o' trade between our countries. He decided to settle in Amsterdam and stayed till he died a couple o' years ago. My mother's still there.'

'I see.' Midori hadn't known anything about the captain's parentage and it had never occurred to her to wonder where he'd acquired his knowledge of English. She supposed she should have asked about his background and credentials before approaching him, but at their first meeting nothing had seemed important other than to secure passage on his ship.

'Can I get you anythin' else, mistress?' Jochem's large, brown puppy-eyes were open wide, as if he were drinking in the sight of her, and Midori had to bite her lip to keep from laughing out loud. No one had ever gazed at her adoringly before, but that seemed to be the case now. She decided to pretend she hadn't noticed.

'The captain mentioned that you could obtain something for me to drink. I assume everyone receives a ration every day?'

'Of course. Right away.' He bowed himself out, still staring at her, but stood up too soon and banged his head on the low lintel. 'Ouch! Sorry.'

Midori hid another smile. The last thing she needed was for him to knock himself out in his eagerness to please. No doubt the captain would put the blame squarely on her if his cabin boy became incapacitated.

He returned not long after with a tankard. Midori accepted it gratefully and took a sip, but almost spat it out again. 'Ugh, what is this?'

'Small beer, mistress.' Jochem looked anxious. 'Y-you don't like it?'

'Well, I … You're sure there's nothing else?'

'That's what we all drink, but I suppose you could have just rainwater as long as we don't run out.'

'Thank you, I'd like that. I could use it to make *o-cha* – green tea. Although I suppose I ought to become accustomed to your beverages.' Midori sighed. 'Is this what you would drink in your country?'

Jochem nodded, still looking uncertain, and shifted from one foot to another.

'Then I shall have to learn.' She gave him a wide smile to put him at ease again, and he blinked. 'For now, however, I'd be very grateful for some plain water.'

'Yes, mistress. I'll fetch it now.'

She didn't see anyone apart from Jochem for several days and the monotony seemed endless. Even talking to Jochem, who wasn't the brightest boy she'd ever met, became a highlight, and she almost started to contemplate venturing up on deck to alleviate the tedium of life on board ship. The captain's warnings about his unruly crew, however, still rang in her ears and she managed to restrain herself. Instead, she tried to occupy her time by writing poems, as well as keeping herself and her little cabin meticulously clean and tidy.

In order to stay fit and healthy she also exercised as best she could in the tiny space, honing her skills with the swords. It wasn't easy, and once when she missed and the sword became lodged in the side of her bunk with a thud, the captain came to investigate.

'Is everything all right?' he asked irritably, when she opened the door to his furious knocking.

'Yes, I'm just practising.' She swished the blade around in a series of movements which had the sword whining through the air within inches of his nose. He took a step backwards and frowned at her.

'In here? Are you out of your mind? There's no room!'

'Nevertheless, I have to try. How else am I to keep my skills? You did say you weren't sure you could defend me, so I must be on my guard.'

He opened his mouth to reply, then shut it again with a snap and walked away without a word. Midori frowned after him.

'I'm very well, thank you for asking,' she grumbled at his retreating back.

'Sword practice? Whatever next?' Nico muttered, although why he felt so aggrieved, he had no idea.

He ought to be pleased she wasn't completely helpless or defenceless, but the thought of a woman wielding a sword as sharp as that made his insides tighten. What if she hurt herself? Or someone else, like the cabin boy, by mistake?

Admittedly, he'd seen her defending herself the first time

they had met and it did look as though she knew what she was doing. Still, it didn't seem right, and he couldn't stop the worries from niggling at him.

Damn, but she was magnificent, fighting like a fury, her beautiful hair flying out behind her like rippling silk. He'd like to spar with her himself, learn a few of her techniques and then show her that not all foreigners were as easily beaten as Barker and his cronies. *But I can't spend time with her and she's better off staying in her cabin.*

'A pox on it!'

He had to stop thinking about her at all or he'd never get this ship home safely to Amsterdam. Let her play with her swords, what did he care?

I'm going to stay the hell away from her.

Chapter Nine

Nico's resolve not to talk to Midori or even go near her lasted two days, then something occurred which made him forget all about it. On the third day he paused for a moment by the ship's railing, leaning his elbows on it to gaze out to sea. Some people found the vastness of the ocean intimidating, but to him the endless horizon represented freedom, and he never tired of looking at it. At the moment the surface of the water was fairly calm, the north-easterly breeze blowing in exactly the right direction to take them towards Java. Nico drew in a deep breath of salt-tinged air, then frowned. He could smell smoke.

Bending over the railing, he looked right, then left and noticed puffs of smoke wafting out of two portholes not far below him. It didn't take him long to realise whose cabin it was. *Midori!*

'What in Hades is she doing playing with fire on a ship?' he muttered and set off towards the hatch at a run. Had she set her bedclothes on fire? *No, that's impossible. The candle of her lantern would never last all night.* What then?

He found Jochem sitting cross-legged outside her door, mending a sail while whistling softly. Nico's sudden arrival had the boy scrambling to his feet, blinking. 'I-is everything all right, Cap'n?'

'No, can't you smell it? Her cabin's on fire!' Nico rapped on the door, shouting, 'Midori? Midori, can you hear me?' He felt his stomach muscles clench. What if she'd been overcome by the fumes already? *Of all the stupid things …*

In the next instant, the door opened, however, and Midori stood there regarding him with slightly raised brows. 'Of course I can hear you, Captain. I should think most of the ship's crew could as well. What's the matter?'

Nico peered into the tiny space behind her and saw smoke curling upwards from a low wooden table. Understanding dawned, but although his anxiety lessened, anger coursed through him instead. 'What on earth do you think you're doing? You brought a *hibachi*?'

He stared at the little Japanese brazier, which looked like a boxy table with a square, copper-lined cavity in the middle. He hadn't thought to check her belongings when they were carried on board, but realised now he should have done.

Midori's eyes narrowed a fraction, but she stayed calm. 'My brother and I thought it would be best if I cooked some of my own food. You did say you would have trouble making the ship's rations last the entire journey, didn't you?'

Nico scowled at her. 'Every captain has the same problem. That doesn't mean I want my passengers cooking for themselves. It's not safe, you could easily start a fire and the whole ship would go up in flames. The only place where fire is allowed is in the cook room, which has a brick floor.'

'I assure you I'll be very careful. Look,' Midori pointed at the *hibachi*, 'I use only a few pieces of charcoal each time to grill fish, which Jochem has been kind enough to obtain for me from your cook, or to heat some water for rice or soup.'

'And if the ship pitches violently, what then? You'll end up with burning coals all over the floor, which, in case you hadn't noticed, is made of wood. Or you'll scald yourself. I'm sorry, but it's out of the question.'

'If the waves are high, I won't cook anything,' she insisted.

'I don't want you cooking at any time!' Nico felt his jaw tightening as he held on to his temper by a thread.

She squared up to him. 'This is *my* cabin, paid for with enough silver to make it my business what I do in here—'

'And this ship is under *my* command,' Nico interrupted, his voice rising now. He saw Jochem stealthily making his way towards the stairs. 'Stay!' Nico barked at the youth. 'I want you to remove the brazier this instant.'

'No.' Midori crossed her arms over her chest and stood her ground. 'I refuse to eat that disgusting mess your cook serves up until I have to.'

Nico was just about to argue back, when he noticed her expression soften. She put out a hand and placed it lightly on his arm, the gesture making an unexpected jolt shoot through his veins. At the same time she looked up at him with those beautiful cat-eyes, so large and luminous in the light reflected from the sea. He felt his antagonism melt away as he drowned in their green depths.

'Can't we come to some agreement?' she asked, her voice low and persuasive. 'If I swear on my honour never to use the *hibachi* in bad weather, surely you can allow me to keep it? I'm not a fool, Captain. I won't go risking my own and everyone else's lives on purpose.'

She held his gaze and although Nico tried to hang on to his anger, somehow he couldn't. He knew she wasn't an imbecile. She'd shown herself to have both intelligence and integrity. And from his short acquaintance with the Japanese, he was sure if she swore something on her honour, she would stick to it.

He capitulated. 'Oh, very well, but if I send word that you're not to use it, you will obey instantly, understand? The weather can change very quickly.'

She nodded and gave him a beaming smile that had his senses reeling. 'Agreed.'

'Good. Well, er ... I'll just ... Good.' He stomped off towards the hatch and up the short flight of stairs, cursing under his breath. 'I should never have let her on board,' he muttered, but deep down he knew the cause of his anger wasn't so much her use of the brazier as the way she fired his blood.

He'd wanted to snatch her up and kiss her senseless.

Midori stared at the *haiku* poem in front of her, then threw down her calligraphy brush in frustration. It didn't sound right. There was something vital missing, but for the life of her she couldn't think what it could be.

> *O distant shoreline*
> *Rocky, unforgiving, hard,*
> *Welcome me back soon*

'Help me, Father,' she whispered, looking round for guidance. Her father had been a master at poetry, writing an entire collection dedicated to Midori's mother, and he'd tried to teach his daughter to follow in his footsteps. No inspiration or help from the spirits was forthcoming at the moment, however, so she had to give up in disgust.

There was a knock on the door and she went to open it. 'Who is it?' she asked, her thoughts still on poetry.

'Jochem,' came the muffled reply and she lifted the heavy bar with a smile. *Someone to talk to at last.*

Jochem wasn't alone, however, and she barely had time to see his frightened eyes before the boy was shoved roughly aside, his head smashing into the nearest wall. Taking the youth's place in the doorway was Barker, the man she'd fought at Dejima. There was no mistaking the large, porous nose and the leering expression. The welcoming smile died on her lips.

'So I was right then,' he murmured. 'The cap'n's been keepin' you all to hisself. That don't seem fair to me. Share and share alike, is my motto. Least when it comes to whores.'

Midori took a step backwards and glared at him. 'I'll

have you know I'm a lady. And I don't belong to the captain; I'm merely a passenger on this ship. Kindly leave my cabin.'

'A likely story,' Barker scoffed. 'And still as hoity-toity, are ye? You'll soon change your tune.' He grinned at her and just before he advanced, she noticed most of his teeth were missing. She tried to duck and reached for her swords, but she wasn't fast enough and he had her pinned to the wall in no time. 'Now then, let's start where we left off, eh?' He imprisoned both her hands with one of his, while his other hand began to grope its way along her body none too gently.

Midori fought back, twisting and turning and trying to kick his private parts, but all to no avail. He may be useless with a sword, but at close quarters he was much stronger than her. She cursed. She had mistakenly thought any attack would come at night, if at all, and had let down her guard. And now she would pay for it. She let out a blood-curdling scream, more furious with herself than afraid. At the last moment, she turned her head to the side to avoid the disgusting mouth which was coming towards hers.

'Get away from me! I'll kill you … swine … *bakajaro* …'

He wasn't listening and Midori felt the panic build up inside her as the anger subsided and fear took its place. Apart from her short time in prison, she had never felt so vulnerable before. She'd always been able to defend herself, but this man wasn't giving her a chance. He didn't fight fair and kept hold of her arms, his big hand a vice around her slim wrists. When she bit his shoulder in a futile attempt to escape his clutches, he threw her down on to the bunk where she landed with a thump. Her knee came up quickly and she managed to hurt him at last, but by now he seemed too far gone to care. It only made him more hell-bent on taking her.

'Little bitch,' he muttered, and she had the distinct impression he was enjoying himself.

Midori screamed again, only to have the sound cut off by

his calloused and filthy hand covering her mouth. She sank her teeth into it, but so hard was the skin she barely made a dent. 'Shut up, woman! This won't take long.'

She felt him fumbling with his breeches, but in the next instant he was lifted off her bodily and flung at the opposite wall. Midori looked up into the furious face of Captain Noordholt, who gave her only a cursory glance before bending down to haul the attacker up by the scruff of his neck. He gave the man a savage shaking as if he were nothing but a sack of grain.

Midori closed her eyes and concentrated on breathing slowly. The thought of Barker's hands on her made her feel violently sick, but somehow she managed to swallow the bile that rose in her throat.

'*Godverdamme*!' In a torrent of words, the captain roared furiously at Barker in Dutch, before seemingly remembering the man was English. As she listened to a further tirade in her mother's language, Midori reflected that it was perhaps just as well she hadn't understood the first part, although the general meaning was certainly clear. Her attacker tried to defend himself, and even took a swing at the captain, but was swiftly knocked down again. Evidently, Captain Noordholt knew a thing or two about fighting.

He bellowed something out of the door and several other crew members came running. Barker was carted off and at last blissful silence descended on the cabin.

'Are you much hurt? Did he …?' The captain looked at her with stormy blue eyes, the light of battle not yet faded away.

She shook her head. 'No. No, he didn't. Thank you, you came just in time.'

'Thank Jochem, not me. He came to fetch me, despite his wound.' She looked around, but Jochem was nowhere to be seen. 'He's having it seen to,' Captain Noordholt explained.

'You'll be without a servant for a while. He's got a large bump on his head.'

'I see. Well, please thank him for me until I see him again.'

The captain glared at her. 'Why did you let him in?'

'Because I thought it was only Jochem, of course. Barker made the boy pretend everything was as normal.'

'You should have checked. Didn't I tell you to be careful?'

'I did! How was I supposed to know he wasn't alone?' Midori snapped.

The captain clasped his hands behind his back as if trying to restrain himself from further violence. A muscle in his jaw twitched. 'I told you this would happen. Do you understand now the difficulties I was speaking of? Why I didn't want you on my ship?' He was almost shouting again, his eyes shooting sparks at her. Midori felt her own anger rekindle.

'I assumed you would be able to control your men during the day, at least, and therefore I wasn't on my guard. I'll not make the same mistake in future.'

'See that you don't. You'll have to arrange a password with Jochem or something.' He was silent for a while before adding, 'Barker will be punished. No one attacks my passengers or harms another crew member aboard my ship. You shall watch. Perhaps it will show you the consequences of your actions.'

'My actions? I did nothing!'

He ignored her protest. 'Kindly bar your door again and don't let anyone else in except me. I will come for you when it's time.'

The lash whined through the air and descended on Barker's back for the tenth time. The man screamed, but still the lash continued its onslaught, relentlessly, rhythmically. His body jerked each time it found its target and blood, mingled with perspiration, ran down his naked back into the waistband of his breeches where it soaked the heavy material.

Nico glanced over to where Midori stood, her face an impassive mask. She stared straight at Barker without so much as a shred of pity or disgust and showed none of the expressions of horror mixed with excitement which were usually to be seen on the faces of a crowd watching someone being flogged. Nico was amazed.

The minute he had left her cabin, he'd regretted his hasty words. *A flogging is no place for a woman.* In a rational frame of mind he would never have insisted on her presence, whether she was the cause of it or not. The problem was that he didn't seem to be able to think rationally where she was concerned and the words had just come tumbling out. The thought of what might have happened to her had horrified him, and he'd taken his anger out on her, even though he knew she wasn't to blame.

He had expected her to retreat to her cabin, faint or even plead for mercy on Barker's behalf after only half-a-dozen lashes. When that happened, he would have been prepared to escort her himself and offer her an apology for subjecting her to such a gruesome spectacle. She hadn't done any of those things. Instead, she remained standing in full view of the rest of the crew, and he could see more than one of them glancing at her in awe and confusion. While some of them flinched in sympathy with their fellow crewmember, she didn't move so much as a muscle.

She looks almost regal. Nico was pleased to see she had exchanged her usual clothing for a more feminine garment. Although her *kimono* was of plain, dark blue silk, with no adornment other than a clan motif and a matching *obi*, nevertheless the material shimmered in the sunlight, indicating its fine quality. *Besides, it's not what she wears, but her bearing which makes her stand out.* No doubt she would have looked the same in homespun wool.

Perhaps I did the right thing after all?

Should any of the others harbour any thoughts along the lines of Barker's, they could now see for themselves what sort of a woman they would be up against. Here was no common tavern wench to be easily persuaded, but a woman of steely determination, as he had witnessed for himself. And he had no doubt from now on she would be vigilant, as would he.

He glanced over to where the English crew members were standing. Barker was usually at their centre, and without him they looked uneasy, yet defiant. Nico frowned. Most of them were troublemakers and he'd keep a closer eye on them from now on.

I should never have hired them. It had seemed expedient at the time to replace those sailors who had died on the outward journey with these willing Englishmen, but now he wondered if perhaps he should have searched harder for Dutchmen.

When the punishment was over at last and Barker had been removed from sight, Midori turned and walked calmly towards her quarters, her back ramrod straight. Nico tried to force himself to look elsewhere, but his eyes kept straying in her direction. Her long, straight hair shone with deep red highlights in the sunshine. It had been loosely tied into a tail as before, and hung down past her backside. And that backside ... Beneath the *kimono*, he could see the swinging of her hips as she walked, calling to him, making him want to run after her and ...

He turned away and stared out to sea, gritting his teeth. 'God's wounds,' he muttered. *She's just a woman like any other and I have to go without, same as everyone else, during this journey.*

'Captain?'

He swung around to find another of his English crew members standing behind him and frowned, even though it was one of the few decent ones. He wasn't in the mood to talk to anyone and opened his mouth to tell the man to go away and leave him alone. The sailor was looking slightly embarrassed, however, and since he was enormous and normally unruffled by even the most unusual of happenings, this made Nico swallow the harsh words out of mere curiosity. In fact, he couldn't remember ever hearing the man speak before, except to say yes or no to an order.

'Yes? Harding, isn't it?' The man appeared to be gathering his thoughts and Nico swallowed a sigh of impatience.

'Yes, sir. I was thinkin', it seems to me you need someone to watch over that there lady for you, so I'm offerin' my services. I wouldn't let no harm come to her, I swear, and I'll kill anyone as comes within ten yards of her with my bare hands.'

Nico blinked. 'I beg your pardon?'

'I said ...' Harding shuffled his feet and stared at the deck.

'Yes, yes, I heard what you said, but why?'

'Well, we wouldn't want this to happen again.' Harding swept an arm out to indicate the scene of the recent flogging where the deck planks were still stained with blood. 'The men were mutterin' and all, and we can't have such a tiny lady bein' hurt again, neither.' He seemed to run out of steam and just stared at the captain while wiping his forehead with the sleeve of a grimy shirt.

Nico frowned. 'And why should I trust her with you?' He looked at the man's arms, which were as thick as small tree trunks, and his beefy neck on top of a massive chest and body. 'Is this another one of Barker's ideas?'

'No, sir. I never bother talkin' to him. Man's a fool and I want nothin' to do with him. But the little lady, sir, I would never hurt her. I have a daughter just like her, all dainty and small, but with a backbone like you wouldn't believe,' Harding said, as if that explained everything. And perhaps to him it did, Nico thought. He weighed up his options, then made up his mind and nodded.

'Very well, Harding, you may guard her, but if you so much as touch one hair on her head, I'll have your guts.'

Harding put his hands up in a gesture of surrender. 'I won't, I swear. She'll be safe with me.'

Nico wasn't sure why, but he trusted this giant and relief flooded through him at the thought that Midori would be properly guarded. 'Come with me then, I'll introduce you.'

Midori hadn't expected to see the captain again so soon, and certainly not with a man-mountain in tow. Mr Harding reminded her of the *sumo* wrestlers she had seen in Edo when she'd last visited that city, although he was surely bigger than any of them because he was so tall as well.

'He is to guard me, you say?' she asked, wondering if Mr Harding would even be able to squeeze through the door to her cabin if he was needed.

'Yes, he volunteered,' Captain Noordholt said.

'In that case, I thank you, Mr Harding.' She bowed to the man, who bowed back as best he could in the confined space.

'My pleasure, mistress.'

The captain gave Harding one last appraising look, then turned to Midori. She noticed the anger was gone from his gaze and, in the sunlight streaming in through the portholes, his eyes were as blue as a summer sky. The sight made her feel slightly breathless.

'You did well up there.' He nodded towards the deck where the flogging had taken place. 'Most people find such sights ... difficult. I'm sorry to have subjected you to it; that was wrong of me. I'm afraid I acted in the heat of the moment.'

'Don't worry, I've seen worse and it was no more than he deserved.'

'Indeed. I doubt there will be any more trouble now. What with Harding to guard you and the example I've made of Barker, you should be safe. Perhaps it would be better if you came up on deck occasionally, instead of hiding away down here? You'll be less of a mystery.'

'I should be glad of some fresh air and exercise. I was merely trying to stay out of the way.'

'I'm sure the odd excursion now and again won't do any harm if Harding is with you. Well, that's settled then.' Captain Noordholt bowed to her. 'And now I'd best return to my duties. Goodbye.'

Midori stared after him and said without thinking, 'He doesn't smile very often, does he?' She'd wanted to see that blue gaze twinkling again.

Harding guffawed. ''Course he don't. Bein' a cap'n is a big responsibility. He can't let anyone think he's soft, now, can he? That would be plain daft.'

'I don't think there's any risk of that,' Midori muttered. 'Now tell me, Mr Harding, why did you volunteer to guard me?'

'Just call me Harding, mistress, everyone else does. And as I told the cap'n, I have a daughter just like you. Wouldn't want no harm to come to her and since there's no one to look out for you here, I just thought ...'

'You're very kind. Please, sit down and tell me more about your family and your country. You are from England, I understand?' Harding nodded. 'Then perhaps you could be so kind as to describe it for me so that I know what to expect?'

A huge grin split Harding's face. 'Of course, it'll be my pleasure.'

Chapter Ten

With Harding shadowing her every step, Midori could go up on deck if she wanted to, but most of the time she stayed in her cabin. Despite what the captain had said, she preferred to keep out of sight and not remind the sailors of her presence on board. The few times she did venture out, however, she forgot about everyone else as she found her eyes straying repeatedly to the captain. The man fascinated her and she studied him covertly, taking in the dark golden hair blowing in the breeze, the blue eyes half shut against the sun's rays and his assured stance as he gave orders.

He's half a head taller than most of the sailors, so I can't really miss him, she tried to justify this unseemly interest in the man to herself. *And he is the captain after all, so he's bound to stand out.* But she knew that wasn't the real reason.

He'd reverted to foreign clothing again – woollen knee breeches, a long-sleeved white linen shirt with a collar, slightly open at the neck, and a leather waistcoat which she'd heard someone call a jerkin. Unlike the other crew members who went barefoot, he also wore hose and leather shoes.

'Is the captain a hard taskmaster?' she asked Harding when she saw him noticing her glance in Noordholt's direction.

'Yes, but he's not unjust,' the big Englishman replied. 'So far as I've seen, he'd never ask anyone to do somethin' he couldn't do hisself. And whenever the weather's been bad, he's helped out. I even saw him up in the riggin' once, though he could've sent someone else.'

Midori was glad to hear it. She also gathered he never raised his voice unnecessarily, despite his stern façade, and didn't need to. And he knew everyone's name and often stopped to speak with individual sailors. This seemed to ensure his commands were always obeyed with alacrity. Several times Midori saw him overlook minor misdemeanours, except to show the crew member in question with a look that such behaviour wouldn't be tolerated a second time. Everyone appeared to respect him, and no wonder, she thought, when he showed himself to be fair in his dealings with them.

One particular incident made Midori warm to him more than ever. The captain was walking along the deck when the youngest member of the crew, a twelve-year-old boy named Ben, hurried past with a bucket of dirty water. As he overtook the captain, he somehow managed to bump the bucket against his legs and half the disgusting contents sloshed out, drenching the captain's shoes.

'Oh, no!' the boy exclaimed, staring at the captain with horror in his eyes. Midori held her breath, expecting dire consequences for the boy. He was obviously too frightened to even utter an apology, but to both his and Midori's surprise, the captain burst out laughing and shook one foot with a rueful expression.

'Less haste, more speed, Ben,' he said and ruffled the boy's hair. 'Try to look where you're going, eh?'

'But, but ... your shoes, sir! I, I'm so sorry, I ...'

'They'll dry, don't worry. Now get on with your work, little one. You're doing well.'

Midori heard Harding chuckle behind her. 'Is he always so lenient?' she asked him.

'With the little 'uns, yes, but not anyone else, although accidents happen and the cap'n's not one to explode unnecessarily. He'd not punish someone for just being clumsy.'

Midori was impressed. The more she learned of the man, the more he went up in her estimation. If only he wasn't always angry with her, but then he hadn't wanted her as a passenger at all.

During a brief walk round the deck at dusk one day, Midori and Harding came across the ship's surgeon, *Mijnheer* de Jong, bandaging a sailor's leg. A nasty gash on the shin was oozing blood and as the sailor jumped and swore every time he was touched, the surgeon had his work cut out to help him.

'Good evening,' Midori said politely and the man replied in Dutch, somewhat distractedly.

'He can't speak to you, seein' as he's Dutch, but I can translate for you,' Harding offered.

'Thank you, that's very kind.'

She didn't really have anything to say to the man, however, but as she watched the surgeon struggle to apply the bandage in a rather clumsy fashion, a thought occurred to her. De Jong was long past his prime. His hands shook slightly and some of the fingers on his right hand were bent by arthritis and obviously painful. 'I don't suppose you need any help with tending the sick and injured? I have some experience of such things and would be pleased to offer my assistance,' she said.

She waited while Harding translated this, and saw the surgeon's eyes light up. De Jong nodded and a torrent of words came out.

'He says you'd be most welcome to help,' Harding replied on his behalf. 'You can make a start with this here bandage, if you have nimble fingers. The surgeon's havin' some trouble, as you can see.'

'I'd be glad to.'

As Midori set to work, Harding grabbed hold of the injured man as if he was afraid he'd lash out at her. Midori smiled and said, 'Please tell him I'll be as gentle as I can.'

Harding did as he was bid and the sailor relaxed slightly.

It didn't take Midori long to tie the bandage neatly in place, earning a look of gratitude from the victim as well as the surgeon.

'*Dank u wel, mevrouw.*'

'You're welcome. Is there anything else I can do? Prepare some ointment perhaps?'

Harding translated and de Jong beckoned her to come along to his cabin. 'He says it's best you come and see what he's got, then you can discuss what needs to be done. Shall we go?'

Life on board a ship the size of the *Zwarte Zwaan* was often dangerous, and Midori was both surprised and pleased to be called upon frequently to help de Jong during the weeks that followed. There were outbreaks of fever, stomach problems and various accidents, and Midori enjoyed having something to do. It helped fill the endless hours that stretched before her each day. With Harding accompanying her she wasn't afraid to tend sick men as they lay in their hammocks, and her skills in preparing ointments and *tisanes* of every description came in very useful. The men seemed to approve of her light touch and no one was disrespectful, at least not to her face.

De Jong was grateful to her. Via Harding he told her this was his last voyage. 'I hope to retire when we return to Amsterdam,' he said. 'I'm feeling my age and I'm not as able to keep up with this work as I did in my youth. Your assistance is most welcome.' The man smiled at her and added, 'I thank God for sending you to help me.'

Nico, meanwhile, was not having a very good voyage. He suffered from a restlessness he couldn't subdue, and he knew the cause of it only too well – he couldn't get Midori out of his mind.

Wherever he went, he caught glimpses of her, or so it

seemed. Her serene beauty and calm demeanour drew him like a magnet. Time and again he found his steps moving in her direction without conscious thought, until he realised what he was doing and turned away again. It annoyed him that she should have this hold over him, especially since he didn't seem to affect her one whit. Although scrupulously polite, she never sought him out.

'Well, perhaps I can change that?' he muttered. Women weren't usually indifferent to him and he'd had no trouble in the past when it came to enticing them into his bed. Why should this one be any different?

Not that I want to bed Midori! Well, he did, truth to tell, but had no intention of going that far. *A little light flirtation wouldn't hurt though, would it?* Just to pass the time. He grinned to himself. Yes, why not enjoy her company while he could? In a purely platonic way, of course.

It was a particularly hot day in the third week of their voyage, and Nico had been walking along the deck, trying to shut his ears to the sound of feminine laughter. It was driving him insane and the Lord only knew what it was doing to the rest of the crew. Low-pitched and musical, it ate away at his senses, teasing him mercilessly. What was entertaining her so? He wondered how Midori could find such happiness in the company of Harding and the cabin boy, not to mention the surgeon.

No reason why she can't be as happy spending time with me, damn it.

His decision made, he walked in the direction of the merriment. As he came nearer, the clacking noise of a pair of dice being thrown against a wooden surface mingled with Midori's laughter and he peered into the small corridor outside her cabin. He wasn't pleased by what he saw, as he didn't encourage gambling among his crew, but it was the perfect opportunity to try and rattle her composure a little.

She was kneeling on the floor, wearing another plain kimono, this time in a dark shade of russet. Her legs were tucked demurely underneath her. Next to her, Harding and Jochem were seated cross-legged, so close they almost touched her.

'What's going on here?' Nico demanded, trying his best to sound stern.

Three surprised faces looked up at him as one, and the laughter stopped abruptly.

'Harding and Jochem are teaching me backgammon,' Midori replied calmly. 'We're playing for money.' She indicated a small pile of silver coins heaped next to her on the floor.

'I can see that.' Nico frowned. 'Should you be gambling away what I assume is your inheritance or dowry?' It occurred to him to wonder if she even had a dowry, and if so, where she kept it hidden. Not that it was any of his business, but he didn't want his crew tempted by the lure of silver as well as her charms.

It was Midori's turn to frown. 'I'm only playing with a small amount.'

'That's what all gamblers say.' Nico nodded as if she'd proved his point.

'She's winnin' Captain,' Harding added. 'Has the devil's own luck, she does.'

'That's neither here nor there. Lady Midori might be winning at the moment, but once the gambling fever sets in, she may not be so lucky.'

'Gambling fever? What's that? I've never heard of such an illness.' Midori looked confused, her usual calm expression slipping a little for once.

Nico hid a smile. 'It's when a person becomes addicted to excessive gaming. They can't help themselves and gamble until they have nothing left.'

'I'm not such a lackwit!'

'Perhaps you don't think so now,' Nico countered.

'I know so,' she said calmly. 'Besides, there's nothing else to do and it passes the time. *Mijnheer* de Jong doesn't need my help today and I can't tidy my cabin and practise swordplay all day. Nor write poetry. Now please, if you don't intend to join us, kindly let us continue with our game. I'm sure you are very busy.' Midori turned back to the game and began to shake the dice inside her cupped hands, dismissing Nico as if he were of no importance. He'd seen the look in her eyes, though, and her cheeks were slightly flushed. She was definitely not indifferent to him at the moment. *Excellent!*

'I shall join you,' he announced and sat down on the floor next to the others, folding his long legs with some difficulty. 'I'll show you what I mean and perhaps when you're penniless you'll understand. Start the game again, if you please.'

Midori threw him a suspicious glance, as if she mistrusted his motives, but rearranged the pieces on the board nonetheless. 'Very well.'

'Jochem, you may begin.'

'Y-yes, Captain.' The cabin boy looked uncertain, but Nico gave him a reassuring nod which put him at ease.

The weather had grown steadily warmer as they sailed south, and the perspiration poured off Harding's bald head as the game went on. Nico could feel his own scalp prickling in the heat, but Midori showed no signs of suffering likewise. From time to time she lifted a fan to cool herself, although she didn't seem to need it very often. It was a beautiful object, richly decorated with coloured flowers on a gold and silver background, an exquisite thing which must have cost a small fortune.

'How do you do that, Mistress Midori?' Harding complained after a while, his face bright red and shiny by this time.

'Do what?'

'Stay so cool. Anyone'd think it was the middle of winter, lookin' at you.'

Midori smiled. 'I have been trained to cope with extremes in temperature. My body accepts them if my mind tells it to.'

'Hmph.' Poor Harding obviously couldn't make his brain understand such reasoning and Midori passed him the fan to relieve his suffering somewhat.

When he gave it back again after a while, Nico said, 'May I borrow it too, please?' Midori nodded and handed it to him. He made sure his fingers brushed hers as he took it, and noticed her twitch a little. 'Thank you.' He looked into her eyes and saw hers widen in response. *Good, she feels the connection between us, too. So underneath the calm façade, she's just like any other woman.*

But he knew he was in danger of being more affected by her proximity than she was by his and he started to regret joining the game. Not only was he uncomfortable in the enclosed corridor where the heat appeared much worse than on deck, but he was having trouble concentrating while sitting so close to Midori. He glanced at her and immediately wished he hadn't. Her dark auburn hair had been pinned loosely on top of her head with what looked to Nico like a pair of eating sticks. Soft tendrils fell forward to caress her cheeks as she concentrated on the dice in her hands. Nico silently gritted his teeth.

No woman should be allowed to look that delectable. He wanted to carry her off to his cabin this instant and …

He stifled a sigh. That wasn't what he'd come down here for. *A light flirtation, that's all,* he reminded himself. And he wanted to find out more about her – her thoughts, her likes and dislikes, what made her happy or sad. *I should just talk to her.* But something held him back.

One thing he did find out, and quickly, was that she was

an excellent backgammon player and Harding had been right – she had the devil's own luck. However hard he tried, he couldn't make her lose and any lesson he had intended soon went out of the window.

'Have you played before?' he asked, knowing he sounded grumpy, but unable to do anything about it.

'Not this particular game, but we have other board games. I played sometimes with my ladies.'

'Your servants?'

'Yes.'

Nico shot her a glance. 'You must miss them. Looking after yourself is surely difficult when you're used to being waited on hand and foot?'

'Not at all. My mother taught me not to rely on others more than necessary and I'm perfectly capable of looking after myself. I was never waited on hand and foot, as you put it.' She gave him an almost mocking bow. 'But I thank you for your concern.'

Nico marvelled again at how different she was from any other woman he'd ever met, so self-possessed, so utterly unruffled most of the time. He looked up to find her eyes sparkling at him, a smile lurking in their depths, dispelling his bad humour. Had she seen through his ruse? *She probably has.*

'Now, if you have finished teaching me a lesson, I find that I am growing hungry, so I think I'll retire to my cabin. Thank you all for entertaining me.' She stood up and bowed, then handed the money she had won to Harding and Jochem. 'Here, you may as well take this back, then we can play again tomorrow. It's only a game after all.' She sent Nico a teasing look.

Touché, Nico thought and scrambled to his feet. He returned her bow with a more European version and couldn't help but smile back at her. 'Minx,' he muttered.

'We'd best be gettin' our rations too, little one.' Harding gathered up the game and pushed Jochem in the direction of the deck. 'We'll be back in a moment, mistress.'

'Thank you.' Midori stopped in her doorway and turned her gaze on Nico. 'Would you perhaps care to have supper with me?'

Nico was torn. This was what he'd wanted, to spend time with her, but now he wasn't sure. It wouldn't be a good idea if he wanted to keep his sanity. In fact, it would probably be downright stupid. *But what the hell* … 'Yes. Thank you,' he said. 'If you're sure?'

'Of course. We can leave the door open and Harding will be back soon.'

Nico hadn't even been thinking about the impropriety of dining with her alone, but he realised now he should have been. He shook his head and followed her into the cabin.

Damn it all, I'm going soft in the head!

Chapter Eleven

'So you believe in fate, do you?'

Captain Noordholt was sitting on Midori's bunk, and looked to be enjoying his meal, although she'd had nothing to offer him except rice and char-grilled fish. She watched as he wielded his chopsticks like an expert, his long tanned fingers not awkward in the least. It pleased her that he'd bothered to learn when most of the other crew members used nothing but a spoon or their fingers.

'Of course. Don't you?' Midori was surprised at his question.

'I've been taught to live according to God's law and that He governs all things, but to my mind, we can each of us change our fate by working hard. I confess I've not seen much evidence that praying has helped me overmuch.'

'Ah, yes, your god.' Midori nodded slowly. She had wondered if he would try to convert her to his faith, as Ichiro had warned her the foreigners would surely do. Harding had told her the crew held morning and evening prayers every day and anyone found missing had to pay a fine. So far, that hadn't included her, but she fully expected to be asked sooner or later.

'You weren't taught about the Christian faith?' The captain regarded her from under swathes of golden hair which had fallen across his cheeks as he bent over the rice bowl.

'Yes, a little, but I chose to follow the Japanese way in such matters.'

'I see.' He seemed thoughtful, then added almost tentatively, 'You do realise that might cause some problems with your English relatives?'

'Yes, I've thought of that and I decided the best thing

would probably be to say nothing. I won't interfere in their beliefs.' The captain stopped eating and stared at her, then burst out laughing. It was a lovely sound, low and rumbling, which seemed to send pleasurable shockwaves right through her, but Midori frowned, unsure of its cause. 'Did I say something wrong?'

She almost didn't hear his reply because she was entranced by the sight of him smiling so broadly. His teeth were white and even, tiny crow's feet crinkled the corners of his eyes and there were grooves either side of his mouth, but they only added character to his tanned face and she found them most attractive. The blue eyes sparkled with amusement. As for his short beard, it was more like very long stubble and Midori was torn between a longing to have him shave it off and running the tips of her fingers through it to see if it was soft or harsh to the touch.

'Not precisely, but I'm afraid it will be the other way round.'

'What will?' His words brought her back to the discussion and she tried to focus on what he was saying rather than anything else.

'About religion. They will certainly try to interfere with yours.' His smile was contagious, so she returned it. His eyes were still shining with suppressed merriment as he shook his head. 'I'm sorry, I didn't mean to offend you. Your way of looking at it was just a little unexpected.'

'I thought England was a free country? I was told no one is burned at the stake there for their beliefs any longer. The good Queen Elizabeth put an end to such practices.'

'Not entirely, from what I've heard, although she was certainly more lenient than the rulers before her. But even if people are not actually killed for their beliefs, it's still an offence to be a heretic. And you can be punished severely in other ways, not to mention ostracised.'

Midori sighed. 'So in England it's a crime *not* to be a Christian, whereas in my country they are persecuted. That makes very little sense.'

'Indeed. If you want to avoid trouble, however, you'd do well to at least learn more about the Christian faith. You might have to pretend to adhere to it. Do you remember anything you were taught?'

'Some.' Midori was reluctant to disclose just how inattentive she'd been. Although Hannah had never tried to force her daughter into listening, she'd done her best to explain about Christianity. But the stories she told Midori of Jesus and his disciples had seemed strange and unreal in the surroundings of Castle Shiroi and Midori had found it hard to relate to them.

Far easier to believe her father's tales of spirits and deities in all the natural things around them, of benevolent *kamis* and ancestors watching over them. His teachings went hand-in-glove with the code of the *samurai* and made much more sense. With hindsight, Midori understood that her father had encouraged her not to listen to Hannah because he was afraid for her. Much as he loved Hannah, he'd never allowed any priests to visit the castle except in the utmost secrecy and Midori had unconsciously followed his wishes by having her mother buried according to Japanese custom and not as a Christian.

'But I don't see what difference it makes to my relatives,' Midori insisted. 'As long as I behave well and perform any duties they require of me, surely that should be enough? I will accept the authority over me of whoever is head of the household.'

'It may not be sufficient. In England, and indeed other parts of Europe, there are several kinds of Christianity. The people who champion each one are rather, shall we say, forceful in their views and tend to be intolerant of each other. Why, in

Holland, there's been a civil war going on for a long time, which is partly to do with differences in religion.' He was looking serious now and Midori listened with a sinking heart as he continued. 'Most of England's population is Protestant and that probably includes your relatives. That means they'll be anxious to ascertain you're not a Papist; that is someone who belongs to the Catholic contingent. If they were to discover you're not even a Papist, but worse, a heathen, they might be horrified.' He shrugged. 'You'll just have to wait and see, though. I may be doing them an injustice.'

'What's a heathen?'

'A non-believer.'

'But I do have beliefs.'

He smiled again, distracting her from the seriousness of their discussion. 'Yes, the wrong ones, in their eyes. I'm sorry, I realise this is difficult for you to comprehend.'

'It's definitely more complicated than I'd been led to believe. I wonder what else I was told that will turn out not to be true?' Midori felt let down, since she'd always taken her mother at her word. She saw now that perhaps Hannah had embellished the stories about her homeland slightly. Or maybe her memories of what it was really like had dimmed with time and to her, England had become a perfect place. 'Captain Noordholt ...'

'Please call me Nico when there's no one else about.'

'Are you sure?' Midori had a vague feeling she shouldn't, but she wasn't sure why.

'Of course. As long as you remember to call me Captain when there are others present.'

'Very well, Nico.' She liked the sound of his name. With its short, sharp syllables it could have been Japanese and a sudden longing for her own homeland swept through her. She sighed, and as if he was attuned to her every mood, his expression immediately became one of concern.

'Is something wrong?'

'No, I was just thinking about my country and how everything was much simpler there.'

'Don't worry, I'll help you to prepare yourself. Can you read?'

Midori nodded. 'Both Japanese and English.'

'Good. Then how about if you read parts of the Bible and I try to explain things to you more fully? There's an English Bible in my cabin. It was Casper's, I mean, Captain de Leuw's; he liked to practise his English by reading it. I'll lend it to you.'

Midori looked into his indigo eyes and felt his strength flow into her. She relaxed. Of course she could do this, there was nothing wrong with her brain and she was quick to learn, always had been. Ichiro had told her she must try to adapt to foreign ways if she was to survive. Now Nico was telling her the same thing. She knew they were right.

'Thank you, I would like that. The sooner the better, don't you think?' She smiled at him again and watched in amazement when his eyes darkened, as if with some deep emotion. All the noises of the ship faded into the background, making her feel they were in a magical cocoon where only the two of them existed. She sat immobile while his eyes devoured her and she couldn't even blink. He held her prisoner with his gaze and although he never touched her, her skin tingled as though he was stroking it.

'Midori ...'

The sound of Harding's voice and loud footsteps in the corridor outside Midori's cabin broke the spell and Nico jumped to his feet in one lithe movement. His eyes held hers for a moment longer, then he bowed and moved towards the door.

'Thank you for the meal, it was excellent. I shall send Jochem to fetch the Bible now.'

Midori was left standing in her cabin with an uneven pulse rate and feeling slightly giddy. Something had stirred inside her when Nico had looked into her eyes, something she had never felt before but knew for what it was – desire. She tried to tell herself it was only because this was the first time an attractive man had actually paid her any attention. But somehow she knew that wasn't the whole truth.

Nico was special and she was looking forward to becoming better acquainted with him.

Nico had marked the parts of the Bible he wanted Midori to read with scraps of torn-off paper, and he went back the next day to see how she was getting on. He ignored the little voice inside his head that whispered it was just a convenient excuse for him to spend time with her. And he was very aware how close he'd come to doing more than just looking at her the previous day, so it was madness to return again.

He went anyway.

Midori invited him in to sit on her bunk, carefully leaving the door open, he noticed, so they were both within view of Harding. The big man was sitting on the steps leading down to her cabin, whittling a piece of wood. She seated herself next to Nico, but with a respectable distance between them.

'I started immediately with the Gospel of St John as you suggested. Since I'm not used to reading in English, it took me a while to get going, but compared to Japanese *kanji*, it's almost ludicrously simple, isn't it? I'm not finding it difficult at all now. In fact, maybe I'll read the entire book from cover to cover.'

'Book?' he queried with a smile. 'It's not just any old book, this one is special so you shouldn't refer to it like that. The Bible with a capital, reverential B.'

'Really? If you say so.'

'I do. And what do you make of it so far?'

'Well, this Genesis bit is very interesting.'

Nico stared at her. 'You're reading Genesis? But I only marked two gospels for you to begin with.'

'I finished those, so I thought I would read some more and I like this better. It's quite a story, isn't it?'

Nico shook his head at her, but couldn't help another smile tugging at the corners of his mouth. 'It's not a story, it's supposed to be accepted as truth. A true Christian would believe that.'

'*Honto?* I suppose it could be true, but …'

'Whether it is or not isn't the point. Believing is key.' And unless things had changed drastically in England in the last thirteen years, her relatives were probably devout Christians. 'So even if you don't think so yourself, you have to respect the fact that others view this as the truth.'

'Yes, I see.' She nodded. 'You know, we have a very similar tale in Japan. It makes me wonder if not all countries have them? My teacher read to me from the *Kojiki* – 'the Records of Ancient Matters' – about the birth of the islands of Japan. I don't know how old your book … sorry, Bible, is, but the *Kojiki* was written more than a thousand years ago, or so I was told.'

'Hmm, well I think the Bible is older than that, but it doesn't matter. You'll need to just accept our ways without questioning them at every turn. Let's see what you've learned so far, shall we? I'll explain as we go along.'

Nico knew this was going to be a challenge, but he was determined to succeed. He had to teach Midori about Christianity or he might as well dump her over the railing right now. Thinking about it, he couldn't help but be amused at the irony of him being her religious mentor. *Me, the most un-Christian member of my own family!* Perhaps she was right and there really was a fate, and at the moment, it was laughing at him.

Chapter Twelve

Their lessons progressed, and Nico came to her cabin most afternoons for an hour or so. Midori enjoyed his company immensely, and found the things he was teaching her fascinating. Sparring with Nico was also a pleasure and she delighted in making him smile at her 'foreign' ideas.

'I think I'd better watch myself, or you'll soon convert me instead of the other way round,' he laughed one afternoon, after she had explained to him in more detail about her beliefs in the spirits of her ancestors. 'Christians would be scandalised to hear me say so, but some of your theories make as much sense as anything in the Bible.'

Midori pretended horror. 'How can you say that? You'll be struck down by lightning instantly.'

He looked upwards as if waiting for God to smite him, then shook his head, the blue eyes twinkling with amusement. 'No, in that case your entire nation would be extinct, wouldn't you say?'

'My point precisely. Personally, I would prefer my spirit to live on in this world for a while so I can watch over my children, if I have any. Why would I want to go to Heaven?'

'Because your children will join you there?'

'That might take a long time, and I couldn't help them.'

Nico shook his head. 'I think you'd best read some more and try to think about it from our perspective. You're going to have to be very careful, Midori. You can't afford to antagonise people if you really want to stay in England.'

She sighed. 'I know you're right. I will try, really I will, but ... Do *you* truly believe in this? All of it?' She indicated the Bible, which was lying open between them on the bunk.

'Well ...' He shrugged. 'I have to admit I was never a very attentive pupil, only learning things by rote when I had to. As I told you before, I'm strongly of the opinion that if a person does his best and works hard, they will reap the rewards they deserve come Judgement Day.'

Midori thought about his words and after a lengthy silence she added, 'Do you think my relatives will mind that I'm different?'

Nico gazed out of the tiny window. 'I don't know. They'd probably welcome you out of Christian duty, but I can't say whether they'll be pleased to see you. I think you have to be prepared to be considered something of an ... oddity, perhaps.'

Midori's heart sank. 'Am I so very different, then?'

Nico didn't answer immediately, and then he turned and put out a hand to run his rough fingers down her cheek while looking deep into her eyes. 'I would say so, yes.' He smiled, taking the sting out of his words by adding, 'But in a good way.'

His smile and the touch of his fingers made her feel all warm inside and sent a spark shooting through her veins. He was so close. If she leaned forward she could ... *No, what am I thinking?* His nearness confused her, but his words weren't exactly comforting and she concentrated on them.

'It would seem I'm doomed to be forever the odd one out.' Midori sighed, despair creeping over her like an insidious poison. All she'd ever wanted was to belong somewhere, to be liked for who she was. Now she was yet again attempting to fit in where she was destined to stand out. Was there nowhere in the world where she would be considered normal?

Nico got to his feet, as if he was restless. 'Your relatives might be overjoyed to see you, who knows?' he said gently.

Midori stood up as well since his height felt intimidating

from her sitting position. He was very close to her in the confined space and she had to look up to catch the sympathy in his eyes. She restrained herself from leaning her head on his shoulder. It was so broad, so near and so tempting, but her problems were not his. She sighed again. 'Yes, you're right, I do hope so.'

'You'll just have to wait and see and in the meantime I'll prepare you as best I can. Your appearance can't be altered, of course, but I think your behaviour will be of more importance.'

Midori resolved to behave impeccably and to that end, took a step back and turned away from temptation.

December 1641

Six weeks after leaving Dejima, the *Zwarte Zwaan* dropped anchor in the placid, muddy green waters of the Java Sea, just outside a walled town. The coast was an almost straight line here and a massive fortress dominated the view along the shore.

'What is this place?'

It was early evening and Nico had brought Midori up on deck himself so she wouldn't miss all the excitement of their arrival. The two of them stood by the ship's railing, slightly apart from everyone else, watching the shore come nearer as the sun went down and the moon swiftly rose in its place.

'It is called Batavia and it belongs to the Dutch nation. It's a sort of general rendezvous for all our ships going to and from the Spice Islands beyond the Straits of Sunda and on the way to India, the China Sea and Japan.'

'I see. And the Dutch conquered it?'

'Yes. It was necessary to acquire a strategic position between the Indian and Pacific oceans, otherwise trade would have floundered. This is ideal as it commands the western end of the Java Sea through which all spice trade has to pass.'

'And the fortress, I assume that's for defence, then?' Midori gazed at the imposing edifice, which was surrounded by a sturdy wall and a moat. Nico nodded. 'Against whom?'

He smiled. 'Everyone, I should think. As I said, this port is needed for the success of the Dutch East India Company, but they're not alone in wanting a foothold in these parts. The Company's governor-general is housed in that fortress, as well as all the senior officials, and of course there's a garrison to defend them. Never fear, we won't be attacked by natives if that's what worries you, although it has happened in the past.'

'I'm not worried …' Midori began, then stopped as she realised he was staring at her in a strange way. 'What is it?'

'Your eyes,' he said, looking into their depths, then nodding towards the water where a moonbeam now lit the murky green of the sea. It made the surface shimmer as if by magic in the half-light. 'They look just the same. Like the moon over green water.' He laughed suddenly and shook his head. 'Sorry, I think your penchant for writing poetry is rubbing off on me. Lord help us.'

Midori opened her mouth to reply, but before she could think of anything suitable to say, he'd already sauntered off to give more orders, beckoning for Harding to take his place beside her. She followed Nico with her eyes for a moment, admiring his tall, broad-shouldered frame and the graceful way he walked, despite his size. Although he was so different from the men she'd been raised with, she didn't find his height and looks strange. After only a few weeks in his company she'd become used to them. In fact, if she was completely honest, she would have to admit to more than that – she found him extremely attractive. His intensely blue eyes in a tanned face, the little crow's feet at the edge of them from squinting at the horizon, the golden hairs on his muscular forearms ... all these things drew her gaze, even though she tried not to notice them.

And what did he think of her? He was taken with her eyes, that much was clear, since this was the second time he'd commented on them. Did he like anything else about her? She thought perhaps he did, but he was an enigmatic man who kept his thoughts to himself, so she couldn't be sure. *And what if he does?* A shiver slithered up her spine and she acknowledged to herself that the possibility tantalised her. *More than it ought to.*

She stood by the railing for quite a long time, thinking about Nico and how far she had come already. Japan seemed so distant, yet sometimes it felt as if this journey was all a dream and she would soon wake up in her own familiar surroundings at Castle Shiroi. The sights, sounds and smells around her were all too real, however, and she was brought back to reality. There was no turning back now, and if she was perfectly honest, would she want to?

The first few days in port were busy ones for the crew, as some of the cargo had to be unloaded in order to be traded for goods that could more readily be sold in Europe. Midori stood on deck with Jochem for hours on end, watching as the men toiled. Harding, with his immense strength, was needed elsewhere.

There were ships and boats of all shapes and sizes around them and people of various nationalities calling out to each other in unintelligible languages. Midori found it exciting to listen to them all and asked Jochem to identify their countries of origin for her if he could. Although she recognised the Europeans, she had never seen any Chinese, Indian or native Indonesian people before. Most of them wore light tropical clothing, even the Europeans.

'The outfits are called sarongs,' Jochem told her.

As it was the middle of December, the heat wasn't as intense as during the summer months. Combined with the humidity it was still warm enough to be uncomfortable though, especially for the foreigners who weren't used to such conditions.

'Won't be much longer now. We've nearly finished.' Harding came up behind them and Midori turned to greet him.

'Then what will happen?'

'The men'll be given leave to go ashore at last. They'll want to celebrate Christmas, I expect.'

Midori nodded. Her mother had told her about this festival, but at Castle Shiroi they had followed the Japanese tradition and only celebrated New Year. 'Is that possible here?'

'Well, not like at home, but no doubt they'll spend every penny they've earned in the grog shops and brothels ...' He stopped abruptly, and turned a bright shade of red. 'Beggin' your pardon, mistress, I shouldn't be speakin' of such things to a lady.'

Midori smiled. 'Please don't worry about it. But tell me, when will I be allowed on shore?'

'That I don't know.' Harding scratched his bald pate. 'You'd best ask the cap'n. I'll fetch him for you.' He scurried off and came back with Nico in tow.

'Good morning.' Nico gave her a brief smile, but seemed distracted. He kept glancing towards the last of the cargo being unloaded. 'Harding tells me you have a question for me.'

'I just wondered when I would be allowed to go into the town.'

'I'm afraid you'll have to wait until I can escort you and right now I have a lot of other things to do. Sorry.'

'If I have Harding to guard me, I should be perfectly safe, don't you think?'

'Possibly, but I would prefer to take you myself as you're my responsibility. Now, if you'll excuse me, I'd better be on my way.'

He bowed to her and left, leaving Midori to wonder at his insistence that he wanted to accompany her himself. 'Is Batavia a dangerous city, Harding?' she asked.

'Well, no more'n any other, I suppose.'

'So why can't I go with you?'

Harding frowned. 'Dunno, but I wouldn't like to go against the cap'n's orders, mistress.'

Midori sighed. 'Very well, I'll just have to wait and see then.'

The captain, however, remained occupied and, for the next few days, Midori waited impatiently for the promised outing. It seemed Nico was busy with disposing of his cargo and finding a new one, and this took up all his waking hours. She sought out the first mate, who was a particular friend of Nico's, and left messages that she would like a word with the captain, but he never came to find her.

On the fourth morning, she temporarily forgot about wanting to go ashore when Harding came to fetch her, looking worried.

'It's the boy, he's not well, mistress. I don't know what to do. The ship's surgeon has gone ashore and I've no experience of these things.'

'Let me have a look at him.'

Harding took her to Jochem immediately and they found him in his hammock below deck, sweat running in little rivulets down his face and bare torso. Midori put a hand on the youth's brow and almost flinched – he was burning up. 'Oh dear, he's caught a fever. Has anyone else been ill recently? *Mijnheer* de Jong hasn't asked me to help him since we arrived here.'

'Some of the other fellows had it a few days ago, but the surgeon said as how he could handle it hisself.' Harding looked ever more worried now. 'Though one of 'em died.'

'I hope it won't come to that, Harding. I think I know just the thing to cure this, but I need a special kind of herb. You'll have to buy it for me in town.'

'Me? But I won't know what it looks like.'

Midori described the herb she was after, but it soon became clear to her Harding wouldn't recognise it. He didn't seem able to grasp the differences between the various plants she was talking about and she knew then she'd have to obtain it herself somehow.

'Never mind,' she told him soothingly, as he was looking more and more flustered. 'I'll go and speak to the captain to see if anyone else can do it. You stay here and sponge Jochem with cold water. Just keep doing that, over and over, until he cools down a little and see if you can't make him drink something. He really must.'

The captain had gone ashore again, though, and there didn't seem to be anyone else about who could be trusted to buy the right herbs. Feeling frustrated beyond belief, Midori finally decided to take matters into her own hands. She went in search of Harding again.

'I'm sorry, but you'll have to take me into the town. Can you find someone to keep sponging Jochem while we're away?'

'I suppose, but are you sure?'

'It's not as if we have a choice. We've got to save the boy.'

Harding nodded. 'All right, I'll find someone to look after him.'

'Meet me on deck as soon as you can,' Midori said and went to prepare for the visit to town. She made sure she had a sharp knife tucked inside her sleeve and enough silver for any purchases she might wish to make, before leaving her cabin.

Most of the men had gone ashore too, and it was eerily silent on deck. There was nothing to be heard except the soft slapping of waves against the hull and the screeching of sea birds. Everyone left behind either sat around desultorily gazing towards land, waiting for their turn to go ashore, or slept in whatever shade they could find.

While leaning over the railing earlier, Midori had noticed the ship's boat was tied to the stern. 'Can we take that?' she asked Harding as he came up behind her.

'Sure an' we can.' He indicated the rope ladder. 'After you.'

Midori didn't hesitate. She swung her legs over the side, climbed down as quickly as her clothing would allow and was soon seated in the boat. Harding followed, nimble despite his size. It didn't take long to reach the shore, where Harding tied the boat up securely, then they set off towards what seemed to be the centre of town.

'Stay close to me, mistress, or the cap'n will have my head.'

Chapter Thirteen

'I'm very sorry to hear about de Leuw. He was a good man. I've known him for years.' Antonio van Diemen, the Governor-General of Batavia, clapped Nico on the shoulder and squeezed it in silent sympathy. 'But you did well to take over and I'm sure the directors will be very happy if you return safely with such a valuable cargo.'

'Thank you, sir. I certainly hope so. But Captain de Leuw arranged it all before his untimely demise, so the credit should go to him really.'

'Perhaps, but you'll be the one to bring it back. That'll count in your favour.'

Nico was offered a glass of wine and then the governor-general changed the subject. 'Have you had a chance to look around here yet? There's plenty of merchandise on offer.' Van Diemen winked at him. 'Trinkets for the ladies, they always go down well.'

Nico had never had anyone to buy gifts for during his travels, but nodded agreement in order to be polite. 'Yes, I'm sure they do.'

'Is there a special lady waiting for you? A wife or fiancée perhaps? If so, you'd best not be stingy.' Van Diemen laughed. 'Your homecoming will be much sweeter if you arrive with a gift in hand, in my experience.'

Nico forced a smile. 'I'll bear that in mind, but no, I'm not married or betrothed yet.'

'Well, if you're hoping to win someone's fair hand, here's your chance. You're in the very best place when it comes to purchasing gifts, I'd say.'

Nico hadn't intended to buy anything, but he didn't want to offend the governor-general when he was being so affable.

He improvised quickly. 'Actually, I was planning to take a walk this very afternoon to see what I could find. Would a length or two of silk be suitable, do you think, or perhaps some jewellery?'

'Knowing the ladies, my friend, a bit of both would be welcome.' Van Diemen smiled. 'Their appetite for such things seems to be insatiable. Not to mention any accessories you can find. Fans are very popular, as are shawls; both always go down well with my female relatives.'

'Oh, yes, in fact, I remember my aunt once saying … *Godverdamme!*' Nico, who was standing near the window, had happened to glance out into the square, where a familiar figure was wandering around, taking in the sights with interest.

'I beg your pardon? Your aunt said what?' *Mijnheer* van Diemen was goggling at him and Nico held up his hands in defence.

'No, sir, I wasn't quoting my aunt, of course not, she never swears. It's just that I've caught sight of M … er, one of my crewmembers out there.' He pointed out of the window. 'This young … varmint has specifically been told to stay on the ship and I don't like my orders disobeyed.'

The governor-general's facial expression relaxed. 'No, of course not. I quite see your point.' He nodded towards the square. 'You'd better go after the culprit then, eh? Before he goes too far. Could get himself into a lot of trouble here.'

'Yes, my thoughts exactly. Thank you, I'll do just that.' Nico bowed. 'Thank you for granting me so much of your time. It was a pleasure to meet you, sir.'

'Not at all, the pleasure was all mine.' Van Diemen inclined his head in return. 'I wish you a safe journey back to Amsterdam.'

Batavia was a delight and Midori wandered around aimlessly at first, simply taking it all in. Harding followed in her wake, keeping her firmly in his sights, but Midori didn't pay him much attention. She was so intent on everything around her that for a while she forgot all about her purpose in coming.

Because the original town had been more or less razed to the ground when the Dutch took it over, she'd been told they had rebuilt it almost entirely in their style. Now she could see what that meant: namely, rows of sturdy, brick houses unlike any she had ever seen before. Most of them faced a grid of tree-lined canals, which apparently provided the main means of transporting goods. The houses had tiny windows and were fairly small and unostentatious. Nevertheless, they were a pleasing sight.

She reached a cobbled square where a much larger building stood. Someone had mentioned a town hall, and she assumed this must be it. A white building, two storeys high with a large entrance and painted shutters, it was impressive. A small bell tower on top of the entrance porch drew her eye and she stopped to admire it for a while, before continuing on her way.

'That's lovely, don't you think?' she said to Harding, who nodded but replied without much conviction.

'Mmm, to be sure it is. Would you like to go find the shops now, mistress?'

'Oh, yes, we mustn't stay too long. Thank you for reminding me.'

Midori soon found the back streets of the town were not as nice as those close to the canals, but she hardly noticed because they had reached the merchant's shops and stalls. First she sought out the herbs she needed for Jochem, and stored them in a small pouch she'd brought for that purpose. That done, she couldn't resist a quick look at all the other merchandise on offer. After all, she might not have another opportunity to come here, so she had to seize her chance.

There was every conceivable shade of silk, as well as leather goods, wooden artefacts, jewellery and much more.

The silver she had brought proved acceptable as payment, though a few of the merchants looked suspicious at first.

'Can you speak their language?' she asked Harding. Although it was possible to haggle without talking, she knew it would be faster if they could communicate.

'Only a few words, but I'll do my best,' Harding replied. 'Most of the people here speak Malay or Portuguese, which are the two more commonly used languages in this part of the world. I know a little of each. Some of 'em might speak Dutch, if we're lucky.'

So engrossed did she become in trying to choose what she wanted to buy, that when she had finally completed her purchases, quite a long time had passed. Panic and guilt welled up inside her. *Jochem – how could I have forgotten about him?* She was supposed to be bringing back a cure for him, not dawdling here among the shops.

'Thank you for being so patient, Harding,' she said to the big man. 'But now we really must be getting back. Let's try and find the quickest route.'

'Er, yes.' He scratched his head. 'That way p'rhaps?' He pointed to the right. Midori wasn't quite sure where they were either, so she was happy to follow his lead. But it soon became clear they should have paid more attention to where they were going.

'I don't think this is right, Harding,' she said and stopped. Just as he was about to answer her, however, another crew member from the *Zwarte Zwaan* came walking towards them. 'Oh, look, there's one of your fellow Englishmen. Jessop, isn't it? Let's ask him the way.'

'I don't know, mistress, he's one of Barker's cohorts.' Harding frowned, but Midori was desperate to get back to the ship now and took no notice.

'Yes, but he's alone, so we needn't worry about that.'

When asked, Jessop – Midori didn't remember whether he was Abe or Peter – seemed only too pleased to show them which direction to go and they followed him quickly. It wasn't long before they found themselves in an even more insalubrious area than before, however. Midori started to feel uneasy and Harding muttered under his breath. Drunken sailors were wending their way along the narrow street, singing loudly and shouting to each other. Some were brawling and others simply slumped in a heap, dead to the world.

'How much fer yer services?' one of them yelled at her in English, but Midori ignored him and scurried on.

'Are you sure this is the right way, Mr Jessop?' she asked anxiously.

'Yes, this is the best short cut. Don't pay no attention to them, they're all three sheets to the wind.'

Midori kept a firm grip on the knife inside her sleeve. She tried to look neither left nor right, preferring to keep her head down.

They turned a corner, and Jessop came to a sudden halt.

'What's the matter? Why have we stopped?' Midori looked around her and noticed that Harding wasn't behind her any longer. 'Harding?'

They were in a tiny alley which appeared to be a dead end. Jessop opened his mouth to reply, a sullen look on his face, but without warning, a hand shot out of a doorway and grabbed Midori by the hand, yanking her inside. It happened so fast she didn't have a chance to react and her knife never even made it out of her sleeve. An arm was firmly clamped around her from behind, pinning her arms to her sides. Although she tried every way she knew of breaking such a grip, it was no use.

'Let me go, you scum!' She kicked and wriggled for all she

was worth. All she received in return was a blow to the side of her head, which made her senses swim, and a stream of what might have been abuse in an unintelligible language. Before she could do anything else, another blow to the head made everything go black.

'Where the hell are you? Damned stubborn woman,' Nico muttered to himself as he walked the streets, endlessly scanning the crowds for a sign of Midori. He wanted to throttle her for disobeying his orders, but he couldn't find her anywhere.

As he hadn't seen in which direction she was headed, he walked around in a huge circle, coming back to the town square several times. Whenever possible, he stopped to question the merchants selling goods he thought she might be interested in, but most of them only shrugged.

'We have a lot of customers, sir, cannot remember each one. Would you like some silk, sir? Very good quality, the lady will like it, I guarantee.'

Nico swore under his breath and ground his teeth in frustration. 'Why can't she ever do as she's told?' he asked of no one in particular, although he knew this was unfair. Midori had done her best to remain inconspicuous on board his ship and had never intentionally caused any trouble. *So why does she have to start now?*

As if to emphasise the misery engulfing him, the heavens opened and torrential rain started to pour down. It doused the streets in seconds and bounced off the nearby roofs. Most of the town's inhabitants scattered like cockroaches in a beam of light, and Nico hunched deeper into the collar of his shirt. It made no difference; the entire shirt was drenched in an instant. Nevertheless, he continued with his search.

When at last a merchant did appear to remember Midori, he was told she had passed that way at least an hour ago, after leaving instructions for her purchases to be delivered to the *Zwarte Zwaan*. The sun was going down and Nico's hopes of finding her unharmed were growing increasingly dim.

Damnation! There has to be a way …

'A few puffs of this, and she might be a bit more amenable.'

The disembodied voice dragged Midori back to awareness through a haze of pain, and a strong smell invaded her nostrils, teasing her senses. She recognised it, but didn't immediately understand its significance. Lightning bolts shot through her head when she opened her eyes, but thankfully the place she found herself in was very dim, giving her eyes more of a chance to adjust.

'She's stirrin'.'

'Yeah, hands off! You can have your turn when I'm done, but I want her good and ready first.'

Midori frowned as a group of faces swam into view, fuzzy at first, then becoming clearer. She blinked. 'Jessop?' she whispered, almost to herself. 'And … Barker?' *Oh, no …* They grinned at her in a leering, malicious way. Midori shuddered.

'So you recognise me, do you?' Barker rubbed his hands together in glee, before turning to issue an order to someone behind him. 'Bring it, then.'

Midori sat up gingerly and opened her mouth to protest. Before she had time to utter a single word, someone grabbed her from behind again and twisted her arms up. Barker suddenly advanced on her with something in his hand. 'Hold her, Abe,' he ordered Jessop, who was standing next to him, looking nervous now.

'Do we really have to?' the man asked.

'Just do as you're bloody well told,' Barker snarled. 'You owe me, remember?'

'Not any more, I don't,' Jessop muttered mutinously, but Barker wasn't listening.

'Do it,' he ordered and Jessop reluctantly bent to perform his task.

'What? I ... umph, mphh ...' A pipe of some sort was stuffed into Midori's mouth, while Jessop's cousin Peter pinched her nose shut. Barker ordered her to breathe in deeply.

She shook her head and tried to wriggle out of Jessop's grip, but a fourth man came to their aid, grabbing her chin. Barker did his best to push her mouth together and his filthy hands on her face made her skin crawl. Despite holding out for as long as possible, Midori was eventually forced to take a deep breath, and as she did so her lungs filled with smoke. She was overtaken by a coughing fit, and the men relaxed their hold sufficiently to slap her on the back.

'What ... is that?' Midori choked out, but she already knew the answer. The smell which pervaded the room was unmistakeable and when she looked around her she could see a pall of smoke hanging in the air, confirming her thoughts. *I'm in an opium den!* She'd heard of such places, but never in her wildest dreams had she ever thought she'd actually find herself inside one.

The decor of the room, such as it was, appeared to be Chinese. Faded red silk lanterns cast a muted glow over piles of cushions, and there were girls lolling about dressed in silk outfits in the Chinese style. Midori thought they must be ladies of the night. Chinamen with long pigtails hanging down their backs scurried about handing customers pipes and other implements. Fear rose inside her. There was an ambiance of evil in this place and it made her want to scream.

Her mother had been given opium in the final stages of her illness to spare her from pain. The strange odour of it had filled the entire sickroom, and it wasn't one Midori would ever forget. She clenched her teeth as the agonising memories of that time briefly returned.

The men around her decided she'd had long enough to recover, and advanced on her again. This time she was a bit faster, however, and managed to whip out the knife from inside her sleeve. She slashed wildly in every direction and had the satisfaction of hearing grunts of pain and a hissed oath from behind her. She was pleased to find that Barker's fighting techniques hadn't improved markedly since their first encounter. Midori managed to cut his arm in roughly the same place she had gashed him with her sword. He screamed and shouted out a string of profanities.

'Hold her, you lackwits!' he ordered, clutching his wounded arm with one hand. 'Are you goin' to let one tiny little woman get the better of four grown men? Pathetic!'

He was so furious, spittle sprayed from his mouth as he yelled. Unfortunately for Midori, his words had the desired effect, and after a further struggle she found herself without the knife and held in a vicious grip once more. 'Keep still, woman,' Jessop hissed behind her and the menace in his voice made her shiver. Barker kicked her for good measure, presumably to expend some of his anger. Then he ripped her clothing from throat to waist, leaving her exposed and humiliated. Midori shut her eyes so she wouldn't have to see the men's voracious expressions.

The whole process of smoking the pipe was now repeated. No matter how much she tried to fight them, she ended up sucking the hateful smoke into her lungs time after time. Her insides felt dry and burning, threatening to burst, and her throat was on fire. Midori coughed until she thought her ribs might crack.

When she was sure she couldn't take any more of it, Barker and his friends suddenly stopped and stood in a circle, staring at her expectantly. Midori frowned, not understanding. Soon, however, her body began to feel strange, floating almost, as if her limbs were no longer part of her. Weightless, relaxed, she sank back on to the cushions placed behind her.

Calm descended on her brain, making her smile up at her tormentors, who all grinned at each other knowingly. Midori didn't care. A state of well-being invaded her entire body, so much so that she stopped wondering about anything happening around her. Instead, her gaze drifted to one of the silk lanterns, studying it in minute detail and admiring its beauty. The rest of the room swam in and out of focus.

'Remember, she's mine first,' she vaguely heard Barker say. 'Is the back room free?'

Midori closed her eyes, giving herself up to the enjoyment of floating freely. Someone picked her up, jolting the pleasurable feeling slightly, but it soon returned. She leaned her head against the shoulder of whoever had lifted her.

'That's my girl. I knew this'd do the trick.' An evil chuckle failed to stir any response in Midori other than another smile.

Time held no meaning and when she was dropped unceremoniously on to another pile of cushions, she didn't know whether a minute or an hour had passed. She didn't care. A commotion broke out around her as she landed with a whoosh and she opened her eyes a fraction to see what was going on. There was a flash of metal and the clang of steel against steel, but Midori couldn't make any sense of it. Slowly, she sank back against the cushions and rested her head. It felt so wonderful, so soft, she wanted to stay like this forever …

Chapter Fourteen

The noise wouldn't leave her in peace. Each clang reverberated around her skull, making her wince, and in order to escape it Midori opened her eyes a crack. She blinked to try and understand what she was seeing, but there was movement everywhere, flashing in and out of her vision. Nico, scowling ferociously and jumping around in what looked like a strange dance. Barker, Jessop, shadowy and vague, joining in. Midori wanted to laugh out loud, they looked so ridiculous.

Tiny heads suddenly became huge and inflated. Faces with grimacing expressions like the strange masks worn by *kabuki* players – absurd, inhuman. Metal, bright as the sun, weaving in and out of the dance, so beautiful. Nico floating above the floor, circling, never still.

The ladies of the night with mouths and eyes wide open, their sinuous bodies merged and separated, like a writhing nest of snakes suddenly joined together into one enormous entity. Shiny clothing turned into smooth reptile skin, flailing arms weaving in and out among the snake's tails.

Midori shut her eyes for a moment. She couldn't make sense of it all.

What sounded like the distant roar of dangerous animals made her open them again, and she saw that Nico was now dancing by himself. The others were all lying down, obviously tired out from their efforts, but howling like dogs in the night. Midori knew how they felt. She was so tired herself, so exhausted. She just had to rest.

He had arrived in the nick of time, and only because he'd hit on the idea of bribing a gang of street urchins. They kept their eyes and ears open and saw everything going on, leading him first to Harding, who'd been hit over the head and left in a doorway, and then to the opium den. *Thank the Lord!* Nico pulled a hand through his hair and drew in a deep breath. It had been very close.

By the time he'd rescued Midori, Harding had recovered enough to take charge of Barker so that Nico was able to carry Midori back to the ship. He sat beside her now, watching over her as she lay on his bunk. He'd brought her to his own cabin, as there was more space and light, but he wished now that he hadn't. The image of her in his bed wasn't one he'd forget in a hurry, even though she was decently dressed now. She looked as if she didn't have a care in the world. Smiling dreamily, she stirred from time to time, but mostly she just gazed into space. Nico wanted to shake her and ask what had possessed her to go wandering around the back streets of Batavia, but he knew it wouldn't have any effect whatsoever. The drug had to run its course.

Harding burst in through the door without even knocking and stopped dead at the sight of Midori. 'Cap'n? Is she …? I'm so sorry, I should've …'

Nico held up a hand. 'It's all right. I don't think she has come to any harm. She's just drugged.' *At least I hope that's the case.* He had no way of knowing for sure, but he wasn't about to tell Harding that.

'Drugged?' Harding stared at her as if he hadn't taken in her appearance before. 'How? I mean, why …?' He walked over to peer closely at Midori, who smiled benignly as before.

'Barker's doing.' Nico's fists clenched involuntarily and he shoved them into his pockets. 'No doubt he thought to ravish her while she was incapacitated.'

'The scurvy worm!'

'My sentiments exactly. Did you take him to the hold as I instructed?'

'Yes and I sent five men to collect the others. They've just arrived. Good thing you bribed the Chinamen so they didn't let 'em escape.'

'Yes, I doubt Barker had paid them as much. Where are his henchmen now?'

'They've been fettered on deck. One of 'em was spoutin' a lot of nonsense, but I think we can make him talk sense a bit later. If he gives evidence, we can hang Barker, though I'd prefer to choke him with my bare hands, the brainsickly little whoreson.'

'No, no, there's no need for that, Harding. The matter will be dealt with properly.' Nico made himself sound calm, when in fact he'd wanted to kill the man, too. He knew he had to stick to the rules, however, and put his own feelings aside.

Harding growled, then glanced at Midori once more. 'You sure she'll be all right, Cap'n?'

'Yes. They made her smoke opium, but it should wear off soon. I've seen it before. A friend of mine was foolish enough to try.'

'Well, I'll go below deck and await my punishment then, sir.'

'Punishment?'

'For not guardin' her properly, like you told me to.'

'Oh, that. Don't worry, I won't hold you responsible. They hit you on the head from behind, you wouldn't have stood a chance. You were only just coming round when I found you. Does it hurt much?'

Harding rubbed the back of his bald pate. 'Just a bit, but it's no more'n I deserve. Although I did try to tell her not to follow that Jessop fellow.'

Nico shook his head. 'And no doubt she wouldn't listen. I know how headstrong she can be and it's not your fault, so don't fret.'

'Thank you, sir. I ... thank you.'

'How is the boy?'

'I've just been to see him and he's still feverish, but someone's been spongin' him and it seems to help like she said.' Harding shrugged. 'I gave the herbs she bought to the ship's surgeon and he said he'd make up a tisane.'

'You'd best return to Jochem straight away then.'

'Yes, Cap'n.' Harding bowed himself out and Nico returned his attention to Midori.

Some time later her dreamy gaze came to rest on him and she smiled a smile so dazzling he had to blink. 'Nico.' She stretched out her arms to him, tempting him to lean forward. Her hands caressed his neck, pulling him towards her. 'Nico,' she whispered again. 'You're scowling today. I don't like it when you're scowling.'

'Midori, you shouldn't—' he started to say, but his words were cut off abruptly when she suddenly put her mouth on his.

He made a strangled sound and tried to pull back, but she twined her arms around his neck and trapped him. He could have used force, he knew that, but her lips were so soft and they were moving slowly over his in a sensuous way he couldn't resist. *Just this once*, he promised himself. *What harm could it do? There's no one to see.* Wrapping his own arms around her, he pulled her on to his lap, holding her so close he could feel her calm heartbeat. She was warm and pliant, and she smelled wonderful, despite the slight odour of opium which still clung to her. When the kiss ended at last, he buried his face in her hair, inhaling its fresh scent and tried not to remember the incredible sight of her naked to the waist.

Dear Lord, but she was perfection itself, with a figure like a goddess!

'Nico.' She repeated his name, over and over again like a

mantra, and he loved the sound of it on her lips. That mouth was too close for comfort, too close to be ignored and so beautiful ...

Nico didn't know how long the second kiss lasted – a minute, an eternity, it made no difference. It felt like a lifetime and he never wanted to stop. The taste of her and her joyful response made him almost crazy with desire, and it was only with the utmost effort he tore his mouth away at last, simply in order to breathe.

Still holding her tight, he could feel her shaking and his own body responded. He bent to recapture her lips, but just then she tensed and let out a moan which sounded as far from desire as was possible. He looked into her face, which had gone deathly pale.

'Midori? What's the matter?'

'I ... I don't feel well. I'm going to be sick. I ... sorry ...' She leaned over and Nico only just had time to snatch up a chamber pot before she cast up the contents of her stomach.

'A plague on it,' he muttered and cursed himself for a fool. Midori had made him forget that the initial stage of euphoria induced by the opium soon wore off and could give way to more unpleasant effects. He should have been on his guard, not dallying with a woman he had no business touching. He swore again, if only to combat the desire that still raged within him.

The nausea continued to plague Midori for another hour or more, then she broke into a sweat and her limbs took turns to cramp up. She doubled over in agony, and Nico massaged the afflicted parts as best he could without removing her clothing. He tried not to notice how soft the skin of her arms was and how perfectly formed the limbs he was touching through the silky material. He gave her some water, then at last she fell into a restless slumber, which by the look of it was broken by nightmares.

Nico collapsed into his chair, exhausted by his efforts and emotionally drained. He closed his eyes and wished himself a thousand miles away.

Nico was kissing her and it was the most wondrous thing. Midori squirmed in his arms, urging him ever closer until they were all but joined up, but just then fear tore through her and she opened her eyes to find that she wasn't kissing Nico, but Barker.

She could smell his fetid breath, see the rotten stumps of his teeth as he smiled in triumph. 'I've got you now, woman. I've got you now …' His laughter echoed all around her and she put her hands over her ears to shut it out, but that only made it louder.

'Let go of me! Leave me alone!'

Barker's voice taunted her. 'I will have you, I will …' His words bounced from one side of Midori's head to the other, making it spin. Weakly, she fought against him, against his voice and that ever-present mouth.

Arms grabbed at her from every direction, holding her down, lifting her up, dropping her and then suddenly throwing her up in the air. Her stomach did somersaults, the nausea rising and falling with the rest of her, and she heard herself cry out. Fingers clawed at her, tearing her skin to reach inside her. Pain exploded in every part of her body.

When at last they let go of her, she opened her eyelids to find herself surrounded by Chinese lanterns. Dusty and blood red, they all had Barker's face stamped on to their surface, laughing again and leering at her. The lanterns swirled around her head in a huge circle, coming closer and closer until each of them attacked her in turn, leaving Barker's mouth imprinted on her skin like leeches wherever he touched her.

Revulsion and horror welled up inside her and she

screamed until one of the mouths fastened itself on to hers, cutting off her breathing. She fought for air, but the mouth wouldn't let go and her arms were held down once more. Her lungs burned, the pain branding her from the inside out, until at last the blessed darkness claimed her...

'Nico? Where am I?'

The weak voice woke Nico some time later. He opened his eyes and realised he'd fallen asleep in his chair, and his body was now telling him just how uncomfortable that was. He tried to straighten his neck, rubbing it with both hands, and then stretched to ease his twisted back.

Midori was still lying on his bunk, staring at him with a strange expression on her lovely face. The memory of how she had clung to him earlier suddenly came flooding back. Nico felt as if someone had punched him in the stomach and drew in a deep breath.

'Nico?'

He brought his gaze back to Midori with an effort. 'You're in my cabin,' he said, 'so I could watch over you until the drug had run its course.'

'The drug? Oh, yes, I remember now.' Her eyes clouded over and she turned her head towards the wall. 'Thank you for coming to my aid. It was you, wasn't it?'

'Yes.'

She glanced over her shoulder. 'Did he ... had Barker ...?' She closed her eyes as if she couldn't bear to say the words.

Nico clenched his fists and stared at the floor. The thought of what she had gone through made him go cold all over. Barker and his cronies had had her in their power for long enough to do whatever they wanted and the worst of it was Nico had no idea whether that included rape or not. There were no outward signs, apart from dirt and bruising, but then he hadn't wanted to remove her clothes to have a closer look. Somehow he'd assumed she would know herself. He wanted to kill Barker with his bare hands for this and for his cowardly way of going about it, too. Nico knew as well as Barker that he could never have bested Midori one-to-one except for when he'd caught her by surprise in her cabin.

'No, he didn't,' he said flatly. If she couldn't tell, there was no point in making her suffer more by adding to her burdens, he reasoned. Midori didn't reply and Nico looked up to find her regarding him with a small frown. 'Are you feeling ill again? Shall I have you carried to your own cabin?'

'Yes, please. That would be ... kind.'

Nico went to the door and shouted for Harding. He heard the message being relayed and turned to reassure Midori. 'He'll be here any moment. Is there anything else you would like?'

'Some water, perhaps? My throat feels as if it's been singed in a fire.' She hesitated, then added, 'Nico, when I was asleep before, I dreamed that you ... that we ...' A faint blush spread across her cheeks as she struggled to formulate her question.

Nico knew very well what she was asking, but had no intention of helping her. In his opinion, it would be best if the entire episode was forgotten. He smiled as if humouring a child. 'I'm sure you dreamed many things. Judging by the smile on your face as you slept, they were very pleasant dreams, too, at least at first. Then came the nightmares. It's all part of the effects of the drug; you must put it out of your mind.'

'I see.' Midori nodded, as if trying to convince herself. She opened her mouth to add something, but just then Harding knocked and came charging into the cabin.

'Mistress Midori! Are you well? I can't believe—'

'Harding.' Nico put a hand on the big man's arm. 'She is very tired and would like to be taken to her cabin. Can you carry her, please?'

'Why yes, of course. Yes, sir.'

Harding lifted Midori almost reverently and bore her out of the door, which Nico held open for them. Nico didn't look at Midori as they went past. If he had, he might have reached out and taken her from Harding's arms to carry her himself. He was strangely reluctant to let anyone else touch her.

When they had gone, he thumped his fist on the wall until the pain became unbearable.

This has to stop!

Midori woke abruptly and found herself lying on her own bunk with nothing but the screeching of gulls to disturb her. She felt dirty and bruised, and her throat was dry and scratchy, but these were minor irritations compared to the turmoil inside her head. As the vague memories returned, she frowned, trying to piece together the fragmented images in her mind. The opium den, she remembered clearly, and the strange feeling of calm which had descended on her, but after that everything was hazy. Barker's face, with its ugly expression, appeared at various stages. He had carried her, of that she was sure, but where to? What had he done to her?

Midori knew what he'd intended, but had he succeeded? Nico had said nothing had happened, but what if he'd been trying to spare her from learning the truth? She needed to know for sure. With determination, she sat up and removed her clothes to check for signs of violation, but didn't find any. There was slight bruising to her upper body, but nothing anywhere else. The relief was so great, she burst into tears.

Nico came in time. He saved me.

Midori hadn't cried since she was a little girl, but now the tears came pouring out in a great, unstoppable torrent. Huge, painful sobs racked her body, and in her weakened state she let them have their way. It was all too much and her mother would have said it was cleansing. *Oh, Mother, if only you were here to guide me ...*

When the tears dried up at last, Midori tried to think rationally. *Samurai* women were expected to kill themselves if their chastity was so much as threatened. If she had still been in Japan, Midori knew she would have been expected to take her own life, since her honour was now gone. In fact, she should have turned the knife on herself immediately, instead of trying to harm Barker with it. But her only thought at the time had been to hurt him.

'I fought as best I could,' she muttered. 'But not even Father could have expected me to beat four men on my own and they didn't fight fair.' Although, as she well knew, that wasn't the point.

There was only one thing to do. *Hara-kiri.*

With gritted teeth, she made herself stand up and seek out her swords. After checking that the blades were honed to perfection as always, she sat down on top of her bunk, cross-legged, and put the two swords neatly by her side. They gleamed and shimmered in the dazzling sunlight streaming in through the tiny portholes. She felt as if they were trying to encourage her with their shining beauty, saying, 'Look at us, we're your friends, we will help you to do the deed quickly.' She took deep breaths to steady her nerves, and tried to clear her mind of everything except thoughts of what she must do, what honour required her to do.

She wrapped a cloth round the blade of the shorter sword and took a firm grip on it about halfway down, then slowly undid her garments and bared her taut stomach. Then she pushed the tip of the sword into the smooth skin until she knew it couldn't go any further without piercing the flesh.

But I don't want to die.

The treacherous thought came out of nowhere, startling

her, interrupting her measured breathing and making her heart thump painfully. When she looked down again, she saw a drop of blood trickle out of a small wound and realised she must have jumped as well, but she hadn't felt anything. She tried to analyse her emotions, tried to make sense of her unwillingness to do what she knew was right. After a while, she came to the conclusion she wasn't afraid of dying as such, nor even of the pain this would entail, but she simply wasn't ready. She hadn't finished living.

That's no excuse. No one has ever finished with life when their time comes. Everyone wants to stay alive just that little bit longer.

And yet, she knew she wasn't prepared for this, the ultimate act.

A small, insidious voice whispered inside her brain, giving her the perfect excuse as to why she shouldn't commit *hara-kiri* – or *seppuku* as it was also known. *My fellow countrymen didn't want me. Why then should I follow their rules?* Besides, had her chastity really been threatened, or was she overreacting? Suicide on such shaky grounds seemed a bit too drastic a step. Another thought occurred to her – *samurai* women were only supposed to commit *hara-kiri* with the permission of their clan leader. As she didn't have anyone here to authorise it, surely she ought to wait?

She closed her eyes and put the blade aside. It was a dilemma, and one she couldn't solve without a lot of thought. She decided the best thing to do for the moment was to bide her time and see what the future brought.

Chapter Fifteen

A day later, just as the new year began, the *Zwarte Zwaan* left the harbour in convoy with a fleet of other homeward-bound merchantmen. All were heavily loaded with exotic goods and, in case anyone should dare to attack them, they were escorted by a couple of warships. It wasn't long before they cleared the Straits of Sunda and reached the open sea. Midori felt an intense sense of relief, as if in leaving Batavia behind she also left the bad memories, but the thought that Barker was still with them niggled at her mind.

'The cap'n will deal with him in his own time,' Harding had told her. 'Let 'im stew for a while first.'

She tried not to think about it, and instead concentrated her energies on making Jochem better. To her delight, he responded well to the remedy de Jong had concocted out of the herbs she'd bought. After that, they merely had to help the boy regain his strength with nourishing broths and the fresh fruit which was available at the beginning of the journey. Jochem was soon on his feet again, back to his normal, bouncy self. He did his best to take her mind off things, and she was grateful to both him and Harding.

Three days into the voyage, Nico came to knock on her cabin door and when she opened it he came straight to the point, looking very solemn. 'Do you want to be present when we mete out justice to your abductors?'

Midori managed to keep her face expressionless, even though her stomach flipped over uncomfortably at the thought of having to face Barker. 'Yes, of course. You mean now?'

'Yes, but if you'd rather not, I will understand. It might

be ... too unpleasant.' His eyes searched hers as if he was making sure this was what she really wanted.

'I need to be there. If you could just give me a moment to ready myself?'

He nodded. 'I'll wait for you on deck.'

Harding escorted her and stood very close to her side, as if trying to imbue her with his strength. Midori appreciated this gesture, although she didn't consider it necessary. It was her duty to watch these proceedings, and she thought seeing Barker punished might help her to combat the nightmares which continued to plague her. She schooled her expression into one of outward calm and watched as Barker and his friends were brought up from the hold, blinking against the piercing sunlight.

A bedraggled individual was dragged forward and Midori realised that it was Abe Jessop. She had thought a lot about his perfidy in leading her to Barker, but she'd come to the conclusion he'd only acted under duress. She remembered something Barker had said which indicated he had a hold over his crony.

'Well, Jessop, and have you thought of anything you would like to tell us?' Nico barked at him in English. 'Remember what I said to you?'

Jessop nodded and darted a look of fear at Barker, who was pretending indifference, although Midori noticed he was shaking slightly.

Nico continued in Dutch for the benefit of the rest of the crew. Jochem, who was on her other side, translated for Midori in whispers. 'We are gathered today to see that justice is done. This lady,' Nico indicated Midori, 'was abducted and badly treated, and I have asked Jessop here to give us his version of events. Proceed, please.'

Jessop wet his lips and cleared his throat several times. 'I, er, that's to say, uhm, he ...' he nodded towards Barker, 'was sure the lady would leave the ship at some point and he made plans to … to abduct her, because he wanted to have some s-sport with her.' His voice cracked and he had to clear his throat once more.

'Go on,' Nico said.

'Barker said as how he'd hit on a really good idea. I was to try and lure her into the Chinamen's area of town, to a place we'd been before.' Jessop took a deep breath before continuing. 'He and the others went on ahead.'

Nico, visibly impatient, interrupted at this point. 'Very well. The lady was then abducted and taken to an opium den, is that correct?' Jessop nodded, while Barker spat nonchalantly on deck, as if the entire proceedings were of no interest to him whatsoever. One of his guards cuffed him hard. 'What happened next?' Nico asked Jessop.

'We helped Barker force the lady to smoke a pipe of opium, sir. She … she tried to defend herself and fought something fierce, but we held her down. I didn't want to, honest, but I owed Barker money and he threatened me and … After that, you came,' Jessop finished lamely, his shoulders slumped, as if in defeat.

'Nothing else occurred?' Nico frowned. 'Was the lady mistreated in any other way?'

'Not that I saw, but then again, Barker did carry her off to a back room, though he can't have been there more'n a few moments when you arrived.'

Barker, who had been standing docilely between his guards until that moment, suddenly sprang to life. Before anyone had time to react, he managed to snatch a knife out of the belt of the nearest guard and then made a dive for Jessop. The man stood stock still, his expression that of a petrified animal. Barker, obviously expecting some resistance, feinted to the left and came up behind Jessop, who still hadn't moved. With the knife at Jessop's throat,

Barker hissed, 'I want you to lower the dinghy now or I kill him. Abe and I are leaving, understand?'

'We're three days out of Batavia. Where do you think you're going in a rowing boat?' Nico asked. He sounded calm, although Midori saw a muscle twitch in his jaw, as if he was keeping himself under tight control.

'I don't care! Anywhere's better than dancin' at the end of a rope here on account o' that whore of yours.' He nodded towards Midori, who sent him what she hoped was a fierce glare.

'Who said you were going to be hanged?' Nico took a step towards Barker. 'You haven't killed anyone, so the cat-o'-nine-tails seems a more appropriate punishment. Now give me that knife and accept your fate like a man. You'll die on the open sea otherwise.'

'D-do as he s-says, John, please,' Jessop begged. 'I'd rather s–stay here and be flogged.'

'Fool! You think we'd survive the cat?' He glared at Nico. 'He'll not stop till we're good and dead.'

'Y-yes, he would. He's a fair man.' Finding some courage at last, Jessop drove his right elbow into Barker's gut and tried to twist away from the knife. But Barker managed to grab hold of Jessop's left arm and pulled him back.

'Traitor!' he shouted. 'Mewling, lily-livered worm!' Then, without the slightest hesitation, Barker sank the knife into the smaller man's back.

A collective gasp was heard from the crew as Jessop froze, made a gurgling noise, then sank slowly down into a lifeless heap. Blood flowed freely, staining both the victim and his murderer, as well as the deck planking. Nico took his chance and before Barker could retrieve the knife, he ran full tilt at the man and knocked into his shoulder. Off balance, Barker stumbled and Nico hit him square on the chin. The blackguard was quickly overpowered and Nico bent over

Jessop's body with a muttered oath. 'He's dead,' he said, unnecessarily.

A murmuring broke out among the crew and there were shouts of 'hang him' and 'keelhaul the whoreson'. Jochem tried his best to keep up with his translations, but the words came out rapidly and disjointed, making it difficult for Midori to follow. She gathered that, although telling tales was never encouraged among the men, outright murder was a different matter altogether. It couldn't be tolerated.

'You think I care?' Barker shouted defiantly, glaring at Nico with hatred in his eyes. 'You was goin' to kill me anyway for darin' to touch your precious whore.' He spat once more. 'Well, I'm glad I had her, and I hope you rot in hell the pair of you!'

Midori drew in a steadying breath and told herself the man was saying such things out of sheer desperation. The words 'I had her' stuck in her mind, however, and echoed round and round inside her brain, even though she knew them to be false. The mere thought of such a thing turned her stomach.

Nico's mouth thinned, but he didn't reply. Instead he turned to the crew and asked, 'Are we all agreed this was cold-blooded murder of the worst kind?' A resounding 'Ja!' acknowledged the truth of this. 'Very well, fetch me some ropes.'

These were soon found and Barker brought forward. He raised his neck in yet another gesture of defiance, but the expected noose didn't descend over his head. Instead, at a nod from Nico, Jessop's body was raised up by two men to stand face to face with Barker, who swore and tried to jerk away. 'What the hell? What are you …?'

'Stand still. You will die with your victim, as is the custom,' Nico said.

'How? What? No! No, you can't … you whoresons!'

The ropes were wound round Barker and the corpse tied securely to him while still leaving the legs free. Barker began to spout obscenities and thrashed around, trying in vain to wriggle away from such close proximity to his victim. He only succeeded in smearing more blood on himself.

'Shut up.' One of the guards cuffed him again, but it had no effect. He continued to shout imprecations.

'Attach the other rope, then throw him overboard. There should be more than enough blood to attract the sharks before Barker has time to drown.'

Nico's orders were executed immediately and Jessop's body hung like a dead weight on his murderer, whose shouting was growing hoarse.

'Does anyone have anything to add?' Nico called out. No one replied. 'Then let's get it over with.'

It took four men to manoeuvre Barker to the railing and throw him over. The assembled crew ran to that side of the ship, craning to see what would happen next. Midori stayed where she was. She didn't want to witness the gruesome spectacle of Barker being pulled along next to the ship. The sharks were never far away and it would all be over in seconds in any case. For her, it was enough that he was gone.

'That was too quick for 'im,' Midori heard Harding mutter soon after, but she didn't care. The only thing which mattered was that Barker couldn't hurt her again.

Nico's voice spoke from just behind her. 'Do you want to stay for the flogging of the other culprits?'

'No, thank you. I've seen enough.' She turned to look him in the eye. 'I believe they may have only acted out of fear of Barker, so perhaps some leniency would be in order?'

Nico nodded. 'I've already thought of that. They'll only be given a few strokes of the lash, enough to teach them a lesson. Let us hope that's the end of the matter.'

Not long afterwards, he came and knocked on her cabin

door again and when she opened it, he came inside and shut it behind him. 'Are you all right?' he asked, putting his hands on her shoulders, staring at her intently.

Midori nodded, but her body was shivering with delayed reaction and he must have noticed straight away. Without a word, he pulled her into his arms and stroked her back in a soothing rhythm while she closed her eyes and gave in to the momentary weakness. It felt so good to be held like that, so safe. She breathed in his unique scent – he smelled of sea, salty breezes, man and some sort of sandalwood soap. For some reason she found it almost intoxicating and she stored away the memory of it deep inside her mind.

'I'm sorry,' she whispered. 'I don't know what's come over me.'

'It's natural you should feel upset. I'm only surprised it's taken this long,' he murmured. 'But it's over. He can't hurt you again.'

'He didn't actually do anything to me; that was a lie.' She felt compelled to tell him that, in order to clear her tainted honour somewhat.

'I'm glad. I didn't believe him anyway.'

They stood like that for a long time, until at last the shivering stopped and Midori started to feel calmer. 'Thank you, Nico,' she said, and pulled away slightly. She had drawn strength from his nearness, but she knew she had to put some distance between them again or she might be tempted to do more than hold him.

'You're welcome.' He bent to place a swift kiss on her cheek, then looked at her once more. 'Will you be all right now?'

'Yes.' And she knew this time she spoke the truth.

Nico deliberately kept away from Midori for over a week to give her time to recover, but finally he couldn't stand it any longer. He had to see her, had to make sure she was still all right. When he knocked on her cabin door and gave her the agreed password, she opened it, looking slightly wary.

'Are you well?' he asked, immediately concerned by her pallor and the way she hesitated before letting him enter. Before, she'd always seemed eager to see him and he had thought she'd enjoyed their discussions as much as he did.

'Yes, thank you. It's just ... you haven't visited for a while so I thought perhaps I'd done something wrong.'

A slight blush stained her cheeks and Nico gathered she was referring to the embrace they'd shared. At the time he had only wanted to comfort her, but he couldn't deny he'd enjoyed holding her and maybe he'd held her a little too closely. That wasn't her fault, though.

'No, of course not. I just wanted to give you time to recover from your ordeal.'

'I see.' An expression of relief flitted briefly across her features. 'That was kind, but there is nothing wrong with me now, apart from my tainted honour, of course ...' She broke off, seemingly mortified at blurting this out. 'Oh dear, I'm turning into a *gai-jin* in more ways than one,' she muttered. 'Please, forget I said that.'

Nico regarded her with his head slightly tilted to one side. 'Tainted honour? Is that how your countrymen would see it? I'm afraid I don't agree and besides, you're not in Japan now. You are on board my ship, where my word is law.' He smiled and took her hands in his, squeezing them. 'Forget what happened, Midori. It's over with.'

She nodded and he noticed her trembling as the slight contact between them sent shockwaves up his arms. He tried to ignore it. She was a beautiful woman and it wasn't to be wondered at if he reacted to her. Any normal man would. That was all there was to it. *She's not for me. At least not here, not now.*

'You're right. I'm on my way to a completely new life, where I'll no doubt have to change my way of thinking in more ways than one.' She gave him a small, slightly wistful, smile that tugged at his heartstrings and made him want to pull her close again. He resisted the urge.

'Yes,' he said, striving for a light tone. 'This is just the beginning of a new future for you. A clean slate. Everything else is in the past where it belongs.' He picked up the Bible which was lying on her bunk. 'So do you feel ready for some more theological debate? I see you've been studying.'

'Yes, please. I need to be prepared and I appreciate you teaching me.'

Nico nodded. He would make sure she knew everything that was necessary for her new life and then he'd forget all about her and return to his own freedom on the seven seas.

It was what he wanted. Wasn't it?

Chapter Sixteen

July 1642

The rest of the voyage back to Europe took seven months. Although it seemed like an eternity in some ways, life on board ship being for the most part tedious, for Midori it went too quickly and she didn't want it to end. The more time she spent with Nico, the more she wanted. He was like the opium drug, something the body craved in ever-larger doses if you allowed it free rein, and she felt as if she could never get enough of his company.

Their daily conversations strayed from the subject of religion, and they discussed everything under the sun. Everything, except one topic – for some reason Nico didn't like to talk about himself.

'There's nothing much to tell.' He shrugged. 'I grew up, went to sea and have been sailing ever since.'

The only other things Midori found out was that he wasn't married, his parents were dead, and although he apparently had a stepmother and siblings, he didn't get on with any of them. Apart from this, he clammed up whenever she tried to ask any personal questions.

Midori knew it shouldn't surprise her. After all, she didn't like to talk about herself much, either, but because he was a *gai-jin* she somehow didn't expect such secrecy from him. It made her wonder what he was hiding, but she had to respect his privacy. In return, she was equally vague about her own upbringing.

The physical awareness between them grew along with their friendship, and whenever their bodies touched inadvertently Midori would feel a strange jolt shooting through her. She was sure Nico felt it, too, but he didn't mention it and never touched her deliberately. It was as if he'd put up a barrier that couldn't be crossed, even though she would have liked to. Midori didn't know if what she was experiencing was merely desire, but she suspected it was something deeper. The question was, what could she do about it?

The answer was – nothing, unless Nico asked her to marry him. She would just have to wait and hope.

Inevitably, there were several storms along the way, but the one that woke Midori up in the middle of the night towards the end of July was far worse than any of the previous ones.

It was the noise from the flapping sails which disturbed her first, sounding like the cracking of a hundred whips at once, accompanied by the keening lament of the wind. As she came to in the darkness, she became aware of the severe rolling motion of the ship, and in the next instant was almost slung out of her bunk by a particularly violent heave. Muttering crossly, she sat up and rubbed at a bruised elbow.

'We're in the Bay of Biscay at last,' Harding had told her only that morning. 'Shouldn't be more'n a few days before we reach Holland, I reckon.'

Midori felt the timbers of the ship shudder as yet another giant wave impacted on one side. 'He may have spoken too soon,' she murmured now.

She turned over and tried to go back to sleep, but it proved impossible. The storm was increasing in strength, rather than the opposite, and Midori started to feel trapped inside her little cabin. This wasn't the way she had envisaged the end of her journey and she most certainly didn't want to die in here. In her mind's eye the walls began to close in on her and she had a sudden vision of the cabin filling with water. Within seconds, she'd be trapped forever in a watery grave.

She tore out of bed and pulled a robe over her night clothes. Without stopping to put shoes on, she flung open the door and staggered into the small corridor. Another wave hit the ship and she was slammed hard against the wall.

'Ow!' She grabbed her aching shoulder and made her way towards the hatch. There was water trickling along the floor, making her feet slip on the wet boards and she splayed her hands on the walls for added stability. It didn't help much, but she managed to keep herself upright.

It took her an age to open the hatch, but at last it fell back on its hinges and she was able to mount the steps to stick her head out and scan the heaving deck. Her long hair was immediately caught by the wind and whipped into a frenzy above her head, but she ignored it and grabbed the sides of the opening to steady herself. The darkness was almost absolute, dispersed only by the occasional bolt of lightning, which showed her the deck was a hive of activity. The scene of chaos stopped her in her tracks.

There were men everywhere, trying to secure ropes, move goods, take down sails and stand guard in case a mast would need to be cut down. She had been told by Harding that this was the usual procedure in an emergency. Now she could see for herself why it might be necessary. As well as warning cries and shouted orders, there was a cacophony of other sounds – screaming gusts of wind, the protest of ship's timbers and the flapping of sails and loose ropes. And above all, the deafening roar of the sea.

Within seconds Midori was drenched through as gusts of rain slammed into her. Icy seawater was sloshing across the decks and one wave found its way to her, making her gasp as it hit her body with amazing force. The salt made her eyes and nostrils sting and, snorting and spluttering, she shook her head. 'Damn you!' she shouted at the storm, shaking an impotent fist at the incredible forces of nature.

In that moment, a figure appeared out of the darkness. 'Midori, what on earth are you doing here? Get below, where you'll be safe, this instant!'

'No, please, Nico, I don't want to die down there. I can't bear to be enclosed like that. It's horrible!'

'You have even less chance of survival up here,' he shouted. 'I've already lost several men; the waves are just too strong. For the love of God, Midori, I beg of you, go below.'

Midori looked up at him, blinking salty droplets out of her eyes to try and make out his expression. Another lightning bolt showed her that he looked grim, but determined. She realised he must feel responsible for everyone's well-being. It was his ship, his duty to steer them all to safety. She owed it to him to help, not hinder his work.

'Very well,' she said, then grabbed the sides of the hatch to steady herself as the ship rolled once more. She went down the steps and he followed until he stood next to her at the bottom. She felt his arm go round her shoulders in a protective gesture.

'Come, I'll take you back.'

Another wave hit the ship and threw her heavily against him. He struggled to keep his balance and she thought she heard a muttered oath. Seven months within hearing of his crew had taught her more than the rudiments of Dutch, including the bad words, and she wanted to utter a few of them herself right now. Ignoring her upbringing as a lady, she did.

'Feel better?' Nico asked, giving her a brief grin. She nodded and smiled back. It was good that he still had a sense of humour, despite everything.

He brought her safely to the door of her cabin. 'Please stay in here,' he urged. 'I really don't want to have to worry about your safety on top of everything else. I'll come and see how you are as soon as I'm able. And try not to worry, we've been through worse.'

She nodded, even though she wasn't sure she believed him. Either way, she wasn't inclined to argue any longer. Shutting the door behind her, she changed into dry clothing and tried to dry her hair. It was a futile effort, however, as she spent the rest of the night being tossed around, ankle-deep in the water which was seeping in under her door. Sleeping was out of the question, so she didn't even attempt to lie down. Instead, she prayed silently to the spirits of her ancestors for assistance. She even prayed to Nico's and her mother's god, just in case it would make a difference. Deep inside, she doubted anyone was listening.

Was this where her journey would end?

She didn't know how long the storm went on for, but it seemed like a lifetime. Hour after hour the waves battered the ship relentlessly, throwing it around as if it was nothing but a toy.

When at last Midori felt the waves calm down and the rolling of the ship ease a little, she was just about to lie down and give in to exhaustion when there was a knock on her door.

'Who is it?'

'Nico.' He gave the password and when she unbarred the door, he stumbled in, one shoulder and arm covered in blood. Midori stared at him, all thoughts of sleep forgotten.

'What's happened? Are you all right?' She tried to see if he was badly hurt, but the faint light of early dawn coming through the portholes wasn't enough to make out any detail.

He closed his eyes in agony. 'Yes, yes I am, but the first mate … I tried to save him, but a spar came down and hit me and I lost my grip.' He covered his eyes with one hand and swore under his breath. 'He was a good man, Midori, a good man and a friend.'

She put a hand on his arm, stroking it with a soothing

motion. 'I'm sure it wasn't your fault. You did the best you could and you have steered the rest of us to safety, haven't you?'

He slicked back his wet hair with one hand and shrugged. 'Yes, I suppose you're right. The worst is over now and we can limp to harbour. Still …'

She tactfully changed the subject. 'Here, let me tend to your wound. Is it deep?'

'No, I'll have it seen to later. I must go and help out on deck. I just wanted to make sure you were all right.'

'Yes, don't worry about me.'

'Good, then I'll come back in a while.'

She sat in her cabin for what seemed another eternity, watching as more light appeared outside the portholes. She wondered what had happened to the other ships in the convoy; they were nowhere to be seen. *I hope they are all right!* The waves were still high, but not threateningly so, and she was even able to eat some stale ship's biscuits while she waited for Nico's return. She could hear the men and guessed they must be clearing away debris and mending things as best they could. She hoped the repairs would be enough to take them safely to their destination.

'I think everything is under control again, or as much as it can be at the moment.'

Nico had come back at last and Midori told him to sit down. Without asking permission she pushed his long, soft golden hair and his shirt out of the way to reveal a nasty gash in his shoulder that was oozing blood. 'I might have to stitch this or it won't heal.'

'Do what you have to, but quickly, please. I must get back to the others as soon as possible.'

'I'm sure they can do without you for a short while,' Midori told him. 'You bleeding to death won't help them much.'

The shadow of a smile tugged at his lips. 'Very well, you may be right about that.'

She fetched the necessary implements and tried not to stare when he pulled the shirt over his head. She'd seen men's upper bodies before, but never one as big or as perfect as Nico's. There were ridges of hard muscle in all the right places, his shoulders and arms nicely defined. She was seized by an almost irresistible urge to run her hands all over him, to feel the softness of his skin against her fingertips, the taut muscles underneath. The sight of fresh blood oozing from his shoulder brought her back to her senses, however, and she set to work as fast as she could. Nico bore her ministrations stoically, hissing in a breath from time to time when she hurt him.

'I'm sorry, but I really think this is necessary,' she said, making the stitches as neat as she could. The castle healer had taught her how and she was grateful for that now.

'I know. I've been through worse.' He attempted a smile and something moved inside her, making her feel warm all over. She wanted more of those slow smiles of his, wanted to hear the deep, husky timbre of his voice, wanted to touch him without hurting him as she was now.

But I don't have the right.

When she had finished, he put on his shirt again and Midori stifled a sigh of disappointment. She could happily have just stared at him for ages. He stood up and took her hand in his and raised it to his mouth for a brief kiss. 'Thank you,' he said. 'I'm grateful for your help. If there are others who need your assistance, may I send them to you? De Jong is very busy and would no doubt appreciate your help.'

He kept hold of her hand for longer than necessary and she put her other one on his arm and squeezed it. 'Of course, and *dō itashimashite*.' He was indeed welcome to her aid any time, she thought. Awareness of him jolted through her and she found herself revelling in the feel of his muscles under the wet garments. Her hands again itched to explore, and impulsively, she buried her face in his wet shirt, grabbing a handful of it to pull herself closer to him. She felt him shiver. There was a feeling of safety, as if she'd come home, but also a pleasurable kind of danger. It was very strange, but she was sure this was where she was meant to be, forever.

'Midori, no. This won't do.' He tried to disentangle himself, although very half-heartedly, his voice sounding almost strangled. He put his hands on her shoulders to hold her away from him.

'Why?' They were still so close she could feel the muscles in his thighs flex against hers. Sparks shot through her and she didn't want to deny these feelings any longer. They only had a few days left. Time was running out and she wanted answers.

She wanted him.

'We shouldn't ... I can't ... I gave my word to your brother.'

'Ichiro would be happy for me. You're a good man.' Her hand came up to cup his chin, the tips of her fingers playing over his lips. The feel of his soft stubble on her palm delighted her and sent another frisson shooting down her arm.

He shook his head. 'You don't know me, not really.'

But Midori wasn't listening. Even though she knew it was wrong of her, she still craved his touch. And she knew he felt the same because his blue eyes were filled with anguish, but also with a longing and desire that fired her blood.

They stood there staring at each other, each one battling with their conscience, but in the end it was as if some irresistible magnetic force was pulling them together and he bent to kiss her, despite his words. It seemed the only thing that mattered right now was this overwhelming attraction between them. There was a tingling feeling wherever their bodies touched. Even the coldness of his wet clothing didn't dispel the warmth generated whenever one of them moved.

Midori closed her eyes. She wanted this man more than anything. She had been given this moment by fate, and she was desperate to show him how much it meant to her. It made her return his kiss with even more passion while she memorised the feel of him, the scent of him, forever. He tasted of salt and wind, and despite his all-night exposure to the elements, his lips were soft and warm. A recklessness sprang up inside her, making her feel wanton, willing him to forget whatever was holding him back.

Eventually, she buried her face in his neck and whispered, 'Oh, Nico, why don't you come with me to Plymouth? Meet my relatives. I'm sure they'll be only too pleased to—'

'What?' Nico pulled away abruptly and stared at her, a frown appearing on his brow. 'Did you say Plymouth? I thought you were going to London?'

Midori caressed his cheek. 'I didn't quite tell you the truth, but I don't want there to be any secrets between us now. I'm going back to my mother's family, the Marston's, and they're in Devon. That's not too far from London, is it?'

But Nico didn't reply to her question. He scowled at her and repeated the words, 'Marston? Your mother?' as if he couldn't quite take them in.

Midori leaned her cheek on his chest and tried to pull him close again. 'Yes, my mother Hannah went to Japan years ago and stayed there. She fell in love with my father you see and—'

Nico took hold of her wrists and put some distance between them. He shook his head, disbelief and what looked like pain in his eyes. 'You should have told me that from the beginning,' he said, sounding stern.

'But what does it matter?' Midori looked down to where

he was holding her away from him and felt as if a chasm had suddenly opened up between them, but she didn't understand why. *Does he hate liars? But I had good reason not to tell him everything about myself, surely he must see that?*

Apparently not. He let go of her and turned away. 'I'm sorry, Midori, this should never have happened. I … I have to go.' He headed for the door without looking back.

Midori stared after him in disbelief, then sank down on to her bunk, feeling cold and numb, as if she'd been the one outside all night. She didn't cry; it was a pointless exercise. Besides, she felt like an empty shell, all her emotions expended. She was now sure that Nico meant a great deal to her, but it would seem there was no future with him. He had been repulsed by her dishonesty and there was nothing for it but to accept that.

She couldn't blame him. Honesty and integrity were the most important things in Japanese society, too; obviously it was the same in Nico's country. *If only I'd told him the truth earlier, perhaps things would have been different? But he wasn't exactly forthcoming himself …* And she still couldn't quite understand why her destination mattered so much to him.

Either way, it was clear he didn't want her. *I have to put him out of my mind.*

Fate had been unkind yet again, but she had lived through this storm, she could weather others as well.

Nico stumbled up the stairs, then turned and made for his own cabin. He slammed the door shut behind him and threw himself down on to his bunk, breathing heavily. Putting an arm over his eyes, he groaned.

'No, I don't believe it! Of all the strange coincidences … How is this possible?'

He swore viciously and cursed fate. *This is too much!*

He'd hoped never to hear the word Plymouth again. It was the place where he'd grown up, the place he'd fled from and tried to forget. *A hell-hole.* And he'd especially hoped never to hear about the Marston family ever again. *Damn them!*

'Hannah,' he muttered. It was a name he'd heard many times and he didn't think there could be two of them. At least not two who had gone to Japan thirty years ago.

'She stowed away on a ship, dressed like a boy. Sailed all the way to the Japans with us, then got herself abducted by a warlord. We managed to retrieve her, only to lose her on the way back to the ship. Drowned in a river, she did. So sad ...'

The words echoed round his brain, the story all too familiar. Whenever they attended a gathering of his stepmother's family, the old tale was told. Hannah had been her sister and their brother Jacob was the man who'd lost her in Japan. Those people weren't just Midori's relatives, they were his as well, albeit only by virtue of his father's marriage to Kate Marston.

'Hell, they're nothing to do with me. Not blood kin, not wanted!' And the feeling was mutual – he had never got on with them and once he'd run away, he'd changed his name and even his nationality to make a new life for himself. He was Nico Noordholt now, Dutch citizen. There was nothing to connect him to Plymouth or the Marstons. *Except Midori, devil take it!*

He stared at the ceiling. *That's not her fault though, but still ... the irony of it!*

'So, Hannah Marston obviously didn't drown, or she wouldn't have had a daughter.' Nico gritted his teeth. 'And the blasted girl had to buy passage on my ship, of all the ones in the world? Damn it all to hell!'

Well, I swore never to go back. She'll have to find her own way there.

And I'm not telling her why.

Chapter Seventeen

July–August 1642

Midori didn't see much of Nico in the days that followed, and whenever she did catch a glimpse of him, it was as if the night of the storm had never happened. He spoke to her politely, just as he'd always done before, but seemed distant. If there was still a spark between them, he gave no sign of it. Midori did her best to pretend indifference as well. She'd had years of practice at hiding her emotions and knew she could do it now, too.

Amsterdam turned out to be a bustling port, just like Nagasaki, but there the similarities ended. Where Nagasaki was surrounded by and built on hills, the Dutch town was as flat as it was possible for a place to be. You didn't approach it directly from the sea, but via the Zuider Zee, a vast yet shallow inlet of the North Sea.

As the *Zwarte Zwaan* glided down the length of it, Midori enjoyed her first view of Holland. Peasants' dwellings abounded, most of them two-storey buildings with a thatched roof, each with a barn or two and a muddy farm yard where animals roamed freely. The lowing of cattle, clucking of chickens and braying of sheep filled the air, mixing with the joyous birdsong of summer. People called out to each other in the Dutch tongue, its lilting cadence a pleasure to listen to. There were young women singing as they went about their daily chores. These sights and sounds lifted Midori's spirits and even the occasional whiff of excessive farm smells couldn't put a damper on things.

I've arrived in Europe at last.

The surrounding landscape, with its trees and shrubs, was a lush green, which reminded Midori of the forests near

Castle Shiroi. The flowers swaying in the breeze added a vivid touch of colour. What fascinated her the most, however, were the distinctive windmills that dotted the countryside. She'd never seen their like and when Nico happened to pass her, she stopped him and asked if he'd explain to her how they worked.

'You really want to know?' He seemed genuinely surprised at her question.

'Of course. I find such information fascinating.'

Nico's mouth curved into a reluctant smile. 'I'm sorry, I should be used to your questioning mind by now, shouldn't I?'

Midori wasn't sure if this was a compliment or not, so just replied, 'Precisely.'

He told her everything he knew about windmills and Midori listened with rapt attention, not least because she still loved to listen to his voice.

As they reached the city of Amsterdam itself, Midori marvelled at the rows of neat and orderly houses, their noble brick façades and richly decorated cornices facing the canals and mirrored in their still waters. She recognised the style of building from Batavia, although Amsterdam was far prettier, in her opinion.

Nico surprised her by staying next to her as they waited for the ship to dock. He still seemed a bit distant, but made small talk as if he couldn't bear a silence between them. 'The city's canals were built as a series of semicircles next to the river Ij,' he told her. 'There are smaller ones running north and south between them as well and narrow, bustling streets among the houses.'

Midori gazed around her. The sheer size of this town would have over-awed her if she hadn't visited the great city of Edo with her father several times.

'There is a stream of goods from all parts of the world

pouring into the warehouses of this town, making it a hive of activity,' Nico continued.

There were foreigners of every description too and, once on the quayside, Midori could hear a jumble of tongues all around her. Nico pointed to some specific races.

'Those men over there are Jews from Spain and Portugal, who have found a haven from persecution here. The tall blond men are from the Baltic States and Scandinavia; they've come to trade their iron ore, wood and pelts for foreign goods. And the rest are a mixture of different European nationalities who flock to Amsterdam for various reasons. It's a huge market place, with goods coming and going in all directions, and the local merchants are making fortunes undreamt of by former generations. I'm hoping one of them will be me.' He let down his guard for a moment and grinned at her.

'Come now,' he continued. 'I'll take you and Harding to an inn before I go and oversee the unloading of the cargo.' As if sensing the question Midori had been about to ask, he added, 'You can't stay at my lodgings. For one thing, it wouldn't be seemly, and for another, there's no room. You'll be more comfortable at an inn. Harding, do you mind keeping Mistress Midori company for a little while longer? Jochem is off home to his family, I understand.'

'Not at all, Cap'n. It'll be my pleasure.'

During their journey, Nico had told Midori a little about the people of Holland and their history.

'They've been at war with Spain for nearly eighty years because its ruler considers himself the head of state for all the Netherlands. The northern states joined together, calling themselves the United Provinces, and have been fighting hard for the freedom to rule themselves.'

'But they haven't won?'

'Well, almost. At least, it's been a long and gruelling fight, but everyone feels they're nearly at the end of it now. The fighting has stopped and peace negotiations have been mentioned, but they're not yet underway. The word is that the Spanish have given up their claim and are prepared to discuss it at last.'

'So really, you're in the middle of a civil war?' Midori couldn't believe the bad luck that had brought her to Europe at such a time.

'Yes, but, as I said, it's nearly over, I think, so you needn't worry. It shouldn't affect you. No one is fighting right now.'

As they walked along by the side of the canals, this seemed to be the case. The people all around them were going about their daily business as if they'd never heard of the word 'war', so Midori began to feel reassured.

'Right, here's the inn I had in mind.' Nico indicated a respectable-looking establishment, which appeared to be clean and neat. 'I'll go and ask for rooms, if you think it will do?'

Midori nodded. 'It looks perfect.'

He returned soon after. 'I've secured two bedchambers and a private parlour for dining. The landlady says you can eat as soon as you are ready.'

'Thank you.'

'I'll leave you to it, then. I've much to do, but I'll come back as soon as I can.'

Nico seemed impatient to go, so Midori didn't try to keep him. In a very short time she was installed in a small, neat room, with a comfortable bed and wash stand, but not much else. She sat down on the soft cover and tried not to feel overwhelmed.

Nico spent the rest of the day making sure his valuable cargo was safely stored in a locked warehouse, with guards posted outside. He wasn't taking any chances and knew there were plenty of unscrupulous people who would happily steal what they could. When he reached his lodgings, which were in the house next to the one that had belonged to Casper, he was exhausted. It seemed the day wasn't quite finished, however, because the landlady told him there was someone waiting for him.

'*Mijnheer* Schuyler, I hadn't thought to see you so soon.' Nico greeted Casper's solicitor friend with a firm handshake. He'd always liked the man, and knew Schuyler would genuinely share his grief over Casper's death.

'I felt I had to come. I was told about the arrival of the *Zwarte Zwaan* this afternoon, but my joy at your safe homecoming was of course dashed by the news of my friend.' Schuyler shook his head. 'He was a good man. I shall miss him very much.'

'As do I.' Nico sighed. He'd had over nine months to come to terms with Casper's demise, but it still felt unreal, especially here where he'd always been only one door away.

'Will you tell me what happened, please? Or perhaps you'd prefer that I return another time ...'

'No, no, of course I will. Shall we go in search of supper somewhere? Then you can hear all about our adventures.'

An hour later, they were ensconced in a corner of a very cosy inn, replete and with a tankard of ale each.

'Ah, I can't tell you how nice it is to eat proper food and drink something that doesn't have to be sieved for maggots first.' Nico smiled at Schuyler. 'You get used to it, but enough is enough.'

'I can well imagine. And yet both you and Casper have been willingly travelling the world for so many years.' Schuyler shook his head. 'I'm afraid I couldn't stomach it myself, even though you've certainly seen some wonderful sights by the sound of it. Now, speaking of Casper once more, did he mention his will to you?'

Nico frowned. 'Yes. I told him I didn't want him to give me anything, but he insisted there would be something. Really, it should go to his relatives, though.'

Schuyler gave a small smile. 'I'm afraid you can't argue with a legal will. The bequest is yours whether you want it or not. He left you his house, but you can sell it if you prefer.'

'What? Why? Shouldn't it be sold and the proceeds divided between his nieces and nephews?' Nico was stunned at the magnitude of this inheritance. Properties in Amsterdam were expensive.

'Casper left them his savings, which were considerable, since he never married and lived quite frugally. No, the house is yours, and everything in it, including the servants, if you want them. I'll inform Casper's relatives, don't worry.'

Nico took a deep breath. 'I don't know what to say. This is entirely unexpected.' He was touched that Casper seemed to have valued him so highly, especially since his own family had been the exact opposite. When his father had died, he'd left his entire estate divided equally between the rest of his children, with not a penny to Nico. The explanation in his will was that he considered Nico a wastrel who needed to be taught a lesson by having to fend for himself. Although there was some truth in this, it had hurt him deeply to be singled out in such a way.

'Just accept the bequest,' was Schuyler's advice now. 'Casper told me he considered you the son he never had and he'd want you to be happy. We can sort out the legalities tomorrow, if you come by my offices. Say mid-afternoon, would that suit?'

'Yes, of course. Thank you.'

I'm the owner of a house, a home. It felt strange to have

somewhere that was really his, not just a rented lodging, but it also felt good.

Nico didn't come back the following day, and Midori decided to explore the town with Harding in tow.

'I don't want to sit around here all day, but is it safe, do you think? I wouldn't want to get into trouble again.'

'Oh, this here place is much more civilised,' Harding assured her. 'And I won't let anyone knock me senseless neither, I swear.'

Midori had to smile at that. 'Yes, we'll both stay away from dark doorways, shall we?' They stepped into the street and she looked around with interest. 'Isn't it wonderful to be on dry land again, Harding? Although the ground still feels as though it's moving a little.'

'Yes, that'll wear off soon.'

'I wonder where the nearest market is?'

'Over that way.' Harding pointed. 'I've spent quite a lot of time here, so I know my way around.' They headed in the direction he'd indicated, walking slowly and taking in the sights and sounds of the bustling city.

'*Goedemorgen, mevrouw.*'

'*Goedemorgen.*' Midori answered the greetings of the merchants with a polite nod of her head and a smile. They gave her some strange looks, on account of her wearing a *kimono* she supposed, but since Nico had told her all manner of people came to Amsterdam, she decided it didn't matter. She felt more alive than she had for months; as if she'd been liberated from prison. Happiness bubbled up inside her.

Midori marvelled again at the orderliness of the canals and houses, and the people hurrying about their business fascinated her. There were the inevitable differences between rich and poor, but most of them looked content, no matter their station in life. The burgomasters and their families, the cream of Amsterdam's merchant class, as Harding explained, cut fine figures in their splendid outfits. Black was the predominant colour of clothing for the rich, but there were other hues as well. Even those dressed in black had used such rich materials their clothing seemed iridescent in the morning light, the black turning to blues and purples in the flash of an eye. Midori made a mental note to purchase some of that lovely dark silk immediately, just because it was so beautiful.

Most of the townspeople wore simple woollen garments in earthy colours, which was presumably cheaper. Midori also noticed a lot of the women wore white caps – coifs, Harding called them – some with lace, some without. 'Why do they do that?' she asked.

'They show whether a woman is married or not, though some wear them anyways,' Harding said. 'It's more proper, see. These are different to the English ones, though.'

'Do you think I ought to buy one?'

Harding guffawed. 'I doubt it would go with your foreign clothes, beggin' your pardon, mistress. Best to wait till you reach England. They'll have their own styles there.'

'Oh, yes of course.'

The market, when they reached it, was everything she could have wished for, and Midori soon found all manner of things to buy. Poor Harding walked behind her, weighed down with parcels, while Midori threw herself into haggling with gusto. The Dutch she had picked up during the voyage stood her in good stead and she was able to hold her own. At the cloth merchant's stall, Midori fingered the costly materials to determine which was of the best quality.

'*Hoeveel kost het?*' She pointed to a length of black silk of the finest kind, happily prepared for a haggling battle. She wasn't disappointed. It took her a long time to make the seller lower the price sufficiently, but in the end they reached a sum that satisfied them both, and she sailed off triumphantly with her neatly wrapped package.

'I knew it, he was a rascal,' she chuckled.

'I'd have given up long since,' Harding admitted. 'You did well. Now how's about we turn back to the inn for some victuals? My stomach's been grumbling this half hour or more.'

'Of course, sorry, Harding. I just got carried away. Let's go.'

'You've done well, Noordholt, we are very pleased with your endeavours. Well, yours and de Leuw's, as you said.'

Nico bowed in acknowledgement of this praise, but tried to keep his expression neutral. He'd gone to report to his employers, before stopping by Schuyler's offices, so that he knew exactly where he stood with regard to remuneration. He was now standing before the *Heeren XVII*, the 'Lords Seventeen' as they were called, the governing body of the Dutch East India Company. It consisted of seventeen directors, although on this particular day Nico only counted fourteen.

The *Verenigde Oostindische Compagnie* was an extremely powerful organisation indeed. It had the right to enter into treaties, maintain military forces and even produce coinage, as well as having powers of government and justice in Dutch overseas territories. To please its directors was most definitely something to be aspired to, as Casper had impressed on him.

Now that he'd achieved that, Nico could look forward to more lucrative contracts, perhaps even a position of some sort. The fact that he wasn't of noble birth made no difference. The Company required only competence, experience and knowledge in its employees. Social rank was irrelevant.

'Nutmeg, cloves, cinnamon, pepper, tea, silk, indigo ...'

One of the directors was reading out a list of the goods Nico had brought back.

'Should fetch a tidy sum.' Another director nodded approvingly. 'Because of *Mijnheer* de Leuw's demise, your share will not be insignificant.' He named an approximate amount that almost made Nico reel, as it was so much more than he'd expected, but he kept his composure somehow.

'Thank you.' Nico bowed again.

'Do you know what is to be done with the money owed to de Leuw?'

'Yes, I believe his solicitor, *Mijnheer* Schuyler, will take care of it.' Nico gave the directors Schuyler's address.

'Thank you, Noordholt. And don't forget to report back to us when you are ready to undertake your next venture.'

With a last bow and a secret sigh of relief, Nico escaped. Standing outside East India House, the company's headquarters, he felt as if he'd faced the Holy Inquisition, even though the directors had been geniality personified. He breathed in the familiar scents of Amsterdam and slowly but surely his heart rate returned to normal.

Now all he had to do was find Midori passage to England and he'd be free to sail the seven seas again.

Chapter Eighteen

Back at the inn, Midori and Harding found Jochem waiting for them.

'At last!' The youth beamed at them. 'I thought you'd never return.'

'We haven't been gone that long, surely?' Midori smiled at him. She'd become fond of the boy and had thought she might not see him again once they docked.

'My mother's asked me to invite you to supper tonight. Said she'd love to meet a lady from such a faraway country. I told her all about you. What do you say, will you come? And Mr Harding, too, of course.'

'Why thank you, that's very kind. I'd love to,' Midori said.

'Excellent. I'll fetch you a bit later on then.' Jochem bounded off, like a young puppy eager to play. Midori realised he must be happy to have some free time after being at everyone's beck and call for so long.

Jochem's mother proved to be a widow who'd supported herself and her family as a seamstress since her husband's death some years before. Her house was somewhat chaotic, but fairly clean. She chattered away excitedly, and Midori did her best to answer all the questions thrown at her by her inquisitive hostess. It was an enjoyable evening, but Midori was happy to get back to the inn at the end of it.

As she and Harding walked through the tap room on the way to their rooms, however, they heard someone calling their names. Midori turned to find Nico sprawled in a chair, with a tankard in one hand and his other arm around a giggling woman who was perched on his lap. The wench was extremely well-rounded, with rosy cheeks, blonde hair and a bosom that was very much in evidence. Nico didn't seem to mind.

'There you are. I was beginning to think you'd gone to England on your own.'

Midori frowned at him, unaccountably annoyed to find him like this, even though she knew it was nothing to do with her how he spent his time. 'Would you have cared? We've not seen you all day.' The words came out before she had a chance to stop them and she gritted her teeth. *Fool!*

'Oh, you missed me, did you?' Nico was slurring his words slightly, so Midori suspected he'd been sitting there drinking for some time. She *had* missed him, but she wasn't about to tell him so.

'No, but you said yesterday you'd return soon. Anyway, we've had supper with Jochem's family. If you'd been here earlier, no doubt you'd have been invited, too.'

'You could have left word.' He scowled. 'I've been sitting here for hours. Was beginning to worry you'd been abducted again.'

'It doesn't look as though you've been short of company.' Midori glanced at the buxom girl who was now leaning her head on Nico's shoulder and twining her fingers in his golden hair, which had come loose from its ribbon, spilling out across his wide shoulders. A pang of jealousy shot through Midori, so strong it almost made her gasp out loud. He wouldn't let *her* touch him like that, but he'd allow a tavern wench any liberties she wanted?

Suppressing these thoughts, she added, 'I'm off to bed. If you can spare the time to see us, perhaps you could return tomorrow morning? We'll be sure to let you know our every movement.'

She turned her back on Nico and the taproom and marched off without even looking to see whether Harding followed or not. Once in bed, it took her ages to go to sleep, however, because every time she closed her eyes, all she saw was the giggling girl's chubby arms around Nico's throat.

'Infuriating man!' she hissed into the darkness. 'I refuse to let him affect me this way. He's made it plain he doesn't want me after all.'

But no matter how hard she tried, she couldn't purge him or that image from her mind.

Nico woke the next morning feeling decidedly bleary. He'd left the inn soon after Midori had gone to bed, refusing the offer of 'solace' from the serving girl. He didn't know why he'd allowed her to sit on his lap when he didn't actually want her, although that in itself was also a mystery. Having been at sea for so long, he should have been desperate for female company, but he'd not been tempted. One look at Midori and any thoughts of bedding anyone else had flown out of his head.

'A pox on it,' he murmured. 'Midori may be enticing, but there are other women who are equally so.' The serving wench just hadn't been to his taste.

Besides, taking Midori to bed would mean having to wed her, he knew that. She wasn't some common doxy, she was a lady. *Marriage? Never!* Wouldn't my erstwhile family love it if I turned out to be so respectable, he thought. And marriage to Midori also meant having to go with her to Plymouth to see that family, which wasn't an option.

What are you so scared of? A little voice inside his head needled him. *Surely they can't hurt you now? You're your own man, very well-to-do after this recent voyage. Why not go back and show them?*

'To hell with that!' he muttered. He doubted they cared what had become of him.

Either way, he knew what marriage did to people and he wanted none of it. He'd watched his stepmother age

173

prematurely, a miserable, downtrodden woman, forever pregnant or with a toddler in tow. And what had she received for her pains? Nothing. The old curmudgeon she'd married hadn't left her so much as a penny, either. Only his children, apart from Nico himself.

'Bastard,' Nico spat. But whereas his stepmother had been offered shelter by her brother, Nico had to find himself board and lodging elsewhere.

'You're more than old enough to support yourself,' Jacob Marston had told him. 'It's past time you stopped gambling and frequenting taverns and did an honest day's work.' It was the truth, but Nico felt it could have been worded differently and he would have appreciated a bed for at least a week or so while he found employment. Marston could even have offered him work in his family's merchant business, but when Nico suggested it he was laughed out of the room.

'I doubt you'd be much use,' was the verdict.

He drew in a deep breath. 'Well, I managed and I've proved him wrong, so no point thinking about it now.' It still rankled, though.

As for Midori, he supposed he'd better try and make up for his boorish behaviour of the night before. Most likely, she didn't care either way, but for some reason he didn't want her to have such a low opinion of him as she'd obviously had last night.

He wanted her to think well of him, although why that should be so, he didn't stop to analyse.

'You've inherited a house, you say?'

'Yes, from my friend, the captain who died while we were in Dejima. Remember, I told you about him?'

Nico had joined Midori and Harding in the private parlour at the inn, but refused any sustenance. Midori suspected he had a sore head and was feeling nauseous, but he didn't look

174

too bad and for some reason that annoyed her. He should have been suffering ill effects from last night. It would have served him right. She nodded curtly. 'Yes, I remember.'

'I've been given the keys this morning, so I wondered if you'd like to come with me to have a look? Harding, what do you say?'

'Not me, Cap'n, if you don't mind. There's an old friend of mine I'd like to see afore I head back to England. If you're lookin' after Mistress Midori anyways?'

'Yes, of course.'

Midori wasn't sure she ought to spend time alone with Nico. 'Is it seemly?' she asked. 'I mean, I don't know what the customs are here, but in my country I wouldn't go about with just a man for company.'

'You did yesterday,' Nico pointed out.

'Oh, yes, that's true, but ...' Midori couldn't tell him that she'd never seen Harding as anything other than a bodyguard, whereas being alone with Nico felt completely different.

'And you've just spent nine months without another woman in sight.'

Midori nodded. 'Very well, let's go,' she said. He was right – what reputation she'd once had was probably gone now, in any case.

They boarded a small boat which floated along the canals at a leisurely pace, giving Midori the opportunity to further admire the city's architecture. Most of the houses were similar in size and shape, with the distinctive gables so common in Holland. But each one appeared to have some architectural quirk or other to show their owners' individuality. Midori thought them all very attractive and the trees that had been planted alongside the canals, with their fresh green leaves reflected in the water, gave an overall impression of beauty and orderliness.

'What are those hooks sticking out of the top of the houses?' she asked Nico.

'They're hoisting beams. Most of these properties belong to merchants and the attic floor of each house is usually used for storing goods. All types of things can be hoisted up there straight from boats or barges on the canal.'

'How ingenious. Is that what you will do, too?'

'I suppose. I hadn't thought about it yet. Usually only part of the ship's cargo belongs to me personally. Each man on board is given a certain amount of space for their own purchases, but it's only a very small part. The main bulk of the cargo always belongs to the Company and would be stored in warehouses elsewhere. But perhaps I'll try my hand at trading for myself a bit more, hiring a ship of my own.'

Nico pointed out the best properties, those of the richest merchants and burgomasters, which were situated on the *Singel* and *Herengracht* canals. His own new home, although not precisely poor, was in a slightly less prominent position on the *Keizersgracht* canal. When they reached it at last, Midori thought it looked to be a fine house, nonetheless.

In the entrance hall, which had a beautiful floor of black-and-white marble tiles, Midori noticed at once the shiny wood panelling and fine landscape paintings on the walls. She gazed around with admiration. 'Oh, this is lovely!'

Nico smiled for the first time that morning and bowed in mock servitude. 'I'm glad it meets with your approval, my lady,' he joked. She shot him a look of exasperation, but found herself smiling back at him anyway. It was good they could joke with each other, despite everything. She reflected that perhaps they could at least be friends, since he didn't seem to want anything else. She couldn't deny she felt at ease with him most of the time. Their minds were so in tune and whenever their eyes met, Midori would more often than not find her own thoughts reflected in the depths of his gaze. It was uncanny.

'Come up to the first floor and let's see what state the parlour is in,' Nico said. '*Mijnheer* Schuyler told me the servants were supposed to have kept the house in order, but with the master away, who knows? He's given them time off at the moment.'

He led the way upstairs to a large room which overlooked the canal. As he threw open the door, Midori drew in a breath of surprise. The parlour was bright and airy, with a polished wooden floor and cushions and hangings of various red hues adding colour to the dark furniture and walls. All kinds of utensils and decorative objects lined the shelves and tables around the room. Blue-and-white china bowls, pewter flagons and even conch shells – each one equally neat and well kept. The whole house had an air of homeliness and warm comfort that was sorely lacking at the inn where she was staying.

'This is a beautiful room,' she breathed. 'You're very lucky!'

Nico looked around, as if seeing it properly for the first time. 'Yes, I am, aren't I? Perhaps I should get rid of some of the clutter, but other than that, it's perfect.'

'Clutter? No, don't, it looks lovely.' Midori felt her cheeks turn red. 'Or at least, that's my opinion. Of course you must do as you see fit.'

Nico raised an eyebrow at her. 'So if you lived here, you'd leave it as it is?'

'Absolutely. But since I don't, it's up to you.' Midori turned away. For a moment she'd found herself wishing with all her heart that she could share this wonderful house with Nico. Perhaps bring up children here. But she knew it was nothing but a silly dream. He'd made that perfectly clear.

'Can we see the rest?' she asked, restless now. 'And then I wish to speak to you about continuing my journey.'

'I've found us passage on a ship that leaves this evening,' Nico told Harding and Midori the following day. 'Can you be ready so soon?'

'Us?' Midori frowned at him. 'I thought Harding was escorting me, since he's apparently going to Plymouth anyway.'

Nico went to stare out of the window, adopting a nonchalant tone. 'I've decided to come with you. I promised your brother I'd see you safe to your destination and I don't want to go back on my word.'

'I can cope,' Midori started to protest, but Nico cut her off by holding up his hand.

'I've already paid, so it's too late to change my plans now. Shall I arrange to have your things brought down to the quay?' He didn't want to discuss why he'd changed his mind because he didn't really understand it himself. All he knew was he couldn't let Midori travel to England by herself. He had to make sure she arrived safely.

'Very well. Thank you,' she added grudgingly. 'I'll go and see to my packing, then.'

Nico watched her go and the thought that they only had a few more days in each other's company was strangely unsettling. He'd become fond of her, used to having her around. *Well, more than that.* He couldn't deny there was an attraction between them. But it was just physical, and he'd get over it. Now all he had to do was deliver her to her uncle and he could put this entire episode behind him and start afresh.

Midori didn't see much of Nico during the four-day-long trip to Plymouth. He seemed withdrawn and brooding, and she couldn't understand why. Harding didn't know, either.

'No idea what ails the man.' He shrugged. 'I did hear as how he's not keen on England, but don't know why.'

'Well, I didn't ask him to come,' she snapped, irritated beyond measure.

On a breezy summer's morning they anchored in Plymouth harbour at last. Midori experienced a mixture of feelings – joy at having finally reached her destination and intense sadness at having to say goodbye to the people who had become her world during the last nine months. Most of all, she hated the thought of having to part from Nico. He'd told her he wasn't staying long.

She knew in her heart that was for the best, but she would have given anything just to spend some more time with him. However, Nico would soon be in the past and only fate knew what lay before her. Since she didn't have a choice in the matter, she was determined to make the best of it, come what may.

They said goodbye to Harding. 'Although I'm only down the other side of the harbour,' he said, 'so I'm sure we'll bump into each other every now and then. If there's anythin' I can do for you, mistress, don't hesitate.'

Midori nodded. 'Thank you for everything.'

Plymouth was nothing like she'd imagined it to be and she wrinkled her nose as she picked her way round all the rubbish littering the narrow streets. 'Why is it so dirty?' she asked Nico as they only just avoided stepping on a rotting animal carcass. It appeared to have been thrown out of a nearby butcher's shop. A cloud of flies hovered over it, buzzing angrily, and Midori swatted at them.

He shrugged. 'Your uncle's house is higher up on the hill, where conditions are slightly better.'

'How do you know?'

'Er, I asked someone.'

Midori hurried on, spurred by a wish to escape the noxious odours. They passed innumerable shops – a candle-maker, a baker, a cordwainer – which looked very different to what Midori was used to. She stopped to inspect some of the wares a few times until she realised the shopkeepers were staring at her, openly curious. She followed Nico with her eyes firmly fixed on the ground after that.

'Why are they staring at me so?' she hissed. 'I changed my clothing, just as you asked.' He'd told her not to wear her most colourful *kimono*, which she'd put on at first in honour of the occasion.

Nico gave her a rueful smile. 'It's still different from what they're wearing, isn't it?' He nodded in the direction of some ladies passing by and Midori saw what he meant. 'We should have bought you garments in Amsterdam.'

'No, I want to arrive in my own clothes.' For some reason she couldn't fathom herself, Midori felt strongly about that. 'No doubt I'll have to adapt later, but today I am me.'

'Well, then, perhaps they are staring because they've never seen anyone so beautiful before,' Nico whispered, sending a streak of warmth down her spine.

'Don't be provoking.' Midori was cross that he'd chosen today of all days to play games with her. He'd never told her she was beautiful before and now it was too late. She marched off with her head held high until she realised she had no idea where she was going and was forced to stop and wait for Nico. He quirked an eyebrow at her, but said nothing more.

Everywhere they went they encountered throngs of people who were none too clean. Assailed by all these odours,

Midori began to feel nauseous and wondered if it would be impolite to put a hand over her nose and mouth. After a while she stopped caring; it was either that or disgrace herself in public. It was a relief when Nico finally stopped at the bottom of a steeply sloping street. He pointed at a house that could be glimpsed at the top of the hill.

'That's your destination, your uncle's house,' he said, his voice a harsh whisper, as if he had to struggle to get the words out.

Midori looked up and saw a four-storey structure, built mostly of grey stone, but with some timber partitions and white plaster at the front. Large windows, with a myriad of tiny window panes encased in lead, spanned the whole width of the house at first-floor level. On the second and third storeys there were smaller windows that overhung the street.

'Are you ready?' Nico asked, pulling her gaze back to him. He shifted from one foot to the other, as if he was impatient to get this over with, but his expression was shuttered.

Midori nodded. Now the time had come she suddenly felt overwhelmed by it all and wished she had stayed a bit longer in Amsterdam before going to face her relatives. Drawing in a calming breath, she reminded herself she was the daughter of a *daimyo* and she feared nothing.

'Just one moment, though.' Nico took a leather pouch out of his pocket and held it out to her. 'Here, you'd better keep this safe somewhere.'

Midori frowned. 'What is it?'

'Half the money your brother gave me. I lied about the price to deter you from coming. Since it had no effect and you're here anyway, you may as well have it.'

'I see. Well, thank you.' She took the pouch, its heaviness weighing down her hand. As she hid it inside her sleeve, she wondered if he was telling the truth or just being kind.

'I will leave you now,' Nico said, 'but if you have need of me, I'll be at the Chain and Anchor inn for a day or two. Send word if—'

Midori interrupted. 'You're not coming with me? Oh, please, just for a short while.' Somehow she couldn't bear the thought that this was goodbye, not so soon. 'They'll think it strange if I arrive on my own, won't they?' she added. 'And they'll want to thank you for escorting me.'

'I doubt it,' he said in a dry tone she didn't understand.

Midori knew she couldn't force him to accompany her, but although she had courage, she'd rather not face her relatives alone when meeting them for the first time. She needed Nico's quiet strength and sent him an imploring glance. A muscle tightened in his jaw and his blue eyes darkened with an emotion that could have been pain or perhaps something else, she wasn't sure. He opened his mouth as if to reply, but was interrupted by a shriek uttered by someone behind him.

'Nicholas? *Nicholas!* I don't believe it …'

Chapter Nineteen

Midori watched as a plump, middle-aged woman came rushing towards them. The lady stared up at Nico, one hand raised to cover her mouth, which was presumably open as wide as her eyes. The woman let out a cry of anguish, then in the next instant, she fainted dead away. Nico sprang forward to catch her as she fell towards the cobbles and managed it, but only just.

'Oh, hell,' he muttered under his breath and lifted her up into his arms, although he held her away from his chest as if he'd be contaminated by touching her.

Midori frowned at him, thoroughly puzzled. 'You know her?'

'Yes,' he said curtly, huffing slightly at the weight of the woman. Without explaining further, he set off up the hill and Midori followed. She had to half-run to keep up with his long, seemingly angry, strides. He stopped outside the house he'd said was her uncle's. 'Would you mind knocking on the door, please? We'd better get her inside.'

All too soon they were passing under a carved stone archway into a dark hallway, its flagged stone floor worn smooth. Midori felt the walls close in on her and suppressed a shiver at the cold which permeated her straw sandals even now, at the height of summer. The maidservant who had opened the door led them into an inner hall where a wide spiral staircase led up towards the first floor. Midori recognised it from her mother's descriptions and felt a tug of sadness. *Oh, Mother, if only you were here with me.*

Nico deposited his burden on a wooden bench which had been placed along one wall.

'If you would but wait a moment, sir, I'll tell the master

you're here,' the servant girl said, wringing her hands while staring at Midori, her eyes almost popping out of their sockets.

Midori wondered if she should have dressed in her finest *kimono* after all, but decided the plain blue one would have to do. Nico had been adamant that the colourful embroidered one she'd brought for special occasions would be unsuitable and she had to believe he knew best. Besides, the blue silk became her well and it showed her father's clan motif, which gave her added courage. Taro Kumashiro wouldn't have let anyone intimidate him, no matter who they were. His daughter was determined to do him proud.

'What is going on here?' A new voice rang out and Midori turned to see an elderly man scowling at them. She guessed he must have come out of the room behind them, as the door was slightly ajar. He was dressed in black woollen breeches and waistcoat, with a white shirt and hose, and plain black shoes. His grey hair was cut just above his shoulders and was somewhat sparse at the front. 'Nicholas! By all that's holy, what are you doing here?' The man's eyes opened wide, his reaction every bit as surprised as that of the woman outside.

Midori frowned. *Yes, what* is *going on here? I'd like to know as well.*

She stared from Nico to the old man and back again. It was plain they knew each other, and she was starting to get angry since she seemed to be the only one in the dark.

The woman on the bench stirred and moaned, her eyelids flickering open. The old man bent down next to her. 'Kate? *Kate!* Can you hear me?' He turned to glare at Nico. 'Couldn't you at least have given us some warning of your arrival?'

'How was I to know the sight of me would make Stepmama swoon? It never did before.' Nico's gaze was colder than Midori had ever seen it, but a muscle jumped in his jaw, showing he wasn't as calm as he sounded.

'Well, you hadn't been gone thirteen years then,' the old man snarled. 'We thought you dead! Kate, sit up, do, Sister. You can't be lying down, you need air.' He helped the woman into a sitting position against the wall, then suddenly noticed Midori for the first time. 'Who's this?'

'This, dear Uncle Jacob, is your niece, Midori. From Japan,' Nico said, crossing his arms over his chest and making the word 'uncle' sound sarcastic. 'Your sister Hannah's daughter.'

Midori couldn't help it, her mouth fell open. *Uncle. Sister.* The pieces of the puzzle fell into place. 'You're my *cousin?*' She blinked at Nico.

He shook his head. 'No, stepcousin. We're not related by blood, but this is your uncle and aunt, in case you haven't gathered that already.' His mouth was a grim line now and his gaze was still frosty.

'My what?' Her uncle stared at Nico, entirely forgetting his sister for a moment. 'That's impossible. Hannah died.'

'Er, no, she didn't, not until last year,' Midori put in. 'I have a letter for you from her which proves it.'

'Well of all the ...' Jacob shook his head. 'This is too much.'

Midori drew in a deep breath, trying to keep her temper in check. She was in complete agreement with him, but the only person she was angry with was Nico. 'Why didn't you tell me?' she hissed at him, while the old man fussed over his sister.

'Because I wasn't going to come this far,' he muttered. 'I was only going to deliver you to the end of the street. You can see why. I'm not welcome here.'

'No, I can't actually. This,' she spread a hand to encompass her confused aunt and uncle, 'could have been avoided. You shocked them on purpose.'

Nico shrugged. 'As I said, I didn't think they cared. And if I'd told you, would you have believed me?'

'Perhaps. Although you must admit it's a bit far-fetched.'

'Precisely my thoughts when you finally told me where you were going.'

'Well, you should have divulged our relationship then!' Midori was exasperated beyond words and couldn't understand what game he'd been playing. 'Why didn't you?' As her uncle had said, it was too much.

'I'm sorry, but—'

She cut him off. She didn't want to hear any more excuses right now. 'Never mind. We can speak of it later,' she said irritably.

'Very well.' His brows drew together and he clamped his mouth shut, glaring at the others.

She decided to ignore Nico for now and went to help her aunt to her feet. 'I'm sorry, Aunt, I had no idea our arrival here would cause such a shock. Please believe me, it wasn't my doing.'

But her aunt didn't seem inclined to accept Midori's help. Her gaze was as frosty as that of her stepson. 'You're my sister's daughter?' she asked. 'My-dowry, did he say?'

'Mee-*doh*-ri,' she corrected without thinking. 'Yes, yes I am.'

'I'd never have believed it if I hadn't seen it with my own eyes. A heathen!'

'I'm not a—' Midori started to defend herself, but Kate interrupted her. She stood up and rounded on Nico instead.

'And as for you, where have you been, you scoundrel? Thirteen years. *Thirteen years!* And not a word to say you're even alive. How could you?'

'Why, Stepmama,' Nico drawled, 'how touching that you've found your maternal instinct at last. A little late, though, wouldn't you say?'

Kate raised her hand as if to slap him, but he caught her wrist easily and shook his head. 'I wouldn't do that if I were you. Not any longer. I've grown a bit, you know.'

'Enough!' Jacob raised his voice. 'You two,' he nodded at Nico and Midori, 'come into my counting room, please. Kate, go and lie down for a while. You can argue with Nicholas later, when you've recovered. I'm not having you faint again.'

They were ushered into the front room on the ground floor, which had a row of windows overlooking the street outside. Jacob seemed calm as he went to sit behind a table covered in ledgers and other papers, but Midori saw him grip the edge so hard his knuckles whitened. With an effort, he smiled at her. The smile looked forced, but it was there, nonetheless. 'My dear, I can hardly believe it's true,' he said to Midori. His voice quivered with suppressed emotion and she hoped it was because he was happy to see her, not the opposite.

She smiled back at him. 'I'm so pleased to meet you at last. Mother spoke of you often.'

'Did she, indeed. Well, well ...' He shook his head. 'But where are my manners? Please, sit down and make yourselves comfortable. Would you like any refreshment, my dear? Nicholas?' He added the last word almost reluctantly.

'No, thank you,' Midori said, wondering how she was supposed to make herself comfortable on a hard wooden chair with no cushions.

'Thank you, but I must be on my way.' Nico bowed to her uncle and then to Midori before moving towards the door.

'Where are you going?' Midori blurted out. She had a sudden urge to plead with him again not to leave her so soon, but she swallowed the impulse. He'd lied to her, or at least withheld vital information. Clearly, he didn't want to acknowledge their kinship, such as it was, so she shouldn't care whether he stayed or went.

'To the inn I told you about,' he said. 'There's no room for me in this house as I recall.'

'Now, Nicholas, you know that wasn't what I meant, and it was a long time ago,' Jacob started to say, but Nico fixed him with a glare.

'Oh, really? Perhaps manhandling someone out of the door means something different to you? Strangely enough, it made me feel rather unwelcome. So, if you'll excuse me, I'm not staying now.'

'Will you come back?' Jacob asked the question Midori wanted to know the answer to as well.

'Are you asking me to?' Nico gave the old man a hard stare.

'Yes, yes, I am. Won't you come for dinner? It would please Kate.'

Nico snorted. 'I doubt it, but very well. Until later.' He nodded to Midori.

She sent him a venomous glance to show him he was far from forgiven. He had some explaining to do, although she wasn't sure she really wanted to hear what he had to say. She'd decide later. For now, she wanted to get to know her other relatives.

The silence in the room after Nico's departure was almost tangible and Midori folded her hands inside the sleeves of her *kimono* to stop them from shaking. Her fingers encountered paper and she remembered the letter she had brought.

'Oh, Uncle, as I said, I have something for you.' She held out the rolled-up missive and watched as he opened it to read her mother's last words to him.

When he had finished, he looked up at Midori with a serious expression. 'So your mother didn't die after all. All these years I have mourned her passing and there she was, alive and well and living with that ...' He stopped abruptly, as if he couldn't bear to utter the rest of the sentence.

Midori didn't know what to reply, so she repeated the tale her mother had often told her. 'She was washed away in a flood and presumed dead, so you left. She was only concussed, however, but by the time she was found and regained her senses it was too late to catch up with you. What would you have had her do? She didn't have a choice but to stay and make the best of it.' Midori didn't add that she had a shrewd suspicion her mother could have left with her brother if she'd wanted to, but having found love with Taro Kumashiro, she chose to stay behind. There was also the small matter of an English husband, a man she had loathed. 'Erm, Captain Rydon, the man she was married to, what became of him?'

Midori knew her mother had briefly been married to a friend of Jacob's, Rafael Rydon, but not by choice. 'I was forced to wed him,' Hannah had explained. 'But we'd agreed to have the marriage annulled as it was never consummated. He promised to see to it the moment he returned to England.'

'Who, Rydon?' Jacob looked surprised. 'He drowned on the same day I thought she did. Just as well, I suppose, or you ... never mind.'

'I don't understand.'

'Don't you? Didn't your mother teach you what's right and wrong? No, I suppose being a sinner herself, that's not to be expected.'

'My mother was a good woman.' Although Midori could see that in her uncle's eyes her mother had committed many sins, she felt the need to defend her. Hannah hadn't done anything wrong in her daughter's opinion.

'I know, but Hannah was always a little ... impulsive, shall we say. She should have been saved from temptation by her family, but we failed her. I, more than anyone else.' He shook his head, his eyes sad. 'Well, it is too late now, but it isn't too late for you, my dear. We'll have to work hard since you didn't even receive God's first blessing, but never doubt we shall manage it, if you're willing, that is.'

'God's first blessing?'

'Not to be born of pagan parents.'

Midori opened her mouth to protest that her parents weren't pagan, then closed it again. There was no point arguing with her uncle and it was probably better to tread carefully at first so as not to antagonise anyone unnecessarily. She bowed her head meekly. 'I see. Will you allow me to stay with you then?'

'But of course. Come now and I shall introduce you to the rest of the household. They should be in the parlour.'

Nico strode down the hill, looking neither right nor left. He was furious, both with himself for his inept handling of the situation, and with his stepmother and Marston for causing such a scene. *Anyone would have thought they cared!*

'The hell they do,' he muttered. Kate hadn't exactly looked pleased to see him, only angry that he hadn't told her he was alive. *As for that old hypocrite Marston ... Bah!*

He acknowledged that he should have found a way to tell Midori they were sort of related before their arrival, but somehow it had never seemed like the right moment. The longer he left it, the harder it became. And it shouldn't have been necessary, since he hadn't planned on seeing her again after today. Even if she'd told them a man named Nico Noordholt had brought her to Europe, they would never have connected that with him, since he'd changed his name. *All would have been well if I'd only stayed away.*

But now she was angry with him and that's not how he wanted to remember her.

'Well, good!' he tried to tell himself. 'If she's annoyed, she won't mind me leaving her here so I can get on with my life.'

But *he* minded, he knew that now. Seeing her there, with her aunt and uncle, she'd looked so out of place, so vulnerable. And his stepmother's instant verdict, 'heathen', summed up how they would view her, he was sure. She'd never fit in here. He'd been mad to think so even for a moment.

So what was he to do? *I need to calm down and think rationally.* At least he had an excuse to return, now he'd been invited to dinner. It was a start.

He took a room at the Chain and Anchor and then headed for the tap room, where he ordered a tankard of ale to help his thought processes. He didn't want company and found an empty table in a corner. His scowl saw to it that no one approached him at first, but after a while a group of men sat down at the table next to his and they seemed oblivious to his bad mood.

'Pardon me, but you haven't by any chance come from London?' the man closest to Nico asked, staring at him with curious eyes. 'Only, you have the look of a traveller about you and we're eager for news.'

'No, I've just arrived from Amsterdam,' Nico replied. 'Haven't been to London for years.' He deliberately kept his answer short and terse, to discourage the men from further questions, but they didn't notice. Instead they moved closer to include him in their conversation. Nico swallowed a sigh and decided not to make an issue of it.

'So are there any rumours going round Amsterdam about us, then?' another man asked.

Nico frowned. 'No, not as far as I know. Should there be?' He hadn't been paying attention to gossip since he'd had other things on his mind while in Holland, but now he began to regret it. He normally kept his ear to the ground and any talk of England would catch his interest.

'Well, we hear all sorts of things, conjecture mostly, I reckon. Some say there's a civil war brewing.'

'In England? Really?' Nico forgot all about his own dark thoughts. This was serious.

'Yes, perhaps. King Charles *has* made poor work of ruling, choosing his councillors badly and not listening to his Parliament, and that's a fact,' someone with an authoritative voice stated. 'It didn't bode well, we all knew that.'

'I've also heard tell he favours Papists,' another man added.

'A pedlar was saying only this morning that Parliament has taken charge of London, but whether it's true or not I've no idea. He claimed the King has gone north somewhere to raise an army.'

Nico was listening intently now. He'd heard this kind of talk before, in Holland, and it sounded to him as though a civil war *was* imminent. If that was so, he'd brought Midori into danger. *Damnation!*

'What are we to do if it's true?' The first man was looking worried. 'Will we have to fight?'

'No, it's bound to blow over soon. The King's been at odds with Parliament for years, nothing new there.'

'I heard the Earl of Bath is trying to rally people to the King's side here in Devon.'

'He'll not have much success.' Someone guffawed. 'Leastways not here in Plymouth.'

'It's still a damnable mess, I tell you,' the first man insisted. 'We may be forced to choose sides.'

'That won't be a problem.' Another guffaw. 'We'll have no truck with suspected Papists, to be sure. But like you said, it'll probably all be over in a trice.'

Nico wasn't so sure. If the King was raising an army, he must mean to use force. *That's if the rumour is true.* He took a large swallow of ale and sat back to look around the rest of the tap room. He became aware of other conversations around him, many of which centred on the subjects of either the King or religion. He also noticed he was almost the only man in the place dressed in anything other than very plain clothing. His indigo-coloured jacket and breeches of finest wool made him stand out like a gold coin in a handful of pennies, despite their simple cut.

'Puritans?' he murmured to himself. *The whole damn lot of them? Surely not!* He'd come across some of them in Holland and knew a bit about their beliefs and customs. He decided to keep his eyes and ears open during his stay in Plymouth. Puritans held extreme religious views and he doubted everyone here followed their thinking. The people in the tap room were probably mostly dressed in this way because it was practical and the cloth cheaper if not dyed in gaudy colours. Still, it wouldn't hurt to find out more, he thought.

He suddenly remembered Marston had been dressed in black and he almost groaned out loud. Jacob had always been inclined to piety, but if he'd gone over to full-blown Puritanism, Midori would find it even harder to fit in than Nico had imagined. *Bloody hell, I've got to get her out of here.*

But how?

Chapter Twenty

Jacob ushered Midori out into the hall and up the wooden staircase to the first floor, then entered a large room at the front of the house. It was the one with windows along one entire wall and obviously the finest room in the building. Beautifully carved dark wood panelling lined the walls and there was a huge fireplace, although not a great deal of furniture. Midori couldn't see any other embellishments either: no hangings or paintings, no cushions to sit on. It was also very gloomy despite there being no shutters on the windows. The glass in the tiny panes was thick and cloudy for the most part, making it difficult to see out and distorting the vision.

She couldn't help but compare this room to the parlour in Nico's newly inherited house in Amsterdam, and decided she much preferred his. With its homely clutter and bright colours it had seemed welcoming, whereas here the room was totally devoid of warmth. Several people were sitting on benches along one wall and they all stood up as Midori entered with her uncle.

'Ah, there you are, good, good. Come and welcome a new member of the family.' The others moved closer, Kate at the head of the group. She'd obviously not taken her brother's advice to go and rest. 'Midori, this is your Aunt Hesketh, my sister Kate, who you've met.' The plump woman looked Midori over again, and the latter remembered to curtsey rather than bow, something Nico had taught her at the last moment. *'Put your elbows on your hips, fold your hands in front of you and look down modestly.'* She followed these instructions, but this didn't seem to find favour with her aunt, who only nodded curtly. Midori suddenly remembered where she'd heard the name Hesketh before and frowned.

'Did you say Hesketh? But I thought …' Midori was sure her mother had told her she'd initially fled England in order to escape marriage to someone of that name; a man she had disliked intensely. That was before the ill-fated union with Rydon, who she'd also detested. Hannah had said her sister, Kate, had married the son of a baronet, so why wasn't her aunt a 'Lady'? Hannah had explained that being a 'Lady' was something to be proud of, like being the wife of a Japanese *daimyo*.

Her uncle ignored the interruption, and continued with the introductions as if Midori hadn't spoken. 'And here is my dear wife, Emma.' A thin woman with white-grey hair, smoothed back under her white coif, came forward and took Midori's hands between her own.

'Welcome to our home, my dear. I hope you'll be happy here. I was sad to hear of your mother's demise. I knew her slightly as a young girl.'

'Thank you, Aunt, you're very kind.' Midori's spirits lifted at this friendly greeting, which served to counter-balance the reception given by her other aunt. 'Should I call you Aunt Emma or Aunt Marston?' She'd forgotten to ask Nico about the correct way of addressing relatives.

'Aunt Marston, if you please.'

'Very well.' *So perhaps Jacob should be Uncle Marston.*

'Now here are our children,' Uncle Marston said, indicating a young man and a girl who stepped forward next. 'This is my son Daniel and my daughter Temperance.' Both were fair, Temperance with hair of a silver-blonde hue, while her brother's was red, although not as vivid a colour as Midori's mother's had been. 'Kate's children and stepchildren have all grown up and live elsewhere,' he added.

'You have a strange name,' Aunt Hesketh commented

with a pursed mouth. 'Couldn't your mother find a Christian one to her liking?'

Midori stared at the woman, surprised at her rudeness. 'I believe my father chose my name. I have green eyes, which is unusual in … his country, and Midori means green. There's nothing strange about it where I come from.'

'You should have a proper name, like Mary, for instance,' Aunt Hesketh insisted.

'If you don't mind, I'd rather keep my own.' Midori felt very strongly about that and she knew instinctively if she gave in to her aunt on this point, she may be giving up a lot more than her name.

'Perhaps this is not the time to discuss such things?' Uncle Marston suggested gently.

'Hmph, well at least she taught you to speak properly,' Aunt Hesketh muttered.

Before Midori had time to reply to this, her uncle's wife put an arm around her shoulders and led her towards the door. 'Come, my dear, I'll show you where you are to sleep, and then it will be time for dinner. We eat our main meal at noon, you see. Is that what you're used to? You must tell me how these things were arranged where you come from …' Chattering on, Aunt Marston shepherded Midori out of the room.

Midori threw a glance over her shoulder at the assembled company, but no one moved or spoke. Her last glimpse of them was another malevolent look from her Aunt Hesketh.

The aunt who should have been a Lady, but obviously wasn't.

The bedroom was on the third floor, directly under the roof, and very small. It contained nothing apart from a plain clothes chest – a coffer, Aunt Marston called it – a single bed and a tiny fireplace. A narrow window let in some light, but it wasn't nearly enough. Combined with the low sloping ceiling and dark furniture, it only served to make the room seem more sombre. In a thin ray of sunshine dust particles rose and fell in a sinuous dance and there was a musty smell which made Midori want to sneeze. She followed her aunt inside and stared at the uneven floor boards, which looked as if the carpenter who laid them had been unable to fit them together properly. She was astonished such shoddy workmanship was tolerated.

'You'll have to share with Temperance, of course,' Aunt Marston was saying, and Midori looked up, startled. The room had seemed small for one person, but for two? Her aunt caught sight of Midori's face before she had time to mask her expression, and added kindly, 'But you can have the bed and Temperance will sleep on the truckle bed, if you prefer. I take it you're not used to sharing?'

'Truckle?' Midori felt as if her brain had gone numb from being bombarded with too many new experiences at once. She stared at the bed, which looked barely wide enough for one. The thought of sharing it with someone made Midori's insides clench.

'Yes, it pulls out from underneath this one, like so.' Aunt Marston half-pulled out a tacky old mattress on some sort of frame from under the other bed.

'Oh, I see. Well, er, thank you, if you're sure she won't mind?'

'Not at all. I'll find you some sheets and a blanket after dinner. Temperance will help you and she'll put some wormwood among the bedding to discourage the bed bugs.'

Midori shuddered. *Bed bugs?* She'd had to live with those on board Nico's ship, but had hoped to avoid them on land.

'Where are your possessions?' Aunt Marston asked.

'Captain Noordholt said someone from the ship would be bringing them this afternoon.'

'Captain Noordholt?' Aunt Marston looked confused.

'Er, Nico, I mean Nicholas,' Midori amended. Had he lied about his name as well? The thought made her furious. She supposed if her other aunt's surname was Hesketh, his must be as well, unless she'd married twice. So why was he known as Noordholt?

'Well, good,' Aunt Marston was saying. 'You can settle in later, then. Did you bring much in the way of clothing?'

'No, I left in something of a hurry and thought to acquire more when I reached England. I bought some material in Amsterdam, though.'

'Excellent. We'll all help you to make something suitable.' Her aunt glanced at Midori's *kimono*. 'Perhaps you could borrow clothes from me until we have a chance to make some for you? We are of a similar size, I think.'

'I … thank you.' The thought of wearing the kind of garments her aunt had on was not an appealing one, as they looked extremely ugly compared to Midori's lovely silk *kimono*, but she resigned herself to her fate. She had to blend in after all, if she wanted to belong.

'One moment, I'll fetch them now.'

A short while later Aunt Marston returned and helped Midori to dress.

'This is a shift. You wear it at all times, to sleep in as well.' A shapeless white linen garment, which reached almost to the floor, was flung over Midori's head. 'Tie the drawstring at the throat and I'll help you with the wrists,' Aunt Marston said kindly.

Midori was then handed something called a 'bum-roll', a sausage-like item stuffed with something soft – 'horse-hair, dear,' Aunt Marston explained – and strings either end, and told to tie this around her waist.

'The roll goes at the back, to give you a more, er … womanly shape, shall we say. Tie it at the front, please. Then put the petticoat on over the top.'

A skirt of very thick wool in an unattractive sludge brown was fastened around Midori's waist. 'It's a little big,' she commented, as it would easily have fit a woman twice her size in girth.

'Oh, don't worry, it has several fastenings.' Aunt Marston smiled kindly. 'I wore this when I was with child and I needed it bigger. It was some years ago now, of course, but it's still wearable.'

Midori tried not to frown at the thought that she was wearing a garment that must be positively ancient.

'Now here's the bodice. This one is sleeveless, as it's summer, but we'll make you one with sleeves for the winter. Lace it up at the front, if you please.' Midori began this process, but was interrupted. 'No, no, not criss-cross. It should look like a ladder, that way you can pull it tighter.'

'Oh, I see.' The bodice, a slightly more attractive russet colour, was snug around her torso and waist, with small square panels flaring out below. Laced up, it kept her bosom in place, but still allowed her to move freely. It would have felt quite comfortable if it hadn't been made of itchy wool. Midori could feel the material through the linen of the shift and tried not to scratch.

'There, now all you need is a collar and a coif.' Aunt Marston handed her a linen triangle and showed her how to arrange it round her neck. 'Probably best if you plait your hair so we can pin it up. My, but it's very long and thick, isn't it! Here, let me help you.' This done, she placed the cap on Midori's head. 'Perfect! You'll have to wear your own shoes for now. I don't have any spares.'

'Thank you.'

'Now then, let us eat. I hope Nicholas has returned by now. Your uncle does dislike tardiness so.'

Midori followed her aunt back downstairs and stood by her place at the table in a smaller room at the back of the house on the first floor. She waited for everyone to sit down on the benches either side of the table, but her relatives remained standing, including Nico, who came sauntering in at the last possible moment. He blinked at the sight of her in her borrowed clothing, but quickly hid his surprise. Everyone bent their heads piously, except for him, as Uncle Marston began to speak. Midori hurried to follow suit.

'Dear Lord, we thank you for the blessings you have brought us today and for the food we are about to receive. We also thank you for restoring to us our long-lost kinswoman, Midori, ...' Nico shot Midori a quizzical look at the mention of her name, but she averted her eyes. '... and Nicholas, whom we had almost given up hope of seeing again. We also ask your blessing, dear Lord, upon ...' Jacob went on praying for what seemed like hours to Midori. Her stomach growled since she hadn't eaten much that morning, but fortunately the noise was drowned out by her uncle's droning voice.

At long last he finished and everyone sat down. Food was brought in by two serving girls and placed on the table, and strange aromas teased Midori's nostrils. Aunt Marston stood up to serve everyone and Midori passed her pewter plate over when asked to do so. It came back with a yellow, glutinous mess on it and a piece of coarse bread. Midori looked at the food with interest.

'What is this dish?' she whispered to Temperance, who was sitting next to her.

'Pottage,' the girl whispered back. 'It's made of peas, milk, egg yolks, bread crumbs and parsley. Sometimes Mother flavours it with saffron or ginger. It must be saffron today – see the colour?'

Midori did indeed. The list of ingredients sounded strange, but she was very hungry and had become used to eating just about anything on board Nico's ship, once the food she'd brought herself had run out. Besides, it would be impolite not to eat what she'd been given, so she bravely sank her spoon into the food. She took a mouthful, quickly followed by a bite of the hard bread. It wasn't bad, but a longing for rice and fish ripped through her, making her catch her breath. She suppressed it. *I have to accustom myself to English ways now, and that includes the food.* Nico had told her they didn't grow rice here, which was a huge disappointment. *I'll never eat rice again!* She pushed the thought out of her mind.

'So what have you been doing with yourself since you left?' Jacob asked Nico, as soon as everyone had been served.

'I've been at sea,' Nico replied curtly.

'For thirteen years? You must have been to many places of interest then.'

'Yes.'

Midori frowned at Nico. He wasn't even attempting to answer Uncle Marston in a civil manner and she wondered what had caused such a rift between them. It wasn't her place to step into the breach, however, so she kept silent.

'I don't suppose they had writing implements where you went?' Aunt Hesketh put in, her tone waspish.

'No,' Nico agreed, as if trying to infuriate his stepmother on purpose. It had the desired effect.

'Well, if you've forgotten how to read and write, I'm sure you could have sent word by way of another seaman.'

'As I said earlier, I would have done if I'd thought you cared. The last time I saw you, you told me you'd be glad never to set eyes on me again.'

'You provoked me! Of course I didn't mean it.'

'Really? You could have fooled me. In fact, you did.' Pointedly, Nico turned to Aunt Marston, who he seemed to like as he addressed her in a much gentler voice. 'And how have you been? You look well.'

'I … er, thank you.'

The meal progressed mostly in silence after that, although Jacob discussed some business matters with his son. Midori assumed he was training Daniel to follow in his footsteps as a merchant. Nico, meanwhile, didn't take any further part in the conversation, but spent the entire time glancing in Midori's direction. She turned away each time she caught him staring though, as she was still angry with him. She wanted to box his ears, but at the same time she took comfort from his presence. At least he wasn't a complete stranger, even though she obviously didn't know him as well as she'd thought she did. *He was right about that.*

She caught the others peeking at her whenever they thought she wasn't aware of it. It made her feel slightly uncomfortable at first, but then she told herself it was perfectly natural for them all to be curious. *Just as I'm eager to learn more about them.*

The pewter spoon she'd been given to eat with seemed large and unwieldy, especially in comparison with the dainty chopsticks she normally used. During a momentary lapse of concentration, she dropped the spoon on to the floor with a loud clatter, and ducked quickly under the table to retrieve it. She could feel her face flaming in embarrassment, but was even more flustered to find herself eye-to-eye with Nico.

'Allow me to assist you,' he said in a loud voice and put the spoon into her hand. 'I must speak with you. Alone,' he hissed.

'I have nothing to say to you,' she whispered back. To her consternation he didn't immediately let go of her hand, but kept hold of it, spoon and all, for much longer than necessary.

'Midori, please …'

'No!' She snatched it back and banged her head on the table in her haste to return to an upright position.

'What's amiss?' Uncle Marston asked from his seat at the head of the table.

'Midori dropped her spoon so naturally I had to help her retrieve it,' Nico said blandly. His stepmother shot him a suspicious look, but Uncle Marston didn't seem to notice.

'Of course,' he said and turned to Midori. 'We all hope you will settle in here very soon, my dear.'

Midori bowed her head to hide her true feelings. 'Thank you. I'm sure I shall.'

'Speak later,' Nico mouthed at her, but she shook her head surreptitiously. She wasn't ready to talk to him yet; she needed to think first.

'Nicholas, a word if you please.'

Jacob ruined Nico's plans to try and catch Midori on her own after the meal. The older man indicated they should go into the parlour, opposite the dining room, and Nico felt he had no choice but to follow. He swallowed a sigh of impatience.

Jacob shut the door, effectively excluding his sister, who'd been hovering behind them. That almost made Nico smile, as he caught his stepmother's affronted glare. She obviously felt she had a right to be present, but Jacob had other ideas and Nico was glad to escape her barbed remarks and accusing looks. He'd forgotten how persistent she could be.

'Please, won't you take a seat?' Jacob indicated two high-backed chairs with armrests next to the empty fireplace. Nico sat down without a word.

'I understand that you feel you were treated harshly after the death of your father,' Jacob began, 'but at the time, I really did think it was for the best.' He waited, as if to see whether Nico wanted to make any comment, but when he didn't, the older man continued. 'You can't deny you were a … shall we say, somewhat difficult youth?'

'No more so than any other.' Nico remembered drinking to excess, gambling with what little money he had and learning about the delights of women, but it seemed to him most of his peers had been the same. It was a time of discovery.

'I would disagree with that.' Jacob frowned. 'My sister frequently asked me to intervene after your father's death, since she couldn't make you see sense. You were running wild and you showed no inclination towards finding permanent employment.'

'I was seventeen and hadn't been taught a trade. I had to take what I could find.' Nico bit his teeth together hard to stop from thinking too much about that difficult phase in his life. He'd felt completely lost. All his siblings and stepsiblings had been given the wherewithal to either start up in business, study or, in the case of the girls, marry. For him, there had been nothing. *And all because my father wanted to teach me a lesson. He could at least have apprenticed me to someone to learn a trade, but even the small sum needed for that he begrudged me. Damn him!* Nico took a deep breath and said, 'Perhaps I was a bit wild, but I could have done with a helping hand. I asked to work with you, but you refused.'

'Because I wanted you to try and find employment by yourself, first. If you came up empty-handed, I would have offered you work, but I knew you would have felt more pride in something you'd managed by yourself. Working with me would have been like taking charity, and sooner or later you'd have resented it. I wasn't going to let you starve, though.'

'That's not the impression I had at the time.'

'Yes, well, you made me angry. You'd just asked me for a loan, and Kate and I felt that whatever money we may have given you would simply be squandered on gaming and ... other things. You needed to be taught a lesson, but we didn't mean for you to leave altogether.'

'Other young men go to sea. It seemed the only option. And once there, I found I liked it.' *No need to go into all the suffering that came first.*

'I understand. You could still have sent us word, once you had ... er, matured a little, don't you think?'

'It seemed pointless and I was a different person.' Nico shrugged. 'Besides, I had no intention of ever coming back. I won't be staying long now, either. I need to return to Amsterdam.'

'Well, it would mean a lot to Kate and me if you would keep in touch from time to time. Can you let bygones be bygones? I apologise for any past misunderstandings between us.'

Nico considered the apology was thirteen years too late, but it sounded heartfelt and it seemed churlish to continue to hold a grudge now Jacob had explained his thinking. Besides, it no longer mattered and Jacob was right – it was all in the past. He nodded, then held out his hand to shake Jacob's, trying his best to suppress the feelings of anger which had simmered inside him for so long.

Perhaps now he could bury the past once and for all.

Chapter Twenty-One

'What is that?' Temperance, who'd just told Midori she was twelve, watched wide-eyed as the latter unpacked her belongings.

'A fan. Don't you have fans in England?'

'Yes, but I've never seen one like that. It's exquisite! May I hold it?'

'Of course.' Midori handed the girl her gilded fan, which was somewhat the worse for wear after much use during the long journey. Temperance opened and closed it with reverence and turned it round several times to inspect the pattern.

'I've never seen anything so beautiful,' the girl breathed.

'Really? Doesn't your mother have fans?' It certainly seemed warm enough in England to warrant the use of one.

'No, she doesn't have any at all,' Temperance confided. 'No one in this house does.'

'Well, you can have this one if you like,' Midori offered. 'I have another.'

'I can? Truly?' Midori nodded with a smile. 'Oh, thank you. Thank you so much.' Temperance held the fan to her chest with a look of pure delight on her face. Then suddenly her expression clouded over. 'But Father probably won't let me keep it.'

'Why ever not? It's only a small trinket.' Midori was confused. What could be wrong with a fan?

'I'm only supposed to own plain things, free from ornament. This is so colourful.'

Midori didn't understand, but she knew one thing when she saw it, and that was happiness. The fan had made Temperance happy and therefore she should have it.

'I'll tell you what,' she said, 'how about if I keep it in my clothes chest, but it is still yours and then it can be our little secret? Or we can find some other hiding place for it, if you like?' She'd been looking around and had already discovered that one of the planks that made up the window seat was loose and made a perfect place for concealing her hoard of silver coins and her two swords.

'You mean it? You won't tell a soul?' Temperance's eyes were huge with a combination of doubt and wonder.

'Never. I swear it by your … the Bible.' Midori thought it was probably the one thing that might convince the girl.

Temperance threw her arms around Midori and hugged her. 'Thank you. I'm so glad you've come. I hope you stay forever.'

Midori laughed. 'I'm not sure everyone else shares your feelings, but thank you for making me feel welcome. Actually, since you're here anyway, could you answer a few questions for me, please? Everything is so new to me and I need to learn quickly.'

'Don't worry, I'll help you.'

Midori smiled. She felt as though she had acquired a younger sister which was something she'd always wanted. Perhaps staying in England wouldn't be so bad after all.

Later that afternoon Midori went downstairs and found her two aunts in the parlour, busy with their sewing.

'Come in, my dear.' Aunt Marston was the first to spot her niece. 'What have you there?'

Midori went up to the two women and gave them each a parcel. 'It is just a small gift which I brought for you. I didn't want to arrive empty-handed.'

'Why, thank you. That's very kind.' Aunt Marston unwrapped the parcel and revealed the length of silk inside. Her eyes widened as she took in its sheen and lustre, but then she shook her head. 'Oh, I'm so sorry, but I'm afraid I can't accept this. It was a wonderful thought, really, but ...'

Midori stared at the shimmering green material and wondered what was wrong with it. She had thought it would suit her aunt's colouring to perfection and brighten up her pale complexion a little. 'You don't like green? Perhaps you could swap with Aunt Hesketh?'

Her other aunt didn't say anything, but was staring at the sky-blue silk in her lap with a mixture of hatred and longing. She looked up, venom in her gaze yet again. 'It's not a question of colour. Or rather, it is, but not in the way you imagine.'

'I'm sorry, I don't understand.' Midori looked to Aunt Marston for an explanation.

'You see, my dear, we don't wear such bright colours. We prefer unostentatious ones, like black or grey. And we don't wear silk either, only wool.'

'Not ever? Not even for celebrations?' Somehow Midori had imagined the dreary clothes were worn only for the sake of everyday practicality. 'But my mother told me about the betrothal party held for you, Aunt Hesketh, just before she left, and she described the dress you were wearing in detail. I was sure she told me it was a lovely rose pink.'

'Enough!' Aunt Hesketh half stood up and had to make a grab for the silk which started to slide off her lap.

Midori recoiled slightly at the vehemence in the woman's tone and Aunt Marston made a calming motion with her hand in her sister-in-law's direction.

'Easy, Kate, easy. Our niece can't be blamed for not knowing these things. After all, over thirty years have passed.' She looked at Midori. 'You see, that was a long time ago and we no longer adhere to the same rules. Now we follow the Bible closely, and it warns us specifically against vanity in our apparel. Surely you can see that something as beautiful as this would be very vain indeed?'

'I ...' Midori didn't see that at all. She understood even less why it was necessary to wear sober, boring clothing in order to believe in something, but she didn't know how to argue her case.

Aunt Marston stood up and came over to take her niece's hands between her own. 'Please believe that we appreciate this gesture most sincerely. We thank you from the bottom of our hearts, but unfortunately we can't accept. Don't be offended, I beg of you.'

'No, no I'm not offended.' Midori thought swiftly and hit on an idea. 'If you can't wear this, however, would it be possible for you to sell it?'

'I suppose so. Why?'

'Well, perhaps you could use the money for some better purpose. I just wanted to give you something. It's the custom in my father's country.'

'An excellent idea. I shall ask your uncle's advice. Thank you again.'

Aunt Hesketh remained silent and when Midori closed the door on her way out of the parlour she saw her aunt fingering the silk before heaving a large sigh.

'Cap'n Noordholt, I hadn't looked to see you so soon again. Do come in, if you please.'

Harding ushered Nico into the tiny house which seemed very shabby in comparison to Jacob's, but still felt much more welcoming. It consisted of only two rooms, as far as Nico could see, but somehow it managed not to appear too cluttered.

'My daughter's out just at the moment, but I'm sure I can find us some victuals if you'd like?' Harding offered.

'No, thank you, I've eaten. I just came because I wanted to discuss a few things with you. Am I disturbing anything?'

'Not at all, I'm a man of leisure 'til the next time I sign on for a journey. Though truth to tell, I'm thinkin' of goin' into business instead. A friend of mine's offered me a half-share in his chandlery, an' I feel I'm gettin' too old for gallivantin' around. I've managed to save enough, so ...'

'Sounds sensible.' Nico nodded.

'And what about yourself, sir? Off back to Amsterdam, are you?'

'Not just yet. That's what I wanted to speak to you about. It's Mistress Midori, you see. I need to get her away from here. In fact, I should never have brought her.' He told Harding about what he'd overheard at the inn. 'I can't make head or tail of all the rumours flying around, but it could be dangerous.' Nico had tried his best to find out, but no one seemed to know for sure.

'I hear tell it's definitely happenin',' Harding said. 'More's the pity. I'm too old for fightin', but I may not have a choice.'

'You really think it'll come to that, here in Devon, too?'

'Aye, I reckon we'll all have to take sides sooner or later. The problem's not goin' to go away this time.'

Nico clenched his jaw. 'That's bad news. It makes it even more imperative for me to get Midori away.'

'I would,' Harding agreed. 'Not the place for a lady such as her.'

'I know.' Nico sighed. 'She's stubborn though, and ... well, I sort of deceived her a little, so she's angry with me now and may not listen.' He reluctantly told Harding about the kinship between him and Midori.

Harding whistled softly. 'Well, I never. Stepcousins, eh? Who'd have thought.'

'Yes, an amazing coincidence, but still, it happened. The point is, if she won't agree to go with me, can I rely on you to look out for her? Should she need it, that is.'

'Of course. Don't you fret, I'll do my best.'

'Thank you, Harding. I'll let you know how I get on. First, I need to find a way of waylaying her so I can speak to her alone.'

How, he had no idea.

'I would like a word with you, Midori, if you please? In private.'

Uncle Marston's voice was pleasant enough as he ushered her into his small study, and the request perfectly reasonable. But Midori still had the feeling she wasn't going to enjoy the ensuing conversation. A week had passed since her arrival in the Marston household, and she knew she'd been under constant scrutiny. It would seem the time had come for the verdict.

'Do take a seat.'

Midori sat down on the high-backed chair opposite her uncle's, folding her hands in her lap and assuming a calm expression. She tried not to fidget, but it was almost impossible, since the woollen bodice and petticoat were making her skin itch unbearably, despite the linen shift underneath. She wondered how long it would take before her skin became used to the scratchy material. Her aunt said she wasn't allowed to wear silk, so her Amsterdam purchases had been swapped for various lengths of wool and linen.

There was a long pause as her uncle searched for the right words. He steepled his fingers together, holding the tips against the underside of his chin. For a while he focused on some point beyond her left shoulder, before fixing her with his calm gaze.

'My dear, I've been observing you for a few days and I hope you don't mind me saying this, but it appears to me you don't quite know how to go on.'

'Oh? In what way, Uncle? I have tried my best to follow my aunts' instructions. I'm learning to make bread, to sew

211

clothes and even to spin wool, although I'm afraid it will take me a while to master that.' Midori knew he wasn't talking about her domestic skills, which probably didn't interest him, but she felt it was better to pretend ignorance. He cut her short.

'Yes, yes, I'm sure you're making excellent progress with such things, and very commendable it is, too. I was rather thinking of your devotions. As you are under my guidance, I would like, if I may, to offer you some instruction in matters of faith.'

Midori couldn't say his offer was entirely unexpected. Although she'd tried her best to join in the daily prayers and hymn singing, the theological discussions had been beyond her and she often found her mind drifting. Obviously, her uncle had noticed, despite the fact that she'd tried her best to hide her inattention.

'It's very kind of you, but ... would you be very upset if I decline? Captain ... er, Nicholas and I had some theological discussions during our journey, but I don't yet feel ready to embrace Christianity fully. I'm sorry.' She hung her head, wondering if he would explode with rage and banish her from the house forever. She had thought for a while that she could adapt to a new faith, but when it came down to it, she found it impossible. *I have to be true to myself!*

'I understand. It must be vastly different to the beliefs you've grown up with?'

Midori looked up. 'Indeed, yes. And I would feel as though I'm betraying my father. It's ... this is difficult for me.'

'Of course, I realise that,' her uncle said in a milder tone of voice. 'Would you like to learn more or are you completely set against it? I'd like the opportunity to change your mind, if at all possible, but I don't want to force you in any way.'

Midori was very relieved to hear that. 'I would be happy

to listen to you, Uncle,' she said. After all, what harm could it do?

'Excellent.' He smiled at her.

'Thank you for being so understanding and for allowing me to stay here with you. I didn't know where else to go and Mother said—'

'You did the right thing. No matter what, we are your family and we're very glad to have you. Think no more about it. Now, why don't you tell me what you and Nicholas talked about, then we can continue from there?'

'He made me read passages from the Bible and then he explained them to me.'

'Did he really?' Uncle Marston looked astonished. 'Well, I never! So his father didn't entirely waste his breath on him then ...' He shook his head. 'Anyway, our Bible is in the parlour and you may read it there as often as you wish. It is kept in a box and I trust you will handle it with care.'

'Yes, of course. Will you tell me which passages to read, please?'

He nodded. 'I'll try to choose suitable ones for you. I'd like you to learn first about the various sins and temptations that are set before us daily. The world is an immoral place, and whatever your beliefs, I must insist you follow mine and your aunts' moral guidance, agreed? There are certain things unmarried young women simply mustn't do. This is not just to do with Christianity, but the code of conduct of English society as a whole, you understand?'

'I promise I'll try my best.'

He continued on in this vein for a while, and Midori listened dutifully. Uncle Marston had treated her with nothing but kindness so far and it wasn't his fault they were miles apart culturally. She was determined to do her best to please him.

'Now don't forget, you may come to me at any time with any problems or questions you may have.'

'Thank you, Uncle.'

Just before leaving the room, she remembered something. 'Uncle Marston, there is something which has been puzzling me all week.'

'Oh, yes?'

'Did Aunt Hesketh marry the man originally intended for my mother, the one she left England to escape from? I was told my aunt was betrothed to another at that time.'

Her uncle's expression turned guarded. 'She did marry Ezekiel Hesketh, yes. She and her former fiancé found they weren't suited to each other and the arrangement came to an end. It's not a subject we normally discuss and it is all in the past.'

'I see. Well, thank you. You've been very kind.'

Midori fled before she could make any more *faux pas*.

Back in the small chamber she shared with Temperance, Midori sank to her knees in front of the minute fireplace. Above it was a wooden shelf, its underside blackened with soot. On this shelf she had placed the two urns containing the ashes of her parents. No one had noticed they were anything other than ornaments, and as they were very plain she hadn't been asked to remove them. A piece of bread and a small mug of cider stood casually between them, as if they'd been left there by mistake. They were Midori's meagre offerings to her ancestors.

She clapped her hands twice and began to pray quietly to her parents' spirits. 'Please help me to fit in here and to learn about their beliefs. Please also intercede for me with our ancestors and make them understand that this is something I'm doing out of necessity. I haven't forgotten your teachings, dearest Father, and never shall. Forgive me for not bringing you offerings every day, but I dare not at present. No one here would understand. And Mother – I know it was your wish that I should come here, so please guide me now so I don't make any more mistakes. I can feel your presence, you are always in my thoughts. Help me, please, I beg you.'

A slight draught stirred up the dust on the floor next to the fireplace, and Midori took this as a good sign. With a lighter heart she bowed once more and whispered, 'Thank you.'

Chapter Twenty-Two

'Mother and I are going to buy provisions. Do you want to come with us, Midori?' Temperance had come into the parlour where Aunt Hesketh, with ill-concealed impatience, was attempting to teach Midori how to darn sheets. It was a boring task and something she'd never had to do before. At Castle Shiroi such things were done by servants.

'Oh, yes please.' Midori stood up, then belatedly looked to her aunt for permission.

Aunt Hesketh nodded. 'Yes, go. We're not making much progress here in any case.' That wasn't quite true, but Midori was too pleased to be leaving and didn't argue.

As the three of them set off, the August sun beat down on them and the air was a shimmering haze through which distant objects appeared unreal. Many of the people they met had faces that had turned an unbecoming shade of pink, and as they picked their way through the personal waste and rubbish which littered the streets, the smell was overpowering. Midori was becoming used to the filth now, although the occasional whiff of something particularly malodorous would sometimes make her gag. She was grateful they weren't headed towards the harbour, though. She'd been there the previous day with Aunt Marston and the stench of the thousands of fish being unloaded and dealt with around the Barbican and Fisherman's Steps was unbelievable.

The heat wouldn't normally have bothered her either, but it made the woollen bodice more itchy. She would have infinitely preferred a cool silk *kimono*, but that was out of the question.

'Your, er, robes are lovely, my dear,' Aunt Marston had said kindly, 'but I'm afraid they really won't do here. You want to be a credit to your uncle, don't you?' And Midori did, so she packed away her Japanese clothing, placing some camphor in between the layers of material to deter moths.

'This way.' Aunt Marston steered a path towards the Guildhall, an imposing two-storey edifice which looked to have been there for some time. One side of it was solid, while on the other side the second floor was supported by a row of arches forming a cavernous open-air hall. In the welcome shade below, market traders were selling their wares, having brought them either in carts, barrels or baskets, and Midori's relations set course for a farmer whose vegetables looked to be of good quality.

As she passed one of the pillars an arm shot out and grabbed Midori's, pulling her out of sight. She started to try and free herself, but when she saw who her captor was, she stopped.

'Nico, what are you doing? Let go of me.' She shook him off and he let her, but looked as though he was ready to take hold of her arm again if she should decide to bolt.

'I need to speak to you and I can't get you alone for a second in that mausoleum of a house,' he grumbled, frustration clearly showing in his eyes. He'd come to dinner several times, but Midori had so far avoided being on her own with him. He held up a hand now to forestall any protest she might make. 'I know you're angry with me, but please, just hear me out. It's important.'

Midori debated with herself, but curiosity won. 'Very well, but hurry or they'll miss me.'

He ushered her out of sight, behind the canvas of a market stall where no one could see them. 'Listen, there are two things I must tell you. The first is that there seems to be a civil war brewing here in England, as well. I don't know if it will affect Plymouth, but it might.' He explained what he'd overheard at the inn.

'That sounds like mere rumours to me,' Midori protested.

'Harding doesn't think so, but I admit it's difficult to tell and it may just be scaremongering.'

'Well, if Plymouth is threatened, I'll just have to help defend our clan.'

Nico shook his head at her. 'You can't fight here, you're a woman.'

'So? You know I'm skilled with a sword and—'

'Midori, I told you, women are not allowed to do things like that in Europe. They stay at home and help look after the household and children. For heaven's sake, don't tell anyone you've been trained in the arts of war. And I hope you've hidden your swords well out of sight?'

Midori frowned at him. 'Yes, but if we're threatened, do you expect me to just watch my family be slaughtered?'

'No, of course not. All I'm saying is it probably won't come to that, so it's best you keep quiet about your abilities. If you really were threatened, of course you must do what you can.'

'Very well, if you insist. And what was the other matter you wanted to tell me?'

'It's about the Puritans.'

'The what?'

Nico turned away from her and paced back and forth. 'It's difficult to explain.' He took a deep breath. 'You remember I told you there were different types of Christians?' Midori nodded. 'Well, some of these groups here in England, and in Holland, too, for that matter, take their Christianity very seriously indeed. They call themselves "godly" or "God's children" and live strictly according to the rules laid down in the Bible. They ... oh, how can I explain it to you? They're simply more intensely Christian than anyone else, almost to the point of obsession. They pray morning, noon and night, read their Bible all the time, discuss theological matters endlessly, and so on. Do you follow me?'

'Yes, but how does that affect me?'

'Because I think Jacob is a Puritan. You must have noticed his sombre clothes and all that praying before dinner? He never stops.'

'Oh, wasn't he like that before?'

'No, not to that extreme. Midori, I can't leave you here with them. You'll never fit in.'

'It's not a problem. I've told him I have different beliefs and he's accepted that. He admitted he'd like to change my mind, but although I'll let him try, he won't. But please don't tell him that.'

'What do you take me for? Of course I won't tell him anything of the sort. But really, he's probably only saying that to lure you in. Before you know it, he'll force you to be baptised or else.'

'No, he won't. He's a kind man and he said I was welcome to stay no matter what.'

'Rubbish.'

Midori glared at him. 'Well, what do you suggest I do instead? It's not as if I can go back to Japan. To tell you the truth, I'm so relieved my uncle is even still alive, I'm prepared to put up with anything. At least now I have a home again, a clan to belong to.'

'But it won't be a home, don't you see? They won't accept you as you are. You'll have to change, much more than I prepared you for. It won't do.'

'I'll stand my ground.'

Nico shook his head. 'I doubt they'll tolerate a non-Puritan in their household for very long, although they will of course expect to have to teach you at first.'

She raised her chin. 'They can't force me and anyway, you're wrong. I don't believe they will.'

'Are you sure you want to stay here? There is an alternative, you know.'

'And what is that?'

He hesitated, as if it was a struggle to utter the words, then said, 'Marry me and go back to Amsterdam.'

Nico knew it wasn't the most romantic of proposals, but it seemed like the right thing to do. He'd never thought he would say those words to anyone, but now he had and it hadn't been as difficult as he'd imagined. He just couldn't see Midori ever fitting in here and he felt responsible for her predicament. He shouldn't have brought her, so it was up to him to find a solution.

'What? You're jesting.' Midori stared at him while her eyebrows came down in a frown.

He shook his head. 'No. You'd fit in better in Amsterdam. There are other foreigners there, one more won't make a difference. You must have noticed, right?'

She glared at him and put her hands on her hips. 'And what makes you think I'd want to marry you? You lied to me for nine months. I didn't even know your real name!'

'Yes, you did, my name *is* Nicholas Noordholt. I changed it when I became a Dutch citizen. I used to be known as Nicholas Hesketh, but since old Ezekiel more or less disowned me in his will, I didn't see why I should keep his name. I owed him nothing.'

There was no let-up in her scowl and Nico could tell she was far from convinced, so he tried to explain it better. 'Look, I left Plymouth because no one wanted me around. My stepmother did nothing when the old curmudgeon beat me twice as much as any of the others. I wasn't her son, so why should she stand up for me? He'd only have beaten her, too. When he died, he left me nothing and the estate was divided between the rest of the children. Kate didn't get anything, either, and went to live with her brother, leaving me to fend for myself. Then Jacob made it clear I wasn't to darken his door, although to be fair, he had his reasons, as he explained to me the other day. Either way, I left to make a new life for myself, determined never to come back. Then I met you ...'

'Fate was obviously unkind to you that day,' she said, her tone dripping sarcasm. 'I'm sorry you had to return here because of me.'

Nico stopped his pacing and stepped close to her. 'I'm sure fate had a reason for bringing us together and I admit I should have told you who I was as soon as I realised our connection. I apologise for that. But there was a spark between us, right from the start, wasn't there? You felt it, too. And I was fighting against it, first because I'd promised your brother I'd protect you and later because I knew deep down it would make me come here. To a place I'd vowed never to set foot in again.'

She looked away. 'I don't know what you mean.'

'Now who's lying?' he asked, softly. He put his hands out to cup her face, turning it towards him, then he bent to kiss her, gently at first, memorising the feel of her mouth, the taste of her. When she made a noise – perhaps of protest, although she didn't push him away – he deepened the kiss and put his arms around her to pull her hard against his chest. It felt so right. She fit perfectly, and he wanted to keep her there so she'd be safe. Perhaps marriage wouldn't be as bad as he'd always imagined. Not with Midori as his wife.

She reciprocated for a while, her tongue sparring with his, but then she suddenly tore out of his grasp and put some distance between them.

'No,' she said, holding out a hand to stop him from coming closer. 'Leave me alone. I'm not marrying a man I can't trust; a man without honour.'

'What? I have more honour than anyone here.' Nico tried to calm his breathing, which was as erratic as his heartbeat. 'And you can trust me with your life. Didn't I prove that to you in Batavia?'

'That was different. And besides, I can't remember much about it, only what you told me. How do I know you weren't lying then, too?' She shook her head. 'It just won't work. A marriage should be based on trust and respect and I thought I was the one who'd been dishonest because I lied about my destination, when in fact it was you who ... No, go back to Amsterdam. You didn't want me before when I ... well, before this. Now it's too late.'

Nico swallowed hard, gritting his teeth to stop himself from hurling angry words at her. He'd done his best, but if she didn't want to be saved, there was nothing more he could do.

'So be it,' he said. 'I hope you enjoy your new life.'

Midori watched him leave with a mixture of anger, despair and longing. Tearing herself away from his kiss was one of the hardest things she'd ever done, but she knew it was the right course of action. She couldn't marry him, not now.

If only he'd asked before and never brought me here.

But he hadn't and now she couldn't be sure anything he said was the truth. There was no denying the attraction between them, as he'd demonstrated so clearly, but she could and would refuse to give in to it completely.

'I'm *samurai*. I will not be ruled by emotion,' she vowed. 'I will do everything I can to fit in here so that I can once again belong to a family. How hard can it be?'

Surely no worse than anything she'd already been through.

The following morning Midori heard angry voices in the parlour and sat on the stairs, unashamedly eavesdropping.

'I can't believe you're leaving again so soon! You've only just got back, after thirteen years. Have you no thought for us? What of your duty to care for me in my old age?' Aunt Hesketh's voice was strident and belligerent.

'How do you know I have so much as a penny to my name?' Midori heard Nico reply. 'Unlike your own children, I was left with nothing, remember? And how is it my duty? If you want to be supported, why not ask them?'

Midori had already been told about Nico's stepsiblings – two brothers in their late twenties who were both clerks, and two slightly younger sisters; one a farmer's wife, the other married to a clergyman. For some reason they'd all moved to Exeter or somewhere near there.

'They have families to look after and it's obvious you've made something of yourself.' Aunt Hesketh sounded defensive. 'Your clothes are of good quality, if a bit on the ostentatious side.'

'Perhaps I stole them?' Nico's voice was calm and controlled, with a touch of sarcasm, but Midori guessed he was holding his temper in check with difficulty. If what he'd told her the day before was really true, she could understand why he hadn't wanted to return. Listening to Aunt Hesketh seemed to confirm his words.

'Now you're being deliberately provoking.' Aunt Hesketh sniffed loudly.

'Well, for your information, I have already given Jacob some money for your keep. You're right and it shouldn't have fallen to him to support you. And since my stepsiblings aren't able or willing to do anything about it, I will, though the Lord knows why …'

'They do what they can, from time to time.'

'Be that as it may, it's all settled.'

'Better late than never, I suppose.'

'A simple thank you would do.' Midori heard the

bitterness in Nico's voice and agreed he had cause to feel that way. Aunt Hesketh was being very trying.

'Of course I'm grateful, but why must you leave again? Jacob said you'd agreed to let bygones be bygones. This has something to do with that girl, doesn't it? I can feel it in my bones, she's a bad influence.'

'Don't be ridiculous. I escorted Midori here because she had nowhere else to go. You and Jacob are her family, don't forget, and you'd better treat her well or else ...'

'I knew it, there is something going on. Why else should you care?'

'There isn't.' Nico's words came out as if through clenched teeth and Midori held her breath, waiting to see what else he'd say. 'Midori is a friend, that's all, and we became acquainted during the journey back. I know she is kind and honourable. She deserves to be treated with respect as your niece, if nothing else. I don't want to hear any more of the "heathen" nonsense, understand? And don't think I won't know, because I will be told, make no mistake. I still have friends here in Plymouth.'

An uncomfortable silence ensued, which was broken by another sniff. 'Very well. I'm sure the girl won't be my responsibility, anyway.'

'Thank Christ for that. Now I need to get down to the ship. Goodbye.'

Midori barely had time to move out of sight before Nico flung open the parlour door and came storming out. He took the stairs down two at a time, sometimes three, and it was obvious he couldn't leave the house fast enough. Midori stood up slowly, her limbs curiously frozen, and blinked hard to get rid of the prickling of tears in her eyes.

'I never cry,' she told herself sternly and drew in a strengthening breath. 'And he's not worth anyone's tears.'

She ignored the little voice inside her head that asked whether she was really sure about that.

Later that afternoon she stood in the small bedroom and rubbed absently at a grimy window pane with the heel of her hand. She looked out towards the harbour. Fishing boats and other sailing vessels of every description and size filled her vision, but the larger ship which had brought her, Nico and Harding from Amsterdam was gone.

She put a hand over her mouth to stifle the cry of anguish that wanted to escape. Despair welled up inside her, but she pushed it down. *I will not give in to these emotions.* She closed her eyes and leaned her forehead against the cool glass.

'Are you all right?'

The small voice behind her made Midori jump and she swivelled round to find her youngest cousin standing by the door, watching her with concern in her eyes.

'Oh, Temperance, you startled me.'

'Sorry, but you were deep in thought. Is something wrong? Is Father cross with you? I know he can be a bit harsh ...'

'No, no he's not.' Midori turned back to the window and stared into the distance again. 'I was just thinking of ... my friends from the journey. Their ship has gone.'

'Cousin Nicholas, you mean? Yes, I heard him say it was leaving with the tide.'

'I know.' Midori tried to make her tone sound even.

'Oh, I forgot!' Temperance put her hand in the pocket of her apron and brought out a somewhat grubby piece of paper. 'He asked me to give you this, sorry.'

'Thank you.' Midori took the note which was addressed to her in bold writing and tried to ignore the sudden quickening of her heartbeat.

Midori,

If you are ever in need of assistance, I beg you will go and find Harding who has promised to help you in any way he can. He lives on the other side of the harbour, in the fourth house on the left facing the quay.

Should you wish to write to me, you know my direction – Keizersgracht canal, Amsterdam.

Yours,

Nicholas Noordholt, formerly Hesketh

Midori balled the missive up in her hand and threw it into the grate. She didn't think she would need to write to Nico, but even if she did, she wasn't likely to forget where his house was situated. And his pointed reminder that he had legally changed his name and therefore hadn't lied about it didn't help. *You still weren't honest with me, so how could I ever trust you?*

The answer was that she couldn't and she'd been raised to value honour above all else. A man without honour was worse than the *eta*, the lowest of the low.

This was her life now and she had to accustom herself to it. But as her breathing became more even, Midori wondered where Nico was now and whether she would ever see him again.

Nico stood by the porthole in his cabin and watched the English coastline sink below the horizon. Inside, he felt numb, as if parts of him were missing, and his thoughts were bleak.

I should never have left her there. She can't possibly fit in. If she won't marry me, I should have found another way.

The guilt ate away at his insides, gnawing relentlessly, giving him no peace.

He clenched his fists. 'It was her decision,' he said out loud.

But they will try to change her. The image of a smiling Midori being beaten into submission by her uncle etched itself on the insides of Nico's eyelids and he rubbed at them to make it go away.

'By all that's holy,' he muttered, 'he's not like that.' Although Jacob had thrown Nico out of his house in anger once, he hadn't actually hit him. *So there's no reason to suppose he will beat Midori.*

Perhaps he should have stayed longer, tried to find out more about the impending civil war before leaving Midori in Plymouth? *How will I know she's all right?*

Ah, but I'm forgetting Midori's own skills in that department. Surely she was fully capable of defending herself? Any soldier trying to attack her was in for a surprise. He couldn't help but smile at that thought.

What if she refuses to do as Jacob asks? He leaned his forehead against a windowpane and closed his eyes. There was a wilful streak in Midori, a steely determination which had helped her to get this far, but it could lead her into trouble. 'I hope she can adapt and accept her circumstances,' he whispered. They would punish her, if not physically, then through other means. *Her lovely hair!* A woman who misbehaved could have her hair cut off as punishment, and even the thought of that made Nico cringe. *Or what if they throw her out?* If Jacob truly was a Puritan, he'd be obsessed with immorality and repress vice wherever possible. A heathen, Midori would not be tolerated.

But she said he'd promised to let her make up her own mind. Would he?

Nico began to pace the small cabin. Should he turn back

and wait until he could be sure? *No, I can't afford to lose any more time.* He had stayed too long in England as it was; he had to report back to the *Heeren XVII* in Amsterdam now if he wanted to continue his career with them.

Harding. Nico had asked the man to keep an eye on Midori somehow.

'I'll pay you for your trouble, of course.' Nico had pressed a handful of coins into the old sailor's palm.

'No, no, that's not necessary,' Harding protested, trying to return the money. 'I'd be happy to help her any way I can, you know that. Fond of her, so I am.'

'Well, keep it just in case,' Nico insisted. 'You may need it for her.'

Harding agreed to that and promised he'd help Midori if the Marstons threw her out.

'Send word to me if either of you need assistance, won't you?'

'Aye, I swear it. Don't you fret none, all will be well.'

Nico ground his teeth. He wanted to believe Harding, but it wasn't ideal. Still, it was the best he could hope for. With a heavy sigh he lay down on his bunk and closed his eyes. He must put Midori out of his mind; she wasn't his concern any longer.

Chapter Twenty-Three

Dear Ichiro,

I am writing to you, as promised, to inform you of my arrival in England. The journey was somewhat eventful, but Captain Noordholt kept me safe. He has now gone back to his home in Holland.

I am slowly adjusting to life here and do my best to please my uncle Marston and two aunts. I am determined to fit in, as we discussed, and apply myself with diligence to learning everything I can, both in regard to religious and domestic matters. I have duties, like helping in the kitchen, not because there is a lack of servants, but because here no member of the household is allowed to be idle. It is a novel experience, but I find I enjoy it and time passes quickly. I have acquired many new skills, such as baking, candle-making and how to make cheese, a staple of the English diet it seems. I think you would like the taste of it – I do.

With my uncle's help, I now understand the Christian doctrines much better. He has made me see what a wise man Jesus of Nazareth (the son of the Christian god) was and that makes it easier for me to follow his teachings on how to behave. It is all beginning to make sense and Uncle Marston is pleased with my progress, although naturally I still follow Japanese customs (albeit in secret so as not to offend my uncle).

I have a young cousin, Temperance, who is very sweet. She is extremely knowledgeable, despite her tender age, and accomplished in most household duties. I find it much easier to learn from her, since she can be relied upon to *explain things in a straightforward manner. In return, I tell her about Japan and our life at Castle Shiroi. She considers this exotic and has an almost insatiable desire for more information. I admit I don't mind satisfying her curiosity as it helps me to keep the memories alive in my own mind.*

I trust you are well, and your wife and the children also. Please write to me if you can.

Your obedient sister, Midori

Midori put down her quill and sighed. She had no idea whether her letters would ever reach Ichiro, although her uncle had said he would try to find a way of forwarding them via the English East India Company's ships to the Far East. She bit her lip to stop the homesickness from flooding her mind and tried to remain optimistic.

I'm sure my messages will get through somehow.

'I'm afraid the ships for the Far East don't leave until earliest January, but if you don't mind travelling north instead, we have one going to the Baltic next. The captain's just been taken ill so we need someone to take his place.'

Nico was in the presence of only one of the *Heeren XVII* this time, which was a lot less intimidating. He hadn't expected to be given employment immediately, so the man's proposal was a nice surprise. Nico felt restless and needed something, anything, to do.

'That would do very well, thank you,' he assured the director. 'I'll go anywhere as long as there is profit involved.'

'Yes, well, it won't be as much as for the Far East journeys, but there are valuable cargoes to be found in the Baltic, too.' The man added with a small smile, 'Your wife will expect you to return with furs and amber jewellery, I've no doubt.'

'I'm afraid I don't have a wife.' Nico tried not to bristle. Why was everyone in the VOC so interested in his marital status?

'Oh, I beg your pardon, only I thought a man such as yourself would have been snapped up by some lucky lady a long time ago.'

Nico tried to smile at the compliment. 'No, not yet, but perhaps I'll purchase some amber just in case.'

'Good idea. Now here are the details of the journey ...'

As Nico was briefed, he tried his best not to think of the only woman he'd ever proposed to. Would she appreciate jewellery and furs? Should he have tried to woo her properly? He doubted it would have made any difference. She placed more value on honour and honesty, neither of which she believed he possessed.

If he ever wanted to win her hand in marriage, he'd have to prove her wrong. *But since I don't, there's no point thinking about it!* Why, then, wouldn't his mind give him some peace?

The truth was he missed her. And he couldn't stop thinking about the kisses they'd shared. His body ached at the mere thought of holding her close. He clenched his jaw.

She refused my proposal. She doesn't want me and there's an end to it.

He sincerely hoped going to the Baltic would keep him very busy indeed.

'Do stop dawdling, girl. I haven't all day, you know.'

'Coming, Aunt Hesketh.' Midori followed her aunt into the house, weighed down by the load of produce they had been to buy at the market, while inwardly seething. She wasn't used to being someone else's beast of burden and the humid late September weather hadn't made her task any easier. Not that she would receive any thanks for her efforts.

Will anything I do ever find favour with this implacable aunt? The very sight of Midori seemed to anger the woman, and nothing could be done to change that state of affairs, apparently. *So much for treating me well, as Nico asked her to do. Nico ... No, I mustn't think of him, he's gone.* But for some reason her mind refused to follow this order.

'I'm going to lie down for a while. This heat is unbearable,' Aunt Hesketh declared. Halfway up the stairs she turned back towards Midori. 'Well, don't just stand there, take our purchases to the kitchen before they, too, wilt.'

Midori hurried to do her bidding, if only to get out of the woman's sight. She shook her head. What reason could her aunt possibly have for treating her so badly?

The kitchen contained only her other aunt, and Midori realised that here was a rare opportunity to find out some answers.

'Aunt Marston, I wonder if I could have a word with you, please?' she said, while piling all the parcels on to the table.

'Yes, of course, my dear. What is it?' Aunt Marston looked a bit like a frightened rabbit, nervously twitching when flushed from its bolt-hole. She always seemed on edge, which was no wonder with a sister-in-law like Aunt Hesketh, Midori thought.

'Uncle Marston said Mr Hesketh was the man my mother was supposed to have married, the reason she ran away, in fact. Can you tell me what happened, please? Why did my aunt end up with him when she was supposed to have married another?'

'Er, well, all I know is Kate was forced to accept Hesketh. There were certain circumstances, and ... Your grandfather had already signed a marriage contract with him, and as the man was willing to take either daughter ... Well, your grandfather could be rather forceful when he chose to be.' Aunt Marston shivered slightly, as if a memory of the old man scared her. She fiddled with her apron strings. 'Was that all? I have a lot to attend to this morning, so if you'll excuse me?'

'Just one more thing, if you please. I don't quite understand the enmity Aunt Hesketh seems to harbour towards me. Nothing I do ever pleases her and I'm trying my hardest, really I am.'

Aunt Marston blanched and gripped the edge of the kitchen table for support. Her eyes darted around as if seeking sanctuary from Midori's questions. 'Well, there was some friction between her and your mother, and perhaps you remind her of Hannah, sometimes. I'm sure that if she's a little harsh, it's just her way.'

Midori could see Aunt Marston was extremely uncomfortable and since she liked her, she didn't want to cause her pain.

'Very well. Thank you for answering my queries, Aunt. It's very kind of you.'

Aunt Marston fled without another word and Midori was left to wonder what exactly had happened between her mother and Aunt Hesketh.

I guess I'll never know.

Nico stood by the railing of his ship as it slowly eased away from Amsterdam and headed northwards. The temptation to turn its bow in a southerly direction instead was great, but he knew it was pointless going back to Plymouth. Even if he went there, he wouldn't be welcomed by anyone, least of all Midori.

'Argh!' He gritted his teeth and gripped the wooden railing hard. *Why can't I stop thinking about her?* It wasn't as if he'd wanted to marry anyone in any case. Marriage was a burden, it tied you down, gave you responsibilities. And he wanted to be free. Didn't he?

He watched the city disappear, to be replaced by flat coastline, and felt a great relief wash over him. Whenever he went to sea, the sense of freedom released the tension he always felt on land. For the next couple of months he'd be too busy to think about anything other than sailing and trade. At least, he sincerely hoped so.

'And when I return, perhaps I'll be sent on another journey to the Far East,' he muttered to himself.

The thought should have filled him with joy, since he knew he'd stand to gain from it enormously, but somehow he couldn't muster up much enthusiasm. *It won't be the same without Midori. All those long months at sea with no one to talk to.* He swore softly and turned from the railing, walking abruptly towards the cabin.

'I've never been lonely before.' He had to conquer those thoughts, once and for all, and accept that Midori was not for him. She'd refused his offer, and that was it.

You didn't exactly pick the best way of asking her, a little voice inside his head needled. He had to acknowledge the truth of that. In fact, once he was back in Plymouth he'd reverted to his old self, almost as if he'd been transported to his teenage years once again. He'd been boorish and grumpy, not to mention presumptuous in trying to persuade her with that kiss. *Was it any wonder Midori turned me down?*

Most women wanted to be flattered and cajoled. He'd thought Midori was different, but perhaps not as different as all that, deep down? Either way, there was nothing he could do about it now.

He took a deep breath and picked up his compass, then went to find the first mate to check on their course.

October 1642

After two months in the Marston household, Midori was beginning to feel a sense of belonging. There were still many things that seemed strange to her, but apart from Aunt

Hesketh, the others all made her feel welcome. This was exactly what she'd hoped for, which was why she wasn't best pleased at the thought that her newfound clan might be threatened by the possibility of an impending war.

Although no one seemed to know for certain how serious the conflict was, there were rumours flying around each day. Midori kept her ears open and at the beginning of October she found that she wasn't the only one.

'I heard today they were asking for volunteers to go with the army to Dorset.' Daniel, who'd been picking at his food that day, pushed away his plate, giving up the pretence of eating.

Midori was surprised. Even at the age of eighteen, he was still fairly shy and rarely spoke, but she knew him to be sensible and intelligent. He'd obviously thought long and hard before raising this topic.

'What nonsense,' her uncle growled. 'There's no need for any armies. This silly dispute will be settled soon.'

'I believe you're wrong, Father. I've been listening, and there's definitely a war coming. Why else would they be recruiting men? Almost everyone here in Plymouth is opposed to King Charles and it's our duty to stand against him, surely?'

'The argument between the King and Parliament will be resolved without any fighting, I tell you.' Her uncle stared at his son, as if daring him to argue further.

Daniel's mouth set in a mulish line. 'War will come, I'm certain of it, and—'

'Enough!' Uncle Marston's fist came crashing down on to the table, sending his knife spiralling to the floor with a clatter. An uneasy silence descended on the table while the two of them glared at each other for what seemed an age. Finally, Daniel averted his gaze, capitulating, and his father picked up his ale.

'There will be no war,' was his final pronunciation before he thumped down his tankard and declared the meal finished.

Midori hoped he was right.

But Uncle Marston was forced to eat his words, at least in part.

'Have you heard that the whole of Cornwall has been secured for the King by Sir Ralph Hopton?' Daniel ventured to ask a few days later. 'It's likely we'll soon come under attack, too.'

'I doubt it.' Her uncle sent his son a quelling look, but Daniel ignored it, obviously too full of news to be stopped.

'Ten thousand Cornishmen have risen in support of the King, I was told,' Daniel reported. 'Just think on it! They're bound to come our way.'

'Rubbish!'

Her uncle was adamant, but as a stream of Cornish refugees, supporters of Parliament, started to cross the Tamar in their search for a safe haven, it became more and more difficult for him or anyone else to ignore the situation. The Corporation of the City of Plymouth began to raise money in order to construct fortifications around the northern part of the town.

'Proves that at least *they* take the threat of war seriously,' Daniel murmured out of earshot of his father, who was incensed because a rate was levied and everyone had to pay their share.

The mayor of Plymouth, Philip Francis, was unequivocally on the side of Parliament, and any Royalists still remaining in the town were arrested. None of this helped in any way to sweeten her uncle's temper, which had been simmering since Daniel had first raised the subject. He handed over his money to the Corporation very reluctantly. 'The futility of all this effort, honestly,' he grumbled.

Nonetheless, Midori noticed he kept an eye on all the various defensive activities going on in and around the town.

'Everyone has been asked to help if they can,' he informed them. Grudgingly he had to spare first Daniel, then Midori and finally Temperance and two of the servants as well, to assist with the building of crude earthworks at strategic points. Even small children had to help to the best of their ability, fetching and carrying whatever they could manage.

'You don't mind all this manual labour, Cousin?' Daniel asked Midori as they worked side by side, their breath emerging as puffs of steam in the cold autumn air. His cheeks had a slightly pink tinge to them, as if he wasn't used to talking to girls, but Midori pretended she didn't notice.

'No, quite the opposite, in fact.' She paused to wipe her brow on her sleeve and smiled at him to put him at ease. 'I like physical activity and to tell you the truth,' she lowered her voice slightly, 'it's wonderful to have this freedom and be away from the house for a while.' Daniel stopped shovelling and stared at her, so she quickly added, 'I mean no disrespect, it's just that I'm not really used to the life here yet.'

'No, no, please don't feel you have to apologise,' Daniel cut in. 'I can understand how difficult it must be for you, coming from such a different background. All the restrictions can become a bit wearisome for us, too,' he admitted, 'although please don't ever tell Father I said that.'

Midori laughed. 'I'm glad you're not offended. And of course I won't tell him.'

Digging dirt was infinitely preferable to the monotony of her days in the Marston household and the hard work dispersed some of her pent-up frustration. Labouring next to Daniel helped her to get to know him better, which was a bonus. It also kept her well away from Aunt Hesketh, who had stopped criticising everything Midori did, but instead glared darkly at her whenever they were in the same room.

'I don't understand why she's so hostile to me,' she commented to her cousins.

'Oh, she's just a grumpy old lady,' Temperance replied, but Midori wasn't convinced. It seemed more personal, somehow.

'Well, I find it very tedious.'

She and the others worked hard and a rampart of the most basic type was soon built, with a turf-revetted front face and an external ditch. In an amazingly short time these primitive earthworks stretched from Eldad Hill in the west to the river Plym in the east, creating a formidable defensive line around the town.

'We'll likely be ready for attack by the end of November,' Daniel said.

'But what if the earthworks don't keep the Royalists out?' Temperance asked, her voice slightly trembling. 'Will … will they kill us, too?'

'No, of course not. They'll not wage war on women and children,' Daniel replied, but as he exchanged a look with Midori behind Temperance's back, they both knew it could happen.

Uncle Marston still refused to acknowledge that war was imminent, but he was proved wrong yet again.

'There was a battle on the twenty-third of October at a place called Edgehill, I hear. The die is cast now,' Daniel told them. 'There's no going back and everyone will be forced to choose sides – King or Parliament.'

'Hmph,' was her uncle's only reply, but Midori knew that for him, the choice was easy. He'd been talking for months about King Charles's ineptitude and arrogance.

'I firmly believe the King has his heart set on restoring the Catholic faith in England,' he'd declared. 'There's bound to be a plot, stands to reason. Well, he has a Papist wife, doesn't he? And he's done nothing to curb her activities in that department. Besides, he has far too much power. Just look at the favouritism shown to his friends.'

Midori's choice was also clear. According to the rules she lived by, her duty belonged to her family. Whatever path they chose, she would follow. Having only been in England for a few months, matters of state meant little to her, but she understood there could be only one ruler of a country. And although she felt it was wrong to fight the King, whom she understood to be England's equivalent of the *Shogun,* she didn't particularly care who won, but honour made her fight on the side of her clan.

'Parliament it is then,' she muttered.

Chapter Twenty-Four

November 1642

'They need more men to defend the town, Father, and I would like to join them.' Daniel, his face flaming with embarrassment, had seized his chance to speak while his father had a mouthful of food.

Uncle Marston choked on a piece of pickled herring and fruit pie, a dish Midori found distasteful. 'What's that? Join the fighting? Not on my life,' he gritted out between coughing bouts.

Daniel bravely tried again, his courage and stubbornness earning Midori's silent respect. 'But, Father, I have it on the best authority that Sir Ralph Hopton is marching this way. He'll try to storm our defences, so every man is needed.'

'You're not going, and that's final. One skirmish and it'll all be over. I have but one son and I want you to take over the business from me, not fight futile wars.'

'Futile! How can you say that, when they're fighting for our freedom to keep our faith? If the Royalists had their way, we'd all be Papists. You said so yourself. And no doubt your precious business would be confiscated to boot.'

'Don't be impertinent. We are amply defended by the force already in place. There's no need for you to go. Your place is here with me, learning to be a merchant. That's my final word.' Midori's uncle looked at his wife, who had gone as white as her starched collar. 'And think of your mother.'

'Oh, Daniel, don't do anything rash, I beg you.' Aunt Marston sent him an imploring look. 'Your father is surely right. And why should you go? You don't even know how to handle a weapon.'

'I can learn, just like everyone else. And someone has to.'

'Well, it won't be you!' His father exploded with rage and a torrent of words poured out of him, the gist of which was that fighting was for people who had nothing better to do and no son of his was ever going to join them. During the entire tirade, Daniel didn't say a word, but his expression remained mutinous.

Midori sympathised with her cousin, but she could see her uncle's point of view, too. Daniel was his only son and he'd never been trained in the arts of fighting. She rated his chances of survival in a battle as fairly low, if not non-existent, and she would have been very worried for him if he'd gone off to fight.

An idea came to her and she mulled it over while slowly chewing her pie. After the meal, she followed Daniel into the garden, where he'd no doubt gone to cool his anger and frustration. She found him leaning his forehead against the trunk of a fruit tree. His breath was coming out in angry clouds of steam and he reminded her of a skittish horse. 'Cousin?' she said quietly. 'May I have a word?'

'If you must, but I'm not really fit company at present.' He looked up briefly, then closed his eyes again. 'I'm sorry.'

'It's all right, I understand. I've come to talk to you about that. It seems to me your father is right in a way, but—'

'Not you as well.' He stared at her and just then he reminded her so much of her mother it made her heart flip over. The family resemblance was clear, especially with that red hair so like Hannah's. Unlike his aunt, however, he also had freckles that stood out against the pure white of his skin.

'Wait, hear me out. I'm with you. What I mean is that you *will* be needed eventually, because I don't think this war will be over quickly. Your father is wrong about that. So if you're patient, the time will come when he'll have to let you go. I thought perhaps you'd like to be a bit more prepared for that.'

'How do you mean?' Daniel glared at her suspiciously.

'Do you know anything about fighting?'

'I can defend myself as well as any man.' His chin rose a fraction and Midori swallowed a smile.

'Yes, but can you fight with a sword? Shoot a bow and arrow?'

'No, not really.'

'There you are, then. I can help you. I learned swordplay, archery and self-defence from my father and brother. If we could find a quiet spot where no one can see us, I can teach you. I would hate to see you march off to be slaughtered unnecessarily. And you wouldn't be doing anyone else any favours, either. You want to help the Parliamentary cause, don't you?'

Daniel frowned at the implied slur to his manliness, but reason won and he nodded. 'Your words make sense, Cousin. I would like to learn. Can you really teach me?'

'Yes. I promise I'm not making it up. I'll prove it to you, but we need privacy. Perhaps the garden at night after everyone's abed?'

'No, they might hear us and it's perishing cold at this time of year.' He thought for a moment. 'We can go down to the sea. There must be some secluded area there where we could practise. What excuse could we give, though?'

'Let's just say we're still needed for digging duties. It's the truth, after all – there is still some work going on – and we don't need to tell them we go elsewhere first for an hour or so.'

'Sounds like a good plan.' Daniel grinned. 'Can we start tomorrow after breakfast?'

'Yes, of course.'

'But what will we use to fight with? I don't even own a sword.'

'I do, but it won't be necessary to use real ones at first. We'll practise with sticks until you know the moves.'

'Right. Until tomorrow, then?'

Midori sent up a swift prayer to the gods that what she could teach Daniel would be enough to keep him safe eventually.

They found a deserted part of the coast where no one could see them and Daniel put down the sack he'd been carrying, taking out its contents. Two sturdy sticks, which he'd cut himself from a copse of trees on the outskirts of town, and a bow and arrows he'd managed to borrow from a friend.

'Is this all we need?' he asked, turning around, then gasped as he took in the sight of Midori removing her petticoat to reveal the *hakama* hidden beneath. 'Dear Lord, but what are you wearing, Cousin?'

Midori smiled. 'You don't honestly expect me to fight in a gown, do you? I need to be able to move my legs.' She demonstrated the split in her skirt-like garment and Daniel's mouth formed a soundless O.

'It – it isn't seemly,' he stammered, turning a dull shade of red. 'I shouldn't have embroiled you in this.'

Midori raised her eyebrows at him. 'As I recall, this was my suggestion. And if it doesn't bother me, why should you mind? Besides, who's to see? Come now, if you wish to learn, you'll need to set aside your prejudices. I may be a woman, but I assure you I can teach you a thing or two. Do you trust me?'

He swallowed, his eyes still wide, but nodded. 'Yes, yes I do.'

'Then forget what I'm wearing and concentrate on this.' Midori picked up one of the sticks and threw it to him, then proceeded to demonstrate basic fighting techniques.

She breathed in deeply of the cold sea air and felt more alive than she had for months. It was so good to be practising her skills again, doing something she was good at. It made her blood sing.

Daniel quickly grasped the rudiments of sword fighting and defence. 'You're doing well,' Midori praised, as they took a short break.

'Thank you. How soon do you think I'll be able to join the army?'

'Not for a while yet. Remember, most soldiers train for years before they are allowed anywhere near the enemy.' Midori didn't want to discourage him, but he needed to be realistic. 'Let's say at least a few months.'

'Months! I may not have that long, so I suppose I'd better learn fast.' Daniel concentrated even harder on Midori's instructions after that.

Towards the end of their first session he shook his head and smiled at her. 'I have to admit, I didn't really believe you, but you've proved me wrong.'

'About what?'

'That you actually knew how to wield a sword.' Daniel looked slightly sheepish. 'You have to acknowledge, it's not something girls are usually taught.'

'Most *samurai* girls are.' Midori shrugged. 'I'm grateful to my father for allowing me to learn, although he may have had his reasons.'

'What do you mean?'

'I think he realised a girl of mixed parentage might have need of fighting skills. He had friends in high places, so perhaps he saw trouble brewing and wanted me to be prepared for every eventuality.'

'I see. A wise man, your father.'

Midori nodded and thought back to the happy times she had spent training in one of the castle's many courtyards. Her father had been so patient with her, encouraging her at every turn, although never allowing her to show weakness. She was extremely grateful to him and wished that he could be here with her now. Quickly she changed the subject before she was swamped with longing for her father's company. 'How are you with a bow and arrow, Daniel?'

'Uhm, not brilliant, but I might be able to hit a barn door at twenty paces.'

Midori began to laugh. 'And if the barn door is an enemy archer coming towards you at a run?'

Daniel cleared his throat. 'I may need a bit of assistance with that. But hardly anyone uses them any more. There are pikes and muskets mostly.'

'Nevertheless, I'm sure it wouldn't hurt to practise a bit. You never know when it will come in useful.'

January 1643

Dear Ichiro,

Although I doubt my previous letter has reached you yet, I thought to keep you informed of what is occurring here and reassure you of my continued well-being as England is in the midst of a civil war.

The town of Plymouth is under siege as of November and although I find it hard to understand how the flimsy defences we have constructed out of earth will keep the enemy out, I have been assured that they will. I cannot but compare them unfavourably to the sturdy stone walls and moat of Castle Shiroi, but warfare is obviously conducted differently here. For the moment, however, we are safe.

You will be surprised to learn that my cousin Daniel, who is eighteen, possessed no fighting skills whatsoever. I have therefore been teaching him and hope this hasty training will be enough. He is eager to fight for his clan, but I am trying to dissuade him until he has learned more as I do not consider him ready yet. Fortunately, he trusts my judgement and so far has listened to me. When the time is right, we will fight together, although my uncle does not believe it will be necessary. I think he is wrong, but we will see.

The beginning of the New Year was not celebrated here as is the custom in Japan. Instead, the birth of the

Christian god's son a few weeks before merited a feast of sorts, although it was a rather poor one to my mind. We merely listened to extra sermons and ate some very indifferent food, since there was not much to be had because of the siege. I did not mind unduly, though. I am used to it now. However, I do miss Castle Shiroi in the snow and the lovely baths in the hot spring. Remember, my mother always said the spring was her favourite place on earth? I can see why now.

On that subject, I do not believe I mentioned previously the curious lack of cleanliness here in general. You will scarcely credit that most people go without a proper bath for months or even years on end! They consider it enough to change their 'linen', or undergarments, and believe staying dirty keeps infections from entering the body. I, on the other hand, am trying my best to keep myself clean according to our customs, you will be happy to hear.

Akemashite omedeto gozaimasu, *brother, I hope it is a good year for you and clan Kumashiro.*

Your obedient sister, Midori

But would it be a good year for her? Somehow, Midori doubted it. Ever since Nico had left, her life had seemed empty and dull and no matter how hard she tried, she couldn't help thinking that perhaps she should have accepted his offer after all. *But would life with him have been any better?* She simply didn't know.

'You've done well yet again, Noordholt. That's three profitable journeys to the Baltic in a row now. Excellent!'

Nico had returned each time from the north with a better cargo than he'd dared hope for and the *Heeren XVII* were pleased. Normally he would have been delighted to have impressed these important gentlemen, but somehow he could barely summon up a smile today, although he tried his best. He felt bone weary, and despondency hung like a heavy, dark mantle on his shoulders.

'I'm happy to have been of service,' he murmured.

'With such a success rate, we believe you may be just the man we need to captain another ship to the Japans,' the director continued. 'Are you interested?'

Nico drew in a steadying breath. This was what he'd hoped for, the goal he'd been working towards for years. Yet now he had it within his grasp, he found he had no enthusiasm for such a long journey. None at all.

He weighed his answer carefully. 'I'm very honoured to be asked, but I'm afraid I shall have to decline this time. I've just received news that my mother is dying and I must hurry to her side. I'm sure you'll understand. She lives in England and with things the way they are over there at the moment, I couldn't guarantee to be back here in time.'

The lie tripped off his tongue easily and he marvelled at himself. He'd never lied to anyone before. *Except Midori*, a little voice inside him whispered. *I didn't lie to her; I just didn't tell her the truth.* He pushed his conscience into a dark corner of his mind and concentrated on the here and now. 'But I would be very grateful if you would consider me for such a position at a future date.'

The *Heeren XVII* looked disappointed to a man, but all nodded assent. 'Very well, these things can't be helped,' the first director said. 'Do please let us know as soon as you are available again.'

'You may be sure I will, and thank you.' Nico bowed and took his leave.

Once outside, however, he cursed under his breath. *I've just turned down the best offer I've ever had, and for what?* A woman he couldn't erase from his mind. He gave a snort of impatience. *This is ridiculous, the world is full of them!* But although he'd tried his best, he hadn't been able to forget about Midori and the problem was, he wanted only her.

'Are there any letters for me, Johan?' he asked his servant as soon as he was back at his house.

'No, *Mijnheer*, not today.'

Damnation! Nico had hoped to find at least a message from Midori waiting for him at his house upon his return from the Baltic, but so far there hadn't been anything. Not even the shortest of missives, and no word from Harding, either. Not that he'd expected there to be, as the man was only to contact Nico in case of an emergency, but still …

'Surely she must have tired of living in a Puritan household by now?' he muttered. Any fool could see she wasn't suited to such a life. Perhaps she had tried to send a message, but it hadn't got through? As he'd mentioned to the *Heeren XVII*, the news that filtered through from England wasn't good. Nico couldn't help but wonder what was happening to Midori and the others, caught up in a civil war. Did they have enough to eat; were they suffering hardship? He'd heard some of the ports were blockaded, so it was a possibility.

'I must find a way to help them and get her out of there,' he muttered. *And a way to make her trust me again and marry me.* Because he knew now he wanted her enough to tie himself down for life. He'd never felt this way about a woman before, but he'd thought long and hard about it. Women had come and gone in his life; none had been important. But Midori was special.

He sighed and left his home again. He would put his affairs in order, perhaps make some investments with the help of *Mijnheer* Schuyler and rent out the house here in Amsterdam, then buy provisions, charter a ship and sail to Plymouth.

And then, somehow, he had to persuade Midori to leave England, because he wasn't coming back without her.

Chapter Twenty-Five

The year had started well for Plymouth.

Hopton had made several attempts on the town, but was rebuffed. When the Earl of Stamford was reported to be marching towards Exeter to relieve that town and those beyond, Hopton wisely decided to move on. He and his Cornishmen left on New Year's Day.

'Excellent! Now we can come and go as we please again,' Uncle Marston was heard to comment.

For Midori the year's beginning had not been as auspicious, however. She was called to her uncle's study one gloomy January afternoon, wondering why, as she'd already had her daily session with him.

'You wanted to see me, Uncle?'

'Indeed. Tell me, what is this?'

Midori was surprised to see her uncle holding up the fan she'd given Temperance all those months ago. He looked for all the world as if he was grasping a viper, the way he held it between two fingers and at a distance from himself. 'Why, it's an old fan,' she replied cautiously, wondering how it had come into his possession.

'I found Temperance with this and she tells me you gave it to her.'

'Yes, I did. As you can see it's not really serviceable any longer, so I saw no harm in letting her have it.'

'You saw no harm?' Uncle Marston looked incredulous. 'After all these months of careful teaching on my part, have you learned nothing? This, this ... object is a gaudy, unsuitable item for a young girl to have. You must have known that, and yet you try to corrupt my daughter by "letting her have it"?'

'I didn't mean—'

Her uncle cut her off, his disappointment and anger almost palpable. 'I thought better of you, Midori. I thought by now you'd come to value the teachings of Christ the way we do, or at least respect the fact that this is how we live, but I see now I was wrong. I wash my hands of you, really I do.'

Midori wanted to rail at the unfairness of his words. She had worked so hard to gain acceptance here. She desperately wanted to belong to a family and have friendship and security, and still her uncle wasn't satisfied. However, she knew if she protested now, she might lose everything. Much as it went against the grain, she had to acknowledge he had the right to chastise her in this way for what she considered a minor transgression. In short, she had to swallow her pride.

'No, please, Uncle Marston, tell me what I might do to make amends. I swear I've been listening to you and I had forgotten all about that fan. I gave it to Temperance at the very beginning, before I understood your teachings properly. It won't happen again. Indeed, I see clearly now that it's a vain item.'

Her uncle drew in a deep breath and let it out in a sigh, his high colour fading. 'Very well, as you seem to be truly repentant, I'll tell you what I propose. I realise I have no authority over your belongings as such, but it would show Temperance at least the error of her ways if you were to burn this. I will tell her to pray to God while you're doing so. She must pray for strength to fight temptation, pray for guidance before acting on impulses like the one that made her accept it in the first place. She ought to have known better. Will you do this for me, please?'

'Yes, Uncle, if that is your wish. I'm very sorry, please forgive me.'

'Of course. Perhaps I was a little hasty in my condemnation. I sometimes forget how far you have come and that you don't see things quite the same way.' He came around the desk and awkwardly patted her on the head. 'Let us put this behind us and move forward.'

Midori was very happy to do so, but as she and Temperance watched the fan burn later, she felt as if she were burning a part of herself. Bit by bit, the old Midori was being eradicated, but there seemed no other way of surviving in England. She must banish all thoughts of her past and embrace her new way of life without reservations, whether she wanted to or not. Even if she wasn't a Christian, she had to live according to their rules if she wanted to stay here. It was a sobering thought. *But what choice do I have?*

Soon after, her uncle had more important things to worry about than whether his niece was behaving or not. Midori and Daniel returned from one of their secret outings to find the house in an uproar. Aunt Hesketh immediately rounded on Midori.

'Where have you been? This is all your fault!'

'What is, Aunt?' Midori looked around to see what household calamity she could possibly have caused now, but saw nothing out of the ordinary.

'Yes, what's amiss?' Daniel added, anxiously.

'Your mother is ill. A putrid throat and persistent cough, enough to shake the rafters. And it's all because of her.' Again Aunt Hesketh looked accusingly at Midori, who frowned as she tried to figure out the connection.

'Midori isn't ill,' Daniel protested. 'She couldn't possibly have passed anything on to my mother.'

'I know that.' Aunt Hesketh cast him a withering glance. 'But if she'd been here to do her share of the chores this week, instead of gallivanting about the Lord only knows where every morning …' Daniel flushed bright red, since Midori had been out training him, but his aunt seemed not to notice. 'Then Emma wouldn't have insisted on going down to the harbour by herself yesterday to choose the fish needed for pickling and salting. In this inclement weather, it was too much for her.'

'I thought she seemed a bit tired last night.' Daniel looked contrite, then took a deep breath. 'Why didn't you accompany her then? Or send the maid with her?'

'We were busy, no one could be spared. I told her it could wait for another day, but she would insist.'

Daniel and Midori went to see his mother together and were not cheered by what they found. Aunt Marston was lying in the canopied tester bed looking flushed and exhausted. The hangings on either side were drawn to keep out any draughts, and a roaring fire warmed the room, the heat almost stifling. It was clear from the beads of perspiration on her face that Aunt Marston was suffering from a very high temperature. Despite this, she was racked by chills so severe her teeth chattered in between the coughing bouts. Her thin body struggled visibly each time these spasms shook her and Midori and Daniel exchanged a worried glance.

The physician, when he arrived at last, pronounced Aunt Marston to be suffering from congestion of the lungs.

'She needs hot poultices,' he declared and charged an outrageous fee for this advice. He also recommended various other potions, which they obtained from the apothecary, but these didn't seem to have any effect. During the night the sick woman's condition worsened and everyone was kept awake listening to the incessant hacking cough. Midori finally dressed herself in her warmest clothes and went to see if she could be of assistance in the sickroom. Aunt Hesketh was there, as well as Uncle Marston, and they both turned grave faces in Midori's direction.

'Is there anything I can do?' she whispered. 'I have some skill with healing herbs.'

'No. She's already had a syrup of hyssop and it didn't help. It's in God's hands now,' Aunt Hesketh replied.

'But I helped the surgeon on board the ship, so I learned a thing or two. Surely, it would be worth a try?'

'You've done more than enough already, now go to bed,' her aunt hissed.

Midori looked to her uncle, but he seemed lost in a world of his own. 'Uncle Marston?'

'What?' He blinked at her, a confused look in his eyes. 'Have you come bearing more soup?'

'Well, no, but I can fetch some if you like.'

'Won't do any good,' Aunt Hesketh cut in. 'She'd only cough it back up.'

Midori stared at the figure in the bed and her heart sank. The scene reminded her so much of her mother's deathbed – the wan face with blue-tinged lips, the frail body and the thin hands on the coverlet. And that cough. Midori could almost feel the pain it must be causing her aunt. If only they'd let Midori help, she might be able to ease the suffering, but without permission she couldn't do anything.

'The flowers ... want them here ... so pretty ...'

'What's she saying?' Her uncle frowned and leaned closer, trying to catch his wife's words.

'It's nothing, she's delirious,' Aunt Hesketh said curtly.

Midori could see her uncle was, for once, unsure what to do. There was great affection between him and his wife, as was clear to anyone who saw them together. Now he was having trouble grasping the fact that his wife was likely dying. Midori put a hand on his arm to gain his attention. 'Would you like me to bring you something, Uncle? Some mulled wine, perhaps? You must have been sitting here for ages. And you can't expect to pray for Aunt Marston's recovery if you take a chill yourself.'

He turned to look at her as if he hadn't really seen her

before. His eyes focused slowly on her face and he managed a small smile. 'Yes, thank you, Midori. That would be kind.' He slowly slid down on to his knees by his wife's bedside. 'And of course I must pray. It's the only thing to be done now. You are so right.'

She slipped out of the room and padded down to the kitchen with a heavy heart. She didn't think any god could save her aunt now.

Aunt Marston only survived one more night. Temperance took the bad news stoically. She didn't cry, but clung hard to Midori's arm.

'It was God's will,' she repeated several times, as if imprinting the words on her memory. Midori knew it was what her father had told her, but wasn't sure her cousin believed this quite as wholeheartedly as Uncle Marston did. She knew from her own experience how lost and bewildered Temperance must be feeling. So she did her best to keep Temperance's thoughts busy in other ways.

Daniel retreated behind a façade of outward calm, and Midori wished there was something she could do to help him, but she knew the only thing that would heal the pain was time. And even that would only take the edge off it.

Aunt Hesketh kept shooting angry glances in Midori's direction. 'Punishment will be meted out where it's due by the good Lord,' she muttered.

'For heaven's sake, Aunt.' Daniel, uncharacteristically, spoke up in Midori's defence, sending his aunt an icy glare. 'My mother would have caught a chill whether Midori had accompanied her or not. And you know full well she'd never have allowed Midori to go on such an important errand by herself. She always chose the fish personally, to make sure she wasn't cheated and given inferior goods, even I know that.'

Aunt Hesketh looked surprised at her nephew's outburst, but walked away without replying. She didn't speak to Midori again until after the funeral, and even then it was only to issue orders.

Well, it wasn't my fault! But Midori decided now was not the time to pick a fight, so she did her best to ignore her aunt's bad-tempered behaviour.

Early February 1643

Nico was pleased to find Plymouth harbour seemingly unaffected by the war as yet. He personally oversaw the unloading of the provisions he'd brought and rented a secure warehouse near the quay to store them in. Then he went to call on Harding to enlist the man's help in finding suitable men to guard his goods.

As he walked in the direction of Harding's house he gazed at everything around him. Nothing about the town appeared to have changed noticeably. The people didn't look as if they had suffered any real hardship, despite the war that was now going on all around them, but there were hardly any smiling faces and he missed the contented expressions of the people of Amsterdam.

He couldn't help but wonder how all this had affected Midori.

'It's good to see you, sir.' Harding grinned in welcome. 'Have you been to see your relatives yet?'

'No, I've only just arrived. Do you know how they are?' Nico thought to himself that forewarned was forearmed. 'I assume there haven't been any disasters as you haven't sent me a message.'

'Well, I heard tell one of the ladies died recently ...'

Nico felt his insides twist as he waited for Harding's next words. Had something happened to Midori? Or had his words to the *Heeren XVII* been some kind of self-prophecy? *Dear Lord, but I wasn't wishing my stepmother dead!*

'… but it were one of the older ones, so I'm sure Mistress Midori is fine.'

'You don't know which one?'

'Sorry, no.'

'I'd best hurry up there to see, then. Will you be so kind as to find me guards for the warehouse, please?'

'Of course, right away, sir.'

Nico was glad nothing had happened to Midori, but the thought of any member of that family dying made him sad. Despite his long absence, he found he still cared about them, more than he liked to admit.

'I suppose it would serve me right if Kate *has* died,' he muttered, regretting the lie he'd told, but there was no taking it back now. He lengthened his stride to find out.

Chapter Twenty-Six

Midori was in the kitchen doing some baking. It was a job she liked. She found it soothing to bury her hands in the soft dough and pummel it into submission. She smiled to herself as she imagined the bread was her aunt's face and gave it an extra punch for good measure.

After Aunt Marston's death, the atmosphere of the house had changed overnight. Where before it had been a sombre, but fairly contented, place to live, now the solemnity took over entirely. With Aunt Hesketh in control of all aspects of housekeeping, everyone was ordered around with never a kind word and more often than not a harsh one. Aunt Marston had been softly spoken, while her sister-in-law had a voice like a general and expected the same kind of blind obedience.

'It's all so depressing,' Midori grumbled to Temperance. 'And why is everything always my fault?' She was usually the one who bore the brunt of her aunt's anger. 'Honestly, it's unbearable!'

But somehow she managed to cope, mostly thanks to her two cousins who helped her in subtle ways whenever Aunt Hesketh's back was turned. She would have loved to teach her aunt a lesson somehow, but punching the dough was the only outlet for her frustration at the moment.

As she shoved the bread into the oven and dusted off her hands, she heard knocking on the front door. Susan, the cook, and the two kitchen maids, were out on various errands and Aunt Hesketh was lying down, so Midori went to see who'd come calling.

'Hello, Midori.'

The deep, husky voice made her look up so fast she almost fell over. She blinked at the familiar figure standing outside the door. 'Nico!' Midori put a hand to her heart to stop it from leaving her body altogether. She took a step backwards to steady herself. 'What are you doing here? I mean …'

He looked the same as ever, apart from his clothes, which seemed more elaborate than anything he'd worn previously. Dressed in black from top to toe, apart from his shirt and hose, he resembled her English relatives. But unlike theirs his clothing was made of the costliest wool and his shirt was of silk which shimmered in the winter sunlight as he moved. She drank in the sight of him – the blue gaze, the sun-kissed hair, his tall, muscular frame – unable to believe her eyes. A warm feeling spread through her and she realised it was pure, unadulterated joy, just from seeing him. Without thinking, she smiled.

He grinned back and bowed with mock politeness. 'It's wonderful to see you, too,' he teased, gently.

'Of course it's nice to see you, but … why are you here? I didn't think you would come back.' For a foolish moment, she'd let herself hope he had come to take her away, but she knew that was merely wishful thinking. She had refused his proposal, so she was no longer his concern. *And I don't want to be! He's untrustworthy, remember? A liar. Or, at least, he didn't tell me the truth …* Her smile faded. She could never marry him, even if he had come back for her. Which he obviously hadn't, as his next words proved.

'I've come to do business with your uncle and to see how you all are, as I promised him back in August.' Nico's smile disappeared as well. 'But I hear I've come too late to attend a funeral. Who passed away? Was it my stepmother?'

'No, Aunt Marston.'

'Oh, poor woman,' Nico murmured. 'How did your uncle take it?'

'He's a bit quiet, but he believes she's in a better place now. Or so he says.'

'Ah, yes, I see.'

'So you're here to do business.' Midori tried to quell the disappointment she shouldn't be feeling, and hid her trembling hands in the folds of her apron. Seeing him so suddenly had made her lose her customary composure and she did her best to rectify that.

'Indeed. May I come in?' He raised his eyebrows at her.

She stepped aside and felt her cheeks heat up. 'Yes, of course, sorry.'

To her surprise, he headed for the kitchen instead of up the stairs and she followed him with a frown. 'What are you doing?'

He glanced at her apron and hands, which were covered in flour. 'I gather I've disturbed you at your baking, so I thought we could talk while you work. I can see the others later. Are you well?'

'I'm very well, thank you.'

'So what happened to Aunt Marston? Was it sudden?'

Midori told him, while busying herself with making up the dough for another loaf.

'So how long are you staying?' she ventured to ask.

'I'm not sure, it depends.'

This vague answer wasn't very satisfying, but it seemed to be all he was prepared to give her as he changed the subject. 'But I want to hear your news. How are you managing here? Have you become a Puritan through and through?' He looked her up and down and she became uncomfortably aware of the dismal clothes she was wearing and the cap she disliked so much. Compared to her lovely silk kimonos, these garments didn't exactly flatter her and for some reason it bothered her today.

'No, but I'm coping all right,' she told him, raising her chin slightly. She was annoyed with herself for feeling at a disadvantage. It shouldn't matter. It was what a person was

259

like on the inside that counted and Nico, of all people, had no right to judge her.

He narrowed his eyes at her for a moment, as if he'd have liked to question her further, then looked away. 'You've obviously done better than I thought.' After a short pause, he turned back to face her again and added, 'But you don't need to pretend with me, you know. I realise it can't have been easy for you and … well, perhaps now that I'm here I can help.'

Midori shrugged and reiterated, 'I'm used to everything now. Uncle and his family have been good to me. This is where I belong.'

Nico's gaze rested on her while he tilted his head slightly to the side and raised his eyebrows as if he didn't quite believe her. Midori stared him straight in the eyes to convince him of her sincerity. She meant what she said and if she was stretching the truth just a little, he didn't need to know that.

She thought back to the way they'd parted all those months ago and realised he hadn't mentioned that. He'd just walked in here, as if nothing had happened between them, seemingly sure of his welcome. From his words, she guessed he'd thought she would have been ready to throw herself on his mercy. *Then he doesn't know me at all.*

'I'd best go and give my condolences to your uncle,' he said. 'I shall see you later, no doubt.'

When he'd gone, Midori went back to her baking, pummelling the dough even harder than before. Life was full of surprises, but why did it all have to be so difficult?

As he walked away from the house later, Nico's feelings were in tumult. He was relieved Midori seemed healthy and well cared for, but he couldn't fail to notice the changes in her. At first he'd had trouble recognising the girl who opened the door as the Midori he knew. The dark grey, long-sleeved bodice and matching woollen petticoat made her blend in with her surroundings, the sombre hues relieved only by a white collar, coif and apron. Her beautiful hair was hidden away – *surely they wouldn't have cut it off?* – and for most of their conversation her face had been as solemn as her clothing.

Her eyes did light up at the sight of me, though. He'd received one of her dazzling smiles, which was wonderful, but she soon schooled her features into a non-committal expression. *What was she hiding?* Was she telling the truth or was she merely trying to allay his fears? *No, I'll be damned if she's as happy as she says she is.*

Harding met him down by the quay. 'What news, sir, of the young lady? Did you manage a word in private with her?'

'I did and she seems well enough.'

'But?' Harding had obviously heard the hesitation in his voice.

'It's probably nothing, but I can't help feeling there's something she's not telling me.'

'Well, I'm sure her uncle's drummed it into her she ain't s'posed to talk to men on her own. Like as not she was feelin' guilty.'

Nico clapped Harding on the back. The man had proved to be a faithful friend and he was very grateful, so he didn't want to burden him with his own gloomy thoughts. 'I'm sure you're right. I was just unsettled by seeing her again. She looked so different. Those clothes ...' He managed a smile. 'It's only on the surface, though, isn't it? Underneath she's still the same.'

'Sure and why wouldn't she be?'

'Well, I wouldn't like to think of her being mistreated.'

'I've seen no sign of that, the times I've caught sight of her. Always seems cheerful enough to me.'

'They're working her awfully hard. Her hands, all red and rough ...'

'Ah, but she's not the kind of lady to like sittin' around all day doin' nothin'. Don't you remember on the ship? Always keepin' herself busy with somethin'. And she'll not let them browbeat her, not her.'

'Yes, you're right,' Nico agreed. Midori had more spirit than any other woman he'd met. And that, unfortunately, would make his own task all the more difficult.

If she'd convinced herself she was happy here, how could he persuade her otherwise?

'So you've brought goods to trade? Not a bad idea at the moment, not bad at all.'

Nico had returned for dinner and, as Midori watched him surreptitiously, it almost felt as though he'd never gone away. The atmosphere round the table was vastly different, however, from the last meal he'd shared with them. His antagonism was gone and it seemed to her that her uncle was looking at Nico with an almost grudging respect. Adult to adult, not adult to sulky boy. It was a welcome change.

'I'm glad you think so. I was hoping you might want to help me find the right buyers,' Nico replied, adding with a small smile, 'with a percentage for your trouble, of course.'

At the thought of a profit, Uncle Marston seemed to come alive. Midori knew there was nothing he liked better than making money and she threw Nico a suspicious glance across the table. Was he deliberately trying to get into her uncle's good graces? And if so, why? He'd never cared before. Nico stared back and, when no one else was looking, he winked at her. Midori frowned. *What game is he playing now?*

He was nice to Aunt Hesketh, too, despite his stepmother's barbed comments about the fine wool of his outfit. 'I told you, I stole it,' Nico said to her with a grin that showed clearly he was joking. 'I'll go back and get some for you, too, shall I, if you like it so much?'

Aunt Hesketh was clearly flustered and looked as though she didn't know how to respond to such teasing. 'Really, Nicholas,' she muttered, but after the meal, when he produced a small gift for each of the 'ladies', as he called them, she seemed pleased.

'You know we don't hold with wearing trinkets,' she reproached him as she pulled a plain silver chain with a small, brown cross on it out of the bit of linen it had been tied into. 'And why are you buying us gifts anyway?'

'You reminded me last time I came that I should have done so. Have you now changed your mind?' Nico teased again, then added, 'It's a religious symbol and it's not of any great value. I picked it up in the Baltic, where you can find amber yourself just by wandering along the sea shore. I'm sure no one could object to something so plain. What do you think, Jacob?'

Her uncle, still in a good mood at the thought of profits to be gained from Nico's goods, gave his consent. 'It's not even shiny,' he agreed.

Midori opened her own little parcel and found what looked like a small, smooth lump of hardened sap hanging off an equally plain chain. Although it wasn't glittering like other jewels, she had a feeling Nico had underplayed its value nonetheless. When she held it up to the light, she could see a tiny flower trapped inside, as if frozen in time. She looked over at Temperance, who was exclaiming over her own necklace. As far as Midori could see, her cousin's was nothing but a polished piece of amber, although pretty when penetrated by sunlight. Temperance said nothing of there being anything inside.

'Yours is special,' Nico said quietly behind her, his voice audible only to her. 'But please don't tell anyone or they'll take it away. Shall I help you with the fastening?'

Midori didn't know what to say. The fact that he'd singled her out in this way made her feel flustered and she wasn't sure she should accept such a gift from him. If she didn't, though, she would have to explain herself and that would never do, either. She hesitated for a moment, then said, 'Thank you.' She handed him the chain and he quickly put it on for her. The brief touch of his fingers on her neck sent a spark shimmering down her spine and Midori had to stop herself from making a sound. She thought he lingered a tiny while longer than he should, but then he moved away to help his stepmother as well, without saying anything else.

Nico took his leave soon after, and Midori was left to wonder once again what he was up to. For she could clearly see he was waging some sort of campaign – the profit for her uncle and the trinkets for the women were only the beginning, she was sure.

What would he do next?

Nico was pleased Midori had accepted his gift, even if she'd done so reluctantly. For once, she'd let down her guard and showed her emotions clearly. He'd read confusion and surprise in her eyes, which was what he'd hoped for. Catching her off balance was the only way to see her true feelings, and that had been his purpose. He had to know if there was any way he could redeem himself in her eyes. If she could forgive him.

Only then could he ask her once again to marry him.

I was a complete idiot the first time I asked her. He should have known he'd been doomed to failure because once Midori decided on something, she stuck with it no matter what. He'd only made matters worse by kissing her, he could see that now. With any other woman, he knew he could have cajoled them into forgiving him for whatever misdeeds they considered he'd done. Midori was different.

Once her good opinion was lost, it would be hard to regain. And he had lost it, no doubt about that. She'd made it clear she didn't trust him; thought him dishonourable and a liar. She wasn't like other women, she couldn't simply be charmed or persuaded by gifts and attention, although he was hoping that might help, hence the amber. She lived by different values and a strict code of conduct. And she wasn't ruled by emotion. *Or at least, not much.*

Nico smiled to himself as he made his way up the hill towards Jacob's house the following day. 'Oh, but she's not as unaffected as she'd like to pretend,' he murmured. That dazzling smile, when he'd caught her by surprise with his sudden arrival, and the frequent glances she cast his way, were proof of that. Not to mention the way she'd reacted to his kisses in the past.

'And you may be stubborn, my lady Midori,' he whispered to himself, 'but I can be equally so. Perseverance is the key. Let the battle commence.'

He arrived just as Midori and her two cousins were leaving the house, all carrying shovels or small pickaxes. 'Good morning,' Nico said, raising his eyebrows at this sight. 'Where are you all off to?'

'Building earthworks,' Daniel said. 'Everyone has to help. You're welcome to come along, Coz.' He looked at Nico's clothing and smiled. 'Although you probably won't want to get that fancy coat dirty.'

Nico grinned back and pretended to cuff the youngster. 'I might join you later. For now, I've got business with your father to attend to and trust me, my "fancy coat" is necessary for that. Where will you be?'

'Near Maudlin, at the moment.'

Nico found them all there some time later, hard at work. He'd changed into scruffier clothes and was fully prepared to do a bit of digging, if that would help improve Midori's image of him. Jacob had told him airily that 'everyone was at it', but Nico was taken aback.

'Bloody hell,' he muttered, looking around. 'I didn't realise the sheer scale of these earthworks.' He was also surprised at the numbers of people helping out and how much they'd built already.

'Yes, impressive, isn't it?' Daniel said, leaning on his shovel as he took a short break. 'But necessary. The Cornishmen could be back any day now so we're adding to what we built last year.'

'It's really as bad as that?' Nico was serious now and drew Daniel to one side. 'I'd thought reports of this civil war exaggerated on the Continent.'

'I'm afraid not.' Daniel filled him in on what had been happening. 'We heard there were reinforcements coming this way, but our Colonel, Ruthven, decided to march into Cornwall without waiting for them. It was a disaster and there've been wounded people streaming back these last few days. I'm sure the Royalists will soon come and besiege us again.'

Nico digested this. It would seem he'd arrived just in time. He glanced at Midori, working diligently side by side with the others, and felt a protective instinct rise within him. *I must get her out of here and fast. The others, too.* Although judging by the determination with which Daniel attacked the earthworks, he guessed he might find it difficult to persuade them to come. Still, one thing at a time. First, he'd work on softening Midori towards him, then she could help him talk the others into leaving. He nodded at Daniel. 'Thank you for telling me,' he said. 'Are there any spare shovels?'

It looked as though he was going to have to dig his way into Midori's heart.

Chapter Twenty-Seven

May 1643

It didn't work.

After kicking his heels in Plymouth for several months, Nico had to concede that his charm offensive simply wasn't working and he was getting tired of the cat-and-mouse game.

Damn, but she's a stubborn woman!

Frustration was eating him up from inside. He was sure Midori was still attracted to him, even if she refused to admit it. Every so often he caught her glancing his way, but when he looked back, she'd turn away quickly. In his experience, that signified interest, but somehow he could never get her alone in order to advance any further. She'd become very adept at keeping her other cousins nearby and she ignored any direct requests for a private word with her or laughed them off as if he'd been joking. And a lot of the time she was nowhere to be found. Nico had no idea where she spent her days, but it certainly wasn't with him.

'Where the hell does she disappear off to?' he muttered.

And how was he supposed to show her he was truly sorry for deceiving her if she wouldn't even talk to him? *I have to find a way.*

But she continued to evade him.

I might as well go and fight in this infernal war, for all the good it's doing me to stay here. But Nico considered wars futile, this one especially, and had no interest in defending either party.

It didn't take him and Jacob long to sell the goods he'd brought, and after that he found himself at a loose end. He'd joined the others in helping to build earthworks, but when that came to a temporary halt he was left with nothing to do again. There wasn't even any fighting to join in, because although the town was briefly under siege during the month of February, that soon ended without any real skirmishes.

'Hah, the Royalists haven't so much as ruffled our feathers,' Jacob gloated. 'Thought they'd cause us hardship, did they? Well, they'll have to think again.'

And it was true, because the Royalists couldn't control the sea front. They tried their best to stop ships going in and out of Plymouth harbour, but their gun batteries along the shore never quite managed it. Out of sheer boredom, Nico went on a couple of short trading journeys on Jacob's behalf. He'd sent the Dutch ship back to Amsterdam soon after his arrival, but Jacob had his own ships which he allowed Nico to captain. Trying to evade the Royalists added spice to an otherwise very dull existence, but come May, he'd had enough.

This isn't why I came to Plymouth.

That morning he'd been helping Jacob fill in some ledgers. The old man's eyesight wasn't as good as it had once been, so he seemed grateful for some assistance. Thanks to the trading ventures, a tentative bond had begun to build between them, although they were both still slightly reserved in each other's company. Neither spoke about the past any longer; it was a subject best forgotten.

'Daniel should be doing the ledgers, but he never seems to be here these days,' Jacob grumbled. 'Those infernal earthworks. You'd think there couldn't be any more to dig by now.'

There weren't, as Nico well knew, but he didn't tell Jacob that. If Daniel wanted his father to think he was out digging somewhere, he had to have a reason for it and Nico didn't tell tales. Daniel was another elusive character, who was seldom to be found. Nico wasn't sure what the youth was up to, but he suspected it had to do with the fighting and he didn't want to make trouble for him. He'd seen the light in Daniel's eyes when he spoke of defending the town and their rights, and it was obvious he was obsessed with joining the army. *Young fool! Who in their right mind wants to fight a war?*

'I believe the earthworks will become necessary soon again,' Nico commented. 'I heard only this morning that the truce is over.' A temporary cessation of hostilities had been agreed between Devon and Cornwall during March, but it obviously hadn't lasted and Nico thought it best to warn Jacob as it would affect trade again.

'Oh, wonderful, that's all we need,' Jacob muttered. 'What else have you heard?' When Nico hesitated, his stepuncle fixed him with a glare. 'Might as well tell me so I'm forewarned.'

'The Earl of Stamford has apparently decided to lead an army into Cornwall,' Nico told him reluctantly. He wondered if Daniel would run away to join up and if there was any way Jacob could stop him. Nico and the old man both knew someone as inexperienced as Daniel wouldn't stand much chance in a real battle. He'd be slaughtered.

Jacob sighed and rubbed his face, as if he was tired of all his responsibilities. 'It's not easy being a father,' he said with a sigh, then looked Nico in the eye. 'I know I have no right to ask, but is there any chance you could have a word with Daniel, try to talk some sense into him? He might listen to you, I know he likes you. If we were really threatened, I realise he'd have to fight, but to go on a wild goose chase to Cornwall ...' His voice tailed off and he sounded so forlorn, Nico put out a hand to squeeze Jacob's arm.

'I'll try, but he's young and hot-headed. He may not listen to me. I'll catch him when he leaves the house tomorrow morning; see if I can get him to talk to me, at least.'

Jacob nodded. 'Thank you. I appreciate the attempt at any rate.'

Daniel's fighting skills had definitely improved and Midori was beginning to think she'd reached the point where she had nothing more to teach him. With the excuse of digging earthworks, they'd had more time of late to sneak off, but as she slipped out of the house the back way once again, she decided to tell Daniel to practise by himself from now on. Any day now, Uncle Marston would find out the earthworks were recently finished.

She joined Daniel at their usual meeting place, several streets away from the house, and they walked in silence towards the deserted part of the coast where they'd found a private spot in which to train.

'So what are we doing today?' Daniel asked, eager as always.

Midori worried that he hadn't understood the seriousness of what he was learning. She felt like shouting at him that she was teaching him to kill other human beings and it wasn't a game, but she knew that wouldn't accomplish anything. She'd prepared him as best she could, the rest was up to fate.

Instead she replied, 'Just practising the moves I showed you yesterday.' She took a deep breath. 'Really, I don't think you need me any more. It's just a question of increasing your stamina now and improving your reflexes. You had better do that on your own. I daren't continue to leave the house so often.'

They had reached the shore, and Daniel stopped and took her hands in his, looking at her earnestly. 'You're right and I can't thank you enough for helping me. I feel so much less ... inadequate now. Really, I thank you.'

Midori smiled at him and didn't resist when he pulled her into an awkward embrace. She'd become very fond of him and was pleased he felt he could hug her like a sister at last. She was about to say he was welcome, when a cold voice cut in.

'Well, well, this is very touching. I'd never have guessed if I hadn't seen it with my own eyes. No wonder you were both absent so much – now I see why.'

Midori couldn't stop a gasp from escaping her lips, and she turned her head to stare at Nico, who came walking towards them. Belatedly, she let go of Daniel and stepped away from him.

Nico stopped in front of them, scowling mightily and with his eyes narrowed. 'So how long has this been going on? And there's Jacob thinking you're both shovelling dirt. As for me, I don't know how I could be so blind!'

'It's not what you think,' Daniel said. 'That's to say ...' He looked at Midori as if asking permission to tell Nico what they'd really been doing. She nodded, so he continued. 'Midori's been teaching me self-defence and fighting techniques. Look, we can show you.'

But Nico wasn't really listening, it seemed. His gaze was boring into Midori's. 'A likely excuse, I'm sure.'

His sarcastic tone made her see red and for once she let her emotions get the upper hand. She put her hands on her hips and glared back at him. 'Well, it's more than you're doing to protect your family,' she accused. 'I don't see you doing anything to defend the town, apart from a little bit of digging. If we were all murdered in our beds, you'd just sail away, wouldn't you?' She knew that was unfair, but she was so angry now she didn't care.

'Is that what you believe?' Nico took a step closer, his eyes dark sapphire slivers that shot angry sparks in the sunlight. 'You really think so little of me?'

'Like I said, I haven't seen you taking up arms on behalf of your clan.' Midori stood her ground. Daniel, wisely, kept silent.

'For the last time, Midori, we don't *have* clans here, not the way you mean. I thought you understood that by now?'

'Uncle Marston and your stepmother ...'

'They're sort of my kin, yes, and I was going to offer to take you all back to Amsterdam to keep you safe, but nothing else. This isn't my fight. I don't give a damn whether King Charles or Parliament wins, so why should I go and kill people in the name of either of them? Why should you?'

'Because it's the honourable thing to do. And you'd only be killing to defend your family.' Midori clenched her fists by her side to keep from hitting him herself. Why couldn't he understand? It was a simple enough code of conduct to live by.

'Oh, we're back to that again, are we? You don't think I have any honour because I withheld some information from you. For heaven's sake, I thought I'd apologised enough for that!'

'It's not an apology I want,' Midori hissed. 'I wanted you to show me what kind of man you are. Words are just that, words. And gifts and charm are all very well, but they don't amount to much if there's no sincerity behind them.'

She saw a muscle jump in Nico's jaw, as if he'd clenched his teeth really hard. 'I see. All right, you want me to go and get myself killed, just to show you I'm honourable and sincere. Very well, have it your way. I'll leave for Cornwall this afternoon. Not that it matters now, anyway. I wish you luck with your marriage.' He turned to point at Daniel. 'And don't you dare follow me, because one pointless death in the family will be enough.'

'What? I—'

'Nico, don't be an idiot.' Midori took a step forward and tried to grab his arm, but he wrenched it loose and started striding off. 'I don't want you to fight anyone just to prove a point,' she shouted after him. 'It doesn't mean anything if it doesn't come from the heart; if it's not your own choice.'

But he wasn't listening, obviously, as he just continued on his way. Midori sank down on to the sand and covered her face with her hands. Hot tears pricked her eyelids, but she refused to let them fall. Nico wasn't worth it. Besides, he'd soon come to his senses when he calmed down. Wouldn't he?

Daniel knelt next to her and said as much, adding, 'I don't know how he could have misunderstood so. It's not as if I've ever made sheep's eyes at you. You're too old for me.'

Midori had to smile at that, even if she felt her smile wobble slightly. 'Thank you, Daniel, that's very reassuring,' she said dryly. 'I hadn't realised I was quite that ancient.'

Daniel grinned back and pulled her close for a hug. 'I was only joking, but I'm sure you know I see you only as a sister. I wish I'd known that Nico doesn't feel the same way. Perhaps I could have helped.'

Midori shook her head. 'No, you couldn't. As I told him, he had to prove his worth to me himself, but not this way ...'

As she thought of him going off to battle she had to fight harder than she ever had before to keep the tears at bay. It was up to fate what happened now; all she could do was pray.

'*Bakajaro!*' she muttered. 'Stupid, stupid fool of a man ...'

But perhaps he was the one who was right? Doubt entered her mind. She'd been in England long enough now to know that not everyone here fought to the death for their beliefs, and honour wasn't as sacred as in her country of birth. She thought of Aunt Hesketh and Temperance – what would happen to them if war broke out properly here in Plymouth? And Uncle Marston, who was too old for fighting?

I've been selfish! She'd been thinking only from her own perspective, whereas Nico hadn't. He'd said he was going to take them all to Amsterdam and safety.

It would have saved their lives. Instead ... who knows what will happen?

'Oh, Daniel, what a mess I've made of things.' She leaned her head on his shoulder and for once felt she needed his strength, not the other way round.

'It will be all right, you'll see,' he said. 'I'm sure of it.'

But Midori no longer believed that.

The anger carried Nico through the following weeks. It was as if he existed in a freezing fog, where nothing seemed real. Enlisting, marching with the army into Cornwall, sleeping on the ground, being filthy and hungry a lot of the time – it hardly registered. He fought in a battle at Stratton in North Cornwall, where the Parliamentarians were soundly defeated, but afterwards he couldn't remember much about it. All he knew was that he survived, although why he was spared when he was one of the few men who didn't care whether he lived or died, he'd never know.

In his mind it was all just a nightmare vision of blood, smoke, screams and the ear-splitting sounds of muskets and cannon. When it was over, he trudged back again all the way to Exeter with what was left of Stamford's army. Despite his inattention, and even though he'd thrown himself into the thick of the fighting, Nico barely received a scratch. It was as if fate was laughing at him.

Midori wants me to show her I can fight for my clan, but when I do, I don't have a single wound to show for it. It made hysterical laughter bubble up in his throat and he realised he needed to get a grip on himself. He looked around and came to the conclusion he had no idea where they were.

'Are we stopping at Plymouth?' he asked the man walking closest to him.

'Plymouth? No, passed that two days ago. They'll have to fend for theirselves, the good Lord help 'em.' The man peered at him. 'Are ye feelin' all right? Hit over the head, were ye?'

'No, I'm well, thank you.'

The man's words jolted Nico out of his numb state enough

for him to start listening to what was being said around him from then on. He gathered Plymouth was cut off from the main Parliamentary forces, the ones he was with, and there was no one to come to their aid. With a sinking feeling, Nico realised Midori had been right and he should have stayed there to fight, but it was too late now.

Midori and the others were on their own and there wasn't a thing he could do about it. Even if he tried to go back, he'd never get through into the town.

Damnation!

'I don't understand it,' Uncle Marston was heard muttering in the days after Nico's departure. 'I thought he was finally acquiring some sense. I did ask him to … but never mind. Perhaps this was his way of helping me.'

Midori exchanged a look with Daniel, but neither mentioned the encounter with Nico. There seemed no point and they soon had other things to worry about. News of the Royalist victory filtered through and everyone knew what that meant – they'd soon be under attack again.

And what about Nico, had he survived? They had no way of knowing.

'You're wanted for more building work. And we're all to be "assessed" for the charges. It's outrageous, is what it is,' her uncle told them one evening. 'Some busybody came to inform me this afternoon.'

Midori wasn't surprised and all through the following weeks she and Daniel, together with Temperance, laboured yet again on the new stone-fronted revetment and parapet being added to the original earthworks to strengthen them. Midori hardly noticed what she was doing, however, as her thoughts kept returning to the image of Nico storming off. *I should have followed him and explained properly. Why didn't I? And how could he reach such a silly conclusion? As if I'd ever want to marry Daniel!* Although she was only two years older than him, she felt vastly more mature and looked on him as a younger brother. Marriage to him was such a ludicrous idea, she didn't know how Nico could have believed it for even a moment.

And yet he had and now he was gone. *And it's all my fault.*

She had nightmare visions of him lying dead in a field somewhere and she knew if only she'd been with him, she could have helped keep him safe. She mentioned this to Daniel, who was working next to her as usual.

'So I was right,' he commented. 'You're as smitten with Nicholas as he is with you.'

Midori shook her head. 'No, he had his chance and he didn't want me. Then he changed his mind, out of some misguided sense of chivalry, and for some reason, because I said no, he decided he wanted me after all. It's complicated.' She sighed.

'I'd say!' Daniel looked bewildered. 'But I think you're wrong. If he hadn't been in love with you, why would it have bothered him to think you and I were a courting couple?'

'I don't know. He's just perverse and obstinate and ...' *the man I love.* She couldn't deny it to herself, but it didn't change anything. He still wasn't the man for her. It didn't stop her worrying, though.

'He'll soon be back,' was Daniel's verdict. 'Like he said, why would he want to fight for something he doesn't believe in? And don't worry about him, he's always had the devil's own luck. Father says so.'

Midori sincerely hoped that for once her uncle would be proved right. The alternative didn't bear thinking of.

Chapter Twenty-Eight

July 1643

Nico had never been to Wiltshire before, but at the beginning of July he found himself outside the little town of Devizes on the edge of Salisbury Plain. It was being held by the Royalists, but the Parliamentarian commander Nico was now following was determined to change this state of affairs.

'Shouldn't be too difficult, by the looks of it,' Nico heard a soldier nearby telling a friend. 'No fortifications whatsoever that I can see. We'll flush 'em out like rabbits in a hole.'

Nico wasn't so sure. By now he'd understood that the commanders of each army were determined men who did nothing without considering carefully first. There had to be a reason the King's men refused to budge and this proved to be the case.

A short siege of the town yielded little result and on the morning of the thirteenth unwelcome news arrived.

'They've reinforcements coming, cavalry from Oxford, so they say. We're marching to Roundway Down.' The message was passed along through the ranks and Nico set off with the others, shouldering his pack and the musket he'd now become expert at loading and firing. Roundway Down turned out to be a hill on the northern side of town, and it wasn't all that far.

'We've got the high ground, the best position,' someone gloated as they prepared for battle, but despite this, the day soon turned into a bloodbath with the Parliamentarians as the losers yet again.

Nico was in the thick of things, firing his musket and moving in for close-up fighting with the bayonet fixed to the end of the weapon and his sword as back-up. It was brutal and gory, like a horrendous nightmare come true, but Nico tried not to think about what he was doing. That way lay madness. Instead, he focused on his opponents – his enemies, as he had to remind himself repeatedly – and just did what he had to in order to survive.

The musket and cannon balls he couldn't do anything about; they took men's lives randomly and without discrimination. Only luck kept those away from him. But the men coming towards him, intent on killing him at all costs, he could and did defend himself against. Time and again he fought back when they charged at him. And he protected his comrades-in-arms as best he could. The fact that they were all Englishmen and he had no real reason to be killing them was a thought best buried deep inside his mind.

This time the Royalists had brought what seemed like thousands of mounted men, who made short work of scattering their foes. Especially those who, like Nico, were on foot. The Parliamentarians ended up in disarray and on the run.

'Retreat, retreat!'

Nico heard the command through ears that were half-deafened by the noise from the cannon, and followed his comrades as they ran through clouds of dust and smoke.

How long will this go on for? Will it ever end, he wondered. No one seemed to know.

August–November 1643

As Midori listened to her uncle and everyone else of note in Plymouth swear a covenant to *'faithfully maintain and defend the towns of Plymouth and Stonehouse'* and not *'accept any pardon or protection from the enemy'*, she wondered where Nico was and if he regretted his hasty decision as much as she berated herself for goading him.

Why did I say those things? I had no right. All through the long, hot summer and the shorter days of autumn, she'd waited and hoped for him to come to his senses and return, but in vain.

'The son of a friend of mine, who's come home to recover from wounds, tells me he saw Nicholas marching with his comrades towards Bristol after the battle of Roundway Down,' her uncle had reported at the end of July. 'But Bristol is now being besieged by the Royalists, so we must assume Nicholas is stuck there.' It was the only news they had of him.

Temperance grew quiet and withdrawn and Midori noticed the girl followed her like a shadow wherever she went, as if Midori was her only security in a world gone mad.

'Are you all right?' she asked her cousin one morning, as Temperance sat staring into space instead of plying her needle as she should.

'What? Oh, yes, I suppose so.'

Midori shook her head. 'You're scared, aren't you?'

Temperance nodded and tears welled up in her eyes. 'It's all so, so ... horrid! I don't know if I can stand much more.'

'I know.' Midori went over to embrace her cousin. At nearly fourteen, she was growing quickly, but her shoulders still felt fragile. 'But you don't need to be anxious, I won't let any harm come to you. Shall I tell you a secret?'

'P-please.'

Midori told her about being able to fight and what she and Daniel had been doing down by the coast. 'So you see, we'll defend you if need be. There's nothing to worry about.' That wasn't strictly true, and they both knew it, but Midori could see she had reassured her cousin a little.

'Thank you, I'm so glad you're here.' Temperance managed a tremulous smile. 'I wish I was brave like you.'

'I'm sure you can be. I have faith in you. And you'll see, when it really matters, you will find the necessary courage. We all do if we have no choice. Now, please don't worry; at the moment we're safe.'

If only I knew that Nico was safe, too!

'Don't fret, Nicholas probably couldn't make his way into the town even if he wanted to.' Daniel, kind as always, tried to reassure Midori.

'I know, you're right.'

From September onwards they'd been under siege again. A substantial number of Cavalier troops arrived, but although there was a lot of skirmishing and raiding, neither side made any serious moves against the other. News eventually filtered through that Bristol had in fact fallen to the Royalists under Prince Maurice, the King's nephew, but still Nico didn't return. Midori began to fear the worst, but kept herself occupied so she wouldn't have time to think about it.

More men were needed every day and the Parliamentarian army began to resort to impressments. No one was safe and, during the sermon on the second Sunday in October, the impressment officers flung open the doors of the church the Marston family attended and marched in, interrupting the minister in mid-flow.

'What is the meaning of this?' he squeaked, dropping the Bible he'd been holding.

'We've come for all the able-bodied men,' the leader said. 'Everyone must do their duty now, else the town will fall into the hands of the Papist Royalists. Any volunteers?'

Daniel was the first to stand up, and to his credit he didn't throw his father a triumphant glance. Instead he nodded at Midori and the others, and slid out of the pew to join the waiting men. His father bent his head and Midori heard him send up a prayer for his son's safety, but he made no protest. Perhaps he had finally accepted the inevitability of this war or maybe he simply took it as his god's will, since it had happened at church. Others soon followed Daniel, some young and some old, and the group was about twenty strong by the time they clattered out of the building.

A hush descended on the congregation after the double doors slammed shut, and all that could be heard was the occasional snuffle as someone's mother or wife tried not to weep too openly.

'Well then.' The minister cleared his throat repeatedly. 'I think some extra prayers may be in order. Let us start with the Lord's own words ...'

Temperance clutched Midori's hand and she could feel the girl trembling. Midori squeezed it back, trying to reassure her young cousin yet again. Then she bent her head and prayed to every god she could think of, including her uncle's, that the skills she'd taught Daniel would stand him in good stead now.

Nico picked up the quill and dipped it in the ink well, but when he put it to the paper, the only thing that appeared was a dark blob.

'Hell and damnation,' he muttered.

'What's the matter, Noordholt, can't find the words to express your undying love?' his comrade, John Stephens, teased. Nico threw him a warning glare, but knew that wouldn't stop the young man.

They'd become friends, or rather fellow sufferers, since the battle of Roundway Down, when Nico had helped the youth flee the field after he'd sustained an injury to his leg. Nico had half-dragged, half-carried Stephens, surprising himself with his determination to save at least one person from the carnage.

At the time he hadn't stopped to rationalise his actions, but he'd reflected afterwards that it was probably because Stephens was so young – only eighteen – and he reminded Nico of himself as a youngster. He had his life before him and Nico wanted him to be able to live it to the full, not die needlessly on some battlefield.

'I'm not writing a love letter,' he said, trying to make his voice sound stern in order to discourage more teasing. 'I merely thought to let my relatives know I'm still alive and likely to come home and plague them once this wretched conflict is over.'

Stephens grinned. 'Nah, you don't fool me. No one would find it that hard to write such a simple message. It's the lover's notes that take time.'

'Much you know about it and you've never met my stepuncle,' Nico said.

'Perhaps not, but I'd wager he's not the person you were thinking of when your eyes went all dreamy like.'

Nico threw the quill at Stephens, who ducked with a gurgle of laughter. They'd been billeted in someone's house, probably against the owner's will – five men in a cramped room, but at the moment only the two of them were there. The others had gone in search of whores, but this held no appeal for Nico and Stephens was still inexperienced when it came to women, so he'd made some excuse to stay behind.

'Be off with you, boy. Find something better to do than annoying me when I'm trying to compose a serious missive.' But he felt a reluctant smile tugging at the corner of his mouth. It was impossible to be angry with Stephens for long.

'Want to tell me what happened? Did she spurn your advances? Or is she waiting faithfully for you somewhere?' Stephens lobbed the quill back at Nico, who caught it in mid-air.

He sighed and turned away. 'Neither. I don't wish to discuss it.'

'Oh, that bad, eh? Well, she'd have to be made of stone to withstand your charm when you set your mind to it. I've seen you, beguiling the washer-women into doing your laundry at half the price.'

Nico closed his eyes. Midori wasn't made of stone, but certainly sterner stuff than the camp followers. She had principles, ideals, and he could never live up to them. *So why am I trying to write her a letter?*

He'd had a lot of time to reflect lately and realised he'd been a fool, jumping to conclusions. Midori hadn't contradicted Daniel when he said she was training him. *But they were embracing, damn it!* There had been something so tender about the scene he'd interrupted he'd been sure they were lovers. And it had made him lose all reason.

They could have been in love. Daniel was more Midori's age and he was a nice boy, even Nico had to admit that. Daniel would never deceive her and he was honourable, just like she wanted. He wouldn't lie and he'd sworn there was nothing going on. *I should have at least listened, let them explain …*

Nico slammed the quill down on to the small table and got up to pace the room. *What does it matter now?* If he survived this war and if Midori wasn't married by then, perhaps he'd try one last time to win her. But at the moment he was stuck here and, having fought alongside the men in his troop, there was no way he could abandon them now. They were his friends, almost like family, and he'd defend them to his last breath. To leave them would be dishonourable in the extreme.

Midori had been right about that and, even if she never found out, he was determined to prove himself this time.

The Royalist forces encamped outside Plymouth consisted of nearly ten thousand men, an awesome sight which made the defenders brace themselves behind their fortifications. Midori wondered how the town could possibly withstand such huge numbers of besiegers, but although one vicious engagement followed another that autumn, they managed to hold out.

If only I could offer my services, she thought. She was sorely tempted, but knew it was impossible. She was needed at home. Aunt Hesketh had slumped into some sort of dark despair after venturing out to see the enemy lines for herself, leaving most of the household duties to Midori and Temperance.

'Why don't you make yourself useful for a change?' she sneered at Midori. 'I need to rest.'

Midori bit her tongue and held back an angry reply, as always. 'No point arguing with her,' Midori told her cousin, who was growing into a proper young lady now, tall and with budding curves. 'Thank goodness I have you and Susan to help, as well as one maid.' The other one had gone home to be with her family. 'Mind you, by rights, you should be running this household, not me, as you know a lot more about it.'

Temperance only smiled and shook her head. 'No, I don't want to be in charge. You're better at that.'

Midori's housekeeping skills may be improving, but she still longed to run off and join Daniel. It would have been good to put into practice all the training they'd done together and help keep him safe. Instead, she had to spend all day cooped up in a house filled with tension, while listening to the booming of cannons and tattoo of drums in the distance and watching Temperance jump at the sounds. The impotence of her situation made her want to scream.

The people in the town were suffering now. The Royalists had cut off part of the water supply and there were food shortages which hit the population hard. Illness was rife and she heard the minister telling someone he was conducting almost seven times the normal amount of burials.

'One hundred and thirty-two souls I buried last month,' the man had said, shaking his head at such an incredible number, 'where normally there would be no more than twenty or so.'

It was not the kind of news Midori wanted to hear.

'What are we going to do, Midori?'

Midori felt Temperance grip her arm as the two of them gazed at the empty shelves of the larder.

'There isn't enough here to survive even a few weeks, let alone the entire winter,' Temperance complained. They had some flour, half a barrel of salted fish, a small sack of dried peas, one smoked ham and a dozen or so chickens scratching around in the garden, but no vegetables of any kind, apart from onions, and the butter and cheese was all gone. 'We can't kill too many chickens or we won't have eggs, either. And I'm so sick of fish broth! There must be something we can have with it, surely?'

'I've tried to buy other foodstuffs in town, but there's not much to be had.' Midori had resorted to bribery, using her precious silver, but even that hadn't had much effect. 'We must hope the siege is broken soon, or that food supplies reach us some other way. In the meantime, I think I have an idea ... Let's go down to the shore. Bring a basket.'

'The shore? In this weather? Whatever for?'

'To gather food, of course.'

'Not more fish, please! I swear I'll turn into one soon ...'

Midori smiled. 'No, we're not going fishing. Come, I'll show you.'

Well wrapped up in shawls and cloaks against the bitter wind coming in off the sea, they trudged down to the shore

285

and made their way to the outskirts of the town. Midori kept her eyes open for any possible attacks, but these were unlikely as most of the skirmishing took place on the northern side of the defences.

'What exactly are we looking for, then?' Temperance's cheeks were red, but Midori decided it suited her and made a welcome change from the winter pallor of most other days.

'Seaweed.'

'What? You're not serious?'

'Of course I am. Certain types are edible, you know, and quite tasty.' Midori smiled at her cousin. 'After all, you've made me eat all manner of strange things since I arrived here. Surely it must be your turn to try something different?'

'I suppose so, but are you sure?'

Midori pulled off her shoes and stockings and waded into the freezing cold water, which fortunately was at low tide. She knew she was right and there should be edible sea plants here, but they would be different to the kinds she'd eaten in Japan, so she wasn't sure she'd be able to find any. *I've no idea which ones are safe to eat, but I'm not telling Temperance that.* She spotted a large, coarse type of a brown hue, its huge fronds divided into flat fingers, which looked similar to one she'd had in Japan. 'This one should be good.' She cut some with a sharp knife and handed it to Temperance to put in their baskets.

'Tangleweed? But it looks so ... so ... slimy.' Temperance made a face.

'Well, so does cabbage when it's been cooked. Once you're used to the texture, it'll be all right. There's not much taste to it other than salt. Oh, and this, this is wonderful.' Midori cut a different type of seaweed, this one much longer and more pointy, which she definitely recognised.

'Dabberlocks,' Temperance muttered. 'Really?'

'Well, we'll check with the local fishermen just to make sure I haven't made a mistake, but these should be good.'

All in all, the expedition was successful and when later Midori served fish soup with seaweed, Temperance whispered that it was most definitely edible and an improvement on their previous meal.

Aunt Hesketh seemed less impressed. 'Has Susan burned the cabbage again? You're not much good at overseeing her work, are you, niece?'

Midori, to whom this remark was aimed, tried not to take offence as she didn't want to tell the others what they were eating. 'It tastes all right to me.'

'Yes, well, perhaps to a heathen it does.'

The look of venom that accompanied this sally was sharp enough to sting, but once again Midori did her best not to react. *Aunt Hesketh is just terrified out of her wits. She doesn't know what she's saying.*

But there was no denying she still hated Midori. *If only I knew why!*

Daniel arrived home a few days later, out of breath and obviously full of news. 'You'll never guess what's occurred,' he panted. 'Prince Maurice has offered us all a pardon if we surrender.'

'Oh, well that's good, isn't it?' Temperance breathed a sigh of relief, her expression hopeful, but her brother turned on her.

'Are you mad? Why should we give in to those Papists?'

'Because we would like to live, perhaps?' Temperance had learned to stand up for herself a little, Midori noted, which was encouraging. 'And they're not really Papists; that's just propaganda.'

Daniel ignored her sarcasm. 'Much you know about it. We'd sooner burn the town to the ground ourselves than give way to their ridiculous demands, or so my commanding officer says,' he announced, proudly. 'We're more stout-hearted than they think.'

Prince Maurice was not impressed with such bravery, however, and was seen to be preparing for a major attack. There was an air of anticipation hanging over both camps and Midori watched covertly whenever she was able to escape from the house. It wouldn't be long now, she reckoned, and she wanted to be prepared. She took to hiding one of her swords under her skirts and made sure a sharp knife was strapped to her leg at all times. She also made Temperance carry a dagger, just in case.

'I wouldn't want you to be defenceless,' she told her, and showed her cousin the best ways of using this tiny weapon, should the need arise. 'You'll have the element of surprise on your side, so you must be prepared to use it to best advantage.'

But would any of them stand a chance?

December 1643–January 1644

Several battles were fought, but Daniel had been right and the town was rewarded for not giving up. The year ended on an extremely positive note.

'He's gone. Prince Maurice is gone!' Daniel reported joyfully. 'Rode away today, on Christmas Day would you believe, even though he'd apparently promised his men they'd be in Plymouth by then. What a wonderful Yuletide gift for us!'

'Let us give thanks to the good Lord,' her uncle said. 'Now perhaps we can get on with our lives.'

'There's still not enough to eat,' Temperance muttered. 'Will we be able to obtain more food soon, Daniel?'

Daniel's joy faded a little. 'To be honest, I'm not sure there's any to be had. I'll keep my eyes open, though.'

Dear Ichiro,

I apologise for the fact that I have not written to you for quite some time, but I did not think my letters would have any chance of reaching you in any case and I have not received any messages from you yet.

The situation here was becoming rather desperate, even for people like my relatives who still had coins to pay with. The war made food scarce and I could not help but wonder how the people of Plymouth would survive the winter. However, I am happy to report that the gods (or the one god, according to my uncle) came to our aid. The townspeople call it 'the miracle of the fish' as literally thousands of pilchards just swam into the harbour, as if directed by the spirits. All we had to do was to scoop them out of the sea. It was a strange sight as hundreds of men and women rushed down to the harbour, us included, and gathered as much of the unexpected catch as they possibly could.

My uncle claims it is a sign that his god is on our side in this war. I do not know, but I am very grateful we need not starve this winter at least.

I pray you are all well and not suffering any hardships at Castle Shiroi.

Your obedient sister, Midori

If only the spirits, or her uncle's god, would bring Nico home as well, Midori thought, then she would be content. But there had been no word from him and no more sightings by anyone they knew.

Oh, Nico, where are you?

Chapter Twenty-Nine

September 1644

Another long march, another battle.

Where are we now? And does it even matter?

It seemed however much they fought, there was never an end in sight and nobody really knew what was going on. Or if they did, they weren't telling the soldiers.

'We won a resounding victory at Marston Moor back in July, all thanks to Lieutenant-General Oliver Cromwell, remember?' Stephens, as always, tried to keep everyone's spirits up. 'It can only be a matter of time before we prevail altogether.'

But although he admired the youth's positive attitude, Nico wasn't so sure. He'd lost count of the number of minor and major skirmishes he'd taken part in since leaving Bristol. The days all merged into a blur and as he grew more and more tired and battle-weary, he stopped thinking about what he was doing and just existed.

As they marched through Devon and he heard someone mention Plymouth, he vaguely contemplated going back, but his previous resolve to stick with his comrades held. He couldn't leave Stephens, even though the boy appeared to live a charmed life. The youth hadn't received so much as a scratch since Roundway Down; Nico himself was never badly hurt, but he didn't escape scot-free.

'Remind me please, where are we exactly?' he murmured as he stood next to the youngster yet again, waiting for orders. 'Not that it really matters,' he added, but he had a bad feeling about this and for some reason he wanted to know the name of the place where he might die.

The Royalists had arrived, hot on their heels, in this

godforsaken corner of England and the Parliamentarians now appeared to be hemmed in somewhere on the coast. If they didn't stand and fight, their only way out would be to throw themselves into the sea.

'Lostwithiel,' Stephens said. 'In Cornwall.'

'Yes, thank you, I know where Lostwithiel is. Now stay behind me if we're going to fight, you cheeky beggar, that's an order.'

No full-scale battle took place, however, but at the end of August, Nico's commander decided to follow Sir William Balfour's cavalry regiment as they attempted to force their way through the enemy line. Once the skirmish was under way, it was the usual chaos and everywhere there were horses: neighing, rearing up, flailing their hooves and trampling anyone unlucky enough to fall. Nico made his way through the mêlée, dodging this equine onslaught with Stephens on his heels, but just as he thought he could see a gap in the fighting, a horse came at him from the right. A large, fuzzy hoof appeared in front of Nico and before he could duck, it connected with his forehead.

It was the last thing he saw before the world turned black and disappeared.

Outside Plymouth the Royalists hadn't quite given up, but the full-scale siege was replaced by a blockade. This continued throughout the spring and summer of 1644 and wasn't as restrictive, as it merely aimed to stop supplies from reaching the town.

'I can't believe how long this war is dragging on!' Temperance complained. Although not as withdrawn and visibly frightened as before, it was clear to Midori that her cousin was always on edge, as they all were.

By September, even Daniel's optimism was fading.

He came into the kitchen one morning, looking

particularly solemn, and said, 'Have you heard the news, Midori?'

Midori had been busy chopping some turnips, newly harvested from their own garden. She looked up from her task and put the knife down, just in case he had something bad to tell her. This seemed all too likely and she didn't want to cut off a finger by mistake.

'No, I haven't been out today. What's happened?'

'They're saying there's been another disaster, somewhere in Cornwall. Lostwithiel, I think. You heard about the Earl of Essex marching Parliamentary troops down there to liberate the West Country, right?'

Midori nodded; she'd been listening to these rumours for months now. 'I know. You wanted to go with him, but Uncle said he'd prefer you to stay here and defend us.' This wasn't quite how her uncle had put it, but there was no point going into that now.

Daniel nodded. 'Well, seems the King followed him and trapped our forces somewhere and all was lost. It's a tragedy.'

He looked so dejected Midori took one of his hands into hers and squeezed it in silent sympathy.

'That's not the worst of it, though,' Daniel continued. 'The Earl abandoned his troops, would you believe, leaving them to surrender alone while he and some of the other officers took a boat and sailed back here, to Plymouth.' He clenched his fists. 'What was he thinking? What kind of behaviour is that for a gentleman?'

'That's appalling!' Midori had been taught to fight to the death for what she believed was right and never give in. She couldn't understand the Earl's actions at all, so she totally empathised with Daniel's anger. 'Any … any news of Nico?' she ventured to ask, although by now she'd almost given up hope of ever seeing him again. Even if he was alive, he was obviously too stubborn to let them know.

Again Daniel shook his head. 'Not yet. We must pray for his safe return.'

But Midori knew this had just become a habit and none of them believed he would come back. Sudden anger surged through her.

'I wish we could do something! I'm so tired of staying in Plymouth, feeling helpless and tied down. I can't stand this waiting any longer! He's proved his point now, so why can't he come home?'

Daniel shrugged. 'Who knows?'

'Couldn't we at least write to the authorities and try to find out if he's alive? There must be someone to ask. Don't they keep records?'

'I doubt it. This war is so chaotic.'

Midori sighed. 'This is all my fault. He was right, he had no business fighting. I wish I could tell him so, before it's too late.' *If it isn't already.*

Daniel patted her arm awkwardly. 'Nicholas will come back when he's ready to, if he can. Face it, there's nothing we can do.'

She knew he was right, but it hurt to admit it, even to herself.

Late the following afternoon there was a thunderous knocking on the front door, and Midori, who happened to be closest, ran to open it. A gust of wind blew a shower of cold rain into her face and she shook herself and blinked away the icy droplets. There was a sodden man outside, leaning on the wall and staring at the ground, but she forgot all about the weather as she stared at the familiar figure.

'Nico? At last!' Her heart made several somersaults, but sank to her stomach as he pushed past her into the hall and collapsed on the wooden bench by the wall, clutching his head. Midori slammed the door shut and followed him quickly, hardly daring to believe her eyes, but terrified by his silence and obvious pain.

'Midori,' he whispered, his voice quiet and hoarse. He looked up briefly and, despite the grime that was plastered all over him, she could see his features were the same, if a bit gaunt. There were grooves of tiredness and pain etched deep around his eyes and mouth. And he was deathly pale, with a rough golden beard, as untamed as his long hair, lying slicked against his skin. The eyes, usually so piercingly blue, were unfocused and narrowed, as if the slightest light hurt.

Midori's heart constricted in a spasm of combined fear and jubilation. *He's alive! Thank the gods! But in what condition?* 'What happened? Where are you hurt? Talk to me, please!' The fear had the upper hand now and she anxiously scanned his body for signs of any serious wounds.

He was wrapped in a coarse blanket, presumably to shield him from the rain, but it was so wet it was dripping puddles on to the floor. It also smelled very strongly of horse. She helped him to remove it while he leaned back against the wall, trying to get his breath back.

'Had a knock on the head ... horse's hoof ... here.' Nico took his hand away from his forehead and pointed to just above his right eyebrow where there was a huge lump with a nasty gash in the middle, bruised and caked with dried blood. There seemed to be something wet oozing out of the wound still, but Midori wasn't sure if that was the case or if the rainwater mixed with dirt just made it look that way. 'Was unconscious, left for dead by the enemies I suppose, but ... hard head.' He tried to smile, a lopsided effort that made Midori's insides twist with love for him. She'd missed him so much and she realised now she didn't care whether he was honourable or not. She loved him just the way he was.

'Foolish man,' she muttered.

He continued, as if he hadn't heard, 'Comrades came

looking for me, found us horses who were only slightly wounded. Rode home ... fast as we could. Managed to avoid capture, travelled at night mostly.' He shook his head and passed a hand over his eyes. 'Sorry, feel a bit faint. Haven't eaten for ... a while.'

Midori could see he was on the point of collapse from exhaustion, hunger and perhaps loss of blood, so she pushed him gently down to lie on the bench. 'Stay still while I organise a bed and some food for you. I won't be long.'

As she turned to head off to the kitchen, Aunt Hesketh came down the stairs. 'Did I hear knocking? Who ... Nicholas!' The older woman almost fell down the last steps in her haste to reach him and cried out, 'What have they done to you? And why did you have to go and fight? Oh, dear Lord ...'

'For the love of God, Stepmama, stop your caterwauling. Please! My head.'

Midori decided Nico could handle Aunt Hesketh, even in his weakened state, and went off to see to everything else. Hot water, towels, clean sheets and warming pans, as well as hot bricks, to ward off any dampness. Susan helped her to bring everything upstairs to a small bedroom under the eaves and eventually Nico was washed as best they could manage, dried and put to bed. A relative calm descended on the household.

'I'll make him a sleeping draught of valerian,' Aunt Hesketh said, and while she saw to that, Midori cleaned Nico's wound and bandaged it. They gave him some broth and the infusion, then left him to sleep. There was nothing else they could do, except hope the damage was not internal and his brain wasn't affected.

'Let us go and pray for his recovery,' her uncle said tersely, having by now been appraised of the situation, 'and give thanks for his safe return. Perhaps now he'll come to his senses and stay here.'

'But we don't know if he'll be all right. How can we give thanks for something which isn't certain? He's hardly spoken a word, just lies there, as pale as death.' Aunt Hesketh had tears flowing down her cheeks and for the first time ever Midori felt some sympathy for her. It was obvious she cared for her stepson after all, and the many months of staring into space must have been partly out of fear for his life.

'He's just exhausted,' she soothed, but Aunt Hesketh only glared at her, as if she knew nothing. Since this showed a return to something like her old spirits, Midori didn't mind too much and made no response.

'It's in the hands of God, as you well know, Sister,' her uncle admonished. 'We can only pray; you know He is testing our faith. We must examine ourselves to see what we have done to deserve these tribulations.'

Years of listening to Uncle Marston had by now taught Midori what that meant. Her family believed if something bad befell them, it was a punishment from God for something they had done, even if it was just a trifling thing, like having vain thoughts or eating too much. Midori couldn't make herself believe that – it seemed to her a bit extreme. But she respected the others' thoughts on the matter and went with them to pray for Nico.

They didn't need to know that she was asking her own gods and ancestors for help, too.

'How are you feeling now?'

Nico had finally woken up and he opened his eyes to find that Midori had brought him a tray of food.

'Have been better,' he replied, half-shutting his eyes against the light coming through the window. 'But at least my head doesn't feel like someone's trying to pierce it with hot irons now; it's just a dull ache.'

He watched her as she put the tray down on the floor next

to his bed, which was low and rickety. In truth, seeing her was all the medicine he needed. Despite the dull clothes and the fact that she'd lost some weight, she was still the most beautiful woman he'd ever met, and he drank in the sight of her. Flawless skin, slightly flushed from her efforts, a tress of auburn hair that escaped the ridiculous cap they made her wear, glinting in the sunlight. Eyes like dark green forest pools, with those long dusky lashes brushing her cheeks. And her mouth, so perfect and soft ...

He cursed himself for a fool. He shouldn't have let her slip through his fingers when he'd had the chance. *How could I not have known I love her?* But perhaps it wasn't too late? He'd done what she wanted him to now, fought for his family's beliefs many times over. Could he find a way to woo her? At least she wasn't glaring at him and he took that as a good sign.

'Here, I've brought you some feverfew. It will help cure your headache. Eat this, please.'

He struggled into a sitting position and she handed him two small pieces of bread spread with a little bit of honey, with raw feverfew in between. He obediently chewed and swallowed, even though the bitter taste of the plant made him grimace.

'You were lucky. I don't know how you managed to get yourself home in that state,' Midori said, as she prodded his pillows into shape behind him.

'It's all a bit of a blur. Several times I contemplated just lying down by the roadside to die, but somehow I continued.' He looked up at her from under lowered lashes, feeling more uncertain than he ever had before in his life. 'I thought "if anyone can heal me, Midori can" but ... perhaps I shouldn't have come back?'

She stopped what she was doing and stared him straight in the eyes. 'Of course you should. In fact, you shouldn't have gone off in the first place. That was my fault and I'm sorry, I … I didn't mean to rile you so.'

Nico took hold of one of her hands and pulled her down to sit at the edge of his bed. 'No, you were right. I'm the one who should apologise. It's my duty to defend you all, just as you said. I see that now. As soon as I'm healed, I'll continue to do that to the best of my ability.'

He saw her gaze become troubled. 'You're going back?'

'To the army? Not unless I have to. It wasn't the most wonderful experience I've ever had and most of my comrades – the men I've been fighting alongside – are gone or wounded. I meant, I'll join the town defenders if they'll have me.' He managed a smile and felt it was another good sign when she returned it. 'I realised while I was away that I wasn't of much use to my family dying elsewhere in the country. I said as much to the others before that last battle, and most of them agreed. One of them, Stephens by name, was the one who found me after the battle. He and a couple of others risked coming back to look for me and helped me escape. He rode halfway home with me and returned to his family over Okehampton way. Had a broken arm, so couldn't fight anyway.'

It had been hard saying goodbye to the boy, but Nico was glad Stephens would be with those he loved, whatever happened. He'd become fond of him during their time together.

He thought he heard Midori sigh – whether with relief or at his stupidity, he didn't know. 'Well, try to eat a little so you regain your strength,' she said and pulled her hand out of his grasp. 'You may be needed for defence purposes sooner than you think. And Temperance and I are planning to wash your hair later. You've been warned.'

'That sounds like a terrible threat – clean hair.' He pretended to be shocked. 'How will I survive?'

'I've no idea. Now eat, please. I'll be back shortly.'

'Yes, mistress, whatever you command.'

The smile she sent him on her way out of the room made him feel better than he had in months.

With a cloth wrapped round his nether regions to preserve his modesty, Midori helped manoeuvre Nico into a large tub which was normally used for laundry. He sighed with apparent pleasure as he sank into the hot water.

'Ah, that feels good. Heat seeping into my aching muscles …' He leaned his head on the rim behind him.

'Your hair has grown so much you almost look like a Royalist, Nicholas.' Temperance regarded him critically, but Midori smiled.

'I like it,' she said. 'It suits you better this way.'

He looked up at her with a grin. 'Then I shan't cut it. Your word is my law.'

'Don't be silly.' She felt warmth creep into her cheeks and turned away. Just seeing him smile at her was having a strange effect and she knew it would almost be torture to handle his soft hair. But it had to be done, as it was so encrusted with grime and blood, you'd never know its true colour. 'Can you sit up a bit please, so I can pour this water over your head?'

He did as she asked. 'I'm sorry, I should be outside dunking my head under the pump, not putting you to all this trouble.'

'Of course not! You're not really supposed to stir from that bed until you've recovered. This won't take long and then you'll feel much better.'

She strived for a brisk tone, because washing Nico's wonderful hair reminded her of the stormy night on board his ship. Touching him in any way was delicious agony, but she had to do this for his sake, as well as the sake of keeping the bed linen clean. For all they knew, his head could be crawling with vermin.

Thankfully, it wasn't, but it took three jugs of water and a large quantity of home-made soap before the burnished gold colour of Nico's tresses could be seen again. As Midori dried it carefully, combing it strand by strand as slowly as she could so she wouldn't hurt him, she couldn't help but enjoy the task. His hair was so soft and silky she wanted to just bury her fingers in it and pull him close. But, of course, that was out of the question.

'You look much more like yourself now.' Temperance grinned at him. 'And less like a poor beggar.'

'I'm glad you think so,' he replied with an answering smile. 'I do feel rather more human now, I must admit. And I could quite get used to having two beautiful ladies wash my hair for me, so feel free to do it any time.'

Temperance giggled and flicked him with the end of a drying sheet. 'Forget it. You can do it yourself as soon as you're well again. We're not your slaves.'

'Alas no, but it was a nice thought. Perhaps I should kidnap the pair of you? Now where could I take you – some place where slavery is allowed. It would have to be the Americas, I think,' he mused.

'Don't even think about it.' Midori joined in the conversation. 'Even if you did, you'd find it difficult to make us do anything for you. Right, Temperance?'

'Absolutely. Midori has been teaching me a thing or two about self-defence, so don't think you can get the better of me.'

Nico chuckled. 'Well, there goes that dream, then.'

'But you're welcome to take me to the Americas if you want,' Temperance added. 'I'd love to travel the world, see new lands. I want adventure, like Midori and her mother had.'

'Lord help us,' Nico muttered, but there was amusement

lurking in his eyes. 'Another hoyden? Really, Midori, what have you been teaching her?'

'Nothing, I swear. I've done my best to persuade her adventuring isn't as great as it's made out to be. If you can change her mind, I'd be eternally grateful!'

'Never,' Temperance declared. 'I may only be able to dream, but you can't change my mind. If ever I get the chance, I'm leaving.' She gathered up two of the ewers and clattered down the stairs.

Midori shook her head and sighed. 'She's been so brave, but this has all been very hard for her,' she murmured. 'It's not how a girl should have to grow up, in a town under siege. It helps her to daydream, I think.'

Nico stood up and she wrapped a huge drying sheet round him from behind, averting her eyes as he discarded the cloth he'd kept round his middle even while sitting in the tub.

'Thank you,' he said. 'Poor Temperance. But then it isn't how anyone should have to live. We'll have to hope there's an end to it soon.'

'Amen to that, as Uncle would say.' Midori handed him a clean shirt and tried not to look as he tied the drying sheet round his hips and pulled the shirt over his head. But her mind had other ideas and she glanced at him from under her lashes, drinking in the sight of him. He was leaner than last time she'd seen him half-naked, and covered in new scars and bruises, but he was still beautiful to her. She felt her cheeks heat up again and swallowed a curse as she turned away. She shouldn't let him affect her this way.

'I'm decent now, so you can look again,' he teased from behind. When she twisted round towards him, he was lying under the covers, obviously relishing the fresh sheets Temperance had put on the bed while he was in the bath. His eyes twinkled up at her. 'I'm sorry I'm not a pretty sight, but hopefully I'll heal.'

'There's nothing wrong with how you look, as I'm sure you know,' Midori answered tartly and gathered up the damp cloths. 'Now I'd better take these downstairs. I shouldn't really be here alone with you anyway. Aunt Hesketh would have a fit.' It was true, it wasn't seemly for her to be alone with him, although as an invalid he surely couldn't be accounted a threat to her virtue, she reasoned.

As she reached the door, she heard him ask in that deep, slightly husky voice, 'Midori, did you miss me?'

She turned slowly and shook her head, keeping her expression solemn. 'No, not at all.' She saw his eyes open wide in outrage, then he registered the fact that her face had relaxed into a huge smile. 'Of course I did, you dolt,' she said. 'You're family and ...'

He raised his eyebrows at her, as if waiting for her to say he was more than that, but she closed her mouth stubbornly. His lips twitched. 'Well, come here and show me how much,' he ordered. 'I haven't had so much as a cousinly kiss to welcome me home.' Despite her best intentions, her legs obeyed his command and walked her back towards the bed. He grabbed her hand again to pull her down on to the edge, but she lost her footing and ended up sprawled on top of him instead, almost nose to nose.

'Well now, this wasn't quite what I meant, but I like it,' he joked, kissing her cheek, then moving along to the corner of her mouth.

'Nico,' she protested, laughing as he put his arms around her to pull her closer. When he kissed her full on the mouth, she pretended to cuff him, but kept their play-fighting to a minimum, mindful of his sore head. She was just about to try and get off him when a cold voice barked at them from the doorway.

'Midori! What is the meaning of this? Get out of here this

instant. Your uncle shall hear of this unseemly behaviour, believe you me.'

Midori scrambled off the bed and straightened her gown. 'But I ...'

'Don't blame Midori, it was my fault,' Nico put in. 'I was only funning.'

'You're ill,' his stepmother said, as if that excused his behaviour, but not Midori's. 'Now go, Midori, what are you waiting for?'

Under Aunt Hesketh's implacable stare, Midori retreated, but not before Nico had sent her a conspiratorial wink. She shook her head at him and mouthed, 'You're incorrigible,' but she was smiling as she left. It was so good to have him home.

There was a bubble of happiness inside Midori, and nothing could dent it for the moment, not even the reprimand she received from her uncle. Just seeing Nico every day, growing stronger and with his bruises fading, was a delight. And even though Aunt Hesketh had assumed the reins of the household again and did her best to keep Midori busy elsewhere in the house, she wasn't able to stop Midori from visiting him occasionally.

'So were you really training Daniel, down there on the beach?' Nico asked on the third day, as Midori busied herself with pouring him a cup of light ale with some willow bark in it to soothe his headaches. Bringing it to him had proved a good excuse for coming upstairs.

She nodded. 'Yes. He was so set on fighting and I couldn't bear to see him go off unprepared. I wanted him to at least stand a chance. So far, he's done all right and Uncle is happy Daniel at least stayed in Plymouth.'

'I'm sorry,' he said.

She looked up. 'For what?'

'Not believing you. Jumping to conclusions.' He shrugged. 'Everything.'

'It's forgotten. Anyway, Daniel tells me I'm too old for him, so I'm afraid my hopes in that direction have already been dashed.' She sent him a teasing smile, hoping he would take the hint. She didn't want to talk about the past, she'd prefer to discuss the future, but so far he'd proved elusive on the subject. Midori was afraid she'd burned her bridges when she had refused his offer of marriage. Although he seemed happy to spend time with her, and flirted outrageously, she wasn't entirely sure what his intentions were now. Since he had faced death on the battlefield so many times, she wondered if he was just amusing himself while he still could. And she happened to be there, available. His eyes lit up with amusement and he chuckled. 'Did he really say that? What a clotpole.'

'Well, I am at least two years older than him. I suppose that seems ancient to someone his age.'

'Lord help me, what does that make me then? In my dotage?'

'Oh, undoubtedly. He's probably surprised you were able to fight at all.' Midori laughed. 'Never mind, I've recovered from that particular disappointment.'

'I'm glad to hear it.' His eyes twinkled at her again and she was pleased to see his gaze was clear now, not laced with pain. When he reached out to take her hand, she didn't resist. His calloused fingers scraped against her own work-roughened ones, and it sent a thrill racing through her veins. 'I suppose you consider *me* old,' he said. 'I have at least ten years on you, I think.'

Midori's brain had trouble focusing on his words. She'd much rather just enjoy the sensation of him touching her, however small the contact, but she tried to muster her thoughts. 'Hmm? Oh, no, I don't judge people by their age.

And you still have the use of most of your faculties, don't you?'

He grinned and pulled her down to sit next to him. 'Oh, yes. Shall I prove it to you?'

As she looked into his eyes, so intensely blue in the light from the window, she thought she saw desire and longing. But then his expression grew serious. He took hold of her other hand as well, stroking her skin with his thumbs. She saw him take a deep breath. 'Midori, I was wondering ...'

She leaned closer, her whole body tingling with anticipation. Was this the moment she'd been waiting for? 'Yes?'

His hands tightened on hers and he opened his mouth to speak, but was interrupted by a hiss of outrage from the door.

'Get away from him, you hussy! How many times do I have to tell you? You're not wanted in here.'

Midori sat up straight and tried to let go of Nico's hands, but he held on. 'Don't,' he said quietly, then frowned up at Aunt Hesketh. 'I'd thank you not to refer to Midori in such terms. She's welcome in my sickroom any time.'

'Yes, I'm sure she is, but I'll not have that sort of thing going on in this house, thank you very much. She can go and work her wiles elsewhere. Ensnaring a wounded man! Have you no shame?' This last was directed at Midori, who gasped at the unfairness of the accusation.

'I'm not ensnaring anyone, and I have a right to talk to Nico as much as anyone else. Besides, I merely brought him a drink.'

'Talking, is it? Pah! You don't fool me.'

'That's enough!' Nico sat up, too, and swung his legs out of bed. 'Please can you hand me my breeches, Midori?' She quickly fetched them for him, but cast him an anxious glance as he pulled them on and stood up, leaving his shirt hanging loose.

'Are you sure you should be getting up? Your head …'

'My head be damned.' Nico fixed his stepmother with a glare, stern enough to make her take a step back. 'I've had enough of your interference and insinuations. What is wrong with you? Why do you persist in thinking the worst of Midori?'

'They're not insinuations. I saw her making sheep's eyes at you only a moment ago. Can you deny it? She's a little fortune hunter, taking advantage of the fact that you're not yourself and …'

'What are you talking about? I may be comfortably off, but I'm not that rich.'

Aunt Hesketh pursed her lips. 'Well, she's been nothing but a nuisance ever since she arrived and now you're here we certainly don't need the extra mouth to feed. I want her gone by the end of the week if she can't behave herself as she ought.'

'Gone where, Stepmother?' Nico's voice was like iced venom and he folded his arms across his chest. 'In case you haven't noticed, we're in a town that's besieged on all sides. Are you expecting her to swim across the Channel, perhaps?'

'Don't be ridiculous.' Aunt Hesketh's cheeks took on a ruddy hue. 'I'm sure she can find employment somewhere in Plymouth. She needs to earn her keep.'

Nico nodded. 'Of course. I was forgetting how little work she does around here, cooking, cleaning and running around all day. And you do so much, overseeing it all.'

The sarcasm in his voice was clear and tipped Aunt Hesketh over the edge. 'She doesn't belong here, I do!' she screeched. 'And I can't stand the sight of her!'

Nico narrowed his eyes at her. 'Now we come to the crux of the matter. What I want to know is why, and I intend to get to the bottom of this.' He headed for the door. 'Come,

Midori, and you too, Stepmama. We are going to see Jacob. I believe he may be able to help solve this riddle.'

'Jacob? Why?' Aunt Hesketh gaped at him, but he ignored her. Instead he took Midori's hand and started down the stairs.

'We're going to the parlour. Now.' His voice brooked no opposition and, to Midori's surprise, Aunt Hesketh followed them as Nico bellowed for someone to fetch Jacob.

'This needs to be sorted out,' he said and threw open the door to the first-floor room. 'Please, sit down.'

Chapter Thirty

Nico and Uncle Marston were on one of the benches by the far wall, while Midori and Aunt Hesketh occupied the two chairs with armrests which had been placed opposite to form a rough circle. Midori sent her aunt a quick glance, but waited in silence for the others to speak. Nico took a deep breath and began almost immediately.

'I think it's time to clear the air, once and for all. There are old grievances in this family which have festered long enough and we need to get them out in the open if we're ever going to move forward. Do you agree, Jacob? You told me it's time to forgive and forget.'

'Absolutely.' Her uncle looked more alert than Midori had seen him for a while, his eyes darting between Nico and his stepmother with interest.

'That's easy for you to say,' Aunt Hesketh muttered, but when Nico fixed her with his blue gaze, she lowered her eyes and her fingers plucked nervously at a fold of black material in her skirt.

'No, it's not easy. When I left Plymouth all those years ago, all I wanted to do was forget you all, and for a while I succeeded. Coming back has opened up old wounds, however, and I've come to realise the only way to heal them is to understand the cause. This isn't just about Midori, although she seems to have been a catalyst of some sort. I believe this goes back much further.'

Uncle Marston nodded. 'He's right, Kate.'

Aunt Hesketh glared briefly at Midori. 'We were all right until she arrived.'

Midori opened her mouth to defend herself, but didn't get a chance.

'If it wasn't for Midori, I wouldn't have returned at all,' Nico stated. 'Would you prefer to think me dead still?' His stepmother gave an involuntary shake of her head and he continued, 'No, I don't suppose you would. Most mothers wish their children to be alive and well, even stepchildren, so I assume you wouldn't go that far. Although admittedly you never seemed to care much when I *was* living here. Perhaps it's time to tell me why? What did I do that was so bad you couldn't bear the sight of me? I know I was a bit wild, but so were many other youngsters and my siblings weren't much better, yet you cared for them well enough.'

Aunt Hesketh struggled for a moment, as if she couldn't get the words out, but then they came pouring through her lips in a veritable torrent. 'You looked like my firstborn, the one I lost and I wanted him so! I thought ... I thought if only I could keep him it would all have been worth it, but it wasn't to be. He was taken from me, while you ... you were as healthy as a stoat. But you weren't mine.' Tears trickled down her cheeks.

'Why was he so important? You had other children of your own, didn't you?' Nico asked, more gently.

'He ... he was conceived before I married your father. He was the son of the man I loved, Rafael Rydon. The one *your* mother married!' Aunt Hesketh turned an accusing glare on Midori. 'It was all Hannah's fault! I should have been married to Henry Forrester – I'd be a titled lady now if I had – but because I was with child, he broke off the engagement. By then Rafael had left and my father insisted I take the man he'd promised your mother to, Ezekiel Hesketh.'

This was news to Midori and all very confusing. She waited to hear more.

Nico raised his eyebrows. 'Surely if Forrester wasn't the child's father, he had every right to be aggrieved. And you loved Rydon, not him. Who was this Rydon fellow?'

'A sea captain, the man I sailed to the Japans with,' her uncle put in and Aunt Hesketh nodded.

Nico frowned. 'Well, had he promised you marriage?'

'No, but if he'd only come back, I'm sure I could have persuaded him. I was young and beautiful, and if I'd presented him with a son ...'

Aunt Hesketh is the loose woman here, not me. Midori would have laughed at the irony if the discussion hadn't been so serious.

Tears continued to stream down Aunt Hesketh's face and her hands pleated and unpleated her skirts repeatedly. 'So I was forced to take Ezekiel and his brats.'

'Brats? That's what you thought of us?'

'No, not really. You were only little and I didn't hate you, of course I didn't, it was just that once I lost my baby, the sight of you always reminded me of him. And because your mother was a cousin of Rydon's, you look so much like him, you have no idea! It ... it was agony watching you grow up.'

Uncle Marston handed her a large handkerchief and she covered her face with it, her shoulders shaking with quiet sobs.

'I understand,' Nico said. 'But it was a long time ago now, and surely you must see that you, yourself, were responsible for what happened? You can't continue to blame others; you must forgive yourself.'

Midori couldn't keep quiet any longer, since she was still puzzled about something. 'But what has all this to do with me? You implied it was my mother's fault you're not Lady Forrester, but she wasn't even here.'

Aunt Hesketh emerged from the handkerchief, her eyes blazing at Midori. 'No, but if she hadn't run away like a hoyden, I wouldn't have had to marry Ezekiel. He should have been *her* husband! I'm sorry, Nicholas, but you must agree he wasn't a nice man and I'd rather have been wed to anyone else but him, but because Hannah escaped, my father was hell-bent on honouring his contract with him. As I was in disgrace, that was my punishment. The stupid little minx, I should have locked her in our bedroom when I went to meet Rafael ...'

'Stones in glasshouses, Kate,' her uncle reminded his sister quietly.

'That's as may be, but now Midori is following in her footsteps.' She glared at her niece. 'It's not just Nicholas she's cavorting with. I know you were sneaking out of the house a while back, no doubt to meet some man. What happened, did he get himself killed so now you have to set your sights on someone else?'

Midori gasped. 'What? No, I never ...' Then she remembered her sessions on the beach with Daniel. She was about to defend herself, but didn't know how without revealing her fighting skills, which would no doubt be another thing against her in Aunt Hesketh's eyes.

Nico came to her rescue. 'Midori wasn't "cavorting" with anyone, I can bear witness to that. She was taught self-defence by her father – it is something that's necessary where she comes from, I believe – and she was passing on her knowledge to Daniel in order to give him more of a chance to stay alive during this wretched war. Is that not so?' He put a hand on her arm and gave her a reassuring squeeze.

'Fighting tricks? A girl?' Aunt Hesketh goggled at them, predictably.

'She's from a different culture, Sister,' Uncle Marston said, smiling at Midori. 'And I, for one, am very grateful for such forethought. Daniel is precious to me.'

Nico looked at Aunt Hesketh. 'So, it seems to me you have only yourself to blame for all this ill-feeling, and you have to come to terms with that. It's time to forget the past and live in the present. You have other children whom you love, grandchildren you ought to see more of and I'm here, whether you like it or not. Neither Midori nor I are going anywhere at present and we are tired of living with your antagonism. It has to stop.'

'I agree with Nicholas, Kate,' her uncle said. 'I've been lenient with you for too long, allowing you to wallow in self-pity and taking out your frustration on those who don't deserve it. Our Lord must think me very remiss in not doing something about it and I will pray for forgiveness. For the sake of your immortal soul, you must change or I'm afraid I can't allow you to stay here. Enough is enough.'

Aunt Hesketh's sobs stopped and she stared at her brother, a stricken expression in her eyes. 'You can't mean that? You need me to run your household.'

'Not any more, Kate.' Uncle Marston's voice was firm. 'Temperance is almost old enough to see to everything, and in any case, my dear niece is here to help her. I would suggest you go and pray for guidance, then come and tell me your decision. If you choose to stay here, I shall expect you to change and there will be no going back.'

Faced with three pairs of eyes, all watching to see what she'd say or do next, Aunt Hesketh suddenly crumbled. Midori would have sworn the woman aged before her eyes, shoulders sagging, face drooping. It was as if all the air left her lungs at once, together with her animosity.

'Very well, I … I see now that my thinking has been skewed. You're right, all of you. I made a mistake and I paid for it.' She looked at Nico. 'I'm sorry, truly sorry …' She blew her nose, then took a deep breath and turned to Midori. 'And I apologise if I've been hard on you. My brother is right, I should remember the words of our Lord – a child is innocent, no matter what their parents have done. And in all fairness, I can't blame Hannah for running from

Ezekiel. I only wish I'd done the same, but I didn't have her courage.'

'Then let's move forward and let bygones be bygones.' Nico stood up and pulled his stepmother to her feet, enveloping her in a bear hug the way only he could. Midori envied the woman, because she too wanted to be in the safety of those arms, but she wasn't sure it was her place.

She watched as her uncle, too, gave his sister an unaccustomed embrace. She was glad the air had been cleared and she hoped it would make things easier.

Easier for Nico to propose again? She hardly dared to hope.

A silence fell over the parlour, but it was broken soon after by the sound of the front door of the house being thrown open, banging into the wall beneath them, and footsteps rushing up the stairs. Nico, who had been about to say something, exchanged a glance with his uncle, who was frowning. *Now what?* He felt emotionally wrung out from the confrontation just ended and wasn't sure he was ready to deal with anything else today.

Daniel burst into the room without so much as knocking. Red in the face and panting, he stopped just inside the door to catch his breath before announcing, 'The King himself has arrived … outside the town. He's brought an army … twelve thousand men they say.' He closed his eyes and drew in another deep breath. 'Saw them coming myself, drums beating, colours flying. Thinks to scare us no doubt, making a big show of it, but we'll show them.'

'Are they poised to attack?' Jacob went over to grab his son's arm, as if he wanted to keep him from rushing off to face such a formidable foe.

Daniel shook his head. 'Not yet, Father, they'll set up camp first, but soon.'

'You'll need all the men you can get,' Nico put in. 'I'll help, but are there any spare muskets? I'm afraid I lost mine.'

'You're surely not fighting? In your condition?' His stepmother stared at him, eyes wide open with incredulity and fear. He wanted to reassure her that all would be well, but he didn't know what to say. How was the town to withstand an assault from such a huge army?

'I'm better,' was all he said. 'My wound is almost healed and I don't suffer from headaches any more.' That was a lie, but they were certainly better than they had been. And he couldn't sit around and do nothing.

He glanced at Midori, who'd remained quiet. He had hoped for a chance to speak to her alone that afternoon, but perhaps now was not the time.

'I'll find you a weapon,' Daniel promised, then turned to Midori. 'We'd best have a square meal now, if you can find something for us? There may not be time to eat later and we'll need the strength.'

'Yes, of course, I'll see to it.'

Before Nico could catch her eye, she'd left the room. He swore under his breath. *Why did the King have to turn up just now? Damn him!*

A half-hour or so later, Uncle Marston came into the kitchen, where Nico and Daniel were polishing off the remains of a stew. 'Hah!' he said, looking unaccountably pleased. 'I've just heard from our neighbour. His Majesty obviously expected the garrison to surrender immediately, as he sent a message saying "Surrender forthwith or be overrun". Naturally he received an emphatic refusal.'

'Should think so, too,' Daniel muttered with his mouth full.

'So what's he going to do now?' Temperance asked. She'd been hovering in the background and Midori had seen her

314

put her hand in her apron pocket several times, as if checking the sharp knife was still in there.

'Well, he was very angry, to be sure,' her uncle replied, 'and probably couldn't believe his ears, but he sent another messenger with the same demand. This time the man was instructed to tell him the town of Plymouth would never surrender to him and if he tried to send a third messenger the man would be hanged.'

'Oh, dear, I suppose he'll definitely attack now.' Poor Temperance was visibly shaking, but her father didn't seem to notice. As Midori had said to Nico, her cousin had tried to be brave throughout the long years of this war, but it was beginning to take its toll on her, as on everyone else. Midori put an arm round Temperance's shoulders to comfort her.

'Aye, no doubt about it,' her uncle said. 'Attack us he will, it's only a question of time.'

Midori took one look at Temperance's expression and thought it best to remove her uncle from his daughter's vicinity for a while. 'Uncle Marston, I do believe Aunt Hesketh was waiting for you to bring more news. I was just about to take her a tray of food. Will you come?'

'Yes, of course. Lead the way, Midori.'

Safely out of earshot of the others, Midori asked, 'Is there any chance we can withstand such a substantial force as the King's?' It sounded impossible to her, but she knew there was no alternative in the minds of the proud townspeople.

'We must. I'm going to join them myself, as is every able-bodied man, woman and child.'

'You are? I thought you didn't want to fight?' Midori was surprised at this about-turn.

'I was being selfish, I see that now. The Lord needs us all to fight for what is right and I should have listened to Daniel. I just didn't want him hurt, but he seems to be managing well, partly thanks to you.' He sent her a smile of gratitude.

315

'It was nothing, but … must you go? I'm sure there are plenty of others who can go in your stead.' Midori considered her uncle too old for warfare. She didn't know his exact age, but guessed him to be at least fifty and she was fairly sure he had never fought before.

He nodded. 'Yes, it is my duty.'

Something else struck her. 'Did you say "every man, woman and child" just now?' He nodded. 'Does that mean I can go, too?'

He put his head to one side as if unsure he'd heard right. 'You want to fight? You're sure of that? I didn't mean it was obligatory.'

'I know, but I want to. Truly.'

'Very well. The time has come for us to stand up for what we believe in.' Her uncle patted her awkwardly on the shoulder. 'I'm very glad you came to us and I'm proud to call you niece. And just in case … you know … I want to thank you for everything you've done, your hard work. I know it's not always been easy for you, but you've done your best.'

Midori smiled at him. 'No, thank *you* for taking me in. I'm very grateful.'

They left it at that, neither wanting to believe it may be their only chance to express their feelings.

Her uncle simply said, 'May God go with us.'

And Midori replied, 'Amen,' as she was now accustomed to. It felt right.

Having left him with Aunt Hesketh, Midori made her way downstairs again, deep in thought. The fact that he had agreed to let her fight showed her how serious the situation was and she could only hope she'd be able to help. The sound of cannon and musket fire could be heard clearly already and she took a steadying breath. It would seem the battle had begun, or at least a skirmish of some sort. The smell of gunpowder was heavy in the air, but strangely, it made her feel calmer.

This is what I was trained for. Father and Ichiro prepared me well; I can hold my own. Whether she lived or died was in the hands of the gods. If only ... but there was no point in regrets. She had to accept her fate, whatever that was.

Nico was the only person left in the kitchen when she entered, and it looked as though he'd been waiting for her. He came forward and, without a word, put his arms around her and pulled her close. 'Midori.' The word sounded like a caress and she closed her eyes to savour the moment. She hugged him back, fitting herself closely to his chest. 'There's so little time and I have to leave,' he sighed. 'Daniel is waiting outside. It's not how I had envisaged spending this afternoon ...' He broke off as if there was much more he wanted to say, but didn't know how.

Midori looked up and smiled at him. 'I know, but hopefully it will all be over soon.'

'Always so positive,' he murmured, staring at her as if he was storing the image of her in his mind. 'I hope you're right.' His gaze grew tender. 'You're the most amazing woman I've ever met, you do know that, don't you?' Before she could reply, he bent to kiss her, properly, deeply, but it was over in seconds and then he was gone.

Midori stood transfixed for a while, then shook herself mentally. He was right, there was so little time and she had things to do.

Chapter Thirty-One

'Midori, what are you doing?' Temperance came into the bedchamber they shared, startling her cousin, who hadn't heard the door open.

'Getting ready to fight,' Midori said, continuing with her preparations. 'I'll be of more use on the battlefield than here at home. And Uncle Jacob said I was needed.'

'He did?' Temperance blinked in disbelief.

'Yes, amazing, isn't it?' Midori managed a smile. 'I'm sorry to leave you with Aunt Hesketh and the servants, but ...'

'Don't worry, we'll do very well here. You go, and rid us of those accursed Royalists. I'll surely go out of my mind if we don't win this war soon.'

Midori noticed the dark shadows underneath Temperance's lovely eyes. It was clear the poor girl was terrified. And who could blame her? 'Are you really sure?' Midori didn't want to leave Temperance if her presence comforted her cousin.

Temperance nodded resolutely. 'Yes, go.'

Half an hour later, Midori was on her way and she soon found Daniel, since she knew where he was stationed. 'What's happening? Any news?' she asked.

He shook his head. 'Not much. I think the King is trying to frighten us, but he'll catch cold at that. He's been making a show of marching his army within sight of the town walls, as if that'll have any effect on us. Much he knows.'

Midori knew Daniel was partly trying to convince himself, but she didn't contradict him. The mind was a powerful thing and if her cousin could make himself believe he wasn't scared, so much the better.

'He's found no openings for an attack either,' Daniel continued, 'even though his soldiers have tried to storm the walls a couple of times already.'

'That's good.'

In fact, the Royalists were beaten off time after time, all through the day, and it seemed the townspeople had luck on their side yet again. A large naval force under the command of Captain William Batten happened to be anchored in Millbay, and when the captain heard what was happening, he decided to put ashore all the sailors to help defend the town. Midori also saw women and children flocking to assist their menfolk – the women by bringing powder, bullets and provisions, while the children fetched and carried whatever they could. They were all likely to be exposed to the most gruesome of sights, but this didn't prevent them from encouraging their soldiers.

'We all want to do our bit,' one woman muttered when Midori commented on it.

As no one was venturing outside the walls to fight a proper battle yet, Midori was content to help the other women for now and, as night fell, she went to sit with them and some soldiers round a small fire. Daniel joined her, eating whatever he was given, and soon after Midori heard the voice she'd been waiting for.

'Ah, Daniel, there you are. I was ... Midori? What are you doing here?'

'I've come to help.' She looked at Nico as he sank down on to the ground next to her. 'You, of all people, should know this is where I belong.'

He frowned. 'I suppose so, but ... I had hoped you'd be safe in your bed.'

'Not until this is over.' To signal the fact that she wasn't prepared to discuss it further, she changed the subject. 'Where are you stationed? On the other side of town?'

'No, I've just been sent over here. Seems more men are needed on this stretch of the defences.'

'Good. The three of us will fight together, then.' She sent Daniel an encouraging smile.

'Excellent,' he said.

Nico still didn't look convinced, but he didn't argue the point. He just muttered, 'No idea how you're going to fight dressed like that, though.' He looked at her long, brown petticoat with a frown.

Midori grinned and lifted up the hem. 'Don't worry, I've thought of that.' Underneath she was wearing a pair of Daniel's old breeches and she saw Nico's eyes widen as he took in the sight.

'You're not serious?'

'Of course. I didn't want to stand out by wearing *hakama*, and it would be impossible to fight properly wearing skirts, so I, uhm, helped myself to a few things. See, I'm already wearing a man's leather jerkin. This way, perhaps I'll fool at least some people into believing I'm a boy tomorrow.'

Nico shook his head, but made no further comment. Instead he tucked into a bowl of broth that someone handed him and Midori was content to watch.

'You might as well go home, Midori,' Daniel said eventually. 'There won't be any fighting until morning and you'll need some sleep to be at your best.' He nodded at Nico. 'You, too. Unless you're on guard duty?'

'No, not tonight. Are you?'

'Yes, but don't worry, I'll be all right. I'm used to it.'

Nico finished his broth then stood up and held out a hand to help Midori to her feet. 'Shall we go, then? The sooner we get to bed, the better. I'm guessing King Charles will have us up betimes.'

She took his hand and allowed him to pull her up. 'Very

well. But send word if anything happens, won't you, Daniel? Promise?'

'I swear.'

As they walked back towards her uncle's house, Midori was surprised to feel Nico's hand closing around hers instead of letting go. His fingers twined with her smaller ones and it seemed they fit together perfectly. Despite everything that was going on around them, she felt safe, protected, just by that small contact between them. They walked in companionable silence until they reached the house, which was in darkness. Outside the door, Midori stopped and turned to Nico, wanting to tell him some of the things that were on her mind, but unsure how to begin or whether this was the right time. 'Nico, will you wake me tomorrow so we can go back together?'

'Of course. I'm not leaving your side. Not until this is over.'

'What, you think I can't defend myself?' She put her hands on her hips, irritation flashing through her. 'I thought I showed you my skills a long time ago. And I've been practising.'

He stepped closer and snaked an arm round her waist, pulling her into his embrace. 'Perhaps I remember them all too clearly,' he whispered into her ear. 'As I recall, you ended up sitting on top of me. And I have to tell you, I wouldn't want you to do that to anyone else. I'd have to kill him, you see.'

Midori felt her body grow hot at the suggestive tone of his voice. She stared at him, although she couldn't make out his expression in the near darkness. 'Nico! You've never … that's to say, I don't know what's got into you.'

'It's *carpe diem*,' he said, nuzzling her right ear, which sent tingling sensations shooting down her spine. 'I heard someone talking about it. "Seize the day." Don't put off doing or saying the things you want to say, because tomorrow it might be too late.'

'I see. And you want to do what, exactly?'

'Go to bed. With you.'

That was plain speaking indeed, but Midori knew it was what she wanted as well and really, was there any reason to hold back? There probably was, but she didn't want to think of that now. She made a token protest. 'But ...'

He cut her words off by putting a finger on her lips. 'Shh,' he said, 'let's not waste our time with talking. Just say yes, please?'

'Yes,' she whispered.

She felt his smile against her mouth as he covered it with his own for a brief, but searing, kiss. Then he took her hand again and pulled her after him, into the house and up the stairs, all the way to his little attic room. They both instinctively tiptoed, although there probably wasn't any need for such caution. Both Uncle Marston and Aunt Hesketh slept like the dead, and Temperance would never think to venture out of her room, nor would the servants.

'I've a mind to see you in those breeches,' Nico whispered, lighting a candle with some difficulty. He turned and helped her out of her petticoat, then ran his hands down her hips and across her behind where the material clung to her. 'Hmm, I'm fairly sure they were never that tight on Daniel.'

'If you're going to make fun of me, I'm leaving,' Midori hissed, but as she pretended to flounce off, he grabbed her arm and pulled her back against his chest.

'I wasn't, believe me. I just couldn't express properly how enticing you look dressed like that. It's driving me insane.' His hands busied themselves with the laces of the bodice she was wearing, and she returned the favour with the buttons of his coat, although it was difficult to concentrate even on such a simple task when Nico's mouth found hers again.

His kisses were everything she'd dreamed of, ever since the night of the storm. Back then, she'd been the one taking the lead. Now their roles were reversed and she found she liked that even better. Although he started slowly, he was clearly impatient, his desire for her firing her blood. She heard Nico groan as she kissed him back with all the emotion she'd been keeping pent up for so long. He tasted of ale and smelled of gunpowder, but underneath was his own unique scent, which she knew and loved so well. She breathed it in and moved her hips so her stomach brushed against the front of his breeches. The knowledge that this enflamed him even further increased her own impatience.

'Do you like that?' she whispered, shy yet wanting to be daring.

'Mm, you have no idea. Feel free to do it again.'

Somehow they both shed their clothing in record time and at last she could feel his hot skin against her own from chest to thigh. She ran her hands over him experimentally, following the hard contours of his well-muscled arms and lean torso. He was so big, so perfect, so ... *entirely mine*. She discovered that she liked touching the hair on his stomach that tapered down towards his groin. Her fingers followed this arrow and then dared to stroke him further down. She heard him draw in a sharp breath.

'Midori.' His voice was even huskier than usual, a sensuous caress as he kissed his way along her collar bone while his hands followed the lines of her body from behind. His touch was reverent, gentle, but her skin was so sensitive now that she felt as if his fingers blazed a trail of fire down her back. He bent to kiss her breasts, first one then the other, then teased the nipples with his lips and tongue while his hands continued their exploration. His fingers found their way between her legs and Midori thought she'd melt into a puddle right then and there. It was beyond wonderful.

'Nico, please ...' She knew what she was asking for, she'd been taught about such things, but she'd never realised how much pleasure was involved until now.

He lifted her quickly and laid her on the rickety bed, pinning her down with his body. She loved the feel of him, despite the heaviness, but he soon supported most of his weight on his arms so as not to crush her. His mouth moved from her breasts to her navel and below, and she gasped as his tongue flicked lower down, sending flames of heat through her veins.

'Dear God, but you're so beautiful,' he whispered. 'A veritable goddess. *My* goddess.' He came back up to kiss her on the mouth while his fingers continued where his tongue had just been. Midori whimpered with need and put her arms around him to make him go where she wanted him. Quickly.

'You're sure this is what you want?' he breathed. 'Me?' He sounded as if he couldn't quite believe it and she knew what he meant. It was like a dream come true. But it was real and she didn't want to wait another second.

'Yes, Nico, all of you. Now.'

No sooner had she said the words than she had her wish. He filled her, body and soul, and she knew this was what she'd been waiting for. And it had been worth the wait. When they moved together as one, she wanted to shout out loud with joy, with triumph.

He was hers at last.

They woke in the early dawn and made love once more, slowly, carefully, as if they were memorising each other's bodies. Afterwards, Nico held her tightly and whispered, 'I wish I could stop time right here, right now, Midori.'

But she couldn't bear to hear him expressing any regrets or even his wishes for the future, so it was her turn to put her fingers on his mouth to shush him. 'Don't. Please. I'm going downstairs now before anyone stirs. Come and join me when you're ready and we'll go.'

He nodded and kissed her one last time before he let her slip out of bed.

Just like the night before, they walked through the streets of Plymouth holding hands and not saying a word. There was no point until they knew what this day would bring.

Chapter Thirty-Two

On this, the second day of the fighting, it became clear the King meant business. The noise, as they approached, was already deafening, with the roar of cannons, sharp cracks of musket shot and shouting of the fighting men all clamouring for supremacy. Nico and Midori made their way to the gate where they knew Daniel was stationed, and looked for him through the smoke and dust that hung in the air like a heavy shroud.

'Where do we report for duty?' Nico asked, following behind her. He tried to keep his tone even, so as not to show how afraid he was. Not for himself, but for her. *What if I lose her now? After last night, how could I bear it?* The thought was like a physical pain and he pushed it to the back of his mind. He couldn't afford to think like that or he'd get himself killed, as well as Midori.

He'd noticed the two swords tucked into her belt, so similar to those of her brother. He knew she'd have honed them to perfection and the thought that she knew what she was doing calmed him slightly. Midori wasn't some helpless female who needed protection; she was a fully trained warrior and he'd do well to remember it. And judging by the training she'd done, even in a small cabin on board his ship, she'd have kept her skills up. He remembered she'd said as much, yesterday.

The thick leather jerkins they both wore would protect them from sword thrusts. He had his own sword, a rapier he'd bought in Amsterdam years ago, hanging on his left-hand side. He carried his musket – a matchlock – and across his chest hung a leather bandolier with twelve flasks called Apostles, each one filled with enough gunpowder for one shot. He also had a larger flask at his waist with more powder for refills, a pouch with 48 musket balls and yards of match wound round his waist, which would be lit at either end before going into battle. *I'm as prepared as I can possibly be.*

'I suppose this is where we need to go.' As Midori spoke, they both caught sight of a redhead coming towards them from the right. 'Wait, that's him I think. Daniel!'

'Ah, there you are at last. You're most welcome, I can tell you.' Daniel, perspiring with his efforts and with streaks of dirt across his cheeks and forehead, pulled Midori close for a quick hug. Midori smiled at him and Nico found he didn't mind. There was no need for jealousy now; she was his and he knew he'd never need to doubt her.

'I can't believe it's all started so early,' she was saying to her cousin. 'We should have come sooner. Now, where are we needed the most?'

'No idea. Come on, I'll find our commanding officer and see what he wants you to do.'

As Nico walked behind them, he decided to follow his uncle's example for once and pray. No one but God could help them now.

They were sent on to the battlefield almost immediately.

'We need every man – and woman – who is able to fight,' Daniel's officer told them grimly, obviously not fooled by her disguise, Midori thought. 'Just follow the others in your troop, but stay towards the back while you get used to things. It can be a bit, uhm, daunting at first.' He looked Midori over one more time, his expression doubtful. 'You're sure you wish to join in the fighting, mistress?'

'Yes, definitely. I assure you I am well trained.' *Although I've never had any actual experience of war.* She decided not to tell him that.

The man's eyes told her he didn't believe her in any case, but on the other hand, he probably didn't care. He waved them on. 'Very well. Off you go, then.'

'Here, you'd best have one of these.' Daniel handed her a helmet he'd been carrying. 'Put on a Monmouth cap first though, or it won't fit you.' Midori donned a small knitted hat and rammed the helmet into place securely. An unpleasant odour emanated from it and Midori wrinkled her nose in distaste. It was also very heavy.

'Do I really need …?' she started to protest, but he cut her off with angry authority.

'Yes, you do. Don't be a fool.'

On her other side she felt, rather than saw, Nico bristle at Daniel's harsh words to her, but she knew her cousin was only concerned for her welfare, so she nodded acquiescence.

Similar conical helmets were worn by hundreds of others around her, glinting dully whenever the sunlight penetrated the clouds of smoke which hung in the air. More smoke issued forth from cannon and muskets all the time and Midori had to blink often to see more clearly through the haze. The feel of the heavy swords at her belt reassured her, as Daniel lead the way.

They smelled the battle before they even came close. The sweet, cloying scent of blood, the stench of rotting flesh, the odour of unwashed bodies exerting themselves to their utmost, all mingled with the acrid fumes of gunpowder. Midori felt her nostrils flare as she recoiled instinctively, her lungs constricting in an effort to take more shallow breaths. *I never imagined it would be like this.*

The mighty blasts of the cannon shook the hillsides and the accompanying screams that rent the air made Midori want to cover her ears. She had heard the sounds men made while suffering extreme pain before, but these cries seemed almost inhuman, like evil *kami* out for revenge. She saw men thrown up into the air as if they were nothing more than rag dolls, landing with a dull thud and the sickening crack of bones breaking.

At first sight of the enemy a frisson of fear slithered through Midori. For a moment she froze next to Daniel, unable to move either backwards or forwards, but after taking a deep calming breath, she managed to make her limbs function again.

'You are the daughter of a *daimyo*, you can do this,' she chanted silently to herself and sent up a swift prayer to her ancestors. 'Father, Mother, give me strength and courage. Help me not to bring dishonour to the family.'

She walked towards the fray, Daniel and Nico either side of her, and tried to empty her mind of all thoughts except those of the coming fighting. She must stay focused, remember all the moves her father had taught her, and above all she must not show fear. *You can do this, you can do this ...*

The reek of panic was all around her, however, basic animal terror, wafting in the breeze, contagious. She knew she wasn't alone and that any sane person would feel the same at such a time, but she also knew she must overcome it or she would die.

'*Never show weakness, Midori. Your enemies will seize on it with glee, remember that,*' her father had said. Midori nodded to herself and squared her shoulders. There would be no outward sign of her apprehension, she vowed.

The beating of drums – the only means of communication on a battle field as it was too noisy to hear shouted orders – made a strange excitement take hold of her as they came closer. She pulled her swords out of her belt in readiness and concentrated on the task before her. 'These men are the enemy, they are scum, not worthy of life,' she told herself fiercely, drumming up feelings of hatred to facilitate the act of killing.

'Are you ready?' Daniel asked and there were murmurs of assent from the men who had accompanied them. With cries of rage, they all suddenly charged towards the enemy, gaining speed as they egged each other on. Midori felt her legs move of their own volition, following the others and she let out the blood-curdling war cry of clan Kumashiro to bolster her courage.

It was time.

By Midori's side Nico also tried to focus on the task at hand. He'd fought in so many battles already by now, but he still wasn't sure exactly what they were fighting for and cared even less. Religion and politics had never been of interest to him, but he'd come to realise it was family that mattered. And since his family were threatened, this must be the right thing to do. He glanced at Midori and saw her determination, her absolute composure, and knew he had to be with her every step of the way.

One thought was clear in his mind – if Midori died this day, he no longer wanted to live, either. But what he wanted more than anything else was to have a future with her, and he'd fight for that as he'd never fought before.

He joined in the war cry and felt his legs gather speed as they charged into the fray ...

Complete and utter chaos reigned.

Once in the thick of things, Midori didn't have a single moment to think about what was happening or what she was doing. Instinct guided her every move. The primeval desire for survival had her jumping out of the way of enemy swords and slashing wildly with her own to kill or maim without discrimination. There was blood everywhere, staining clothing, pouring into the ground, raining down in tiny droplets, spraying through the air. Midori felt its metallic taste on her tongue and swallowed hard, revolted and excited all at once.

She soon realised that the imaginary battles in her father's courtyard were a far cry from the reality of war. Here there was no quarter given, none expected. Each individual was intent on killing his opponent and the bloodlust she saw in the eyes of those around her chilled her to the bone, although she knew it must be reflected in her own eyes. It was an insanity which had her, and everyone else, in its grip; relentless, omnipotent.

There seemed to be some method in the madness occasionally. With banners flapping in the breeze, the two sides advanced towards each other in formation from time to time. Musketeers kneeled in tiers on the ground to fire salvos into their opponents and Midori heard more than one shot whistle past her ears. When the men in the first row had finished, the next stepped forward to fire in their turn and so on, sending off a never-ending stream of deadly musket balls, some of which found their targets in the ranks of Parliamentarians.

The pikemen were easier to pick off with a sword. Gathered in groups, their pikes held at shoulder height to charge their opponents, they looked like nothing so much as unwieldy hedgehogs performing a strange dance. Midori didn't hesitate to attack them at every opportunity, and more than one billowing white shirtsleeve soon turned crimson with enemy blood from her efforts.

One pikeman turned unexpectedly, however, and surged towards Nico, who was busy fighting someone else. Midori reacted instinctively, swivelling round to pierce the man in the back with her sword just as his pike glanced off Nico's arm.

'Jesus!' Nico jumped and sent her a wide-eyed glance. 'Thank you. That was a bit close!'

Midori smiled, but didn't tell him her blood had turned to

ice in her veins at the thought of just how close she'd come to losing him.

She had never been so tired in all her life, but nor had she ever felt as alive. Each moment she managed to keep from being killed became precious, something to be savoured. Her senses took everything in, storing up the images for processing later. For the time being she couldn't afford to think about what she was seeing or doing, only act and act swiftly. Wielding her swords furiously, she slashed her way through enemy soldiers, a dull satisfaction filling her each time she struck home.

'Holy Mother of God,' she heard Daniel hiss the first time he saw Midori's swords in action. 'Those are unbelievably sharp!' But he soon had to concentrate on his own battles. He and Nico fluttered in and out of Midori's vision, and although it was each man – or woman – for himself, they all kept an eye on each other's backs.

For a while she felt invincible, then weariness set in and with it the fear came creeping back. *What if I don't have the strength to keep going? Or I slip up in my concentration; become a liability rather than an asset?* To keep up her courage she shouted out war cries in her father's tongue, some of which made her opponents stare at her in horror. She wondered fleetingly if they thought her a magical creature cursing them, such were their expressions. She was soon quite hoarse, however, and had to desist. The constant smoke around them made her throat so dry she couldn't stop coughing.

Although she would never have admitted it to anyone, it was an unutterable relief when darkness descended at last and the fighting had to stop for the night. In her haste to reach the camp fires, she tripped over a dead body, but managed to retain her balance. She looked around to make sure no one had seen her. *I won't have anyone think me weak.*

Chapter Thirty-Three

'Have you seen your father?' Midori asked Daniel as she and Nico sat together on a boulder next to him, catching their breaths and eating some dry bread and cheese. It seemed to be the best thing on offer and she didn't care as long as it was edible.

'Not recently. He was over on the western side because some friends of his asked him to join them.'

'I hope he's all right.'

'Yes. I told him there was no need for him to fight, but he's a stubborn old man.' Daniel sounded as if he wasn't sure whether to be annoyed with his father or admiring of the old man's courage.

'I know. I tried to dissuade him as well, but once an idea takes root, there's no turning him, as you well know. Runs in the family, doesn't it?' She punched him lightly on the arm and he retaliated in kind, but with a grin on his face.

'I'm glad you came,' he said, before standing up to stretch. 'But now I must be off. See you both later.'

Nico, who had been silent throughout this exchange, put an arm round Midori. 'Are you all right? Any cuts or bruises that need tending?'

She shook her head. 'Nothing major. You?'

'I'm all right, I think.' He gave her a lopsided smile which melted her insides. 'Although in truth, I'm so tired I'm not sure I'd notice.'

'I know what you mean. Shall we just rest here for now, in case we're needed?'

'Yes. I've promised to take my turn at guard duty. Do you mind not sleeping in a bed?'

His eyes told her he did. Despite the weariness, she knew

he desired her and it sent a tingling through her veins. She leaned over to give him a quick kiss. 'Yes, I do mind, actually, but the sensible part of me says I should stay put.'

He sighed. 'Yes, mine, too.' He reached out to smooth away a strand of her hair which had escaped the cord she'd tied it back with. 'When this is all over, we'll spend a week in bed, agreed?'

She nodded, going along with his pretended optimism. 'Absolutely.' And although she noticed that he didn't mention marriage as part of his plans, she was past caring. Besides which, she'd already given herself to him, so she was to all intents and purposes a fallen woman.

The thought didn't worry her in the least.

The fighting continued at daybreak. Midori felt as if she was in the grip of a hideous nightmare, where everything was repeated *ad infinitum*. The stench, the fear, the noise and gore were all the same as the previous day, the only difference being that Midori's limbs grew more and more reluctant to obey her. Her muscles screamed in protest, but no matter how many men she fought, there were always a hundred more to take their place.

Faces darted in and out of her line of vision in an endless stream; contorted with rage, frowning in concentration, gaping in wide-mouthed pain, triumphant, defeated, frightened. Midori wanted to scream at them to give her some respite, but there was no stopping them. The hours passed and she began to ache unbearably in every part of her body. There were bruises and cuts everywhere today; she'd lost count of the number of times she had been hurt. She had to stop repeatedly to wipe the perspiration and grime out of her eyes, and she saw Nico and Daniel do the same. Both men had insisted on flanking her yet again, each obviously determined to protect her, as she was trying to do the same to them. She had to admit she was glad of their presence. It made her feel safer.

The battle raged on. 'Is it never going to end, damn it?' she heard Daniel cry out once, but it seemed the answer was no.

Midori's breathing became laboured and her sword arm leaden. *I can't go on, but I must, I must* ... It was an effort to simply remain upright and she had to pause repeatedly for short rests. It was just after one such break that disaster struck.

A cannon ball thudded into the ground next to them, splintering a small tree nearby and sending up a shower of dirt and debris. A sharp pain tore through Midori's right thigh. She heard Nico and Daniel shout her name in unison as she felt her leg give way. She cried out, the ground hurtled up to meet her and then everything turned black.

'Nooo!' Nico heard himself scream, but it was as if the sound was coming from somewhere else as he watched Midori crumple next to him.

He exchanged glances with Daniel and saw the shock and horror that must be mirrored in his own eyes. Somehow, after her heroic efforts the day before, Nico had convinced himself Midori would be all right and they'd get through this somehow. He'd forgotten about the cannon, the unseen foe that could strike at any moment.

For an instant he froze, unable to make his limbs move in any way, while a cold sweat of fear broke out across his body. Then a cry from Daniel alerted him to the danger of an enemy soldier on his left and with an enormous effort of will he somehow made himself swing around to deal with the man, before turning back to Midori.

She's not dead. She can't be dead. I won't let her, damn it!

'Watch my back!' he shouted at Daniel, who nodded and

darted forward to shield Nico while he bent to pick her up. He put his ear to her chest briefly and heard the reassuring thud of her heart beat. It was all he needed for now. 'Follow me,' he ordered and set off at a run towards the earthworks. He didn't wait to see if Daniel did as he'd asked; he trusted him.

As soon as they were safely behind cover, he put Midori down on the ground, shrugging out of his jacket to put it under her head. Daniel appeared next to him, silently helping him to lift Midori on to a blanket someone brought.

'She's breathing,' Daniel said.

Nico nodded. 'Yes, but look at her leg. A splinter from the tree, I think. It's got to go.' There was a huge gash in the breeches she'd been wearing and the material was covered in blood, the stain spreading rapidly.

'Her leg?' Daniel blanched under the grime that covered his face and blinked at Nico.

'No, you dolt, the splinter.' Nico tried to make his tone sound light. It wasn't a joking matter, but the last thing he needed was for Daniel to turn faint now. They had to help Midori together. 'Is there a surgeon about?'

'I don't know, I'll ask.'

Daniel hurried off, but came back shaking his head. 'Can't find one, they're probably all busy.' With bleak eyes he surveyed the carnage all around them as everyone seemed to be bringing the wounded back here.

'Then we'll have to extract it ourselves. I've seen it done on board a ship. Hold her for me, will you?'

'Me?' Daniel's voice squeaked slightly, like that of an adolescent, and Nico could feel the fear emanating from him. It was as nothing to the terror he felt himself, but he knew he had to act quickly if Midori was to have any chance of survival at all. He gritted his teeth and fixed Daniel with a stern glare.

'Yes, you. I need you. She needs you. You can do this, all right?'

Daniel nodded and drew in a deep breath and swallowed hard. 'Yes, yes I can,' he said.

'Good man. Oh, look, she's stirring. Damnation, I was hoping she'd stay unconscious for a while longer, but it can't be helped. Hold her, please.'

Nico took a deep breath himself. This was going to be hell.

'Midori! Midori can you hear me?'

She opened her eyes slowly and at first saw nothing but sky, then Nico's face swam into focus at the same time as pain exploded in her leg.

'Nico?'

'Yes, I'm here. You've been hurt and I'm afraid we have to hurt you a bit more, else the risk of infection will be too great. You must be brave now. Do you want something to bite on? Some strong drink?'

'What are you going to do?' She looked from one man to the other, but neither would look her in the eye. 'Tell me! I need to know.'

'You have a piece of wood in your thigh, a giant splinter. It has to come out quickly before it goes in deeper, or you might lose the entire leg. I'm sorry.'

Midori gritted her teeth and nodded. At least they weren't cutting off the whole limb, or at least, not yet. 'Very well. Extract it.'

She could still hear the sounds of battle, although slightly more distant now, and realised she was lying on the hard ground next to a tree with something softer for a pillow.

'I'm going to put a strip of leather in your mouth so you don't bite your tongue,' Nico said. 'All right? Here we go.'

Midori nodded; she'd seen the ship's surgeon do that to

his patients and knew it made sense. She bit down on it, trying not to gag at its foul taste.

Nico advanced on her with a small sharp knife and she closed her eyes. Daniel took one of her hands in both of his and squeezed, trying to imbue her with his strength. Then he lay down gently across her torso, pinning her down. 'Sorry,' he murmured. 'Have to do this.'

'Are you ready?' Nico's voice came from the other side of Daniel.

'Mm-hmm.' Midori braced herself. Almost immediately pain sliced through her as Nico began his task and she hissed in a breath through her nose. Her teeth gripped the hard leather strip so tightly she thought they might break. As Nico continued, she couldn't stop a moan from escaping her throat, then the pain became so acute blessed darkness descended on her again and she knew no more.

'Will she live?'

'Yes, I think so. She's a fighter, as we all know.'

The disembodied voice sounded slightly disapproving as it floated into Midori's brain and niggled at her until she struggled to open her eyes. She saw nothing at first except the colour white and wondered if she was still unconscious. Then she realised she was staring at Aunt Hesketh's apron and her aunt was kneeling next to Midori's bed, bandaging her wound, while Temperance hovered nearby.

With an effort she turned her head and saw Nico standing by the door, a worried expression on his face. As her aunt finished the task, the dull fire burning in Midori's leg turned into stabbing pain, and she drew in a sharp breath, which the others heard.

'She's conscious again.'

'Midori, how are you feeling?' Nico came forward, a frown creasing his forehead and his deep-set eyes full of concern.

'A bit … sore.'

Aunt Hesketh put a hand on Midori's forehead and nodded to herself. 'No fever yet,' she muttered. 'Did you use a knife?'

Nico nodded. 'Yes. My ship surgeon once told me he always cleaned the rust off his knife blades with wine before performing any surgery, but all I could find was someone's flask of strong cider so I used that. And I put it in the fire to cauterize the wound after. Is it still bleeding?'

'A little, but I've put some cobwebs on it, so it's almost stopped. I'll leave it for a while before making a comfrey poultice to stop it festering, but she should have willow bark or feverfew now. I'll go and find some.' She left the room with Temperance, leaving Midori alone with Nico, who sat down gingerly on the edge of Midori's bed.

'You're in good hands with my stepmother,' he said softly, and smiled when he saw the look of scepticism she managed. 'Really. I know you've had your differences, but that's in the past now, and when she takes charge of something, she does it to the best of her ability.'

'I suppose you're right,' Midori reluctantly conceded. 'Are you well? The splinters didn't hit you or Daniel, did they?'

'No, we're both unharmed. Daniel is still fighting; he said he couldn't be spared. I carried you back here, but I'll have to go in a while and …' He didn't finish the sentence. They both knew what he'd be going back to.

'Of course, I understand.' She tried to smile, but it was beyond her at the moment.

Nico was staring towards the window, so Midori couldn't see his expression, but she heard the catch in his voice as he said, 'I thought I'd lost you, Midori, and I just wanted to die myself.' He turned back to her. 'You must get through this, do you hear me?' Midori was taken aback by the emotion blazing in his eyes, but at the same time it made a warm feeling spread through her veins.

'I will. Just you look after yourself. You can't spend a week in bed with your mistress if you get yourself killed, you know.'

'Mistress? You thought …? For heaven's sake, Midori, I can't believe you still think me so dishonourable!'

'No! I'm the one who has thrown away my honour. What happened the night before last was … well, it was my choice and I don't regret it. Really, it's all right.'

Nico took her hands in his and leaned over her so his face was very close to hers. 'No, my love, it's not "all right" at all, if that's how you're thinking. I thought you understood – I love you. I want to marry you. But there seemed no point making plans when there is every possibility one or other of us might not live to see the end of this week.'

'You love me? Truly?'

'Of course I do, you goose.' He shook his head. 'Although why, when you persist in thinking the worst of me, I've no idea.'

She raised her hands to pull his face down to punctuate her words with kisses. 'I don't. Think. You. Dishonourable. I love. You. Too. With all my heart.'

He smiled then and kissed her back, but carefully, tenderly, as if she was the most fragile thing on earth. 'So you'll marry me, then?' he whispered.

'Yes, of course. I've never wanted anyone else.'

'Good, then I've got something to look forward to when I come back.'

The thought of him having to return to the battle put a dampener on Midori's joy, but she glanced towards the urns that were still on the little mantelpiece of the bedroom and sent a swift prayer to her ancestors.

'Please, keep him safe for me. He's precious and I can't lose him now!'

Chapter Thirty-Four

Plymouth continued to hold out and on the fourteenth of September the King's frustration got the better of him and he withdrew to the north the following day, leaving Sir Richard Grenville to blockade the town once again.

'Thank heavens for that! The fighting is over for now,' Daniel exclaimed, barging into Midori's sickroom with barely a knock. He was limping, but it didn't seem to bother him and she couldn't see anything else wrong with him, apart from bruises. Temperance, who was with her, frowned at him and tried to remonstrate, but he was bubbling over with the good news and he wasn't alone. A great cheer went up from the exhausted defenders, which echoed through the town. Midori smiled at Daniel, sharing his joy despite her weariness.

'You can have a well-earned rest now,' she said.

'Yes, the Lord knows we need it. The Royalists must have lost their will to win, else we should have had to give way soon. I've never felt so tired in all my life.'

'Lucky for us they didn't know that,' Midori commented.

As Daniel turned to leave, Nico entered the room, looking as if he'd been running. 'Daniel, Temperance, I'm so sorry to be the bearer of bad news, but … your father,' he said. 'He collapsed and died. I think it was all too much for him. He should never have fought in the first place.'

'Father? Surely not?' Temperance stared at Nico as if she didn't believe him.

Daniel shook his head. 'What? But the battle is over and …'

Nico sent his stepcousins a look of deepest sympathy. 'Yes, but he had a seizure of some sort, so I'm told. They'll be bringing him shortly.'

'Oh, no!' Midori felt sadness wash over her and in her weakened state she couldn't stop a few tears from trickling down her cheeks. *When is all the dying going to end? I'm so tired of it.* She stretched out her arms to Temperance, who broke into noisy crying as she took in the news at last, and collapsed to lean her head on Midori's shoulder. Midori held her close and looked at her other cousin. 'Daniel, I'm so sorry, but at least he died doing what he believed was right,' she said, hoping to comfort him.

Daniel visibly pulled himself together. 'Yes, you're right. When I last saw him he told me it was time for him to make a stand. Everyone was needed and he knew it.'

'It was a desperate situation,' Nico added. 'And he always did what was right. I honestly didn't think the town could withstand the King's forces, but somehow it was accomplished and it was thanks to men like your father.'

Daniel nodded slowly. 'Yes, we have to be grateful for our deliverance, however high a price we've had to pay for it.'

Midori's recovery was slow, even though the dreaded wound fever never set in. Nico waited anxiously for the first few days, sitting by her side as much as he could. She was asleep for the most part, dosed with some concoction of Kate's, and to her obvious sorrow wasn't able to attend Jacob's funeral. But she was clearly in pain. Nico found it hard to see her like that and would have liked to crawl into bed with her to just hold her in his arms. Out of respect for his late stepuncle, however, he did no such thing. For once, he decided, he was going to do things Jacob's way – the right way.

Even when she began to heal she looked as weak as a newborn lamb, but her spirit returned and Nico had trouble persuading her to remain in bed for far longer than she would have liked to.

'You'll be up and about soon enough,' he soothed. 'Then we can be married and start our life together.'

'In Amsterdam?'

'Is that where you'd like to live? I thought you wanted to stay here,' Nico said.

'Well, you said I'd fit in better there, although as long as we're together, I don't mind where we are.'

'That's good to know, because I've had some news. The solicitor, Schuyler, has sent me a letter, enclosing one from the *Heeren XVII*.'

'The VOC directors?' Midori frowned. 'What do they want with you?'

'They wrote to inform me the position of chief factor in Dejima is becoming vacant soon as they've recalled that fool Corneliszoon. They're wondering if I'd be interested in taking over.'

'Dejima?' Her whole face lit up and Nico could see he'd been right in thinking she'd be pleased.

'Yes. I thought since we can't live in Japan itself, this would be the best alternative. At least you'd be closer to your brother there. You may have to pretend to be my Japanese concubine, as females aren't normally allowed at the trading post, but if you don't mind that, I'm sure it could be done.'

Midori looked slightly dazed and a small frown appeared on her smooth brow. 'Dejima?' she repeated, and Nico began to get worried. Perhaps he'd misread the situation?

'You don't want to go back after all?'

'No, I mean yes, of course I do! It would be wonderful to be closer to Ichiro and to Japan, but that means leaving everyone here behind. And what about you? Your home is in Holland. You have a house, you like it there.'

'Don't worry about that, it won't be forever and we can come back for visits. I found Japan a fascinating place and I think I could be of more use to the company than the

343

present chief factor. Especially if I bring my own translator.' He grinned at her. 'So do you want to go or not?'

Midori threw her arms around his neck and kissed him. 'Oh yes, please. It sounds like a wonderful compromise. I wonder if we can visit Ichiro in secret?'

Nico laughed. 'If I remember him rightly, he'll arrange it somehow. He had the look of someone who brooks no opposition when he sets his mind to something. A bit like you, actually.' He kissed her back before she could protest, then added, 'You don't think he'll mind about our marriage?'

Midori shook her head. 'He wanted me to be happy and I am. He'll be pleased for me.'

'Very well, I'll go and send a reply to the *Heeren XVII* straight away, then. And don't you dare leave that bed – I want you fully recovered as soon as possible.'

'I won't move so much as a muscle, I promise. Only hurry, before they change their minds!'

'Well, this might keep you busy while I'm gone.' He smiled and pulled something out of his sleeve, which he handed her. 'Here's the letter you've no doubt been waiting for. Let me know what news your brother sends you.'

'At last!' Midori seized on the missive and unrolled it, scanning the words as fast as she could.

When Temperance came into the room some time later Midori beamed at her. 'I've finally had a message from my brother. Everyone is well and waiting for news from me. Thank the gods!'

As soon as Midori was able to stand on her leg again, they were married and Daniel, as the head of the Marstons, proudly gave her away. The entire family attended and even Nico's siblings and stepsiblings came, which pleased Midori no end.

'See, you do have a clan after all,' she teased.

'Yes, I suppose so,' Nico agreed, 'and now I'm older, they don't seem quite as stuffy or, in the case of the younger ones, annoying.'

'Nico!' Midori protested, but she could see he got on well with them really.

Best of all, however, she found Harding and Jochem waiting to congratulate them after the service. She hadn't seen Harding since before the siege and had feared the worst.

'I invited the boy,' Nico told her, although Jochem wasn't so much a boy as a man grown now. 'He's to sail with us to Japan.'

'My sailing days are over though,' Harding said, 'but I wish you the best of luck and hope to see you when you come back.'

In the end, it took over a year before they finally set sail for the Far East, as there were so many loose ends to tie up first, but Midori was glad because by then it was clear that her relatives would truly be safe from now on.

The town of Plymouth had continued to hold out and remained steadfast to the Parliamentary cause. It was attacked once more soon after the New Year in 1645, but the Royalists couldn't breach the defences and in the middle of March they were ordered to march to Somerset. A small force was left behind, but they made no attempts to take the town. By the end of the summer, the war was all but over.

All over England the Royalists were being overwhelmed. There was fighting throughout Devon, but relief came at last in the shape of General Sir Thomas Fairfax and the so-called New Model Army, instigated by Oliver Cromwell, but trained by Fairfax. They proved unbeatable. As they drew nearer the desperate Royalists tried to bribe Plymouth into surrendering by offering its commander ten thousand pounds and command of a Royalist regiment, but he refused.

On the twenty-fifth of March 1646 General Fairfax rode into Plymouth. All the inhabitants turned out to watch, including Midori and Nico, who were leaving for Amsterdam the following day. They joined the other members of the Marston family in celebrating, while the sound of three hundred cannon echoed through the streets. It was a joyous sound this time, not the ominous herald of disaster it had been previously, and made everyone smile.

As Midori looked around at her relatives, she was pleased to note how happy they all seemed, apart from Aunt Hesketh. But then she knew her aunt was sad to see her stepson go, especially now there was a newfound rapport between them.

'Don't worry, we'll be back in a few years,' Nico had soothed her. 'Time passes quickly and we promise to write to you. And who knows, we might even bring you back another grandchild or two?'

To Midori's delight, Daniel had a new glow of confidence and maturity which had been lacking before, and seemed relaxed and at ease. She knew this was because he and Nico were now equal partners in the family business, and although Daniel would be running the English side of it, Nico would be sending him goods to trade with.

'I can't think of anyone I'd rather work with,' Daniel had told her, and Midori could see Nico was as ecstatic as she was to finally feel a true sense of belonging within the family.

'Is it really over? Is this the end of the fighting?' Temperance's cheeks were pink with excitement and relief as they stood watching the general passing by.

'Indeed it is. You can sleep soundly in your bed now,' Daniel reassured his sister. 'The Royalists are well and truly beaten.'

'It will almost seem a bit flat,' Temperance said wistfully.

'Are you mad?' Daniel stared at her, but she was no longer

looking at her brother. Instead she had turned to Midori and Nico with pleading eyes.

'I want to go to Japan, too. Please may I come with you, Midori? I would so like to see your country and it would be such an adventure. Please, please?'

Midori didn't know what to reply. 'But we may be there a long time, Temperance. It's not really the place for a young single woman. In fact, you wouldn't be allowed.' Midori didn't add that her little cousin was turning into quite a beauty as well, and may be a temptation for the men sent to work in the East, far from their wives and family.

'Couldn't I dress as a boy, like your mother did? I don't mind, only please let me come. I'll do anything, help you with housework or, well, anything. I so want to see everything you've told me about. It sounds magical.'

Midori looked at Nico, who smiled back and shrugged. 'It seems to me the young lady has made up her mind. If we don't take her, she'll find a way to go there by herself, as your mother did, so she'll be safer with us.' He shook his head ruefully. 'The Marston women are a stubborn lot and I can only hope the good Lord gives me the patience to put up with it.'

Midori punched him lightly on the arm as everyone laughed, and he swept her into an embrace. 'You're sort of a Marston, too, and you know you'll enjoy every minute,' she murmured, and he didn't deny it, because it was the truth.

One year later, almost to the day, the *Zwarte Zwaan* glided into its anchorage outside the strange, fan-shaped island of Dejima. The familiar sights, sounds and smells of Japan assailed them and, standing on deck, Midori felt a profound gratitude to the gods and spirits who had kept her safe throughout her adventure. Now she was embarking on another, of an entirely different kind, but she was ready to face anything as long as her husband was by her side. She squeezed his hand, too choked with emotion to say anything, but she didn't need to say a word.

They understood each other perfectly.

Author's Note

This story is based on real historical events. By 1641, the Japanese ruler, the *Shogun*, had decided to evict all foreigners except the Dutch (the Portuguese, last to go, left in 1639). This included all the children of foreigners, whether half Japanese or not. Christianity had already been banned for some time and any Christians found hiding were executed, so although my heroine Midori is fictitious, her plight would have been all too real.

Whereas before, foreign traders had been based mostly in Hirado, a port slightly further north, this changed after the expulsions. The Dutch were forced to move to the small island of Dejima in Nagasaki's harbour and they were not permitted to go anywhere else. Japan was, to all intents and purposes, closed to the outside world for the next two hundred years.

The events I describe happening in Plymouth during the Civil War are also historical facts. It was a time of great turmoil and it must have been incredibly difficult for the average Englishman to decide which side to support. Although I admit that personally I would have been on the side of the Royalists, I have tried to show what was occurring without any personal bias. Since my heroine and her family are staunchly Parliamentarian, I had to argue the case for the 'opposition', as it were, which was a very interesting exercise! However, I could see the point of view of both sides, and obviously they each considered that they were right at the time, which made it easier.

I have stuck to true events as much as possible (seen through the eyes of the Plymothians) and hope I've got it right – any mistakes are purely my own. I believe Plymouth was the only West Country town not to fall into Royalist hands and to remain Parliamentarian throughout the war, which was quite a feat. Of course, we all know their triumph was not to last, but although Charles II was reinstated, English royals never again had the same kind of power, so the way the country was governed changed forever. I only wish poor Charles I hadn't had to lose his head for this to happen, so sad!

I tried not to use real people for this story, preferring to make them up, although some, like the various commanders during the war, had to be mentioned by name. The Chief Factor at Dejima wasn't called Corneliszoon, but Antonio Van Diemen was the Dutch Governor-General of Batavia, and I used a little bit of 'poetic licence' in his conversations with Nico. I hope his descendants won't mind!

About the Author

Christina Courtenay lives in Herefordshire and is married with two children. Although born in England she has a Swedish mother and was brought up in Sweden. In her teens, the family moved to Japan where she had the opportunity to travel extensively in the Far East.

Christina is vice chairman of the Romantic Novelists' Association. In 2011, Christina's first novel *Trade Winds* (September 2010) was short listed for The Romantic Novelists' Association's Award for Best Historical Fiction. Her second novel, *The Scarlet Kimono*, won the Big Red Reads Best Historical Fiction Award. In 2012, *Highland Storms* (November 2011) won the Best Historical Romantic Novel of the year award (RoNA). And *The Silent Touch of Shadows* (July 2012), Christina's fourth novel, won the award for Best Historical Read at the Festival of Romance.

www.christinacourtenay.com
www.twitter.com/PiaCCourtenay

More Choc Lit

From Christina Courtenay

The Scarlet Kimono

Winner of the 2011 Big Red Reads Best Historical Fiction Award

Abducted by a Samurai warlord in 17th-century Japan – what happens when fear turns to love?

England, 1611, and young Hannah Marston envies her brother's adventurous life. But when she stows away on his merchant ship, her powers of endurance are stretched to their limit. Then they reach Japan and all her suffering seems worthwhile – until she is abducted by Taro Kumashiro's warriors.

In the far north of the country, warlord Kumashiro is waiting to see the girl who he has been warned about by a seer. When at last they meet, it's a clash of cultures and wills, but they're also fighting an instant attraction to each other.

With her brother desperate to find her and the jealous Lady Reiko equally desperate to kill her, Hannah faces the greatest adventure of her life. And Kumashiro has to choose between love and honour …

Prequel to The Gilded Fan

Visit www.choc-lit.com for more details including the first two chapters and reviews, or simply scan barcode using your mobile phone QR reader.

Trade Winds

Short-listed for the Romantic Novelists' Association's Pure Passion Award for Best Historical Fiction 2011

Marriage of convenience – or a love for life?

It's 1732 in Gothenburg, Sweden, and strong-willed Jess van Sandt knows only too well that it's a man's world. She believes she's being swindled out of her inheritance by her stepfather – and she's determined to stop it.

When help appears in the unlikely form of handsome Scotsman Killian Kinross, himself disinherited by his grandfather, Jess finds herself both intrigued and infuriated by him. In an attempt to recover her fortune, she proposes a marriage of convenience. Then Killian is offered the chance of a lifetime with the Swedish East India Company's Expedition and he's determined that nothing will stand in his way, not even his new bride.

He sets sail on a daring voyage to the Far East, believing he's put his feelings and past behind him. But the journey doesn't quite work out as he expects …

Prequel to Highland Storms

Visit www.choc-lit.com for more details including the first two chapters and reviews, or simply scan barcode using your mobile phone QR reader.

Highland Storms

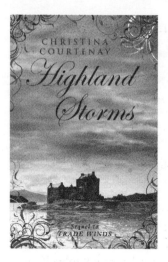

 Winner of the 2012 Best Historical Romantic Novel of the year

Who can you trust?

Betrayed by his brother and his childhood love, Brice Kinross needs a fresh start. So he welcomes the opportunity to leave Sweden for the Scottish Highlands to take over the family estate.

But there's trouble afoot at Rosyth in 1754 and Brice finds himself unwelcome. The estate's in ruin and money is disappearing. He discovers an ally in Marsaili Buchanan, the beautiful redheaded housekeeper, but can he trust her?

Marsaili is determined to build a good life. She works hard at being a housekeeper and harder still at avoiding men who want to take advantage of her. But she's irresistibly drawn to the new clan chief, even though he's made it plain he doesn't want to be shackled to anyone.

And the young laird has more than romance on his mind. His investigations are stirring up an enemy. Someone who will stop at nothing to get what he wants – including Marsaili – even if that means destroying Brice's life forever …

Sequel to Trade Winds

Visit www.choc-lit.com for more details including the first two chapters and reviews, or simply scan barcode using your mobile phone QR reader.

The Silent Touch of Shadows

Festival of Romance

Winner of the 2012 Best Historical Read from the Festival of Romance

What will it take to put the past to rest?

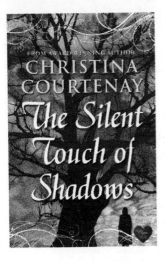

Professional genealogist Melissa Grantham receives an invitation to visit her family's ancestral home, Ashleigh Manor. From the moment she arrives, life-like dreams and visions haunt her. The spiritual connection to a medieval young woman and her forbidden lover have her questioning her sanity, but Melissa is determined to solve the mystery.

Jake Precy, owner of a nearby cottage, has disturbing dreams too, but it's not until he meets Melissa that they begin to make sense. He hires her to research his family's history, unaware their lives are already entwined. Is the mutual attraction real or the result of ghostly interference?

A haunting love story set partly in the present and partly in fifteenth century Kent.

Visit www.choc-lit.com for more details including the first two chapters and reviews, or simply scan barcode using your mobile phone QR reader.

More from Choc Lit

If you loved Christina's story, you'll enjoy
the rest of our selection.
Here's a sample:

The Road Back
Liz Harris

When Patricia accompanies her father, Major George Carstairs, on a trip to Ladakh, north of the Himalayas, in the early 1960s, she sees it as a chance to finally win his love. What she could never have foreseen is meeting Kalden – a local man destined by circumstances beyond his control to be a monk, but fated to be the love of her life.

Despite her father's fury, the lovers are determined to be together, but can their forbidden love survive?

A wonderful story about a passion that crosses cultures, a love that endures for a lifetime, and the hope that can only come from revisiting the past.

Visit www.choc-lit.com for more details including the first two chapters and reviews, or simply scan barcode using your mobile phone QR reader.

The Silver Locket

Margaret James

**Winner of CataNetwork Reviewers'
Choice Award for Single Titles 2010**

**If life is cheap, how much is
love worth?**

It's 1914 and young Rose
Courtenay has a decision
to make. Please her wealthy
parents by marrying the man
of their choice – or play her part in the war effort?

The chance to escape proves irresistible and Rose becomes a
nurse. Working in France, she meets Lieutenant Alex Denham,
a dark figure from her past. He's the last man in the world
she'd get involved with – especially now he's married.

But in wartime nothing is as it seems. Alex's marriage is a
sham and Rose is the only woman he's ever wanted. As he
recovers from his wounds, he sets out to win her trust.
His gift of a silver locket is a far cry from the luxuries she's
left behind.

What value will she put on his love?

First novel in the trilogy.

Visit www.choc-lit.com for more details
including the first two chapters and
reviews, or simply scan barcode using
your mobile phone QR reader.

To Turn Full Circle
Linda Mitchelmore

Life in Devon in 1909 is hard and unforgiving, especially for young Emma Le Goff, whose mother and brother die in curious circumstances, leaving her totally alone in the world. While she grieves, her callous landlord Reuben Jago claims her home and belongings.

His son Seth is deeply attracted to Emma and sympathises with her desperate need to find out what really happened, but all his attempts to help only incur his father's wrath.

When mysterious fisherman Matthew Caunter comes to Emma's rescue, Seth is jealous at what he sees and seeks solace in another woman. However, he finds that forgetting Emma is not as easy as he hoped.

Matthew is kind and charismatic, but handsome Seth is never far from Emma's mind. Whatever twists and turns her life takes, it seems there is always something – or someone – missing.

Set in Devon, the first novel in a trilogy.

CLAIM YOUR FREE EBOOK

of

The Gilded Fan

You may wish to have a choice of how you read
The Gilded Fan. Perhaps you'd like a digital version
for when you're out and about, so that you can
read it on your ereader or anywhere that you can
access iTunes – your computer, iPhone, iPad or a
Smartphone. For a limited period, we're including a
FREE ebook version along with this paperback.

To claim, simply visit ebooks.choc-lit.com
or scan the QR Code.

You'll need to enter the following code:

Q011307

Introducing Choc Lit